GILGARRAN'S WILL

GILGARRAN'S WILL

Martin Salter-Smith

Best wishes Vera

Martin Salter-Smith

18/9/06

Soldiers are citizens of death's grey land
Drawing no dividends from time's tomorrows.

'Dreamers' - Siegfried Sassoon (1918)

Paperback ISBN 1 904908 78 0

Produced by

Central Publishing Services
Royd Street Offices
Milnsbridge
Huddersfield
West Yorkshire
HD3 4QY

www.centralpublishing.co.uk

Martin Salter-Smith was born in Liverpool. He has worked as a language teacher and mountain guide and now lives in Cumbria, close to the hills. He has also published *Our Stolen Years*, a compilation of his parents' wartime memoirs and letters, numerous magazine articles and several booklets of poetry.

Prologue: 1944 – Belgium

It is the sixth autumn of the War, and at last, the Wehrmacht is going home. The supreme fighting machine of the Third Reich, the greatest Army the world has ever seen, is broken. In the East, the Russians are pouring forward, avenging their people's suffering with untold savagery. The cities of the Reich are in flames, and wiser generals than Hitler are desperate for the peace that the Allies will no longer countenance. Retreating before the onslaught in Normandy, the Germans abandon Paris and are pushed back rapidly from the Somme to Brussels. Along the borders of the Fatherland, the wounded army gathers itself for the final defence, and the Allied advance peters out. For a fortnight, the British XXX Corps kicks its heels, waiting for Montgomery's new attack. Sporadic fighting takes place between German units withdrawing from positions overrun by the rapidity of the advance and patrols of British soldiers sent out to intercept them.

On this September evening, two of these soldiers are alone in a wood not far from the capital, Brussels...

They work quickly and methodically, the only sound their occasional grunt of exertion, and as they turn the damp earth, the edges of their entrenching tools gleam dully in the moonlight filtering thinly into the dark place which they have chosen. An owl hoots from the edge of the wood, and as if in answer an unseen creature screams in the darkness, seeming very close and almost human.

"What the hell was that?" The corporal's voice is a taut murmur.

The other soldier, a private, pauses in his digging, motionless and listening intently. The vixen calls again, from a little further away, and he relaxes and smiles, his teeth showing white against his camouflaged face.

"It's only a bloody fox, you thick Scouse bastard!"

They chuckle quietly at their own nerviness, and carry on with their macabre job. The ground in the wood is marshy in the hollow where they are, and the recent rain has softened it further. It is hard work, however, carrying and dragging the bodies deep into the wood and digging down far enough to hide them and to cover them with soil and then heaps of broken branches.

At first they had thought of leaving them where they lay, scattered by the vehicle, one hanging grotesquely from the door, another sprawled by the roadside where the pounding machine-gun bullets had hurled him to the ground.

The skirmish had been short and fierce. Separated from the rest of their patrol, the two infantrymen were heading back across country to rejoin their unit. The light was fading, and they were about to cross a narrow lane when the hoarse roar of a truck's engine made them draw back into cover under the eaves of the wood, where the shadows were dark. Then the vehicle came into sight around the corner, swastika pennants still snapping defiantly on the wings, but mud-spattered and lurching crazily over the potholes.

The two soldiers saw the black uniforms, and the silver glint of the SS badges on their collars; the corporal didn't hesitate. He brought the Bren gun up and squeezed the trigger, swinging the barrel in a slow, caressing arc that took in the whole of the front of the truck. Glass showered from the windscreen, and the driver bobbed like a marionette as the heavy rounds ripped into him. The truck careered into the shallow ditch and ground to a halt, the engine sputtering and dying; the German in the passenger seat twisted sideways and struggled awkwardly to get out of the stricken vehicle, his machine-gun bouncing in his grasp from the recoil of wild, un-aimed shots. The private, half-hidden in the shadows of the trees, dropped to one knee, and took rapid aim with his Lee-Enfield, snuggling the butt quickly and firmly into place. As he closed one eye and squinted down the sights, he remembered his training and saw not a man, not even an enemy, but a target. He absorbed the recoil in his shoulder, and the .303 bullet took the SS man square in the chest. He slumped from his seat, sliding headfirst down onto the running board, his feet still trapped in the cab.

A third SS trooper leaped from the back of the truck, steadied himself and paused, feet braced apart like a toy soldier, facing them while he blazed away with his machine-pistol. For a moment, all was noise and confusion. The bullets went high, tearing through the branches above the Englishmen's position, and they felt leaves and broken twigs pattering down onto their tin helmets. The corporal opened up again with the Bren, and the German turned to run. He had taken only a couple of strides before the bullets found him. They caught him in the back, and he stumbled forward, threw up his arms, and fell onto his face with a cry.

After the heavy thumping of the Bren, the silence was palpable. In the distance, the occasional crump of shell-fire could be heard, but close to, the only sound was the ticking of the truck's engine as it slowly cooled, and then the soft, summery cooing of a woodpigeon some distance away. The corporal lowered the Bren and whistled softly through his teeth. Turning to his companion, he jerked his head towards the vehicle, now motionless apart from one lazily spinning wheel, and they began to approach it, slowly and carefully, one from each side. They crept round behind the truck, and peered in under the canvas top. An SS Sturmbannführer was slumped in the back, his uniform torn by bullet-holes, his sightless eyes staring upwards. There was nothing else in the truck apart from a pile of kitbags, a large stack of boxes and sacks, some ammunition belts, helmets and a few articles of uniform.

"You must have got the bastard with that first burst, Corp!"

The soldier's voice was strained but excited.

"That's four more Krauts who won't be pulling back beyond the Rhine!"

Leaning against the back of the truck, the corporal took a crumpled packet of Woodbines from the breast pocket of his battle-dress blouse, shuffled a couple out of the pack and offered one to his companion. They lit up, cupping the matches in their hands, and drew deeply on the cigarettes, relaxing as they drew the smoke down. When they had half smoked them, they nipped off their cigarettes and put them behind their ears, saving them for later, and then climbed into the truck for a closer look at its contents.

When they jumped down again, their faces were grim with determination beneath the camouflage boot-polish they both wore. Darkness was coming on, the moon was rising and they still had some way to go before they could rejoin their unit. But before they set off, they knew they had a job that needed doing.

Moving corpses is a difficult task. They are heavy and difficult to get hold of; they are soft and pliable and sagging; and worst of all, they are frightening. There is an inescapable feeling that some sort of life may still be in them. Both soldiers had fought their way from the D-Day beaches and through the terrible Battle of Normandy. They were inured to the sights and sounds of sudden death, and knew the shapes and the smell of its aftermath; but they found the next couple of hours unnerving. More than once they paused in their work with an indefinable feeling of being observed.

They had to try to carry the dead Germans deep into the wood, so as to leave as few tell-tale traces as possible of having dragged them there. Then the hard work of the digging began. Tree roots and stones made the work tedious and frustrating, but the ground was soft, and eventually they had excavated the shallow graves where the SS men would lie, far from home and family, mouldering in the earth of a country which had once felt the arrogant tramp of their jack-boots.

At last it is done. They cover the turned earth with dead and broken branches, and sweep over the tracks as well as they can to hide any obvious traces of what has gone on in that place. As they leave the wood, the corporal suddenly hesitates, then crouches and picks up something from the ground. In the moonlight they can see what it is: a torn swastika armband. He looks at it for a minute, turning his head slightly as if listening to the sounds of the night, then stuffs it into his pocket.

They emerge once more cautiously into the lane, where the stricken German truck still lies lopsided in the ditch. They can smell diesel, dripping from the punctured fuel tank. The corporal pauses and glances at the private, who nods slowly. A tossed grenade, a quick burst from the Bren, and flames roar up, enveloping the vehicle. The two soldiers run silently away, as the fire finds the ammunition and the fierce conflagration is punctuated by the sound of intermittent explosions.

The corporal hoists the heavy Bren gun onto his shoulder and they melt effortlessly into the shadows. By tomorrow the SS truck will be just another relic of the German retreat, a burnt-out wreck by an anonymous wood, a rusting and meaningless metal carcass guarding a bitter secret.

Chapter One: Liverpool 1990

Five priests stood in purple and gold chasubles before the altar, offering up prayers for my dead brother. Incense rose from the swinging thurifer, its pungent scent hanging on the air under the arched and painted roof. I tried falteringly to join in with the half-remembered hymns, while the organ thundered, transporting me back to the High Masses and sunny Sunday mornings of my distant childhood, when I still believed. Then one of the priests, from Jack's school, strode gravely to the marble pulpit and spoke a commendation describing in glowing terms a person I hardly seemed to have known, and whose final actions had left me confused, disorientated and angry.

The congregation of a few former colleagues, friends and half a dozen relatives, including a frail and temporarily confused old Aunt Emily, had been bolstered slightly by one or two nurses from the hospital where Jack had spent the last couple of months. As we emerged from the church into the flat grey light, they took the trouble to have a word with me.

"A real gentleman, your brother ..."

"Never complained ..."

"Pity there aren't more like him ..."

But what did they know of him? What did I, in the end, know of him? And what, if anything, did I understand about our relationship?

They shook my hand, whispering and inhibited by the unfamiliar atmosphere of the Catholic church with its candles and shrines, the congregation genuflecting and making the Sign of the Cross with fingers dipped in holy water. They were obviously glad to escape into the fresh air outside, and I knew how they felt. It was nearly thirty years since I'd made my escape, and stopped attending church regularly.

I was seventeen then. At first I'd started attending evening Mass, to avoid going with my parents on Sunday morning; then I began to go out at six-thirty and walk around the darkened winter streets, pretending that I'd been to church. When they asked me which priest had said Mass, and who I'd seen there, I had to make it up, and eventually I got tired of the pretence and told them the truth.

If you haven't been a Catholic, it's hard to imagine the shock that runs through a family when one of them decides to give up the Faith. After all, if you're not a Catholic, you're on the way to Hell, or at least to Purgatory, where the poor souls go who aren't yet ready for the pearly gates. My family were pretty undemonstrative, but underneath they were really worried about me. Jack, my elder brother, whose Catholicism was considered unshakeable, was deputed to take me for a brisk walk one Saturday afternoon, during the course of which he had obviously been briefed to find out what was the matter.

"I gather you're having problems with your Faith, Mark?"

"No, not really."

"So why have you stopped going to Mass?"

"Because I don't believe in it any more."

A pause.

"What exactly do you have problems with? Remember, Mark, some things demand Faith. You may have to believe them without fully understanding them in human terms. The Trinity, for example … transubstantiation …"

Don't patronise me …

"Too right I don't understand them, because they don't make sense. The New Testament, as you, I'm sure, well know, was written by a few of Jesus's mates. OK, so we accept that he was a good bloke and wasn't afraid to say what he thought, but they blew it up out of all proportion, and invented half of it anyway. You could probably do the same with Martin Luther King, or Bob Dylan. All the rest, the Mass, Communion, fish on Friday and so on, is an accretion of mumbo-jumbo designed to keep the peasants in thrall to the clerics."

I was exasperated and, in those days, quick to scorn. There was a long silence before Jack spoke again, this time coldly and with careful emphasis.

"You realise that what you are saying is blasphemous. I don't like the tone of it. It borders on the sacrilegious. You will need to confess this."

He turned his gaze on me, his eyes blue like my father's, but more piercing, and his expression sterner than my father ever managed. He had never been one to suffer fools gladly, and the frequently harsh assessments he made of other people seemed to me to sit oddly with his professed Christianity.

I laughed sarcastically.

"Either you are joking, Jack, or you don't understand me. I don't believe in Catholicism any more, I'm not going to church any more, and I'm certainly not going to confess my innermost thoughts again to some alcoholic Irish shirt-lifter in a black dress."

This time I thought the silence would never end. We walked on down the windswept suburban road, the sunlight occasionally shining through the clouds, to gleam on the swirling litter of crisp packets and chocolate wrappers. I felt tense. I knew I had gone too far. I also knew I would be leaving Liverpool soon for the new horizons of university, and thought that this life, this stifling life of home and church, could be abandoned and left behind for ever. I did not realise then that the ties of family and religion are not so easily broken, that the past does not, after all, disappear into a black hole, and that words once spoken resonate through relationships and throughout the years.

Jack walked on, eyes fixed on the ground, his hands clasped, as always, behind his back, his sports jacket flapping open at the front. After a while, I tried to engage him in conversation on other topics, but he merely grunted. I pretended to be nonchalant, but I knew my words had troubled him deeply, and I felt a knot of apprehension in the pit of my stomach.

No further word was spoken on the subject, either then or later, and eventually I kidded myself that the topic was closed. Over the months and years that followed, after a period of brittleness, our relationship returned slowly to one of apparent outward harmony, although the unquestioning, carefree friendship of our childhood was long gone, and gone for ever. Eventually, I came to consider myself as an agnostic, while my family were still Catholics, and I thought that was the end of the matter. But there was much, much more to it than that.

The church of Our Lady of the Rosary is hidden in a tangle of narrow terraced streets in Wavertree, away from the main road, in an area which has so far escaped demolition and modernisation. It has changed little in my lifetime, except that now there are tightly parked cars everywhere, and satellite dishes on the roofs. When I was a child the streets were empty of cars, but full of kids playing football and riding bikes, women walking to the shops, men in long mackintoshes and cloth caps coming home from work; a working-class neighbourhood of old-fashioned values and limited aspirations.

The black funeral cars and the hearse came slowly down Sycamore Street and drew up in front of the church, the coffin was carried swaying slowly down the steps, and almost inevitably, the raindrops began to weep from a slate-grey sky as we prepared for Jack's last, sombre journey to the crematorium.

I had been with him a week earlier as he fought for breath, the life inexorably choked out of him by the merciless illness. His face was gaunt and his short brown hair thinned by the drugs they had pumped into him. I had to lean close to catch his words.

"I've made sure Emily will be all right. She can carry on living in the house ..." – a pause here for breath. After a short while he went on. "And you two seem to be doing quite well, you and Jenny. So I've also left some money to Phil ..." He gasped again for air.

"You'll have to speak to Phil about the house ... I've made the best arrangements I could ..."

"Don't try to speak any more, it's okay. I understand." But I didn't really. Not then, when he told me the bare fact that he'd left something to a former pupil; not later when the whole truth came out. I knew that Phil Sullivan had been one of Jack's sixth-formers, a clever historian who had gone on to study for a degree at Oxford, and I had met him several times at the terraced house shared by my brother and aunt since my father's death the previous year. I had never been able to get more than a couple of words out of him, and had frankly given up trying. As a result, I knew little about him, apart from the fact that he was training as an accountant. But it struck me as odd that Jack would leave money to him.

Jack was a traditionalist, and true to form, he died in the cold grey hours before a January dawn. I was drunk when he died. Jenny and I were staying with Liz and Derek, friends from the early days in Liverpool. We had enjoyed a relaxing meal together, and thinking Jack would last at least a few days longer, had found release from the tensions of that week in one or two bottles of good red wine. When the phone call came from Broad Green hospital, waking me from a deep drink-thickened slumber in the middle of the night, my speech was barely coherent and I was in no state to drive. We took a taxi through the darkened streets in order to sit mournfully together by Jack's bedside. I stared bleakly across the shadowy room, my thoughts maudlin and alcohol-driven.

I remembered our childhood together, our story-telling sessions in the cold bedroom on the top floor, and our different dreams of the futures we would have. I mused on the long summer holidays in North Wales, roaming the fields and woods and helping on the farm near where my father had later bought a cottage for his retirement. I thought of our school years, working hard to get to university, myself always following, as it seemed, in Jack's footsteps; always a little in awe of him.

And now he was gone. We would never bandy quotations or swap jokes again. I felt alone, and very low. Hours passed unnoticed, and morning was coming, but it was still very dark outside when the nurse put her hand gently on my shoulder.

"We'll have to ask you to leave now. We need to move your brother's body before the other patients awake. I'm sorry."

Riding back in the taxi I was suddenly very sober. Not only had I lost my older sibling, which made me suddenly very aware of my own mortality, but there were many things to sort out. Aunt Emily, for a start. She had lived all her life with our family, from the days when my father, returning from the War in 1945, had moved in with my mother, who had spent the war years keeping house for the family.

When their parents died and their brother left to get married, Emily had remained and stayed with us all through our lives. How would she cope on her own? At eighty-nine she was old to be living alone for the first time. Social Services would help, no doubt, but there was no question of us leaving our home in the Yorkshire Dales to look after her. Nor would she want to leave her home and friends to come and live with us, when we were both out at work all day.

At least Jack had said that Emily would be looked after in his will, and that the house would be hers to live in. Or so I thought he had said. I'd assumed that Jack would leave the house to me, as it had passed to him when my father died, but if he wanted to leave it to Emily, that was also fine. Obviously, I assumed I'd get the cottage in Wales, although I was more bothered about the sentimental aspect of that than the financial benefit of it. But something nagged at the back of my mind.

"You'll have to speak to Phil about the house," he had said. Why would I have to speak to Phil? I remembered that Jack had said he'd left Phil some money – doubtless a gift of a few hundred pounds, perhaps even a few thousand, which would have to be sorted out. But what involvement could he possibly have with the house? I tried to push it to the back of my mind. I had funeral arrangements to think of, death certificates to collect, friends to notify, and most of all, Emily to look after.

The next day I went round to the house with Jenny to break the news to Emily. She seemed shell-shocked by the whole business. She'd been ill herself, and was just recovering. Now she found that one of her nephews, the one who had shared a house with her all his life, had died at a comparatively young age. I thought bitterly that the death of a son or daughter, or in this case a nephew, going as it does against the normal flow of life, is always more affecting than that of a parent, someone whose life seems to have run its course.

Emily had always had a reputation for poor health, sickly as a child, and prey to infections, bronchitis and pneumonia. Yet here she was, at 89, still keeping going, while Jack, who until this last illness struck him down, had been remarkably healthy, had died.

We made milky coffee, and sat talking quietly in the kitchen. The electric fire was burning in front of the old stove, which would never now be lit again. Overhead, tea towels hung from the drying rack, and watery sunlight crept in through the window which looked out onto a small back yard, and beyond that, the backs of other houses, walls, rooftops and blank windows.

"At least I'll still have the house, I hope. Jack would have wanted me to have somewhere to live."

Emily's voice was weak.

"I don't know what he's done about the cottage, though. I know Jack had some money saved. I helped him with that, when he got sick. I wanted to make sure he wouldn't go short if he had to stop work. But I don't know what he will have done with it.

6

Probably given it to charity."

Her smile was feeble.

"You two will be all right though, won't you?"

There was an earnestness, almost a pleading in her features that unsettled me. I knew she would want the best for us. Emily had always stood by us, never letting her deep Catholic faith, and my lack of it, come between us. She had been generous enough never to show disapproval even when Jenny and I started living together, and afterwards when we refused to get married in church.

"I'm not sure yet which of us Jack's left the house to, Emily, but the first thing now is to make sure you're all right."

Emily sat forward in her armchair, turning her head slightly to catch my words, her hands folded in her lap. She was wearing one of the brightly coloured pinafores that she always wore during the day.

"I know your father would have wanted you to have the house and the cottage, Mark. And if I did get the house, I'd only have to leave it to you in a few years anyway."

"Don't be morbid, Emily. You've got years in you yet!"

I tried to sound more cheerful than I felt.

Later that morning, Father Byrne, the parish priest, a quietly-spoken elderly man with a soft Irish accent, called to pay his respects. We chatted, as is often the case in such circumstances, in a fairly desultory way as we drank tea from Emily's best china in the front room. Priests are at least fairly used to being involved in the aftermath of death, and spare the bereaved the "I don't know what to say" routine.

"You'll miss your brother. We all will."

"I know; but to be honest, we hadn't seen too much of each other in the last few years. Until his illness, of course."

"A great shame. He was a fine man. Still, your faith will be a wonderful support for you in this difficult time."

I stiffened, and put down my cup with a slight rattle in the saucer. Father Byrne seemed to assume I was still a Catholic. Or did I detect a slight note of irony in his tone? I didn't know whether to put him right before we went any further. It seemed in a way unnecessary and perhaps slightly offensive to tell him at this juncture that I didn't believe in anything the Church had to offer; on the other hand, it felt deceitful not to. I felt again the adolescent fear of confronting the centuries-old weight of expectation, guilt and unspoken threat that the Catholic Church relied upon to discourage dissent.

Before I could say anything, the priest put his hands together and bowed his head.

"Let us say a prayer for Jack, and for those of his family left behind. *Our Father, who art in heaven…*"

I glanced across at Jenny, who smiled gently and nodded almost imperceptibly. We bowed our heads and joined in with the prayer, mumbling quietly, while Aunt Emily spoke the well-known words in a surprisingly strong, but slightly quavering voice. Although embarrassed by the assumption of my continuing Catholicism, I could not help finding the prayer quite moving in the circumstances. The thought came to me then, that for the priest, if he knew the truth, and certainly for Emily, I was not a man who could be thought of as having no attachment to religion, but would for ever be a "lapsed" Catholic.

In the afternoon we had a visit from two priests from St Luke's College where Jack had been Deputy Head up until his retirement on grounds of ill health. One, Father Kelly, was the Headmaster, a broad man with a bluff manner and a shining pink face.

"He was a great loss to the school, your brother."

He looked at me over his rimless glasses, and smiled.

"I remember all those trips to the Highlands he would organise for the boys. And what a strong walker he was! Walked the legs off me the time I went with them!"

He clasped his hands over his ample stomach.

Yes, I thought, you probably would find walking difficult, even at Jack's pace. We all know that he loved the Highlands, and enjoyed his walks there, but he was never a hardy mountaineer. However, I would imagine sampling the malts would be more your line.

"There are several of us who would like the opportunity to concelebrate Jack's Requiem Mass," Father Kelly was continuing." I've already spoken to Father Byrne, so if you've no objection, we'll all be there together. Five priests at the altar together. Now there's a fine thing!"

The other priest, Father Murphy, smiled and nodded in agreement.

"Of course, Father" – the word was out before I could stop it, although I hadn't intended to give him the honour of that title. It reminded me too much of my childhood, and of the guilty pressure of trying to think of sins to confess, at eight years old.

"We'd be delighted," I heard myself continuing, "and Jack would have been greatly honoured."

I, too, I realised, would be strangely pleased that my brother's passing was to be recognised in this way. Not many people had so many clerics assembled together to mark their passing. Father Kelly rose with some difficulty from the low armchair, and shook my hand.

"We'll see you on Thursday, then, at Our Lady's"

"Thank you, Father," – there it was again "and thank you for coming."

The day was wearing away, and after the shock of Jack's death and the visits from the priests, together with lack of sleep, we were all tired. The yellow streetlights had come on and were glaring intrusively at the windows, even with the curtains drawn. We were debating what to do about tea – nobody felt like cooking – when, with something between surprise and shock, I heard the front door open, and a moment later Phil Sullivan appeared in the room, the house key still in his hand. He stared at me without speaking, his eyes hard in his pale face.

"Hello, Phil. I didn't know you had a key to the house."

"Of course I have. Jack gave it me a while back. I come and go as I please."

I felt my hackles rising.

"That may have been the case when Jack was alive. Now that Emily's on her own, I don't think it's really appropriate. I'd rather you gave back the key."

"Why? What's it got to do with you? I'm entitled to do what I like!" His voice was scornful.

"I don't think so." I tried to keep my voice calm, but it was beginning to tremble with anger. "This is my house now, and I'll decide who comes in here. I've Emily's welfare to think of. She's lived in this house all her adult life, and I want her to go on feeling as secure as possible here."

Phil laughed.

"Unfortunately, whatever you may think, it's not up to you any more. Jack was a good friend to me, you know, as well as a teacher." As he spoke, I felt myself turn cold. *You'll have to speak to Phil about the house...* suddenly, with a feeling of horror, I guessed what was coming next. Shocking and unlikely though it was, I knew what he was going to say.

"The house is mine now," he went on. "Jack left it to me. Have a look at this. It's Jack's will."

He pulled some sheets of paper out of his jacket pocket and thrust them at me. They were covered in Jack's small, scrawled writing, blue fountain pen on white paper. Typical of Jack to write his own will. I scanned them in panic haste.

"...being of sound mind..." really? *"...I leave everything to Philip Sullivan...Emily to be allowed to continue living in the house...my brother to be allowed to choose a memento of me..."*

There was lots more, details of gifts to various friends, clauses defining what was to happen to the house after Emily's death, arrangements for my father's cottage in Wales, and a substantial bequest to Jack's former school, but the bare fact remained: at a stroke, he had left nearly everything that belonged to him and our family to a former pupil whom I hardly knew.

I was horrified. I felt my skin going clammy. Not just because Jack had given everything away, but the fact that he did not once mention me by name in his will...*my brother – my nameless brother...* I felt like a stranger, dismissed by Jack not only from the house, but from his life. I couldn't understand it.

I looked up, the papers crumpling in my hands. Phil was smiling broadly.

"Bet that's put your nose out of joint, hasn't it? You thought you could just turn up and inherit everything. But it doesn't work like that. And, by the way, I've already taken a photocopy of the will, so don't get any ideas about destroying it." He reached out and took the sheets from my trembling fingers.

I felt like punching his sneering face. But what would be the point? It was Jack who had done this to me, to us. I didn't care that he had given all his own money away to a comparative stranger, although that was odd enough, especially when I knew that Emily had helped him to build up his savings during his illness. But what right did he have to give away the family home and my father's cottage, and leave Emily at the whim of someone who was not even a relative?

I felt stunned and humiliated, and hardly aware of what was happening.

"By the way," Phil was saying, "Jack did leave something you might want. I certainly don't want it. I'll go and get it."

He turned and went out of the room, and I heard him running up the stairs. He reappeared very quickly with a battered cardboard box, which seemed to be crammed full of old papers, magazines and various other stuff.

"It was your dad's. Some of his things from the War, I think. Jack left everything to me, but you can have this, if you want it." His tone was dismissive, almost contemptuous, as if he was tossing me a half-gnawed bone.

I took the box from him wordlessly. At that moment it seemed a bonus to get anything that had belonged to my family.

"See you at the funeral, then." Phil's voice was sarcastic.

"Yes, I'll look forward to that." It was clear as could be from my tone of voice that it was the last thing I was thinking.

I kissed Aunt Emily, who looked bewildered and upset. She might have been about to say something, but thought better of it. Clutching the box as a shipwrecked man clings to driftwood, I let Jenny lead me to the car and drive me back to our friends' house.

My mind was in turmoil. Why had Jack done this? Why, at the end, had he denied our brotherhood, our friendship? And why would he give everything to Phil? None of it made any sense. But there had to be a reason, an answer of some sort. I was not going to leave it at that. I was determined to find out.

Chapter Two

A road runs around Sefton Park, ringed by substantial Victorian houses built for wealthy merchants in the days when Liverpool was one of the world's major ports, its prosperity founded on sugar, cotton, and the slave trade. Many of these houses are now divided into flats, while several have become hotels which seem to specialise in catering for functions. It was in one of these, the pretentious but faded Hotel Sonata, that Jack's post-funeral buffet was held.

Such gatherings tend to be morose occasions; the only plus being the fact that it gets the family together, as well as friends of the deceased. The rain was still puddling drearily in the gutters, and the cold, fitful wind slapping in our faces when Jenny and I arrived from the crematorium with Aunt Emily to join those who had gone straight to the hotel. The food was laid out in an upstairs room, and we were offered glasses of medium sherry from a tray on arrival, although I was more in need of a pint.

Some of Jack's friends and colleagues from St. Luke's were there, as well as one or two friends from his own schooldays. There were a couple of cousins that I hadn't seen for ages, and Emily's sister-in-law. And, of course, Phil, in a striped grey suit with wide lapels that made him look like a used car salesman, smoothing his way around the room as if he was the host, offering drinks to people and accepting their condolences with all the mournfulness of a bereaved relative. Some of the people there obviously seemed to know more about Phil's relationship with Jack than I did, and expected him to be very upset, but few of the staff from St Luke's even knew who I was. Maureen, the school secretary, a small, plump woman in her fifties, whom I had met once or twice, made a point of coming over to speak to me, along with the Head of History, a woman only slightly younger, but well-preserved, tall and slim with shoulder-length auburn hair tinged with grey, and a ready smile.

"I just wanted you to know how much we'll all miss Jack. It was such a tragedy when he had to leave the school, when he got ill. We were both very fond of him. If there's anything we can do to help, just ask. Ruth and I would love to come over and visit Emily. She's such fun!"

"That's very kind of you, Maureen," I answered, thinking: *strange how other people see our relatives. Emily I thought of as charming, loving, supportive...but **fun**?*

"I'm sure she'd love to see you. It'll be difficult for her to get used to being on her own."

"Yes, how do you think she'll manage? Do you think she'll want to move?"

"She won't move. She'll manage, and a little bit of support from ourselves and friends like you two will probably be all she needs."

Ruth put her hand on my arm.

"Jack was a lovely man, Mark. You should be very proud of him. Old-fashioned, but a gentleman. He could be a bit abrasive at times, when others didn't live up to his standards, and some couldn't cope with that. But I enjoyed working with him very much, and found him very courteous."

"Thanks. I appreciate that."

But I didn't really. I was seething. How could all these people think that my brother was so marvellous? They had no idea of the bombshell he had dropped on me. Now he was dead, I had no way of asking him about it, or confronting him. Not that he would ever have told me what he was thinking. He kept his emotions too close for that. The whole thing seemed like a macabre joke that he had played with his last breath. I turned away and walked to the bar to get a drink.

I bought a pint of bitter, and turned away from the bar with it.

"So what *did* he die of then, your brother?"

The voice boomed in my ear, and I recognised two teachers, one of whom was Steve Tomlinson, the Head of PE from St. Luke's. He was a powerful-looking man in his late thirties with a rough complexion and a strong Liverpool accent. It had always surprised me that Jack would be so friendly with him, but he had once told me that he admired Steve's clear-mindedness and dogged refusal to be cowed by senior management.

But it was the other man who had spoken. I had met Bob Downs once or twice, but had never warmed to him. Dark-haired and rather overweight, with soft, plump hands, he was a colleague from Jack's previous school, the all-boys Paduan College. I had a vague memory of some friction between him and Jack, covered up by spurious friendliness.

"I'm sorry. It's Bob, isn't it?" I played for time, wary that there was some hidden agenda behind his question.

"That's right, Mark. My condolences." His voice was insincere, and the hand he offered for me to shake was moist and gripless.

"You know when we first heard that Jack had started taking time off school, to be honest, some of us thought he was swinging the lead a bit."

"He didn't have that reputation though, did he? He loved teaching."

"That's right. That's why it seemed so out of character. But nobody knew what was wrong with him. It sounded a strange sort of illness. Apparently he was OK when he had time off, then felt sick when he came back to work. A lot of us feel like that!" He chuckled, and took a pull at his pint.

"It wasn't like that though. He really ill."

"Oh, of course! Don't get me wrong!" He re-arranged his features hastily into a look of serious concern.

"We heard that he'd got ME. Which we know now is a real medical condition. But was that what Jack had? You must know."

I realised that I didn't, in fact, know exactly what had been wrong with Jack. Of course, I'd seen the effects, and had talks with the doctors about their prognosis. But I didn't have a name that I could flourish to finish off the conversation. Bob was looking at me expectantly.

" It was a breakdown of the immune system. It caused his liver and lungs to stop functioning over a period of time." As soon as I spoke, I realised how it might sound.

Bob looked at Steve, and I fancied that an eyebrow was raised. He put down his drink.

"I thought so! A bit like AIDS, then? That attacks the immune system, doesn't it?"

"Well, yes, but I don't think it was that. I'm sure it wasn't."

"What makes you so sure, if you don't know what it was?"

I raised my glass and took a drink to cover the expectant silence.

"I just know it wasn't. Why should it be?" But the seed had been planted, burrowing into my mind, looking for something to feed off, to grow …

Bob bought another round of drinks, lining them up on the bar. He was drinking faster than he should, and so was I.

"Why should it be?" he mused, echoing my words as he counted his change and slid it carefully into his trouser pocket. He gazed up at the ceiling. "And why shouldn't it be? You must have heard all the rumours about Jack?"

"What rumours might they be?" My tone was icy, although my hand trembled, spilling liquid onto the bar as I picked up my fresh pint.

"Well, he was always very fond of the boys. He was a very *attentive* form teacher …"

"Of course he was! That was his job. He liked his pupils. He believed in getting involved with the boys." Again, too late, I realised how that sounded.

"Exactly! But don't be naïve, Mark. Jack was more than just a teacher to some of those boys. If I said to you that he liked little boys, perhaps you'd catch my drift." His smile had turned to a leer.

Suddenly, I had a cold, empty feeling in the pit of my stomach. Jack had never been one for girlfriends. I couldn't remember him ever talking about girls. And he had often told me how much he liked the first year pupils when he started working at the Paduan College. It all began to seem so obvious, and I felt a fool for not putting two and two together earlier. At the same time I was angry with Bob Downs for saying these things about Jack, when we had only just come from his funeral. This was a family affair, and I couldn't even remember having invited Bob when I went through the list of names in Jack's diary.

" And another thing," – *would he not leave it alone?* "I hear Jack's left pretty well everything to a former pupil. Someone not a million miles from here. Why would he do that?"

"I don't know, Bob." *News travel fast,* I thought, *and it must have come from Phil.* I was sure that neither myself, Jenny nor Emily had mentioned it. Emily hadn't really taken it in yet, anyway.

"You tell me."

Steve Tomlinson leaned forward in front of him.

"Leave it, Bob. You've said enough already. More than enough."

Bob ignored him.

"Well, Mark, look at it this way. If a teacher died and left all his possessions to a former *female* pupil, one who wasn't related in any way to the family, there would only be one conclusion, wouldn't there? So don't you think that in this case the evidence points to the fact that Jack was having an affair with young Sullivan?"

I swung at him, knocking glasses wildly from the bar as I did so. My punch went awry, fortunately, skimming his chin and landing in the soft flesh of his well-padded shoulder. Steve grabbed me and pushed me back. Jenny, who had been standing nearby and had overheard the last part of our conversation, screamed my name and leaped to my side, clutching my arm.

"Don't, Mark, don't. He's not worth it."

I knew he wasn't, and I also had a horrible feeling that he had hit on the truth. I didn't want to admit it about my own brother, but in the circumstances, what other explanation could there be for the turn that events had taken concerning Jack's death and his will? And given that he had hurt me so badly, why should I worry about his reputation?

Few in the room had been aware of the nature of the fracas. Emily certainly hadn't heard any of it, and most other people affected ignorance. Bob left soon after, and it was not long before other guests began to drift away with the usual thanks and offers of support. Soon it was over, and I was quiet and thoughtful in the car as Jenny drove us back to Aunt Emily's house.

Shocked though I was by my conversation with Bob Downs, what he said had made sense, and if I was looking for an explanation of Jack's will, painful though it was, I seemed to have found it. The one thing it still didn't explain was why Jack had cut me out so brutally, but given the state he was in over the last month or so of his illness, I began to assume that he simply wasn't thinking straight, or perhaps had been overly influenced by Phil.

At least, now the funeral was over, we could concentrate on getting Emily organised in the house with whatever help was necessary; and when that was done, head back North, forget about it all and get on with our lives.

We took Emily back to her house and made sure she was settled in. The home help was coming later to sort her out with a meal, and Emily's sister-in-law had promised to pop in later to check on her, so we went back to Liz and Derek's in Aigburth for the evening.

"How did it go?" Liz wanted to know, coming through from the kitchen with a pot of tea on a tray.

Jenny flopped down on the sofa, kicking her shoes off and pushing her blonde-streaked hair back behind her ear

"Well, you know what funerals are like, Liz. Never a barrel of fun. But this one was a bit more tense-making than usual. Mark tried to start a fight!"

"Oh really, Jenny! Do you have to be so irritating? You know what was going on!" I looked at her sourly, the after-effects of the alcohol making me even more miserably bad-tempered than I felt.

"So-orry, I didn't mean it like that."

"Well, why did you say it then!"

"Leave it, Mark. Don't be so sensitive."

"Of course I'm bloody sensitive. So would you be in the circumstances!"

"I'm sorry. Liz, ignore us." Jenny apologised. We're a bit on edge at the moment."

Liz stood in front of the fireplace, hands on hips.

"I'll go if you want me to. But it might help just to tell me all about it."

We'd already told Liz and Derek about the contents of Jack's will, and they were as horrified as we were. But telling them of the insinuations about his sexuality was another bridge to cross.

She poured the tea, passed round the biscuits and listened while we explained what had happened.

"Well, Mark, it must have been awful hearing it like that, from someone like this Bob Downs, and I wouldn't have blamed you if you'd dropped him. But at least you know the truth now…"

"If it *is* the truth," I interrupted, still unwilling to believe that Jack had been involved in a variety of unattractive sexual activities, some of them probably illegal.

"It sounds possible. In fact, probable. You've said yourself how you always wondered why Jack never had any girlfriends when you were growing up. And it does explain why he's left nothing to you, and everything to a former pupil. If he was that close to Phil, he would want to leave things to him, and it makes the fact that he cut you out less of an insult to you."

"But he hardly even mentioned me in the will."

"No. I know that's really hard to bear. But remember, he was very ill. It's probably best not to dwell on it too much."

"I'd find that easier if he hadn't left Emily living in a house that doesn't belong to her. How's she going to feel?"

Liz shrugged.

"You'll just have to make sure that she's OK. Make sure that Phil doesn't do anything to upset her. I know you can do that."

It was later that evening, after dinner, that the phone rang. Liz went to answer it, and came back, frowning, into the room.

"It's for you, Mark. He didn't say who it was."

I went through into the hall, and picked up the phone which Liz had left lying on the small table.

"Hello," I said cautiously. "Mark Gilgarran speaking."

"Hello Mark. It's Steve. Steve Tomlinson."

"Hi, Steve."

"I got this number from your Aunt Emily. I thought you were staying there."

"No, we're with some friends. We've just been talking all about this afternoon's little charade."

"Yes, I wanted to speak to you about that. Bob was well out of order."

"He was probably only saying what everyone thinks." I suddenly felt cross again and a little tearful at the same time.

"Well, you're right, Mark. There's been a lot of rumours over the years. But there's never been any real evidence. Some people just don't like it when someone's a bit different. They can't understand it, so they make things up to explain it. Maybe it tells you more about Bob Downs than about Jack."

Get to the point...

"I wanted to have a word with you, Mark, because I've got my own theory about what's been going on."

"What theory is that then Steve?"

"I don't want to talk about it on the phone. Can we meet?"

"Tonight?"

"Why not? In the bar of the *Black Bull* in half an hour? Say ten o'clock?"

"OK Steve. I'll see you there."

"I don't think you'll regret it. I think you'll be very interested in what I have to say. It could change everything for you. And I'm not exaggerating!"

It could change everything. What on earth could that mean? I was intrigued. I picked my coat from the stand in the hall, and called through to the others.

"I'm going out. I'll be about an hour." Then I stepped into the winter street and closed the door behind me.

The *Black Bull* stands in what was once the village of Woolton, but which has long since been swallowed up in the outskirts of Liverpool. Apparently it used to be a droving inn, although you wouldn't think so now with all the main roads round there. It's an attractive pub, though, and a pleasant place to meet on a bright summer's evening, surrounded as it is by buildings whose dark red sandstone has been quarried over the centuries in the local area. On this January evening, however, the streets were damp and empty as I drove there, my route cutting across the wide dual carriageways and past the parks that make this area of the city so attractive.

Steve was already seated in the bar when I arrived. He rose to his feet and shook my hand warmly.

"Pint, Mark?" he asked, stepping up to the bar.

"Cheers. Thanks, Steve."

We sat down again with our drinks.

"So, Steve. What is it that you can tell me? What's your theory?"

He seemed to hesitate. Perhaps he was thinking better of sharing it with me. Perhaps it was too far-fetched after all. Maybe he thought I would laugh, or lose my temper. He didn't strike me as a man who acted frivolously, but rather as one who expected to be taken seriously. I sensed his dilemma.

"Tell me, Steve," I said, more gently. "I want to know the truth, whatever it is. As long as what you say is based on fact, and you're not just taking the piss, I want to know what you're thinking. Don't worry, I won't lose it again like I did this afternoon. I know you're not Bob."

He looked as if he had reached a decision.

"Well, Mark, some of what I've got to say is fact, but some of it's guesswork. But you've got to believe I'm not making this up for the sake of it. I was very fond of Jack too, and I want to get to the bottom of all this. I think we'll all benefit in different ways if the truth is known."

"Go on, then, Steve. Tell me what you know."

I was starting to get impatient.

"I'm not sure where to start, Mark, and I'm not very good at telling stories, so I'll try the beginning. This goes back twenty-five years or so now. I was a pupil at the Paduan College when Jack started there. It was his first teaching job, and he was still learning his trade, but he inspired me with a love of history. He made it come to life, and he made us work hard. I took history at A level before I went to PE College in Loughborough. Jack was unusual, even then."

You don't need to tell me that...

"He used to wear a three piece suit to school, and a college tie. Trousers with turn-ups – this was the late sixties, remember – and short hair. We respected him, although we thought he was a bit square. But the women liked him, because he was so courteous to them in the sort of way that was going out of fashion. And one or two of them obviously didn't just like him. They wanted to get close to him. And one of them was Ruth."

"Ruth?" My voice expressed my surprise. "Ruth who teaches at your school now, at St Luke's?

"That's the one. She was teaching there then, as well. They were in the same department. They got very friendly. Then, one half-term, Whitsun it was, a friend of mine, Barry McHugh, was on holiday with his parents in North Wales, near Lake Vyrnwy. They saw Jack and Ruth coming out of the hotel there, obviously together. They walked out onto the dam and looked over, and Ruth put her arm round his shoulder. Then she kissed him on the cheek. That was enough for Barry. It was all over school the following week, and I'm afraid we made things quite uncomfortable for them. You know what little bastards even nice kids can be. They just don't think. They don't realise how much they can upset people. In fact, I was pretty embarrassed about it all afterwards.

"That summer, Ruth left the school, and the rumour went around that she was pregnant. People saw her around Liverpool for a little while after that – you couldn't fail to notice her with that hair, it was like a flame flickering down the street – then she disappeared, and nobody saw her for ages."

"So what? You're not suggesting that it was Jack who got her pregnant, are you? I mean, it's interesting that Jack had some interest in women, but I can't see him getting up to anything like that. And it was a long time ago. It doesn't necessarily change anything, does it?"

I thought: *One minute my brother's a homosexual with an interest in small boys; now he's fathering illegitimate children. I can't cope with all this*

Steve was obviously eager to continue with his story.

"So you think it doesn't change anything? Doesn't it? No, you're right, on its own it doesn't. But listen to this. When Phil Sullivan started at the College, I was his form teacher. He had a lot of problems settling in, and always seemed as if he had the weight of the world on his shoulders. He was bullied, as well, and then he started truanting. It was because of that that I got involved, and found out that Phil lived with foster parents. The Newmans were a middle-aged couple who had a house on a council estate at Dovecote. Smashing folk they were, down-to-earth working-class people – you know the clichés. George was a bus driver; Elsie was a dinner lady at the local Primary School. They were very worried about Phil, and between us we managed to get him back to school, and stopped most of the bullying. After that he made good progress, but he was never a happy boy."

"This is all very interesting, Steve. But what have Phil Sullivan's problems at school got to do with me, or my brother?"

"Good question, Mark. I'm just coming to that. When I was talking to George and Elsie, we got on to the subject of their financial situation. Neither of them was well paid, but their house was very well-equipped, and Phil had good clothes, a telly in his bedroom, a brand-new bike and so on. Not a fantastic lot, but more than you might have expected. They seemed to be coping remarkably well. They got money from Social Services, of course, for fostering Phil, but that's not a great lot. Then one day when I called in, we got chatting, and Elsie told me something interesting."

Steve paused and took a drink from his pint.

"Go on, Steve. What was so interesting?"

"Apparently, Mark, they got money paid into their bank account every month. A fairly substantial amount, enough to more than compensate for looking after a growing young man. They'd asked who it was from, but the bank couldn't tell them, the source was supposed to remain anonymous. However, a few months previously they'd changed their account, and there'd been a problem with the transfer of the standing order. Because of that, the first month they'd got a cheque sent through – the only time this happened – and there was a signature on it.

"The signature was J. Gilgarran."

"Jack!" I almost exploded. "Jack was sending them money? For Phil? Why? Why on earth…?"

"Think about it, Mark. Put two and two together. You brother is paying money every month, apparently, to support Phil Sullivan. Phil was born in 1969, shortly after Ruth Morris left the College. You were away at university then, remember. The rumour goes around that she's pregnant, and we think she may have had an affair with Jack shortly before that. He's a Catholic – he can't be seen to have had an affair, and an illegitimate child. What would that have done to his family? And to himself and his career, for that matter."

"But he could have married her. That's how most people regularise the situation."

"Maybe he didn't want to marry her. Maybe she wouldn't marry him. Who knows? Anyway, can you think of any other reason why your brother would be paying money every month towards the upkeep of an apparently unrelated child?"

I took a long drink from my pint, reluctant to answer.

"No, I can't, Steve."

"And think about this, Mark. You brother lived all his life in a small terraced house. He ran a Vauxhall Nova. Yet he was a Deputy Head when he retired, a single man with no expensive habits or hobbies. He should have been able to afford something better, a nice detached house in Woolton, or Aigburth, and a better car. Why did he never move? Emily often complained, when I was round there, about how cold the house was in winter, and he didn't even have central heating put in. Why would that be, unless there was some drain on his resources that used up his disposable income?"

"I don't know." I was finding this all hard to digest. Steve seemed to have done a lot of thinking about this. It all began to fit together, and seemed plausible enough. The most shocking thing, and the most unpleasant pill to swallow was the thought that Phil Sullivan might be my nephew. If I found him more sympathetic it wouldn't be so bad, but as it was I couldn't see him as anything other than a stranger, a usurper of my family's inheritance.

"What about the Newmans, Steve?" I asked. "Phil's foster parents. What did they say about the money coming from Jack? They must have known he was one of Phil's teachers"

"They said nothing. They didn't know why he was paying the money, but they realised it was meant to be a secret, so they kept it that way. I don't think they would have mentioned it to your brother."

I stared at my beer, pushing the pint glass in small circles around the table, centring it on the beer mat. There was one other thing still bothering me.

"What about Jack's condition? I never really found out what it was, except that it was something to do with his immune system. And you heard what Bob Downs said about that. He drew the conclusion that it was AIDS, and he's probably not the only one. And you know what that could mean."

"Well, yes, I thought that too. But I visited Jack several times in hospital, and had a word with the doctors. They were a bit cagey about the diagnosis, and they were especially reluctant to talk, with me not being family. But one of the younger housemen did tell me what they thought it was. He was quite proud to be involved, because Jack's condition was pretty unusual."

"Go on," I urged, as Steve paused.

"I didn't quite catch the name at first, I have to confess But I knew it was some sort of -oma. He said it was called after the man who identified it. It's very rare, apparently."

"Typical," I interrupted. "Typical of Jack to go for something no-one's ever heard of."

Steve smiled a bleak and humourless smile, and I sensed his

disapproval. He hesitated, then went on.

"They don't know what causes it, and they obviously don't know how to treat it. It attacks the sinuses, then the lungs and kidneys. But there's no connection with AIDS, so any insinuations that might follow from that, you can forget."

"Are you sure?"

"As sure as I can be. I checked it afterwards in a medical dictionary. I'm pretty sure I got the right thing. Wegener's granuloma. It was a bit vague, but it seemed to say that it wasn't certain what caused it. Didn't mention AIDS at all, though."

"Well, that's a relief. But all this still doesn't prove that Jack wasn't attracted to young men, does it?"

Steve gave me a long hard look. Then he sat back and sighed wearily.

"Mark, if what I've just told you is true, and I believe it is, Jack certainly wasn't having an illicit relationship with Phil. He was his father, for heaven's sake. I know that must be a shock for you, but surely better than the alternative.

"Jack was a good teacher; and he either wasn't bothered about relationships with the opposite sex – with either sex, in fact – or else his affair with Ruth was something he never really got over, and he never wanted another relationship after that. Whatever the case is, I don't think you should go on worrying about him being a rampant homosexual. That's just not the man I knew."

"You seem very sure about all this, Steve, but I'm still not totally convinced."

"Honestly, Mark, if you don't mind my saying so, you're not being very loyal to Jack."

"Frankly, how do you expect me to feel? No, I don't feel very loyal to him. He's just given away everything that belonged to our family. And on top of that I've just found out that he's got an illegitimate son that he's been hiding for over twenty years!"

The anger and resentment were trembling in my voice. I took another drink. The barman was going round collecting glasses. I looked at my watch and saw that it was eleven o'clock. I'd been out much longer than I thought, but hoped Jenny wouldn't be worrying about me.

"I'll have to go, Steve. And thanks for sharing all this with me."

"Don't mention it, Mark. I was very fond of Jack. I must admit I was a bit shocked myself when I found out about him and Ruth, but it seems to have been a youthful indiscretion that came back to haunt him. Fancy living your whole life with that in the background!"

"Yes, it's weird to think about it. And I never even suspected it. But we never really talked about anything very personal, I suppose."

I finished the dregs of my pint, and handed the glass to the barman.

"What I still don't understand is why he didn't even mention me in his will. OK, so he was going to leave everything to Phil, his son. I can understand that now, even if it doesn't make it easy to accept. But not to even mention me, and to just bequeath me a "memento." Why would he do that? It's that that hurts most."

Steve looked at me and shrugged helplessly.

"I don't know, Mark. I always got the impression that he was fond of you. But I think he was a bit confused, and some of the things he said were rather strange in the latter stages."

"Yeah, that's what one of our friends said, too. I shouldn't take it too much to heart." I smiled weakly. "Oh well, thanks again, Steve. I'd best be off."

I rose to go, and Steve walked to the door of the pub with me. Outside, in the cold air, we shook hands and I got into my car and started the engine. I sat collecting my thoughts for a moment, then eased it into gear and pulled carefully out into the road.

After the morning's rain, the roads were still wet, although the air had cleared. There was little traffic about as I drove slowly back towards Aigburth. My mind was in turmoil and I wasn't concentrating on my driving. When I reached Liz and Derek's, I saw a parking space at the last minute and braked sharply without signalling. I hadn't noticed the car behind me, which had to swerve and pull out round me. I caught a glimpse of the passenger's short fair hair as he peered angrily at me, and I waved absently in a gesture of apology. As I got out of my car, it accelerated away. Something about it seemed a little unusual, but I couldn't put my finger on it. By the time I got my key in the door, I'd forgotten about it.

Jenny and the others were in bed when I let myself into the house. There was a light burning on my side of the bed, but Jenny had obviously been asleep, or nearly. I tried to undress quietly, but she half-turned under the bedclothes.

"You're late."

"I know. I'm sorry."

"Steve have anything interesting to tell you?"

"Yes. Quite a lot. I'll tell you in the morning."

She must have been tired, because she didn't quiz me any further, and soon the sound of her regular breathing showed she was sleeping. I cleaned my teeth and got gently into bed, but I couldn't sleep.

Steve's theories kept going through my head. Was he right? Had Jack been hiding a secret all these years? And if so, was it really the secret Steve believed he had uncovered, or the secret Bob Downs had suggested? The facts and the fancies kept running through my mind. Whatever the truth, he wasn't the brother I thought he was. Did it matter now what the truth was? Could it change anything, or should I just let it lie? Forget it, I told myself. Go home and get on with your life.

But, I thought again, why *would* Jack do what he'd done in his will? Why had he cut me out of it? Was Phil his son, or something else? I had to know, even if it changed nothing. I had to dig a little deeper. But where to start?

I tossed and turned until late in the night, when I finally drifted into a fitful sleep.

Chapter Three

"So why don't you do something about it?" Jenny's tone was harsh. "You've been moping around all the time since we got back from Liverpool. You say it doesn't matter, but you're obviously thinking about nothing else. You talk about nothing else. It's been weeks now. It's driving me up the wall."

I'd told her everything that Steve had told me, but she wasn't as shocked as I thought she'd be. I knew that she'd always thought Jack was pretty odd, one way or another, and this seemed like proof to her. But since we still didn't know definitely whether Steve's version of the facts was true or not, she seemed to be keeping an open mind.

"I'm sure you'd be a bit preoccupied if it was your family, and your inheritance, Jenny."

"Yes, OK, but I'd probably do something about it."

"Like what? What can I do?"

"Oh, for heavens' sake, Mark! Either you do something, or you forget about it and we get back to normal."

"So what do you suggest?"

"I would have thought it was pretty obvious!"

"Go on then, enlighten me!"

Jenny turned away from the bay window, where she had been gazing across the meadow towards the river. She folded her arms and gave me a challenging look.

"Don't tell me you haven't thought of it yourself. If you think Ruth is the mother of Jack's child, go and ask her." Her tone was abrupt.

She was right, I *had* thought of it, but it was too bold, too committing a step. To me, with my conventional life, it smacked too much of the private detective, the opening of a television drama. The most exciting thing ever did was climb a few mountains, and these days I seemed to do less of that and spend more time pottering in the garden. And there were other obvious problems that had suggested themselves to me.

"What if she won't tell me? Or doesn't tell me the truth?"

"Then you're no worse off. And at least you've tried. But I'm sure if you go to her house, speak to her and look into her eyes – watch her reactions – you'll find out something."

"It all seems a bit scary. A bit of an imposition …"

Jenny took a pace nearer me and spread out her hands, the fingers splayed in an impatient, stabbing gesture.

"Either do it, and do it soon, or shut up about it. I'm getting sick of the whole thing! If you must know, I'm getting pretty sick of your pathetic behaviour!"

She stormed past me into the kitchen and I swore quietly under my breath. Things hadn't been great between us for a while and as the time went by there seemed to be less and less affection left in our relationship. Sometimes I felt she blamed me for our childlessness, and the fact we hadn't made love for many months wasn't helping things. I knew she was under pressure with her job, and now we had Jack's death and Emily's situation to think about, but I was still hurt and angered by her reaction and apparent lack of support.

Her caustic words, however, were enough to finally spur me into action. I realised immediately that I had no idea where Ruth lived, but that wasn't a big problem. I could easily find out. I picked up the phone and dialled Steve's number.

However, when he answered the phone and had listened to my request for Ruth Morris' phone number, he was unable to help at first.

"Sorry, Mark. I'm not sure I've got it. No, it's not in my address book."

I was taken aback. I was certain he would know Ruth's number.

"Are you sure, Steve? Well, there must be someone you know who's got it."

"Let me think …" he paused. A long pause.

Then: "Maybe I can get it through directory enquiries. I think Jack mentioned she lived in Princes Road or somewhere like that. I'm sure they'll find it for me. Can I get back to you?"

"It's all right, Steve. I can try myself. Don't worry about it."

Another pause.

"Oh, it's here, Mark. On a scrap of paper in the back of my address book. Sorry about that."

He read the number out and I noted it down.

"By the way, Mark, you realise she may deny it anyway, don't you?"

He sounded anxious, concerned.

"Of course, Steve. But thanks anyway. I'll let you know how I get on."

Despite the poor reputation of Toxteth, many of the impressive Georgian houses in Princes Road have been renovated over the years and turned into good quality flats, with high ceilings and old plaster mouldings, and large windows overlooking a tree-lined road. Ruth Morris lived in one of these. The number Steve had given me turned out not to be the right number after all – maybe it was from a previous address – but as it turned out I'd been able to find her number myself quite easily and quickly, through Directory Enquiries. Now, seated in her living-room in the Sunday morning sunshine, while she made coffee in the kitchen, I found evidence of her lifestyle all around me. Overflowing bookcases, piles of exercise books, a battered briefcase and a good quality CD player with various opera recordings lying around, were all typical of a single teacher.

But the shelves and walls were also covered with all sorts of artefacts – masks and pottery pieces that looked as if they had come from the heart of Africa; pan pipes from South America and a Berber *kellim* rug in front of the fire. I knew that over the years she had several times taken a break from working in this country to travel, earning a living by teaching English as a Foreign Language. Each time she had returned to Liverpool, and she had been working at St Luke's for some time until Jack's illness and subsequent retirement gave her the chance of taking over his job.

She came back through with a couple of china mugs steaming with the aroma of real coffee, and set them down on the low table. She sat on the sofa, leaning against the arm, and stretched her legs out. Her long red hair, streaked with grey, was piled up and pinned rather untidily on top of her head, and in the loose *djellaba* she was wearing she had the air of a student. It was easy to imagine how attractive she must have been in her youth.

"I'm glad you called, Mark. Jack used to mention you often."

"Did he really?" I tried to sound neutral, but sensed that there was bitterness in my voice.

"Yes, over the years he talked about you a lot. I know he

worried about you. All those jobs you had before you settled down to teaching!"

It was true that I'd done a variety of jobs before my family were finally able to breathe a sigh of relief when I went into the so-called "profession" of teaching; but even then – even now – I didn't really consider myself settled.

"I know Jack worried about me. But did he tell you the real reason?" I guessed that if Ruth and my brother had been as close as Steve had suggested, they must have discussed such things.

She took a drink from her coffee mug, eyeing me thoughtfully over the rim.

"I'll be blunt," I went on. "Did he ever mention to you that I was no longer a Catholic? Or, as he would say, no longer a *practising* Catholic?"

She put her mug down carefully on the coffee table.

"Of course he mentioned it. It upset him quite a lot, I think."

"Enough to cut me out of his will?"

She shrugged.

"I really don't know, Mark. I do know that he was very friendly with Father Kelly, the Headmaster, and that he – Father Kelly – had no time for non-Catholics. Perhaps he exerted some influence. Who knows?"

She spread her hands in a gesture of incomprehension.

"And who do you think would know why Jack would leave everything to Phil Sullivan?" My voice sounded artificial, almost trembling, in my attempt to keep it even. "Would *you* know?"

Ruth hesitated for a moment, her expression clouded, then pulled a face and shook her head.

"I'm sorry, Mark, I've no idea. I'm as puzzled as you about that."

"Are you sure? I get the impression you knew my brother rather well. Very well, in fact."

"I'm not sure what you're getting at, Mark." She looked genuinely surprised.

I could feel myself getting impatient.

"What I'm getting at, Ruth, is that you and Jack were very close back in the late sixties. And that Phil Sullivan was born shortly afterwards."

She put her spread hand against her chest just below her throat, in a gesture of amazement. Then she put back her head and laughed.

"You're not suggesting that Phil was the outcome of an affair between myself and your brother?" She laughed again.

"So you think I'm Phil's mother? Don't be ridiculous!"

I stared at her stonily.

"You don't deny that you had an affair with Jack? Or that you went away with him to a hotel in North Wales?"

The smile faded and she shook her head wearily.

"Not that again, Mark! I thought that had been forgotten long ago. Yes, I went to a hotel with Jack. But it wasn't really what everyone thought. We had become very close, and I was really fond of him, but it wasn't that sort of relationship. Jack would never have had an affair with me, however attracted we were to each other; he valued his religion too much. I'm not sure, though, how I would have reacted if he had wanted to take things further. He was always a little awkward with women in those sorts of areas anyway, so the question never arose. But we went away to Wales to do some walking together, that's all. We had separate rooms even. But Jack was very preoccupied at the time."

"How do you mean, preoccupied?"

"He said something had happened. He'd found out something which would change his life." She paused, her green eyes far away, searching her memory for those long-gone days.

"Did he say how? Did he say what it was?"

"No. He wouldn't tell me. He said it was something that had to remain hidden. He said it wouldn't be fair to tell me and burden me with that secret. Always the gentleman! But he was obviously very upset and confused. I just did what I could to comfort him and support him."

I didn't know whether to feel relieved or not to discover that Steve's theory appeared to be wrong. There seemed no reason at all to disbelieve what Ruth was telling me, but it really solved nothing. I suddenly felt ashamed of my intrusion into her past, and of my allegations.

"I'm sorry. I didn't mean to be intrusive. I just need to find out what really has been going on, and why Jack's done what he did. It's really preying on my mind now."

"I can understand that, Mark. But I can't help you. Really I can't."

"I think I know that now. But is there anyone who might help? Anyone who could point me in the right direction?"

There was a long pause. Then, as if suddenly remembering something, she sat up and leaned forward.

"You could try your dad's cottage, Maes-y-Bryn. You know Edie Barton's living there now. That woman who was very friendly with your dad. She might know something."

"What would she know?"

"I don't know, really. I only met her once or twice when your dad was alive. But there seemed to be something unusual about the relationship. I couldn't really put my finger on it. But she might know something. It's worth a try, anyway."

"Thanks, Ruth." I finished the dregs of my coffee and put the mug down.

"I'll get from under your feet. And I'll follow up your suggestion. I'll go and see Edie Barton."

I got up to go and Ruth came over and kissed me on the cheek.

"Good luck, Mark. Let me know if you get to the bottom of it. I'd like to know, too."

She waved goodbye from the window as I got into my car and pulled out into the traffic. So far, I knew no more about Jack's motives then on the day of the funeral, very little about his sexuality, and nothing new about his relationship with Phil. All Ruth had really told me was that Jack had a secret. I knew I had to try to find out what that secret was.

I glanced at my watch. I still had plenty of time to get out to my father's cottage in Denbighshire and speak to Edie Barton before setting off home.

Beyond Queensferry the road rises steeply into Wales. New dual-carriageways have obliterated the old roads and the café at Ewloe where I used to stop on a Sunday morning with the cycling club. But further on, as the Llandegla moors come into view, the landscape has changed much less. It is a countryside of isolated hill farms and sloping fields with trees and hedges bent by the wind, and in the distance the hazy purple heather of the moors, where buzzards rock on great pale wings.

As I crested the brow of the hill near the *Cross Keys* inn a curlew swooped across the marsh, its liquid call bubbling down the sky, and surprised rabbits scattered in a roadside field. I turned off onto the narrow lane which led to Maes-y-Bryn and drove slowly down between the bare hedges of early spring, lost in thought about what I might discover from the coming interview. I pulled off the lane and parked the car in the little lay-by opposite the cottage. To my right, in the reed-encroached field where I had first learned to shoot, a piebald pony was grazing. To my left, in the still air, smoke was rising vertically from the cottage's old stone chimney. In the verge by the wall, snowdrops were pushing their delicate heads through the grass. In the March sunshine, although the afternoon was by now quite well advanced, it was surprisingly warm when I got out of the car.

I had met Edie Barton once or twice, but only briefly. I had paid her little attention, and could remember little about her. As far as I knew she was in her mid forties, and went to the same church as my father. She lived on her own in a nearby village, in a rented terraced house. They had become friends and had helped each other out with lifts and shopping and so on, but I had been surprised to find that they were close enough for my father to want her to move into the cottage after his death. I was even more surprised when Jack's will made it clear that although he was leaving Maes-y-Bryn to Phil Sullivan, Edie was to be allowed to go on living in the cottage for as long as she wanted. I was quite intrigued to meet her.

The woman who opened the door looked younger than I expected. In her sleeveless white top and short denim skirt, she could have been in her thirties. Her eyes, deep blue against the tanned skin of her face, betrayed no obvious sign of recognition until I introduced myself.

"It's Mark. Harry's son. We've met before, once or twice. I don't know whether you'll remember me. I hope you don't mind my calling like this."

"Oh, yes. Mark. No, of course I don't mind!"

She smiled brightly and pushed her blonde, permed hair back from her face in a nervous gesture.

"Come in!"

She led me through into the living room, a light, cheerful space with lots of pine and bright colours. I hardly recognised it. My father had converted the cottage himself when he bought it, getting water laid across the field and adding a bathroom and kitchen, but he had done it on a shoestring, with a second-hand bath and sink, and uneven tiles on the kitchen floor, and it had never felt really modernised. Edie, or someone, had obviously spent some money on it since then, knocking through walls and opening it up, adding work-surfaces in the kitchen, re-tiling the floors and decorating it throughout. I had to admit it looked better. Even the wood-burning stove was an improvement on the old fire, which used to be so difficult to light.

"Sit down, Mark. I'll put the kettle on."

I sat down on the sofa and looked out over the garden which had always seemed a little out of control. My father had been more interested in growing potatoes and vegetables, and I think he also liked the feeling of being on the verge of the wilderness. I remembered spending hours strimming and cutting grass, only to find on my next visit that it was just as bad as before. Now, there was a neat lawn, the bushes had been cut back, and there were flowerbeds around the edges.

Edie came back through with a tray loaded with a brown teapot and home-made scones and jam. She put it down and sat next to me on the sofa.

"It was terrible news about Jack," she said quietly, in a voice that betrayed Liverpool roots. "I'm sorry I didn't get to the funeral. I was just too upset. First Harry – I was still getting over that, really. Then Jack ..." Her voice trailed away.

"Don't worry. It's a long way for you to come. There were a lot of people there anyway. Five priests at the altar, celebrating the Requiem Mass, would you believe!"

"I do believe it. Jack was so involved with the church and the school – those priests were friends as well as everything else. It doesn't surprise me at all. I'm glad he had a good send-off. He deserved it!"

She smiled weakly.

"Tea?"

She leant forward and picked up the teapot, her left hand resting on the lid to hold it in place. As she poured the tea, I couldn't help noticing how brown her arms and shoulders were. For the first time I saw her as an attractive woman, rather than just as someone my dad had known. Jack had spent a lot more time at Maes-y-Bryn than I had – in fact he had helped my father to buy the place – and would have had the chance to get to know Edie a lot better than I did. The thought began to cross my mind that maybe she had something to do with Jack's "secret" which he had confided to Ruth Morris all those years ago. But how could that be? Unless she'd been around for a lot longer than I realised.

She passed me my tea and a plate with a buttered scone, picked up her teacup and sat back on the sofa, crossing her bare legs and showing what suddenly seemed like a disturbing amount of smooth brown thigh.

"So what brings you out here to see me, Mark? Or was it just your father's cottage you came to check on? I *am* looking after it, you know!"

"I can see that. It looks great, but very different from when my dad was alive. I suppose I'm quite nostalgic about it really. We spent a lot of time in these hills when we were kids. Not here, of course, it was another cottage a mile or two away. It had no running water and no electric light in those days. But we loved it. We spent a lot of time there. And then when my dad bought this place it seemed like a permanent link to our childhood. I must admit I haven't really been here since he died, but it was nice to know that it would always be in the family. That's why I was so shocked when ... when ..."

I paused lamely, not wanting to give too much away too soon, but Edie had picked up on it. She smiled sympathetically, and carried on where I had left off.

"... when you realised it had been given away." She nodded thoughtfully. "I can understand that, Mark. You come back to Liverpool to bury your brother and find he's done some very strange things in his will. It must be very upsetting for you."

"It is, Edie, but I don't know what I can do about it, apart from trying to work out his motivation. Find out why he did the things he's done."

"So you came to see me because you thought I might be able to shed some light on it?"

I nodded sheepishly.

"I thought you might know something, Edie. My wife thinks I should just accept the situation, and get on with it, but I can't help feeling that I'm missing something. I started wondering about Jack's will, and it seems as if something strange is going on. Maybe I'm over dramatising things, but I can't help thinking that there's some secret that Jack had, that I know nothing about."

I deliberately didn't want to mention my chat with Ruth Morris. But I wanted Edie to tell me anything she knew that would be helpful.

"Jack and I were friends as well as brothers," I went on. "At least, I thought we were. So when he left everything to Phil, including this cottage – my dad's cottage – and didn't mention me in the will, it didn't seem rational. But Jack *was* rational. He didn't do things without a reason, even if his reasons were sometimes based on a different view of life from my own. So why? I've heard the rumours, of course, about his sexuality, but I can't say that I believe them. I don't think that had anything to do with it.

"You're involved, though, Edie. You're living at Maes-y-Bryn. There must be a reason for that. People, even Jack, don't usually leave their father's house to be lived in by a friend on a peppercorn rent for no good reason. So, why are you here? I don't mean to be nosey, but you must know something about his motives. Can you tell me anything that will help me to understand?"

Edie drained her teacup and set it back carefully down on the tray. She turned towards me, pulling her legs up underneath her on the sofa, but at first she didn't look at me, gazing instead at the floor. After a pause, she began to speak softly.

"You're right, I knew your brother quite well. Very well, I suppose. He used to come out here often at weekends and in the holidays to see his dad – your dad. He'd often bring Emily with him, and sometimes Phil. And I'd see your dad at church on Sunday mornings, and he'd bring me back here for coffee. If it was a nice day we'd go for a stroll over the mountain or down the lanes to the *Rose and Crown* for lunch. Or just sit outside in the sun, chatting or doing a bit of gardening. It was always very peaceful and calm."

Her face was wistful.

"After the life I've had, it was like a little piece of heaven. A magic world." She paused and sighed heavily, then reached back onto the little table behind her for a box of tissues. She pulled one out and dabbed at a tear.

36

I felt faint stirrings of jealousy of the picture she was painting. I should have been there. I should have spent more time with my dad. Perhaps if I had, I would have been closer to them all, Jack wouldn't have left everything to a stranger and I wouldn't be behaving like a second-rate private detective.

"That all sounds very cosy, Edie. How long had you known my dad and Jack?"

"A few years. Five, maybe more. It was after my last relationship broke up. I'd been living with a guy in Liverpool, and we came to Wales when he got a job near Queensferry. Then things started to go wrong between us – he hit me once or twice – and eventually I left. I had a friend in Tyddyn-y-Bont and she told me of a house to rent in the village. It was just a terraced house, a cottage really, but it was enough for me. To begin with I did some cleaning jobs to make ends meet, and I worked in the village shop. Later, I took a secretarial course at the college in Wrexham, and for the last few years I've been working as an administrator for a little firm in Mold.

"I met Harry – your dad – at church in Mold. He used to run a bookstall at the annual fête and one year I offered to help out. We got on well, and started to give each other lifts to church and so on, or do bits of shopping for each other. Then he invited me to Maes-y-Bryn one weekend, and I met Jack. After that it became quite a regular thing, like I just said, to spend time together. Sometimes on a Saturday evening we'd have a meal together, either here or at my place in Tyddyn-y-Bont; or we'd go out together to one of the pubs for a meal. Jack would drive us. If it was late when we got back I'd often stay over. I suppose that was when our relationship really started."

I sat up straighter on the sofa, waiting for Edie to continue. I could feel the sweat prickling under my arms, and my throat felt dry. If she had been having an affair with Jack, and if Phil was their son...no, that couldn't be right, I was getting confused – they'd only known each other five years...but if Phil was *her* son, and Jack was in love with her ... that could explain her part in all this. But in that case why didn't she come to the funeral? And what might she be able to tell me about Phil?

Edie didn't go on talking, but got up and walked in bare feet across the sheepskin rug to the window. She stood looking out at the Scots pine in the garden which I could see blackly outlined against the darkening sky, stained blood-red by the sinking sun and streaked with bands of silvery cloud. The afternoon was passing quickly away.

I cleared my throat. My face felt hot and my pulse was racing, but I decided to confront her there and then.

"So you were having an affair with my brother? Is that the explanation of all this … this … will business?" I felt relieved that it was out, and hopeful that I was getting to the bottom of it all.

Edie turned back from the window to look at me, but in the fading light I could hardly see her face, just her outline and a gleam of blonde curls. There was silence for a moment and then I could see she was shaking uncontrollably. I was worried I had gone too far, been too abrupt, upset her badly. But her next reaction astonished me, as she put her hands up to her face and began to laugh out loud.

"Jack? An affair with Jack! You are funny, Mark." She laughed again, then paused thoughtfully, as if unsure how to continue.

"No, no, you're right, sort of…I *was* having an affair, and it had been going on for years. But not with Jack, nice though he was."

Another pause, then as if she had come to a decision about what to tell me, she went on.

"No, Mark, I was having an affair with Harry. Your dad! And you mean to say you never realised!"

I was stunned. It had literally never crossed my mind. I never thought of my father like that. He had been devoted to my mother, and would never have strayed, I was fairly sure of that. But she'd been dead for over ten years, long enough for a man to get over his wife's death and to feel the need of female company, especially if he lived alone in the countryside, as my father had. And when I thought again of my father, it was not so strange that he should attract a much younger woman. He had kept his military bearing, and his body was still hard from chopping wood, digging the garden and taking long walks in the hills and fields. Nor had he lost too much of his wavy dark brown hair.

A gentle man, despite his wartime experiences, my father was always quiet, verging on the taciturn, and like most men of his generation and social class, not given to open displays of emotion, or discussions of intimate secrets. The more I thought about it, the more reasonable it seemed that he might have had an affair without my knowledge. *And maybe more than one...*

With a jolt, I remembered what Steve had said about the cheque paid to Phil's foster-parents. It was signed *J. Gilgarran*. We had both assumed it was Jack. But my father's real Christian name was John, which he'd always disliked, preferring his middle name of Harry. That was why, when he passed the name on to my brother, he used the diminutive form of Jack. Perhaps ... perhaps ... it seemed impossible, but perhaps Phil was in fact my father's son – and if so, my half-brother. My lip curled in distaste at that idea, and at the thought that perhaps my father wasn't the faithful husband I had always imagined.

But even if this theory was correct, it appeared that it still could have nothing to do with Edie, who had known my father for not much longer than she'd known Jack. So who could the mother be? The more theories I had, the less clear everything seemed to get.

"I loved Harry, you know." Edie's voice broke into my thoughts once more. She switched on a lamp in the corner, then came back and sat down on the sofa again, this time a little closer to me, so that the fragrance of her perfume surrounded me. She gazed straight at me as she went on.

"He was a good man. He looked after me, made me feel safe in a way no man had done before." She put her hand on my arm.

"You were lucky to have a father like that. It's something I never had. Oh, Mark, I miss him!"

She began to sob, and as she did so she leaned towards me. Instinctively, I put my arm around her shoulders, and she laid her head against me. I reached for a tissue and handed it wordlessly to her. She blew her nose and then stayed pressed against me. I could feel the warmth of her, the rise and fall of her distressed breathing, the softness of the brown skin of her upper arm under my hand. We sat like that for some time. Slowly, her trembling ceased. Then, after a while, she sat up, kissed me softly on the cheek and said with forced brightness:

"Will you stay for something to eat? I really don't want to eat alone tonight."

I glanced at my watch. I was amazed to see that it was

already well after five o'clock. I really should be getting back to Yorkshire. But I still only had half the story. A good reason for Edie to be living in my father's cottage; but no explanation of why Jack had left everything to Phil, or why either he or my father was already paying money for his upkeep at least fifteen years ago. I took a quick decision.

"I'd love to, Edie. That's really kind of you. We can cheer each other up, I hope. But you must let me help you with the cooking."

"No need!" she said, almost bouncing up off the sofa. "You open some wine – that's a man's job – and I'll see to the food."

Half of me was hoping she would get something ready quickly and I could be on my way – Jenny would be waiting for me – but half of me was anxious to find out more from Edie, and, if I admitted it, I was finding her company attractive. I watched the sway of her hips as she vanished into the kitchen, re-appearing shortly afterwards with a bottle of Shiraz, a corkscrew and two large glasses.

I opened the wine and poured it out, then took one glass through to Edie. She was chopping peppers and mushrooms and throwing them into a brown earthenware casserole dish which already contained some chunks of steak.

"I'm doing a *boeuf bourguignonne* in the oven, Mark. Less fattening that way. Hope you like beef!"

"I love it, Edie, but won't it take a long time? I've got to get home sometime tonight."

She turned and looked up at me. There were creases at the corners of her bright blue eyes, and her nose wrinkled mischievously.

"It'll be a couple of hours. But we can occupy ourselves, can't we?"

She reached out and smoothed my collar with her left hand. I couldn't help noticing that she still had the chopping knife in the other. She must have seen my glance.

"Yes, Mark, you'd better stay or else." She waggled the knife theatrically.

"We've still got a lot to talk about. Or we could watch a bit of telly. Or…"

She twirled round, picked up her glass and took a drink, eyeing me over the rim. Was I mistaken, or was she flirting with me? I realised, with a shock, that if she was, I didn't really mind. I could see now very clearly why my father would have found her attractive.

While the dinner was cooking I busied myself making sure that there was enough fuel in for the stove. First, I raked out the ashes and took them outside, filled the coal-scuttle and added some to the stove. Then I went across the yard to the old pig-sty which now served as a wood-store. The moon was rising and the yard was bathed in silvery light. I brought back an armful of logs and stacked them in the fireplace, then placed several in the stove, letting it draw slightly to make the flames leap cheerfully behind the glass. With the curtains drawn it was a warm and comfortable place to be.

Edie put some music on. She had quite a good selection of fairly popular classical music, and we listened to Bruch's violin concerto, or maybe it was Mendelssohn's – I can't now remember which. We chatted again, and I tried, as subtly as possible, to find out what she knew about Phil, but she seemed content to answer my questions obliquely, without giving any definite answer. My tentative suggestion that she might have some relationship with Phil was met with a laugh. Perhaps she didn't know any more than she admitted.

"Jack was unique," she told me at one point. "Once he'd decided something he went ahead. If Phil was his favourite pupil, and he thought he needed the money, he'd give it to him. I know he thought you and Jenny were all right financially. I've got the cottage – you know why – and Emily's in the house in Liverpool. So he's only given away his savings. He didn't have to give them to you, you know."

"I know that. But why didn't he mention me at all in his will?"

"I don't know, Mark. That was Jack for you though. Staid but ultimately unpredictable."

"And did you know, Edie, that either he or my dad – I'm not sure which – was paying money for Phil's upkeep years ago, when he was with foster parents?"

"Were they?" She tossed her hair nonchalantly as she asked the question, although I sensed she already knew, and her reaction was surprisingly dismissive.

"Maybe it was something like Action Aid. They paid money

every month to support an orphan. You never know."

Maybe she was right, although I was by no means convinced. But I got no more out of her on the subject, and I was gradually becoming more interested in other aspects of the evening than my investigations.

I suppose I should have phoned Jenny to let her know something about what was happening, but we hadn't parted on very good terms. I still felt aggrieved at her attitude. I'm not a very good liar at the best of times and I certainly didn't feel like ringing to let her know I was spending the evening with another woman.

On the other hand I wondered sadly whether, at this point in our relationship, she would even care.

.

Chapter Four

Scented candles flickered in the corners of the room, and the stove hummed softly, creaking occasionally as a log settled and flared. The wine had gone to my head, and together with the warmth had lulled me into a state of relaxation where the normal run of my life and my responsibilities belonged to another world. The atmosphere seemed dreamlike, shut in from the gathering cold of a winter's night in my father's cottage, about to have dinner with his former mistress. Dinner – and what else?

Suddenly shocked at the reality of the thought, I sat up and looked again at my watch. Time had slid by and it was now nearly eight o'clock. I'd have to take a decision. If I didn't go soon I would be so late home that it would be difficult to explain. I dithered. What should I do? What could I say to Edie?

I looked up and saw she was standing in the doorway, holding the hot casserole dish in both hands with a tea towel.

"Checking the time again? Want to get back to your wife?"

Her expression was flat and her eyes were cold. She banged the dish down on the table.

"Don't let me keep you, Mark!"

She stormed back into the kitchen. Horrified at the change in her mood, I went after her. She was standing at the sink, shaking with great sobs. I put my hands tentatively on her shoulders, which were stiff and unyielding.

"I'm sorry," I murmured.

"No you're not! You don't care! Nobody does. I'm almost part of your family, but no-one cares about me or how I'm getting on. I've lost Harry, and now I'm stuck out here on my own. You came just to find out what *you* want to know, and now you can't wait to get away! What's wrong with you? What's wrong with *me*?"

She covered her face with her hands. She sounded so wretched that I just had to find the words to comfort her, tell her I wasn't going to leave her alone that evening, that I wanted to stay with her.

Gradually her sobbing stopped and her shoulders softened. She turned to look up at me, her eyes gleaming with tears. She put her arms round me and hugged me to her, and I felt the warmth of her body against mine. A smile trembled at the corner of her mouth.

"Oh, Mark, thank you. You don't know how much it means to me."

I kissed her forehead, then pushed her gently away from me.

"Come on, Edie. Let's eat."

Gradually the atmosphere eased, and as we settled down at the table I began to forget my worries and accept what was happening. I opened a second bottle of wine and poured it and we drank to each other's health. In the subdued light, her eyes, so recently weepy, now seemed to sparkle at me. There were still things I wanted to know about her.

"So you've no family, then, Edie? You've never been married?"

Did she hesitate for a moment?

"No, Mark, I've never been married. I've never had that comfort and stability. I was adopted, you see, and since then I've always had to look after myself."

Maybe that explains why you took up with my dad – not just a lover but a father figure as well.

"You must have had a lot of admirers though. You're a very attractive woman."

She shrugged.

"I've had a few. There's been a couple since Harry died. They get so possessive though, these local blokes. I went out with one a few times – he was a building contractor, and he seemed very kind and understanding at first. He helped me a lot with all this." She waved her hand around the room. "But he got a bit too heavy in the end. He was very jealous. One day he came out to see me and found me sunbathing in the garden. I love the sun and I like to sunbathe naked when I can."

I had a momentary, unbidden image of Edie lying unclothed and unconcerned on the lawn, soaking up the warmth and the light. It was not an unattractive thought.

"Anyway, he went mad, saying what if someone else had seen me without my clothes on, and trying to tell me what I could and couldn't do, so I stopped seeing him. He still phones me up, though, and talks about me in the village as if we were still going out. I went out with one of his friends as well for a while, and between them they talk as if they have some sort of rights over me. I don't think either of them can face up to the idea that I might prefer to go out with someone else! I sometimes worry that one or the other is going to turn up here one night."

The thought of some hefty builder turning up while we were eating began to preoccupy me, but the idea was soon pushed from my mind when I felt Edie's bare foot against my leg, her toes probing up inside my trousers.

"Try this!" she said.

I looked up from my plate and saw that she was holding out a piece of beef, speared on her fork. It hovered before me, and her eyes were fixed on mine. I leaned forward and she slid the meat into my mouth, where my teeth closed around it and pulled it clear of the fork tines. She smiled slowly and lowered her eyelids.

I remembered the chicken-eating scene in the film of *Tom Jones*, and recalled how shocked my mother had been when, as a teenager, I'd gone to see a film in which unmarried people had sex. How things had changed.

I tried to keep my voice steady.

"How about a shallot?"

I proffered it carefully, and with eyes still half-closed she parted her lips just enough to receive it. A small trickle of gravy ran down her chin. She remained motionless, then slowly and delicately raised her napkin and wiped it away, still gazing at me steadily.

For a moment, the atmosphere was charged with sexual tension. I could feel the excitement within me, and the saliva in my mouth. Then I saw that she was trying not to giggle, the set of her mouth began to dissolve and suddenly it was too much and we both burst out laughing.

I raised my glass, holding it carefully by the stem, and touched the rim to hers, with a clear chime of crystal. The candlelight gleamed on the dark purple wine as she took a mouthful

"Cheers!" I murmured. "I'm glad I stayed."

After the meal Edie made coffee and we finished off the wine. I was still sitting at the table, when she went to the front door, opened it and looked out.

"What a fantastic night, Mark! Let's go for a walk!"

She spun round, beaming and enthusiastic like a little girl. I couldn't have refused her, even if I'd wanted to.

"Come on, let's go!" she exclaimed, and reached out her hand to pull me to my feet.

I grabbed my fleece from the back of the sofa and followed her.

Leaving the lighted warmth of the cottage, the air struck chill. Pale stars pricked the night sky, but the moon was riding high and once my eyes were accustomed to the darkness, it was light enough to walk safely without a torch. We climbed over the rickety old wooden stile from the garden, and set off up the steep slope of sheep-bitten turf and whispering reeds that I remembered so well. At the top of the field we passed through a gap in the broken-down wall and the lake came into view, a lane of moonlight shimmering down its centre. We walked quietly towards the water's edge, where the silver ripples lapped gently on the shore. The old boathouse threw angular dark shadows and the heather-clad hill behind it was outlined against the sky like the humped back of some great slumbering beast. We walked a little way around the lake, taking care on the narrow path, and paused where the way leads off up what we used as children to call simply The Mountain.

"Beautiful, isn't it?" I murmured.

"Yes, Mark, it is."

"Coming from the city, this was the first place where I knew silence, and darkness. Now even that's being stolen from us."

I turned to look at the faint yellow glow in the northern sky, which rose from the expanding built-up areas away towards the Dee Estuary.

"But I still have my memories of when the language of these hills was Welsh, before the electricity pylons marched across them, and the roads were driven up to every farm. Now where can you go to see a hayrick built, or a cow milked by hand? I'm glad I knew it before all that changed."

My tone was bitter, but Edie sighed sympathetically.

"I know. The whole place must have memories for you, and it certainly does for me. Happy ones. But it's cold, isn't it!"

Edie shivered and folded her arms around herself, and I

noticed then that they were bare and that she had brought no coat. I took off my fleece and wrapped it around her shoulders, and she sighed gratefully and pulled me towards her, her upturned face smiling at me, silver in the light, her eyes laughing and her breath clouding in the cold air.

It was then that I kissed her, no conscious decision taken, but the moment and the moonlight and the companionship of the evening combining with her warmth under my fleece and her yielding as she pressed against me, to make the impulse irresistible. I kissed her long and hard, and her mouth was soft but eager; and when we stopped my arms were around her and her head pressed against my shoulder for a while. Then she stepped back and took my hands.

"Let's go back"

We walked back in silence. Just below the boathouse hill something made me turn fleetingly to look at the moon, which seemed almost to be resting on the hilltop, and I thought a shadow passed dimly before it, a creature of some sort, watching us perhaps; a sheep, or a fox? Maybe it was just a scrap of cloud, although the night was clear. I peered into the thin light, but nothing moved again. I shrugged and went on.

The short grass on the hillside was beginning to crust with frost and we trod carefully back down to where the cottage window glowed, a single point of warmth and life shining in the empty darkness. As we were getting over the stile, we were suddenly startled by a clatter in the underbrush by the hedge, and we froze, motionless, Edie grasping my hand tightly. Then we relaxed, and she laughed softly as we saw the elegant pale shape of the barn owl swooping across the garden and away.

The warmth in the cottage was luxurious after the cold outside. I sprawled on the sofa, near to the flickering stove, my eyes feeling tired from the combination of fresh air, a long day and a little too much alcohol. Edie locked the door, then came over and gently ruffled my hair.

"Do you fancy a nightcap, Mark? Brandy, whisky?"

I knew I shouldn't. I'd had enough to drink already – too much really – if I was going to drive home. I knew I should be going. I'd found out what I could about Edie's relationship with Jack and my father, and although I was surprised to realise that

I'd flirted with and kissed my dead father's mistress, I could still walk away now and we could just be friends. I really should get going. I sneaked a look at my watch without moving my head. I didn't want another outburst from Edie. It was very nearly midnight, and home was a good two and a half hours' drive away. How would I explain that when I got back? And how, on the other hand, would I tell Edie I was leaving, without another explosion?

"I'll have a whisky. Just a small one," I heard myself saying.

Edie went to get the drinks. She seemed to be gone a long time and my eyes began to close. I heard the last log settling in the stove, and the sound of water running in the bathroom. Then I heard her calling.

"Your drink's ready. If you want to come and get it."

Naively, I wondered why she wasn't bringing it to me. Sleepily, I got up and went out into the tiny passage from where the kitchen and bathroom opened. They were in darkness. From the foot of the stairs I could see light shining from above.

"Ma-ark…" her voice called down to me in a sing-song, beckoning tone. I swallowed. My throat felt dry. I had a good idea what was going to happen. Slowly I mounted the stairs in the half-light and turned through the doorway into her bedroom. She was sitting up in bed in her nightdress, a glass of whisky in her hand. There was another one on the bedside table, where, next to a pile of books and magazines, a candle also burned. In the shimmering circle of light her hair looked almost like a blonde Pre-Raphaelite and the perfumed atmosphere was one of peace and calm.

"I thought you might like to tuck me in." She patted the edge of the bed provocatively, gesturing to me to sit down. She handed me my whisky, and we clinked glasses and took a drink. We sat in silence then, slightly awkwardly, drinking until our glasses were empty. Edie put hers down on the table.

"Are you staying, then?"

I hesitated. My last chance to say no, to get away, not to get involved. The pause grew.

"OK. Say nothing!" – a flash of temper. "Don't take a decision, then. Do what you like! Go now, if you want to. I'm going to sleep now."

She snuggled down ostentatiously, turning her head away

from me and shutting her eyes. I paused again, indecisive. Minutes passed.

A vein beat softly in her neck. Gently, carefully, I bent down and kissed it. She moved luxuriantly, her eyes still closed, then sighed and grasped my hand firmly, pushing it down under the duvet, and I felt the cool skin of her belly and, with increasing excitement, the soft swell of her breasts above her ribcage.

Her nightdress slid effortlessly up and over her head, and then there was fumbling with my belt and my clothes until I could join her beneath the duvet. There was no hesitation now, just wordless haste and purposeful caresses. I slid between her spread thighs, she lifted her hips urgently to meet me and the heat of her body enclosed me. She made love like a wild creature, her breathing almost hoarse, her suntanned body moving unceasingly in the candlelit shadows, hands clawing at me, muttering gasped words into my ear. I had no thought of leaving now, no thought at all except of the moment. The consequences could take care of themselves. I relaxed and let events take their course, until finally she squealed, animal-like, then shuddered and lay still.

After the candle had guttered out, we lay conjoined in the darkness, our limbs entwined. Eventually Edie turned over without a word and slept, and I felt her buttocks hot against me in the warmth of the bed as I drifted into satisfied unconsciousness.

Half asleep, I saw the barn owl flying in my dreams again. I jerked awake. Something about it had bothered me, and now, suddenly, I realised what it was. Of all birds, the barn owl is perhaps the most silent. It doesn't clatter in the undergrowth. Pigeons do, but not, usually, at night. *So what did?* Whatever had made the noise that startled us had startled the owl as well. What was it? Edie's disgruntled suitor, perhaps? I lay awake, straining my ears anxiously, but all was silent. Gradually I relaxed, and later slipped unknowing into sleep.

Chapter Five

When I awoke it was daylight and she was gone. Her perfume lingered, but her side of the bed was already cold. I lay for a while trying to make sense of what had happened over the last twenty-four hours. I knew now why Jack had allowed Edie to lay claim to the cottage, and I knew that Jack had not had an affair with either Ruth or Edie. But in terms of progress in unearthing Jack's real motives I was back to square one. Nothing there had really changed.

But one thing was certain and could not be changed – I had slept with my father's mistress, a woman who in different circumstances might have become my stepmother. Had she really found me so attractive, or in her state of loss, was I just a substitute for my father? And what more would she expect from me now?

Last night it had been easy to live in the moment; now my thoughts turned to Jenny, who would be worrying about me and might even have phoned the police. What would I tell her? Would she leave me if she found out what had happened? Our relationship had been fragile enough for some time; when I thought about it again, on balance I wondered whether she would be worrying about me at all.

And what about school? I hadn't let them know I wouldn't be in. I glanced at my watch. Nine o'clock! My pupils would be shoving their way into the classroom, bags swinging, waiting for me to quieten them and settle them down. They would neither know nor care where I was. But my Head of Department would. I should phone the school.

I rolled out of bed, picked up my scattered clothes and stumbled down to the bathroom. After a shower I felt better, although my head was still thick from the previous night's drink. Feeling unjustifiably sorry for myself, it was easy to convince myself that I really was ill when I phoned the school and spoke to the secretary. I told her that I wouldn't be in for the rest of the day, and she grunted non-committally and said she would pass the message on to my Head of Department.

The smell of coffee drew me to the kitchen, where the filter machine was still switched on and the jug half-full. Next to the machine was a scrawled note – *Gone to work. Help yourself to coffee.* Nothing else – no greeting, nothing. I poured myself a mug and made some toast. As I sat pensively eating by the window, my eye fell again on the note. It was obviously torn from an office memo pad, and at the top was the name and phone number of an engineering firm in Mold, presumably where Edie worked, although she hadn't mentioned much about it.

Should I ring her at work? I felt that I should, just to say hello, check she was OK, say how much I'd enjoyed being with her, despite my misgivings, despite any complications. I couldn't just go off like that without a word.

The girl who answered the phone was bright and cheery. Of course she knew Edie.

"Who should I say rang? I'll pass the message on when I see her."

"Can't you put me through to her now?"

"I'm sorry sir, she's not in work today. She phoned to say she was taking a couple of days off. Urgent family business."

I put the receiver down thoughtfully. Where was she? Where had she gone that meant taking time off work? I looked at her brief note again, seeking inspiration. As I turned it to the light I saw the impression of some other writing on it, a phone number that had obviously been scribbled on the sheet above and had gone through to this one. I could just make out the code – *01425* – but the rest of the number was harder to decipher. It meant nothing to me anyway. I shoved it into the pocket of my fleece, drained my coffee mug and, with a last look round, made for the door.

Outside it was a cold still morning, but with a scent of coming spring in the air. I decided to take a walk before setting off in the car, hoping it would clear my head and give me a chance to reflect. I set off up the hill, retracing our steps of the night before. At the far end of the lake I began to climb the slopes towards the trig. point on the summit, such a long way when we were small, but now a gentle stroll. I paused part way in the ascent and moved out from the path onto a small rocky outcrop, looking north to the Clwyd hills, rolling away towards the Irish Sea. As I did so a movement caught my eye.

It was almost windless up there, and apart from the cry of a planing buzzard, and the fussing of rooks in a wood some distance away, the moors seemed still and lifeless. But in the shallow heather-filled gully below me a man was moving. There was nothing so unusual about that – shepherds and walkers crossed these moors from time to time – but something was wrong about this figure. Bent double, he seemed to be trying to keep out of sight, but there was nothing else moving up there to hide from. Except myself.

If I hadn't changed my route slightly to look at the view I would never have seen him, but I got the impression he already knew where I was. The glimpse I got of him showed that he was wearing jeans and a leather jacket, and town shoes – not a walker then, nor a shepherd. My presentiments of the night-time came back to me. Was this Edie's spurned lover come to get his revenge? Was it him I had seen last night on the hilltop, and had he then startled the barn owl from cover? Had he been spying on us all evening?

I didn't want to wait to find out. I turned and hurried back down the hill, passing the gully before he could reach the top. I saw him then a few yards below me, and he saw me. He straightened up, whistled and I saw him point, perhaps to a second person who was out of my sight. I broke into a run along the path just above the lakeshore, which cuts across the slope where the hill is steepest. The water was calm, almost glass-like, and all at once my eye was caught by a reflection which made my heart jump. What I saw was the figure of a man, distorted by the faintest of ripples, as he launched himself at me from above.

Forewarned, I twisted as he landed, and just about managed to avoid being knocked down. Luckily for me, he tripped and staggered, and seeing him off-balance I barged into him and pushed him violently. His arms windmilled for a second, then he toppled off the path, tried vainly to stop himself on the greasy rock slabs, and slipped the remaining six feet or so into the icy water.

I ran. If these men were seeking revenge for being rejected by Edie, they seemed to be taking it rather seriously, and I wasn't going to hang around to chat. I reckoned the man in the gully would stop to help his companion out of the lake, and I hoped desperately I would have time to reach the car. My heart pounded and my feet slithered; over the broken wall, down the bank, over the stile and out through the gate, fumbling with the car keys.

As I started the engine I saw them coming and heard them shouting to each other. It didn't sound like English, and at that distance I couldn't make out whether it was Welsh either, but I didn't stop to check. I screeched away in a cloud of gravel, down the narrow road, hammering along between the hedges. Fifty yards down from the cottage I passed a car pulled in under the branches – theirs, no doubt. There was something familiar about the car, but I was further down the road before it struck me. It was a BMW, like the car I had seen that night outside Liz and Derek's. A coincidence, surely? I could think of no reason why Edie's admirer would have been in Liverpool then.

I concentrated on my driving, charging down the lane, swerving round the bends, clipping the grass verges, hoping I didn't meet a tractor or a herd of cows. At one point I caught sight of the BMW far behind in my mirror, but I had a good lead and the other car's greater speed was less important in these lanes. Eventually I emerged on a bigger road, turned sharp right and shortly after, swung and skidded left into the maze of roads between there and Mold which I know like the back of my hand. Being chased by another car is more frightening in real life than it is at the cinema. Every vehicle you see seems to look like the one you are trying to avoid; but the further I went the safer I felt.

Beyond Mold I began to relax. There was no sign of the BMW, and in any case, surely they would have given up by now. It couldn't matter that much to them. Could it?

On the motorway my breathing settled back to normal. I just wanted to get home. The whole incident of my visit to see Edie seemed increasingly bizarre and surreal, but as I got nearer home the problem of explaining my absence to my wife and my employer began to prey on my mind. As I turned from the village street into the driveway by the side of our house, the old converted grey stone barn buildings looked comfortingly familiar. I got out of the car and looked around. I felt as if the whole world knew what I had been up to and were pointing metaphorical fingers at me. In reality, there was not a soul in sight, not even a curtain twitching down the street.

In the house, however, there was a shock for me. There was a note on the kitchen table – I was getting used to this by now – from Jenny.

Gone to stay with a friend. I need some space. I phoned Ruth. She told me where you'd gone. Why didn't you come home, or ring? I can't take all this. Jenny.

In a strange way I was relieved that I didn't have to face her and explain myself. I knew I should be upset, but there were too many other emotions churning around for me to worry about my marriage at that moment. I noticed that she hadn't said when, or if, she was coming back. I went up to our bedroom and looked in the wardrobe. She'd taken a load of clothes with her, but that meant nothing. She always took too much stuff, even for a weekend away.

As I closed the door and turned away, my eye was caught by something in the bottom of the wardrobe – the cardboard box containing my father's things which Phil had thrust at me when we met at the house in Liverpool. I'd stuffed it in there when we got back and never looked at it. On an impulse I pulled it out. Maybe something in there would tell me more about my dad, or even give me some clues as to what was going on now. I carted the box down to the kitchen, made myself some lunch – cheese on toast and coffee – and began to go through the contents. It looked as though they hadn't been disturbed for many years.

There was a musty, dog-eared D-Day newspaper, wartime magazines, copies of messages to the troops from Montgomery and Eisenhower, notebooks, faded unwritten postcards of Rouen and Brussels – a lot of stuff that was interesting from a historical point of view, but not very personal. But then I found his dog-tags, the identification that every soldier wears around his neck, with the number marked on that no soldier ever forgets. Attached to them was a small crucifix. This was more like it.

There was also an old tobacco tin that chinked when I picked it up. Inside were his medals – the '39-'45 star, the Normandy campaign, and incredibly, the red, white and blue ribbon and heavy silver of the Military Medal. I remembered then that he had mentioned it on one occasion, at Christmas when he'd drunk a little, but generally he hadn't talked about the war very much. I didn't know where, or why, he'd won his medal. I'd thought at the time that if *I'd* won a medal for bravery I'd want everyone to know; but then if my mates had been killed on the day I won it, perhaps it would have seemed tarnished by the memory..

Next I found a tattered brown envelope full of old photographs. There were holiday snaps and formal portraits. My parents on their wedding day, my father stiff in his uniform. But the one that intrigued me most was near the top of the pile. Taken at the dinner table in a room I didn't recognise, it showed my father in his infantry battledress, his cap tucked under one epaulette, half-turned to the person beside him. Fingers interlaced, and forearms resting on the table, he is caught by the camera, smiling, laughing almost, with a special light in his eyes. Turning to gaze at him with an equal sparkle is an attractive young woman, with wavy fair hair and a patterned dress. It is not my mother, and I don't recognise her. Yet they seem at ease with each other. I put the picture thoughtfully on one side.

There were more papers in the box, and as I moved them I saw some red material peeping out underneath. I pulled at it carefully, and as I eased it out I found myself holding a torn red armband with a black swastika in a white circle sewn onto it. The material was stained in places, and something about it made me shudder slightly. I imagined it on the arm of some German soldier, and wondered what had happened to him. By the look of his armband, something gruesome. I put it on one side and delved again into the box. There were some documents in German that at first glance meant nothing to me. Lists of names, places and items with comments next to them, all closely typed. A lot of the people's names were French, as were the towns and villages listed, but my German isn't good enough to read stuff like that without a dictionary. It all looked rather official in a Teutonic sort of way, and quite boring.

Then suddenly I was filled with excitement and anticipation. Under all the old papers was a substantial pile of letters without their envelopes, and beneath them again, a number of slim diaries. This was more than I could have hoped for. I lifted them out the letters began to read.

They were roughly chronological, but sporadic. They started in 1941, when my father was called up from his job in the Cotton Exchange, to join the Liverpool King's Regiment, and ended around the middle of 1945 when he was demobbed. I was taken aback by how literate my father seemed. Of course, letter writing is a lost art nowadays, and the most I usually manage is a hasty note or a card, but my father, for all his lack of formal education, was an intelligent man, who, in today's world, would doubtless have gone to college or even university.

The first few letters described his basic training and various postings and exercises in different parts of England. After looking at some of these, I put them on one side. I was eager to read more about his active service. I searched through until I got to June 1944, but it was not until I found a letter dated July of that year that he began to talk about Normandy and the D-Day landings.

Fascinated, I read his rather matter-of-fact description of how they had come ashore.

"My darling Sarah,

It's a month to-day – or rather four weeks – since I arrived in France. We were on the boat for hours before sailing. We started off at 7 o'clock on the Monday night – 5th – and before we were out of the harbour were ordered below. Although we were crowded together, we had a bunk each and were provided with one blanket, which was ample. Our craft wasn't very big. I suppose the sea was calm really to a sailor, but our craft rolled quite a lot, and the engine kicked up a terrific din. I lay on my bunk and became accustomed to the rolling, but then it would start to toss, or the engines would change their tempo, and I thought I'd never sleep. We were provided with three vomit bags, but I didn't need mine. Eventually I fell asleep and slept fairly steadily until we were called on deck at four o'clock, in the dark. As it grew lighter we began to see more and more ships, until eventually we saw the coast of France, and as we came closer could see hundreds and hundreds of ships of all sizes.

The land sloped very gradually upward from the sea and as we wormed our way closer inshore I could see our troops along the beach and on a road leading up from the beach. There was a lot of gunfire and bodies on the sand in between the barbed wire and other obstacles. A landing craft came alongside and we jumped down into it. It wasn't easy for us, loaded as we were, because the edge of the smaller craft was one minute close enough to step onto and the next far below – we had to step onto it as it came up. Eventually we were all in two of them and headed for the shore. The landing craft drew closer and closer to the beach and eventually the front went down and we stepped out into two or three feet of water.

We were all pretty scared, I think. Bullets were pinging off the sides of the craft, and as soon as the front went down one of the men was hit and fell forwards into the water. We were pretty lucky, though, and I was glad we weren't in the first wave of assault. Most of us got out OK and waded towards the shore. It was like a bad dream, trying to run and splash and stumble through the water with our heavy loads, holding our rifles up to try to keep them dry.

We ran straight up the beach, through a gap in the houses and onto the road leading inland. A few men were hit by machine-gun fire, but most of our section were OK. The houses looked exactly like they did on the pictures we'd been shown, which was comforting. I think they'd taken them from old holiday postcards. We had to keep moving until we were well clear of the beach. The ground was pretty well blasted and churned up, although the road itself, apart from its dustiness and general lack of repair, didn't seem to have been damaged. Most of the houses we saw at first were very badly knocked about..."

The letter went on to describe the confusion of those first hours ashore with the mass of shipping and landing craft crowding in from the Channel, the shouted orders, the bustle, the chaos, the sound of engines, the rumble of gunfire from the sea and inland. The screams of wounded men, the medics rushing about doing what they could; the rattle of machine-guns and the crump of shells, the planes sweeping overhead, the bloody firefights with the German defenders in their pill-boxes and gun emplacements. And finally, the men of my father's unit re-assembling, exhausted after the adrenalin-pumping terror of the day and the long night-time passage from England, marching inland along a dusty road to bed down in a field under foreign stars, with the enemy held tenuously at bay. Poignantly, he finished the letter:

"...That was the end of my first day in France.
"I'll never forget the view of the Channel when we looked

back on our climb from the shore – I've never seen so many ships all at once and I don't suppose I ever will again. I've been told that the people used to wonder why we were taking so long to come, but when they saw the immense amount of shipping and supplies of all sorts they wondered at our having come so soon…"

The following letters described the tedium and the fear, the deaths of comrades, the battles and skirmishes as the Allied armies fought their way towards Belgium. The hours went by unnoticed, and by the time they got to Brussels, I realised with surprise that it was going dark. I paused in my reading to switch on the light and draw the curtains.

I went to the drinks cabinet, poured myself a whisky, sat down again and carried on going through the letters. It was some time later that I suddenly stiffened with concentration, re-reading part of one particular letter that seemed significant. It was dated 6th September 1944.

"We went out on patrol yesterday near the front line, looking out for German stragglers. You know how they are retreating, and they're trying to escape in all sorts of conveyances, including farm carts and bicycles. It makes the locals laugh to see them – they were so arrogant when they arrived as conquerors a few years ago. Anyway, we've advanced so fast that some of them are caught behind our lines, and it's part of our job to look for them and make sure they don't cause any mischief.

" We didn't find any Germans, but I picked up this armband and I thought you might like it as a souvenir. Whoever owned it must have been keen to get rid of it…"

I put down the letter and picked up the swastika armband which I had looked at earlier. It was torn, which might explain why it had been lost. On close inspection, the brown patches on it looked very much like bloodstains. This seemed a strange souvenir to send to a wife back home. It had obviously appeared significant to my father at the time, and I wondered why. I pondered for some time, fingering the red cloth which had once graced the arm of a living German soldier. A member of the Wehrmacht, the Regular Army, perhaps, or one of the hated but fierce-fighting Waffen SS?

As I sat in thought, my eye fell again on the diaries. They were slim volumes, varying in size and shape and dating from the mid-thirties. Amongst them were several which were identical, black bound with faded gold leaf lettering. I guessed that these covered the war years, probably a standard format for soldiers, bought at the W.V.S. canteen or somewhere similar. I hunted through them with bated breath. 1941…1942…1943… The next one, and the last one, was 1945. I searched through all the diaries again. It wasn't there.

I slumped back in my chair, frustrated. This was typical! The one diary that related to the same period as the letter was missing, and any information it held was gone. I took a long gulp of my whisky. Gradually I calmed down and began to think about it.

There was one diary missing from the sequence, and it was the one I most wanted to read. Perhaps that was why it wasn't with the others, then, because it *was* significant. I sat motionless, cudgelling my brains. Then it came back to me and with an audible cry of excitement, I turned to the pile of papers that I had first taken from the box. Amongst them were some notebooks which I had moved just before I found the dog-tags and medals, and yes … amongst them was a black diary, identical to the others but unremarkable on its own, and with it a tattered address book. The fact that they were separate from the others suggested, perhaps, that my father might have been looking at them comparatively recently before he died.

I riffled through the pages of the diary. They were week to a view, not designed for lengthy journal writing, but my father had crammed in quite a lot in his small, neat writing, onto pages yellowed now and smudged in places. Serving soldiers don't have too many appointments – life at the cutting edge of the Army's advance is not organised like that – but he had used it to record a lot of things that happened. Unit movements, advances, haircuts, pay parades, guard duty, visits to friends, football matches, Ensa concerts …. I didn't know quite what I was looking for, but it was none of those things.

Then I found it.

"5ᵗʰ September 1944.

Patrol. Skirmish with SS truck. 4 dead. Pte & I buried them and everything else.

Share later."

That was it. A few lines in a cheap diary, easily overlooked. And this referred to the day when he had written in his letter *"we didn't find any Germans."* Yet he had. By the sound of it, he had been involved that day in a fierce gun battle. Why hadn't he mentioned it? Maybe he didn't want to frighten his wife back home; and yet, elsewhere in his letters he had written graphically about the dangers of war, the beaches, the bullets, the shellfire and the bombs. So why had he not spoken of this incident? And what had they buried along with bodies that they could share later? Why bury the bodies in the first place?

The rest of the diary entries seemed to yield no more information, so I closed it and dropped it into the box again, but as it fell, a sheet of paper which had been tucked inside the back cover slipped part way out of it. I picked it out. It was a map, an Army map of part of Belgium. It was folded and faded, blotched with brown and tatty round the edges, the creases nearly worn through. I opened it carefully, spread it on my knee, and studied it closely. It was a map of the area to the south-east of Brussels, and I saw that south-west of a village called St Hubert, there was a wood, and next to this was a cross marked in pencil. Why was it marked? A target, an enemy strongpoint, a rendezvous ... or something else?

I turned the map over, and caught my breath in excitement. On the back was a hand-drawn map, in pencil, showing just St Hubert and the wood, and the access tracks leading into it. Another cross marked – what? Distances were given in paces from two track junctions. It seemed pretty obvious from this that the map had been hastily drawn to indicate, for future reference, exactly where my father and his mate had buried the dead Germans, and something else.

But what else? Another mystery. I'd started out on Sunday morning looking for the answer to one question, and now, instead of an answer, I had another question. Was there any link between the two? It appeared to be the case from my father's diary that he and another soldier, a private – I knew that my father was a corporal by now – had had some sort of battle with SS men in a truck, had wiped them out, and had found something of value which they had buried, and had planned to come back for it. Was it Nazi gold, I wondered, excitedly. And had they ever retrieved it? It seemed unlikely – we'd never had any money at home, no more than a man could bring home from an ordinary office job, such as my father had. Or had he found it again and shared it with his companion? Was it not gold, but something else? How could I find out? I didn't even know the identity of his comrade-in-arms, no name, not even an initial.

I glanced again at the swastika armband. Had it come from one of the SS men killed by my father and his mate? The thought made it seem more unpleasant and threatening than before, but it might explain why he had picked it up and kept it, to remove a last shred of evidence.

I passed my hand over my eyes. They were tired, and so was I. My watch showed me that it was ten o'clock, and I had been sitting reading letters and diaries for several hours. I'd had no dinner, either, and I was hungry.

I made myself a sandwich and boiled the kettle for a cup of tea. While I was eating, a plan formed in my mind. It was obvious, really. I could think of no other way of finding out what had happened on that September day in 1944; on the spur of the moment I decided to take the bull by the horns. It was a spontaneous decision, and most of my acquaintances would say it was out of character. I was normally a man to weigh the pros and cons of a situation before taking a decision, and by then it was often too late. Perhaps it was Jenny's absence that gave me a feeling of freedom and irresponsibility I had not felt for a long time. But now, for better or worse, Jenny wasn't there to worry about. As for school, I could phone the next day and tell them I was still ill. After all, I would be back in a couple of days.

I was going to Belgium, to find the village of St Hubert, and the wood on the map, and I was going to ask questions until I got some answers.

I threw some clothes into a bag, got my passport out of the desk drawer, and put the diary and map in with them. As an afterthought, I put in the old address book I had found, and the photograph of my father and the mysterious woman. Then I had a shower and went to bed, setting the alarm for five o'clock. I would have a long drive, and I wanted to get away early.

Chapter Six

It was dark at five when the shrilling of the alarm startled me awake. I surfaced reluctantly, convinced I had only been asleep for a couple of hours, although I had in fact slept soundly through the night. Turning on the shaded bedside light, I lay in the semi-darkness of the room, warm and comfortable under the duvet, while sleep gradually changed to wakefulness. Should I get up? Or simply snuggle down and doze off again? Should I bother with my plan of the night before? After all, no-one but me had any idea of my project. Nor, I guessed, would anyone really care. Maybe I'd give it another hour in bed, and then see how I felt.

After a few minutes I heard the hoarse roar of an engine in the village street, and the rattle of milk bottles as Eddie Carr did his delivery round. I thought of him getting up in the cold of a winter morning, scraping the ice off the windscreen, handling the chilling bottles while folk like me were still abed. I thought of the War, of soldiers like my dad, snatching sleep in all weathers with little hope of a hot breakfast, carrying on fighting for day after day with no prospect of real rest and comfort.

I felt suddenly ashamed of my sloth, and my lack of determination. I threw back the bedclothes and swung my legs out of bed. It was cold in the bedroom. The central heating was still set to come on at seven o'clock and I had forgotten to re-set it. I padded to the bathroom and took a quick hot shower, shaved and cleaned my teeth. Then I went down to the kitchen, poured myself some cereal and made a cup of tea. Eating and drinking quickly, I was ready to leave by half-past five. I put my fleece on, and as I did so, I felt a piece of paper in the pocket. I fished it out, and saw that it was the note Edie had left for me, with the indecipherable phone number. Remembering something I had once read, or seen on a TV programme, I got a pencil and softly shaded over the impression on the paper. To my delight, the number appeared, not clearly, but easy enough to read – *01425 58996.* I felt like a real detective now. Unfortunately, the number meant nothing to me. I didn't even recognise the code. I put the paper back in my pocket, picked up my bag and turned the lights out.

Outside, in the semi-darkness of our driveway that the lights in the main street didn't penetrate, I unlocked the car and dropped my bag into the boot. I paused in thought for a moment, then went back inside, and looked again through the pile of my father's letters. I grabbed the ones that seemed to relate to the time he had spent in Belgium and stuffed them in an envelope file. Then, to be on the safe side, I picked up the whole box of stuff, went back out to the car and put everything in the boot.

I scraped a thin layer of frost off the windscreen, got in and started up the engine, its quiet growl sounding deafening in the early morning peace of the village. I eased into gear and pulled out into the slumbering street, where it seemed that all the parked cars were still sheathed in sparkling white. The windscreen of one car, however, parked on the double yellow lines near our turning, was clear. As I swung out round it I noticed smoke coming from its exhaust and realised its engine was running. Then I recognised it. I had seen it before, in the narrow lanes around Maes-y-Bryn, hunting me down.

As I passed I thought I saw a figure, or figures, hunched in the seats. It was facing in the opposite direction to me, and I was reassured by the fact that they would have difficulty turning round if they wished to follow me. I looked anxiously in the mirror as I drove away down the street, but the car didn't move. Perhaps they expected me to behave like a creature of habit and were dozing, off guard, trying to stay warm through the long night. At any rate, they made no move to follow me. Once I was out of sight, I relaxed. If they wanted to attack me again, or warn me off, they had missed their chance.

I wove my way carefully through the network of narrow roads that is the shortest way to the M6, and joined the traffic already streaming down the motorway. Somewhere in Staffordshire the sun came up in the clear sky like a molten ball, with a brief promise of good weather, but clouds were already building, swallowing the light into dreary greyness, and by the time I reached Hilton Park the sky was blank and the traffic at a standstill. I pulled off into the services and treated myself to an expensive cooked breakfast and some coffee. Then I phoned school to say that my cold had turned to bronchitis, and it was unlikely that I would be in all week.

By the time I had finished doing that, the motorway was

beginning to flow again, and I carried on under dispiriting watery clouds, flicking the wipers intermittently to shift the dirty spray which accumulated continually on the windscreen. Past Birmingham and on to the M1, the lorries and motorcars became gradually less packed. At the junction of the motorways, I headed south.

Since I had left on the spur of the moment, I had had no time to check ferry sailings from Felixstowe directly to Belgium, so I decided to head for Dover, from where the ferries left more frequently, catch a boat to Calais and drive north, past Dunkirk and Lille to get to Brussels.

I crossed the Thames at Dartford, picked up the M2 and eventually came down the steep hill to Dover and turned into the ferryport. Seagulls were calling, the air had the tang of salt, and I felt that faint stirring of excitement that all Englishmen feel when they are about to take ship, even a short-haul car ferry. We are all mariners at heart, I thought, an island race to whom the sea is a highway, but also our first line of defence. Looking along the sweep of the White Cliffs, I thought how Hitler's hopes of invasion had been dashed in 1940, partly by the bravery of a few young men flying bullet-holed "crates", and partly by a short 22 miles of water, so inoffensive on a summer's day, so wild and treacherous in a winter gale.

Today the water was dark and glassy, stretching ominously and impenetrably away into the shape-changing sea-fret, and the ship rolled slowly as we hit the long, low swell beyond the sheltering arms of Dover Harbour. It was afternoon now, and I was hungry, so I went to the self-service cafeteria and had some lunch. There were few people around – on a weekday in March there are not very many holidaymakers or noisy school parties travelling, and the boat was calm and peaceful.

Afterwards I went on deck, and leaned on the rail, peering into the mist and pondering. It seemed surreal to be travelling off on a quest like this, when I should really be at work. What would my colleagues say if they knew? They would be covering my lessons at this very moment, and might be justifiably angry if they found that I was not lying ill at home. Jenny would probably be furious, but I was getting used to that idea.

And where was Edie? After an intense evening and night together, she had disappeared without a word, unless you counted the brief note she had left. Two emotions vied within me, and I realised I was keen to find out more about her on both counts. On the one hand I was very curious to know more of her background, as I was convinced now that there was a lot to her that she hadn't told me; and on the other hand, I wanted to feel her warmth again, hear her voice and see her teasing eyes sparkling up at me…I started, and shivered, not just with the damp cold of the sea. What was I thinking of? I had had an unexpected night of passion with someone I hardly knew, and now I was letting myself think I was falling in love with her. *Grow up,* I told myself. *By all means, find out more about her role in your family's affairs, but don't kid yourself about anything else.*

And yet … I couldn't help thinking about her…

Northern France seemed featureless and unprepossessing on this dank grey afternoon. The villages lacked the charm of regions further south, the houses suburban, often terraced in the English style. Factories lined the busy motorway and slag-heaps from the coal-mines poked their conical snouts into the darkening sky. By the time I reached Lille, it was raining and spray was showering across the windscreen, the wipers struggling while I peered anxiously at the unfamiliar road-signs. Lorries choked the inside lane, and blurred, blinding headlights surged in my mirror out of the deepening gloom. My spirits were sinking fast, evening was approaching, and as yet I had nowhere to stay. I hoped I would reach St Hubert in time to get a room and something to eat.

Darkness came as, with a sense of relief, I left the motorway and headed across country on minor roads to find the village I was looking for. Several times I had to stop at poorly signed junctions to search on my road map for the correct route; several times I thought I had made the wrong turn, but finally I saw the sign – *St Hubert 1km.* I breathed a sigh of relief. I was looking forward to getting there after a long and unexpected day's travel.

The village looked neat and prosperous, with new developments of upmarket detached houses, and the centre, when I reached it, appeared to have retained much of its old charm. Nosing down a narrowing street past parked cars, I emerged in a square with a stone fountain, cobbled with rain-slicked setts and lit by elegant cast-iron lamp standards. The lights shone like haloes through the misty squalls. Shops, shuttered at this hour, lined the square, where quite a few vehicles were parked. There was the usual *boulangerie*, a butcher's and a small supermarket, but there was also a hairdresser's, a rather smart clothes shop and one or two arty-looking *boutiques*. It appeared, from first impressions, that the populace of St. Hubert had an enviable lifestyle. No doubt, I guessed, many of them commuted to well-paid jobs in Brussels.

A couple of small bars caught my eye, then the sign *Hotel de la Paix*. It seemed promising, and with luck they would have a room available. I pulled into a parking space and turned off the engine. I sat for a moment listening to the ticking of the engine as it cooled. I closed my eyes and massaged them with my thumb and forefinger, realising now that I was tired and a little disorientated, remembering why I was there, in Belgium, but craving more than anything a drink, a rest and something to eat.

I got out of the car, locked it and walked into the hotel. Coming in from the dark, the brightness took me aback, and I think I blinked at it. The door opened straight into a large bar, which was lit by chandeliers of electric candle bulbs. The walls were lined with mirrors engraved with 1920s adverts and Toulouse-Lautrec drawings, and the bar-top itself was polished copper. The floor was of scrubbed boards, and the tables and chairs retro copies of pre-war elegance. At the back I could see a dining-room, the tables already laid with white cloths, flower-painted crockery, and wine-glasses. It wasn't what I had imagined. I had expected a drab, functional sort of place, with faded posters, dog-eared newspapers and a resident drunk. This was better! I began to cheer up a bit.

A few men, regulars by the look of them, were sitting at tables, quietly chatting. Another man leaning on the bar acknowledged my entrance with a nod, and I smiled in reply. An attractive young woman with bobbed blonde hair and a low-cut dress was perched on a bar-stool watching a game show on the television. As I approached she slipped from the stool and went behind the bar.

"*Monsieur?*"

"*Une bière, s'il vous plaît.*"

"*Stella ou Amstel?*"

"Stella, s'il vous plaît."

I waited in silence while she poured my drink. I was thirsty after the journey and a beer seemed like a good starting point. She placed the glass carefully on a beer-mat on the counter.

"Merci, Mademoiselle."

"S'il vous plaît, Monsieur."

I took a long drink of the cold liquid, while the girl opened the electronic till, picked out the change and turned to hand it to me.

"Pardon, Mademoiselle...vous avez une chambre pour ce soir?"

She smiled briefly at me, pulling the reservations book towards her. I held my breath. I didn't fancy heading out again into a wet night in search of accommodation.

"Une personne?"

"Oui." I nodded.

She scanned down the page.

"Une nuit seulement?"

I guessed I might want to stay longer than one night.

"Non. Deux. Peut-être trois. J'ai des affaires ici."

"Oui, monsieur. Pas de problème. Numéro douze, premier étage."

I breathed a sigh of relief as she held out a key with a large brass number 12 attached.

I went back out to the car, got my bag and went upstairs. The rather narrow, gloomy room, typical of many such old hotels, was cheered by bright wallpaper and there was a duvet on the pine bed. The en suite bathroom was clean and well appointed, and the power shower was a luxury I wasted no time in wallowing in, gratefully washing away some of the grime and tiredness of my trip. I wasn't here on holiday, but it was a relief to find myself in reasonably comfortable surroundings. I didn't have much to unpack, but before going down to eat I got out the file with my father's letters in, and browsed through them again.

I read once more, and with greater attention, the vivid descriptions of the welcome the Allied, and especially British, troops got as they advanced through France and particularly Belgium, the flags waving, the bottles of wine that had been saved to celebrate the Liberation, the crowds pressing in on both sides as the men struggled to get their transports through the narrow streets of the towns. Girls jumping up onto tanks and jeeps to give flowers to the soldiers, the cheering, the weeping, the bands playing the Marseillaise and "Tipperary".

There were also descriptions of the devastation – the burned-out vehicles, the ruined buildings, the bodies of soldiers awaiting burial, the stench of dead cattle and horses lying in the fields. Joy was balanced with sorrow at the horror of it all, and over and above everything else, the hinted fear of action in which my father's unit was intermittently involved.

I reached the point at which I had stopped the night before, with the mention of the swastika armband found by the wood. The next letter spoke of the following week, and a visit to a café in the village of St Hubert.

"...it's more of a small town than what we would call a village. It was good to have 48 hours off patrol, and we were determined to enjoy ourselves. The town was celebrating the presence of their liberators – we're absolutely "it" at the moment. They've waited so long and haven't got over the joy of our being here.

The café we went to was quite a big place – part of a rather shabby hotel – with a good dance band (even the smallest place has a band, however small). The café was full of people going round – imagine Christmas Eve or New Year's Eve at a dance and magnify it a thousand times and you'll have some idea of what it was like. The place was very crowded but we pushed our way in and were looking for a seat when the band struck up the National Anthem and everyone stood up, then the Marseillaise and everyone sang it, then God Save the King and those who could sang, then the U.S. National Anthem.

Then the band played "Tipperary". Before we knew what was happening we were grabbed by some of the local girls and were dragged around and round the place – in and out the tables, round and round, in and out, until we were hot and weary, every soldier the girls could lay hands on, until there must have been hundreds going round. The band wasn't allowed to stop for a long time. It wasn't a case of dancing, but running, hopping, skipping, etc. – just an outlet, and it goes on every night at the moment. The band played "Tipperary", "Run, Rabbit, Run" "Siegfried Line" and others. It was a very good band and it's a pity there wasn't a proper dance floor. They also played "In the Mood" and "Tiger Rag".

When the band did stop we were besieged for souvenirs and I couldn't get away without parting with my cap badge. The recipient, one of the girls who had dragged us on to the floor, kissed me on both cheeks when she finally got it…"

I laid the letter down, imagining the scene that my father described. To be young and abroad, hailed as heroes surviving the heat of battle as part of a victorious army riding hard on the heels of a retreating foe; to be cheered and welcomed by grateful people, kissed and fussed over by pretty girls – what could my generation experience to equal that? No wonder, I thought, that many men recognised the War as the time when they were, if not at their happiest, then certainly at their most alive.

And had I, by chance, found myself staying at the very hotel that my father had visited over forty years ago in a brief moment of relaxation during the push north through Belgium?

I picked up the diary, and flicked through it, looking for the matching dates.

10th September 1944
Off duty. Went to café. Dancing. Girl took cap badge.
11th September 1944
Confession (in French). Went for drink with Sophie later.
12th September 1944
Patrol.
13th September 1944
Moved out in trucks – heading for Berg-en-Dal. Will we be back?

So. My father had met a girl – here, perhaps, in this very hotel. Was she the woman in the photograph I'd found? I didn't think so. He'd moved on two days after they'd met, so he obviously hadn't had an ongoing affair with her – this Sophie.

The crucial question, however, was whether he'd mentioned the stuff, whatever it was, that I guessed he and some unnamed private had rescued from the SS and buried in the wood not far from the village. Had he mentioned it to this girl, who presumably lived in the area? Had she told anyone else? I sensed that I would have to tread carefully when I broached the subject. I put the letters away, slipped the diary and address book into my pocket and went down to dinner.

The bar was busier now, with men drinking beer, watching the TV, chatting to the barmaid. A group of young women sat at a table drinking cocktails and giggling, and in the corner some older men, elder statesmen of the village, all berets, hard hands and walking sticks, were seated in the companionable silence that comes from a lifetime spent in each other's company.

I went through to the restaurant and seated myself where I could see the comings and goings of the place. There was a *menu du jour*, with several choices for each course. I like that. It makes choosing easy, and suggests that the chef has taken special care with each dish. I chose the *soupe de poissons* followed by *boeuf en daube* and asked to look at the wine list. It was surprisingly extensive, mainly French reds, and whites from Alsace and some of the better German vintages.

I went for a bottle of *Fitou* and sipped it while I waited for the waitress to bring the food. It was excellent and would taste even better with something to eat.

While I sat there I watched the other people in the restaurant. Some couples, one or two family parties, a table full of businessmen. Most of them were fairly local, by the look of it. They seemed to know each other, and there was a lot of kissing and handshaking when a new group came in. They all greeted me politely with a formal "*M'sieu!*" but I got the impression that it was quite unusual to see a stranger in there.

I was browsing through my father's diary again, trying to glean further information from it, when my meal arrived. I put the diary away and concentrated on the food, which was excellent. By the time I'd finished my pudding, it was well after nine o'clock, the restaurant was full and the bar was busy. It was obviously the place to be if you lived in, or near St Hubert.

I left a tip for the waitress, got up and went to the bar, easing my way through the crowd of people. Although my French is reasonable, I'd never pass for a Frenchman, or a Belgian, come to that. It was no real surprise, therefore, that after I'd given my order for a beer, I heard a gravelly voice in my ear.

"*Anglais?* English?"

I turned and saw a creased brown face with a day's growth of stubble smiling at me from a few inches away and breathing pastis fumes in my direction. A navy blue beret was slightly askew atop a head of cropped grey hair. Interesting how it always seems to be the older men who speak to you first.

"*Oui*, yes," I answered cautiously. *"Je suis anglais,"*

"It is the first visit in Belgium?"

"Yes, it is."

The distant look in his eyes and the slight slurring of his speech suggested that he had drunk more than one pastis in the last couple of hours.

"You like it here?"

"I think so, so far. I've only been here a few hours. I arrived this afternoon. From England."

"I hope that you will like our country."

"Well, my father did. He was in Belgium in '44."

He straightened up from where he was leaning on the bar counter, picked up his glass and clinked it, with a slight effort of concentration, against mine.

"*Santé!* '*44! La libération!* Tommies. We love the Tommies."

He nudged me with his elbow and winked conspiratorially, then jerked a thumb towards his own midriff.

"*Henri, je m'appelle Henri.*"

He held out a big rough hand which seemed to envelop my own.

"Mark," I replied, raising my voice above the hubbub. *"Enchanté!"*

He half-closed his eyes, as if with an effort of memory, then he began to sing in a surprisingly tuneful and robust voice.

"...Is a long way to Tipperary, is a long way to go..."

He stopped singing abruptly and grasped my elbow.

"Here! I want that you meet my friends!"

He stepped back and, turning, drew me forward so that I could be introduced to the three men he was with, two perched on bar-stools, another one leaning on the counter. I'd been wondering where to start asking questions, if I needed to do so to find out more about my father's references to the area. I wasn't sure whether I should just take the map and start exploring on my own, but I guessed that at some stage I'd need some local inside information. And this was better than I could have expected. A casual introduction to a group of men who, by the look of them, would have been around during the war. And they'd been having a drink, so their tongues might well be loosened. I felt quite excited.

"Pierre, Marcel, Maurice! Regardez! Mon ami anglais!"

I moved into the space in their circle that had opened up for me, and smiled and nodded a greeting to the others.

"Who's your friend, Henri?"

Pierre spoke in French.

"Mark. He's English. His father was in Belgium in '44 with the British Army. He's just arrived here today."

"Ah, the English Tommies. Our liberators!" Pierre looked dreamy.

"I remember it as if it was yesterday. They came here like a gale, sweeping the *Boches* away. One hundred and twenty kilometres from the Somme in one push. Brussels, Antwerp, liberated by the Tommies. The Germans didn't even have time to run away. Some of them were wandering round for quite a long time, trying to get back to their own lines. The English? Yes, we love the English! They liberated our country. But the French? Pah!"

He made a dismissive gesture with his hand.

"So why don't you like the French?" I wanted to know.

"The French? The biggest army in Europe in 1940, always boasting about it, and about the Maginot Line, and when it came to it, how long did they last against the Germans?"

"*Hé*, be fair, Pierre," Marcel interjected. "Who could have stood up to the Panzers when they attacked? We couldn't, could we?"

"You're right, Marcel, you're right. We're only a small country. But we didn't sign an armistice like the French. We didn't collaborate with the Germans. Pétain? He was as bad as Hitler! And De Gaulle was only interested in winning France back, not in helping to free other countries or win the war!

"But the British? That's another story. Churchill, Montgomery – they stood up to Hitler and without them all Europe might have been Nazi now. So cheers to the British!"

Pierre raised his glass and there was much clinking and drinking and laughter and slapping me on the back, although I felt rather guilty since I hadn't even been born in 1944, let alone serving in the army. I was happy to bask in the reflected glory, though.

When we'd all calmed down a bit, Marcel turned to me.

"So what brings you to St Hubert, then?"

I hesitated.

"Business, holiday …?"

"Holiday," I answered, hoping that would be the end of the matter. I was reluctant to reveal the purpose of my visit straight away.

Marcel looked thoughtful.

"Not many people come here on holiday, *monsieur*. It's not what you might call a popular holiday destination. Most people stay in Brussels, or the Ardennes."

"True, but this is a nice hotel. And I can visit Brussels and Waterloo from here. Then I may move on to Dinant and explore from there."

Maurice had been watching me carefully. In appearance, he was better-groomed than his friends, his clothes more stylish and expensive. He seemed at first more reserved than the others, but when he spoke he quickly gave the impression of a man who was used to being listened to.

"You said your father was in Belgium in '44. Whereabouts exactly was he?"

I took a drink of my beer and thought about my answer.

"He was in lots of places as they travelled through. But he spent some time here."

"Here? In St Hubert itself?"

"Yes, I believe so. A few days."

"And did he say anything about our village?"

"A little. Not much."

There was a pause, during which everyone seemed lost in thought. Henri took a drink of his pastis, and Marcel rolled himself a cigarette.

"Was there much fighting round here?" I asked, hoping to draw them out on the subject.

"Yes and no," answered Pierre. He went on:

"When the British advanced through here, they pushed the *Boche* back very quickly, so there was not a great battle here. But, as I said, many Germans who had not been able to retreat were trapped behind the British lines. Many patrols went out and caught the ones who were left behind. The Resistance dealt with others. Some tried to disguise themselves, some got help from collaborators. Although by then most of the *collabos* knew which side their interest lay…"

Maurice caught his eye and gave an almost imperceptible shake of the head, and Pierre stopped talking. He spread his hands in a gesture of *what more can I say?* and smiled.

I got the impression there was something they were reluctant to talk about. I decided to take the plunge.

"Do you know…or did you hear about some SS men near here? A truck that was ambushed, perhaps, by a British patrol…?"

Maurice cut in sharply, any friendliness gone from his voice.

"There were many Germans near here, monsieur. We don't remember all the stories. Why should we?"

"These SS men," I persisted, "their bodies were buried in a wood near here. That's unusual, isn't it?"

"I've never heard of that, monsieur. Never heard of such a thing. I don't know where you got the idea from"

Maurice picked up his drink and turned away with an air that told me the conversation was over. I decided to try one last question.

"Do any of you know of someone called Sophie? She'd be about your age perhaps."

I thought I caught an exchange of glances, as if they were surprised by my question. Pierre looked at the others, and then at me, as if he might be about to say something, but Marcel cut in.

"Sophie? No, I don't think so. Anyway, it's a common name."

They turned their backs and began to talk rapidly amongst themselves, effectively excluding me from any further conversation. I leaned on the bar and drank deeply of my beer. My throat felt dry and my heart was pounding. These men knew something, and didn't want to talk about it, which suggested it was both important, and a secret. But what should I do next? I hadn't come all this way just to go home again without getting to the bottom of it, and the reactions of Henri and his friends suggested that I had touched a nerve. Maybe I had interpreted my father's diary correctly. I gazed sightlessly into my drink and pondered.

"Psst!"

At first I didn't realise he was trying to attract my attention.

"*Monsieur!*"

I turned to my right and saw that someone had sidled down the bar towards me. A slightly built man in his forties with smooth black hair and a face like a stoat, he was wearing a cheap blouson-style leather jacket, and turned-up jeans over cowboy boots.

"I couldn't help overhearing your conversation, *monsieur.*"

He spoke in a hoarse whisper, as if afraid of being overheard. He looked nervous and his hands shook as he took a cigarette from its packet and lit it. He drew on the cigarette and blew the smoke out sideways.

"I may be able to help you."

"Really? How can you help?" I didn't much like the look of him. I thought he might just be trying it on, wanting money perhaps, and I didn't really want to commit myself.

"You were asking about the War? A fight with some SS soldiers, whose bodies were buried in a wood near here?

"That's right. I did mention it. What about it?"

He leant forward and muttered quietly, almost whispering:

"I can show you the wood, if you want."

His whisper wasn't quiet enough, because suddenly Maurice detached himself from his friends, and with a movement as swift as someone half his age, sprang between me and my new companion, who flinched and raised his hands instinctively to protect himself, in the manner of someone who is used to being bullied.

"*Fils de pute!*" Maurice spat at him. "*Ta gueule!* Shut up! What do you know anyway? Don't tell your stories to strangers, Alain! It can be bad for your health!"

Alain stared at him sullenly, his mouth working but without uttering a sound. Maurice grabbed him by the front of his jacket and pulled him close. The bar had gone quiet.

"*Tu m'écoutes?* Are you listening to me?" Maurice hissed. "Now, do as I say, and get out! *Fiche-moi la paix!*"

He dragged the younger man effortlessly towards the door of the café, opened it with his left hand, and shoved Alain through it and out into the street. He walked back past me, dusting his hands together and fixed me with a piercing stare. He nodded at me and murmured *"M'sieu"* in mock greeting. I smiled weakly at him and turned away.

I waited till the conversation had started up again and things had got back to normal, then finished my drink and slipped outside. The rain had stopped and the atmosphere was clearing, although rags of cloud still streamed across the face of the moon. The square was quiet, the shuttered buildings blank and eyeless, their stepped gables blackly outlined against the lighter sky. Above my head, the hanging *Hotel* sign creaked in the wind.

My thoughts were racing. If my conversation with Pierre and his friends had made me fairly sure that I was on some sort of track, Alain's words and Maurice's reaction to them had made me certain. All of a sudden it was all terribly real, no longer just a few words hidden in an old diary of forty-five years ago, but an event that had affected the inhabitants of a Belgian village and could still stir violent emotions. It made me nervous to think of it, but at the same time more determined to get to the bottom of it all.

The air outside was cold and I shivered, folding my forearms around my body. As I turned to go back into the hotel, a figure emerged from the shadows. It was Alain. He beckoned to me, and I went to meet him as he stepped back into the black shade thrown by the building.

"What is it?" I hissed.

"You want to find the wood? I can show you."

"*C'est gentil*. But why? What does it mean to you?"

"The wood? Nothing. There's nothing there anyway."

"So why are you telling me about it?"

"You are English. You come back for what's yours, maybe?"

"Maybe."

"You come back with soldiers, I help you…"

As he spoke, the door of the hotel swung open, throwing a square of yellow light onto the pavement. The figure of Maurice was framed in the doorway. He peered intently up and down the square, then turned back inside. When I looked round, my eyes now more accustomed to the darkness, Alain had vanished. I heard the light patter of his running footsteps as he made off.

Shaking my head, I went back into the hotel and without pausing in the bar, went upstairs to my bedroom. I had just shut the door when I heard the creak of footsteps on the old floorboards of the landing, and the sound of somebody going quietly downstairs; then I heard the door into the bar open and close again. I paid little attention to it until I looked around the room. The file with the letters in was lying on the desk, but I was almost sure I had left it on the bed. My bag had been moved as well, but a quick check showed nothing missing. Had someone from the hotel been in to tidy the room? It seemed unlikely at that time of night. Or had someone slipped in to search through my things?

I wondered who would have access to my room. I didn't much like the thought of being spied on, and I wasn't impressed by the thought of someone coming back during the night. I toyed with the idea of jamming a chair under the door handle, but the handle was in the wrong place and the chair wasn't the right sort. I cleaned my teeth, got undressed and went to bed. I started to make a mental review of what had happened during the evening, but I was so exhausted I fell asleep almost instantly.

Chapter Seven

Clumps of trees swam out of the mist, brooding dark islands in the pale wash of morning. With each exhalation of mine into the cold air, water vapour hung in clouds, and my own muffled footfalls and the sound of my breathing were all I could hear. Alongside the pooled and muddy track, droplets sparkled on grass stems and spiders' webs, and the swelling, dormant earth of the fields on either hand, pregnant with summer corn, was sheened with wetness.

I was glad of the mist. Unwilling to risk my car down the unsurfaced track, I had walked from the outskirts of the village, and at first felt highly conspicuous. I imagined unseen eyes watching my progress from silent windows, although when I turned to look, the houses showed no signs of life and there was no-one in sight. Soon the mist screened me from view. Map unobtrusively in hand, I headed for the wood, which was marked as lying a couple of kilometres from the village. Post-war developments had encroached on some of the fields, which confused me at first, but after a while I recognised the features on the map – a water tank, an old shed, a track junction. Other rough tracks led off across the flat farmland and green pathways separated cabbage fields and potato crops. Without cattle or sheep to be seen, although cultivated, it seemed a bleak landscape.

At one point, rounding a bend where the grass grew tall in the verge, my heart missed a beat as I heard a loud and unfamiliar thudding. Then two large hares swerved past, narrowly missing me and closely avoiding a painful collision. With ears laid back and long legs driving, they followed their graceful course across the fields and were soon lost to sight.

The wood drew steadily nearer, the blurred grey outline resolving itself into individual trees, and I turned the map over to inspect the sketch which would show me exactly where to look. Then I heard what I didn't want – the sound of an engine approaching. I looked around, instinctively seeking cover, but there was none, short of throwing myself in the muddy irrigation ditch. I had a very strong, almost irrational fear of being accosted and having to explain myself. I was on no public footpath, and had no recreational or business reason for being there. As I looked round wildly for somewhere to hide, it was suddenly too late.

Out of the murk behind me there surged a dirty red Toyota pick-up, rocking slowly through the potholes, its fat tyres splashing muddily through the puddles. It drew to a halt next to me, and the driver leaned out of the open window. He jerked his head, shapeless in an old trilby hat, in my direction

"Où allez-vous, monsieur? C'est pas publique, ici, vous savez!"

"Promenade," I answered. *"Touriste,"* although I knew as I said it that I was probably the first tourist to ever take a walk down that glutinous track, and my answer was far from convincing him.

He stared at me for a moment, and I realised I was still holding the map in my hand. He looked at it quizzically and I stuffed it hastily into my pocket.

He gave a humourless smile, his mouth a steely line in a red-veined, weather-beaten face.

"Promenade? Pas possible! C'est privé."

I stood my ground and smiled and shrugged non-committally, deciding it was as well to admit to as little knowledge of French as I could get away with.

He tried a different tack.

"C'est dangereux, monsieur." He indicated the back of the truck's cab with his thumb, and following his gesture, I saw a shotgun lying on the seat. He tapped his watch, then pointed to the jackdaws which we had disturbed from the trees, flapping and cawing, and mimed a shooting action.

"Paf! Paf!"

Then he stared at me with a look of pure unfriendliness. If he wanted me to think that he and possibly others would be shooting rooks and crows there later, and that I should avoid the area, I didn't believe him. But there didn't seem much future in ignoring him. I raised my palms to him in a gesture of compliance, and set off back the way I had come.

He waited until I had gone some distance, then trundled slowly past and stopped again well ahead of me, watching me suspiciously in his rear-view mirror. I kept walking, and he checked on me all the way back to my car. He watched me get in and drive off before he disappeared. I should have felt nervous, or even frightened, but instead I felt angry and frustrated.

I went some way out of the village towards the main road before I stopped in a small lay-by. I dug the map out of my pocket and stared at it again, hoping for inspiration. The map was old and faded, and there were no colours on it, making it difficult for modern eyes to read. But looking at it again, I saw something staring me in the face. I had tried to approach the wood by the shortest route from the village, ignoring the tracks on the far side, which seemed tortuous and a long way to walk. But now I saw that what I thought was a track passing close to the other side of the wood had a number marked on it. It was a minor road, and therefore tarmacked, and although it meant driving about twelve kilometres, I could reach it from the main road. Fired with new hope, I turned the key in the ignition and put the car into gear.

Where the lane ran by the wood, there were trees on both sides of the road, although on one side it was only a narrow screen, unmarked on the map. Looking in the other direction I could see that the wood rose gently towards me from the far side, where I had been earlier, to meet the road here. There was a wide verge – ten yards or so of rough grass, and I was able to pull the car under the edge of the trees, being careful to park it where it would not be bogged down when I came to set off. I felt much more comfortable here, with no buildings in sight, and hidden from view. I locked the car and got out the sketch map.

It made much more sense from this side. It showed the access tracks from the lane, and by following one of them I should be able to reach the junction and pace it out to reach the spot marked by the cross. And then what? Suddenly I was scared of what I might find. I was about to enter the trees when, as an afterthought, I went back to the car and opened the boot. I always carry a spade in the car in winter in case it snows and I have to dig myself out, or shovel grit. I lifted it out and took it with me.

Under the trees the pale light was filtered through the branches. The track was overgrown with tall wet grass and brambles, and dead trees lay across it in places, but it was still easy enough to follow. The wood looked as though it had once been coppiced in parts, but had been left to its own devices for many years. It was quiet and although I tried to tread softly, a twig breaking under my foot sounded like a gunshot to me, and I paused for a moment, my heart pounding. Then I went slowly on.

It wasn't far to the track junction and from there I carefully paced the distance marked in what I hoped was the right direction. I reached an area where the trees were far apart, but the undergrowth was thicker, and the floor of the wood swelled into a sort of mound. I left the spade there as a marker and went to find the other path junction. This was a little harder to detect, where the growth of many years had obscured the paths. However, after a little while, I found it and paced back, stumbling over lying branches and trailing brambles. This time I passed a few yards from where I had left my spade, but roughly where the two lines intersected, behind the mound, there was a hollow of softer ground where the grass and the weeds grew thick and rank. I took my spade and made the first cut.

I dug down a couple of blade depths and found nothing. I tried again a few feet away with the same result, finding the soil easy to turn, but obstructed with thin roots and occasional stones. I knew that men in a hurry, burying bodies or whatever else, would not dig a six foot grave, so whatever lay there should be fairly near the surface. I tried a couple more places, digging down to a depth of about eighteen inches with no result. Was I in the right place? I paused and leaned on the handle of the spade. The wintry sun was by now burning off the mist and filtering through into the wood. Sweat was pearling on my brow, and I was hot inside my clothes with the exertion. I dug again.

After twenty minutes I had found nothing, and my exploratory holes had spread right across the hollow. Had the bodies been moved? Had somebody come back for whatever else was buried there? I began to feel that my search would yield no clues after all to what had happened on this spot forty-odd years before. I straightened up and stretched my back.

As I did so, a pigeon exploded out of a nearby tree and clattered off, startling me so that I jumped. Suddenly alert, I thought I caught a movement a little distance off through the wood, and as I did so I heard the terrifying bang of a shotgun. Pellets tore through the air above me, and I was spattered with debris of torn bark and smashed twigs. I flung myself face down on the ground and in the echoing silence that followed, birds squawked and scattered from the wood. Within seconds, there was another loud report, and this time I was sure the shot was lower over my head.

I pressed myself into the damp ground. *Now* I was frightened, really frightened, and I could do nothing for a moment but stare blankly, my heart pounding. A few inches from my eyes I could see wet grass stems spattered with disturbed soil, the fine tendrils of a root system, an earthworm wriggling to safety...and then my eyes focused on something else, a glint of silver in the earth, something that was not part of the natural floor of the wood.

I slowly stretched out my hand and reached for it, loosening it with my fingers, and drew it clear of the ground in which it had lain buried. Discoloured, mildewed though it was, I recognised it instantly for what it was. **SS** – the lightning flash collar insignia of the Waffen SS. My hand closed over it. So it was true, something had happened in this wood, although the man Alain had said there was nothing here. What had he meant by that? I was so close to finding out what really lay there, beneath the earth of this Belgian wood. But even as I thought about it, I heard faintly the solid click of a reloaded shotgun snapping shut, and then the heavy tread of someone coming through the bushes, very close now.

If it was the farmer I had seen earlier, I hadn't liked the look of him, and he seemed to mean business now. If it was someone else – who knew what they might have in mind. I didn't wait to find out. I jumped up, grabbed the spade and ran, bent double and weaving from side to side. Another shot rang out, deafeningly, but he was aiming high again and missed me, whether deliberately or not I didn't know.

I fumbled out the car keys as I ran, nearly dropping them in the process. I jerked open the door of the car and was away from that grass verge with spinning tyres and the engine roaring. In the mirror I saw the shapeless hat and the raised shotgun of the farmer, and I wondered: was he just scaring off a trespasser, or was he also involved in this mysterious affair?

Back in St Hubert it was a normal morning. Women were

shopping, and chatting in the street, their baskets full of baguettes and fresh meat from the butcher's. The square was quite empty of cars, suggesting that most of the inhabitants had driven off to work elsewhere, in Brussels perhaps. In the sunshine there was nothing threatening about the place. One of the hotel staff was sweeping the step and greeted me with a friendly *"Bonjour."*

Inside, Alain was at the bar again, sipping a *petit blanc*. I got the impression he was something of a fixture, tolerated even though some might treat him with contempt. I also gathered that whatever he said was filtered through a permanent veil of alcohol. I wanted to speak to him again, so I greeted him cheerily and ordered a *café au lait* from the blonde girl behind the bar. She brought me the coffee, and another drink for Alain, then disappeared out the back, and through the closed kitchen door I thought I heard her speaking on the telephone.

"Well, did you find anything, *monsieur*?"

"Only this."

I held out the SS badge on my palm. Alain drew in his breath sharply.

"So you found the place. Do you know what happened there, *monsieur*? Do you know exactly?"

"No, that's what I came to find out."

"And you want me to tell you. It's risky, you know. And I'm not sure I can remember it all."

He looked around suspiciously, then took a packet of cigarettes from the pocket of his scuffed leather jacket and lit one. He drew on it without speaking, concentrating instead on placing his lighter on top of the packet and lining it up carefully on the bar.

In the silence I took a bundle of francs out of my wallet and slid them along the counter to him. He pocketed them without a word, and took another deep draw on his cigarette before he spoke.

"Ah, yes, it's coming back to me now. 1944. The British arrive. Many people suddenly were very brave and pretended to be in the Resistance, but before September 3rd, our *Libération*, they were too afraid. The Germans were not bad to us here in Belgium. My parents had an *alimentation* which sold many things to them for good prices. My father didn't care for the Resistance; they caused too much trouble. The War was no problem for us. Then the British came. The brave people here – suddenly brave, when they'd grovelled in fear for four years – took out those they called *collabos* and stripped the women and beat the men. Then they hung them in the square. From the lamp standards. My father was one of them. Bastards!"

He spat on the scrubbed boards. A long pause ensued. Alain flicked ash nervously from his cigarette I tried to jog him into continuing.

"This is very interesting, *monsieur*, and no doubt very sad for you. But what's the connection with me?"

"With you, *monsieur? Ah, oui.* The connection is this, perhaps, because you are the only Englishman to come asking about it. So I guess it may concern you personally in some way. When the British troops came, there were many fights in this region with the Boches who were trying to retreat. Near the wood that you know of, retreating SS troopers in a truck met a couple of British soldiers. In the battle that followed, the Germans were killed. The soldiers buried their bodies in the wood. And with them they buried something else."

He took a drink and let the silence draw out before he went on.

"Gold. Nazi gold. Well, French gold, Belgian gold, to tell you the truth, *monsieur*. Many Nazis stole what they could from the occupied countries. Their pension fund."

He smiled wryly.

"These SS men were transporting – protecting – some of what their superiors had stolen. But they lost it here and no German ever knew what had happened to it."

"But how did you find out about it?"

"It's a small village, monsieur. And a lot smaller in 1944. Secrets were hard to hide. From the Boches, yes. From outsiders. But not from the locals. The English soldiers hid the evidence of the bodies. The truck was burnt out. There was nothing to show what had happened. But one of the soldiers had had a liaison with a local girl, and his tongue was loose…"

As he spoke, the barmaid came back through from the kitchen and began to polish glasses and put them away, standing close to the counter. Alain stopped speaking abruptly.

"Let's sit over here, monsieur."

He led me across to the far end of the room, where we sat

down in a quiet corner. Before Alain could continue, however, we heard the sound of a car driven quickly up to the hotel, then footsteps, and the door swung open.

The man who entered paused briefly, looking around, and the barmaid nodded almost imperceptibly in our direction. He came straight towards us then and Alain stiffened, with the hunted look of a startled animal.

"*Va t'en, Alain!*" The voice was quiet but commanding, and Alain stood up immediately, giving me an apologetic, almost pleading, look, and made for the door.

The newcomer, a tall, solidly-built man of a similar age to myself, settled himself on the bench seat that ran along the wall, turning himself towards me with his legs crossed and his arm stretched along the back of the seat. He was casually but smartly dressed, his trousers creased and his shoes polished, and, like Alain, he wore a leather jacket. However, where Alain's jacket was cheap and stiff and worn, this man's was expensively cut, and the soft Spanish leather did not creak when he moved.

I was tense, wondering who he was and what he wanted. I was nervous, because I knew now that there were people in the village to whom this whole thing was real and personal, and were prepared to use, or threaten violence to keep it all hidden from outsiders. He fixed me with his penetrating blue eyes.

"So, *Monsieur* Gilgarran, you are interested in our village."

I must have looked surprised when he used my name, for he went on.

"Don't forget, you signed the hotel register yesterday. Yvette told me your name."

He indicated the girl behind the bar as he spoke. I thought rapidly. I didn't want to show that I knew as much as I did.

"Not so much your village, *Monsieur…*" I paused, inviting him to respond with his name, but he merely stared stonily at me, so I went on.

"It's more that I am interested in certain aspects of the war. I am making a study of the thefts the Nazis made of jewellery, paintings, gold and so on; all the plunder that they took from France and other Occupied countries, and the reprisals they carried out on the populace who tried to stop them. I believe something of that nature may have happened here in St Hubert."

A pause. He gazed at me sceptically. I was trying to think of something to back up my story. Then a memory came back of a visit I had made with Jenny to a village near the Dordogne many years ago.

"As it did at Oradour," I went on.

"The Germans massacred eight hundred people there, men, women and children, because they believed they had stolen a consignment of Nazi gold. They destroyed the village. It was terrible, barbaric…"

"That is just a theory, monsieur, you must know that. No-one has really proved what the motives of the Germans were. And this is not Oradour. No-one was massacred here. And no Nazi gold was found here."

His casual rebuttal irritated me, when I knew he was lying. The challenging question left my lips before I could think better of it.

"So what about the SS troopers buried in the wood?"

"Who told you that story, *monsieur*?"

"Alain told me about it. He explained about the fight with the British patrol, the burying of the bodies, the Nazi gold …"

He cut in sharply.

"Alain is a drunkard. He has a fertile imagination. He is also a man with a grudge. His parents were *collaborateurs*, and they supported the *marché noir*. At the Liberation, the local people carried out reprisals of their own. Unfortunately, Alain's father was one of those who were summarily executed, without a trial. Regrettable, but" – here he shrugged – "these things happen in wartime. Alain's mother was shunned by many, and he grew up hating his place in this small village. He has wasted his life trying to get his own back. Telling stories to strangers is one of his methods.

"I suggest, *monsieur*, that you stick to tourism."

Angered by his tone, I reached into my pocket and pulled out the SS insignia I had found, tossing it contemptuously onto the table. He raised an eyebrow.

"So?"

"I found that in the wood."

Again, his answer was smooth and dismissive.

"*Monsieur*, there are such things scattered all over Belgium. Two great wars have been fought this century over our soil. This is not England. All sorts of reminders of those, and earlier conflicts are turned up by farmers' ploughs every year. One little badge means nothing. Put your souvenir back in your pocket and take it home with you. A present from Belgium."

"And if I decide not to take your advice? What if I decide to stay and ask a few more questions?"

"I would not recommend it."

His tone was coldly menacing now, but I was still not prepared to back down completely.

"And why should I take your advice, *monsieur*. I don't know who you are. You haven't even told me your name."

He leaned forward, and his jacket fell open slightly as he did so. I felt myself turn cold as I caught sight of the butt of a gun holstered under his armpit. Was this real, or was I dreaming? Fear crept over me. This was more than I expected, and at a stroke my bravado dropped away.

"You do not need to know my name, *monsieur*." His tone softened slightly as he continued. "But you may call me Jean-Luc. However, we are unlikely to meet again. Certainly not here."

His tone was final. I put the badge back in my pocket and stood up. He rose and shook my hand in a grave and courtly manner. As he did so, there was something about him that seemed strangely familiar.

"Bon voyage, Monsieur Gilgarran. Enjoy the rest of your stay in Belgium, and a safe return home."

He turned abruptly and strode from the bar, calling goodbye to Yvette as he left. I went pensively to my room to collect my few things. It seemed my investigations had come to a standstill, and the risks to my safety seemed to be accumulating. I was going to take Jean-Luc's advice.

I left Belgium some time after mid-day with a feeling of relief. I drove slowly through the motorway traffic and into France, where I stopped at the services for a bowl of salad and a *café crème*. Evening seemed to be approaching, although it was actually the back end of a cold and dismal afternoon, when I reached Calais and booked into a cheap hotel. I took a stroll round the town and dined later on in a fish restaurant near the harbour. I was trying to reassure myself that I was just a tourist on a short break, but images of a man in a leather jacket with a gun kept creeping unbidden into my thoughts. I hoped I had extricated myself in time from any involvement that might be bad for my health.

The next day, on the early morning boat crossing, normality seemed to be resumed. I treated myself to a full English breakfast and browsed for a while in the shop, buying a copy of the *Times* and a CD compilation of World War Two songs. As I did so, the events of the last couple of days receded into a graphic, but hopefully momentary aberration from my normal life. I'm not used to being threatened and shot at, and the whole thing had already assumed an unreal quality.

I sat quietly by the window, looking out over the grey sea, and tried to review what I knew. But as I went over it in my mind, I realised that this was in fact very little. Looking carefully again at the diary entries I saw that my interpretation of "*Buried them and everything*" could be wrong. Did it refer to the SS, as I'd at first assumed or maybe, more likely as it seemed to me now, to British comrades killed that day? "*Share later*", looked at closely, might really say "*shave*". Silly though it might sound, it could be that. Some of the diary entries were, after all, very detailed and mundane. I knew my father set great store by cleanliness, even when roughing it, and elsewhere in his letters had even commented on the fact that shaving in the evening saved time in the morning before parade.

The map with the cross on it gave no indication as to what it marked – again, had I jumped to the wrong conclusion? True, Alain had talked about the incident in some detail, but I recalled now that he hadn't mentioned it until he'd overheard my conversation and knew what I was looking for.

As for being shot at, I had been on private property and the farmer had warned me he would be shooting there later. Maybe that was all there was to that. And the antipathy of the locals could be simply an understandable desire not to have outsiders raking up the village's painful wartime past. Even my father's references to the girl he had met seemed less significant now. After all, none of the men in the bar had recognised the name Sophie. Maybe my father had got the name wrong. Maybe she was from another village.

On the other hand, there was the SS insignia – but, as the mysterious Jean-Luc had pointed out, there are a million such souvenirs in the earth of Belgium and Northern France. There was the fact that he carried a gun – maybe he was a policeman of some sort. There was the attitude of the locals, as if they were hiding something – or had I just been tired and overly suspicious, hoping to find proofs for my own theories? I didn't know. There were too many *maybes*.

As the White Cliffs separated themselves from the murk, I began to look forward to getting home and getting my life sorted out again. I decided I would do well to forget all the business of stories about Nazi gold, SS men and village girls. In my emotional state, I had probably read too much into it all. I could be back in school next week – no doubt they'd be pleased at my dedication at getting back in so soon when I'd been so poorly. I could start to patch things up with Jenny, and I would have to try to forget about Edie…

"…drivers are requested to rejoin their vehicles…"

The loudspeaker announcement intruded on my thoughts. I got my things together, including the book I had brought with me to while away the crossing, but which I hadn't got round to opening. I went down to the car with the sparse crowd of passengers, and drove with some feeling of relief down the ramp onto English soil. I'd already decided to call on Emily on the way back, to see how she was doing.

I turned left out of the ferry port and up the steep hill towards the M20. It was still only eight o'clock and I hoped to be in Liverpool by early afternoon.

Chapter Eight

"Jenny phoned, you know. She wondered whether you might be here. It was a bit of a shock, hearing it like that from her. I do hope you can sort it out, Mark. She's a lovely girl. You should try to make it work..."

"I know, Emily, I'm sorry. I should have rung you. I don't really know what's going on myself. I'm sure it'll sort itself out, though."

This was the first step, I thought, in getting things back on an even keel. Emily was a bit of a rock, never really disapproving, but too often disappointed by me. I hoped this time that it wouldn't be long before she was happy again with my situation.

I'd rung Emily from a crowded Knutsford services to tell her I'd be calling on my way back from Belgium – although I didn't mention my business there – and we'd had a bit of late lunch when I arrived. Time had passed now after the shock of Jack's death and the funeral, and Emily had regained some of her old poise. Despite her age, she insisted on looking after herself, and as usual, had got a light meal together for both of us. Now we were sitting in the kitchen drinking the obligatory milky coffee. I felt tired and a little disorientated, but the familiar surroundings of the house helped to reassure me, and talking to Emily, who had always been there to turn to during my childhood and adolescence, was a calming influence.

I'd told her a bit about what I'd been up to: the friction with Jenny, my trip to Wales and then to Belgium. I didn't, of course, mention the fact that I had actually slept with Edie Barton. That would be pushing her understanding and forgiveness too far at this point. Emily knew by now about Maes-y-Bryn. She had seemed shocked at first to find that Phil was now the owner of my father's cottage, and perplexed by the fact that Edie Barton was living there.

We hadn't talked about it since she first found out, but the fact that I'd been to the cottage meant that we spent some time discussing it. Emily wanted to know how the place was and whether Edie Barton was looking after it. We chatted for some time about Maes-y-Bryn, recalling happier times there and our holidays in the area. Eventually I managed to steer the conversation round to the question I had never really put to her.

"So why do you think Jack left Maes-y-Bryn and this house to Phil?"

Emily fumbled in the pocket of her apron for her small lace handkerchief and blew her nose.

"I don't really know, Mark. I'm not sure I can answer that question. More coffee?"

"No thanks. And he never mentioned me in the will. What do you make of that?"

"I can't really say."

She got up with an effort.

"I'll put the kettle on again. Father Byrne said he might call round this afternoon."

While Emily was in the kitchen lighting the gas under the kettle, the front doorbell rang. I went to answer it. Outside, the day was fading and the street lights coming on. Children, returning from school, were calling to each other, chasing each other with bags swinging. On the corner of the street the lights of the shop were shining out, and on the main road buses, cars and lorries were rumbling and flickering past.

Father Byrne stood on the step, his face pale under the brim of his hat in the sickly yellow glow from the nearby lamp. In the gap at the throat of his long dark macintosh, which hung limply from his narrow shoulders, I caught the white gleam of his dog-collar.

"Good afternoon there, Mark. Would Emily be in?"

His voice had an artificially cheerful tone, but the effect was lugubrious. I found myself almost unconsciously mimicking his southern Irish accent and manner of speaking when I replied.

"She is indeed. Will you not come inside, Father?"

The word seemed anachronistic and dusty on my tongue. I stepped aside to let him into the hallway, and he took off his old-fashioned black trilby and went straight through into the kitchen with the air of a man who felt at home in the house and knew his way around. By the time I had closed the door and followed him through, he was seated by the table, and in the manner of Catholic priests everywhere, was waiting for the woman of the house to bring him a cup of tea.

Emily made a pot of tea and put it on the stand on the table, snugging the knitted cosy down around it.

"I'm so glad you called, Father, even though I've got unexpected company. Mark's just on his way back from Belgium." She smiled at me as she spoke, but I rather wished she hadn't mentioned my trip abroad. It wasn't something I wanted to talk about at the moment.

"I'll let it draw for a minute, Father. I know you like it strong. Not like Mark. When he makes it it's so weak it couldn't stand up on its own. I think he just shows it the teabag."

"Sure, Emily, and you know how to make a fine cup of tea for a man."

Father Byrne chuckled and I smiled wanly. After a pause he went on.

"So how would you two be managing now without Jack? Sure and you lost a fine fellow there."

"If you say so." I grunted. The priest's tone was light and he sounded admiring of my late brother, but I felt surly and antagonistic. He frowned at my reply.

"And what would you be meaning by that, Mark? Do you not miss your brother?"

"Not as much as I might have done." I didn't really want to say more to this man of a cloth which I didn't consider holy, and whom I had no real reason to respect.

Emily broke the silence that followed, by pouring tea for us all.

"Mark feels upset by what Jack put in his will, Father. And by what he didn't put – I told you about that, didn't I? I think it's really stopped him grieving for Jack. Which is good in one way, but a bit sad. They were very close as children."

I was flabbergasted and felt betrayed. At first I couldn't believe that Emily had talked like that to someone outside the family. But once again I had underestimated the strength of the Catholic community, and the trust and faith that even intelligent women like Emily, from an older generation, placed in their priest. I was seething, but I said nothing. Father Byrne was watching me thoughtfully over his tea cup. Then he put it down with a slight clatter in the saucer.

"Perhaps I can help you with that, Mark," he said gently. "Sure and it's a hard thing to come to terms with, but I might be able to explain things so that you wouldn't be worrying now and tearing yourself up about it. If you'd just wait while I finish the tea, perhaps you'd take a little walk with me and we can have a quiet chat. Set your heart and mind at rest."

The last thing I really wanted was a heart to heart with an Irish Catholic priest – I'd left all that behind a long time ago. On the other hand Father Byrne sounded so sincere and his tone was so caring that it seemed churlish to refuse. And there was always the chance that I would learn something from him that would shed light into some corner that I had overlooked in my search for the truth.

"All right then, Father. I'd appreciate that. Just finish your tea and I'll go and get my coat."

Penny Lane had changed since the Beatles wrote their song, and the street sign was no longer being stolen every week by fans of the famous Liverpool group. The chandler's where we used to buy paraffin for the stove was now a wine bar, and the corner shop where I would once run after Sunday lunch for a family block of ice cream was now a tanning studio.

Night had fallen. Making desultory conversation, we walked down the road, now busy with evening traffic, and followed it to where it reared up over the railway line. We stopped and leaned on the bridge.

"You have brought it on yourself, you know. All the business about Jack's will, and the houses, and Phil. It's your own fault."

The change in Father Byrne's tone was breathtaking. The languid brogue had all but disappeared and the ingratiating charm was gone. His words fell like physical blows. I bridled, and replied acidly.

"Could you perhaps be more specific?"

"Certainly, my son, I'd be delighted."

I'm not your son; and oh, yes, I bet you're going to love this.

"You know, Mark, being born a Catholic is a great privilege and also a great responsibility."

Father Byrne did not look at me as he spoke. He leaned his forearms on the brickwork, his hands clasped together, and gazed back down the railway line towards Liverpool, his face in shadow below his hat.

"Your parents were Catholics, and so is Emily. Your brother, Jack, was a devout Catholic. You, on the other hand, have let them down."

"We all make our own decisions. I chose to reject the Catholic faith. In fact, I chose to reject all religions. I haven't been a Catholic since I was a teenager."

"Correction, Mark. Whatever you think, you are still a Catholic, but, unfortunately, a lapsed Catholic. It's not so easy to reject something with the power of the True Faith, of the Catholic Church. It may be that you don't go to Mass now, or to Confession; you may not have been for most of your life; but you were baptised a Catholic and you cannot erase that fact."

"It may be a fact to you, but I consider it meaningless."

"Meaningless it may seem to you at present, but you cannot see the end as yet. Emily prays to St Jude for you every day."

"St Jude?"

"The patron saint of hopeless cases."

"But if it's hopeless, what's the point of prayer?"

"She may have no hope, but she has Faith."

"And what sort of religion substitutes blind Faith for human hope?"

"We cannot see all things, and therefore we must place our trust in God. He moves in mysterious ways and men cannot explain in human terms all the developments in Heaven."

I grunted, unwilling to argue further along these lines. A train appeared, speeding down the track towards us, two-tone horn heralding its approach. The brickwork vibrated slightly as it passed underneath us. I moved away from the parapet of the bridge, and Father Byrne turned to follow me. We walked on down the opposite side of the bridge, and turned left, passing alongside the railings of Liverpool College sports ground. Eventually I broke the silence.

"You said you could explain Jack's will. Can you?"

"I think so," he began carefully. "To begin with, I suppose you realise that you father would still have loved you if you'd kept the Faith?"

"My father did love me. I know that."

"He did his best. But your denial of the Church hurt him deeply. That's why he left the house to Jack."

"Don't be ridiculous. He left Jack the house because he and Emily were living there!"

I tried to sound dismissive, but the seed of doubt had been

sown. Father Byrne went on remorselessly.

"Jack, too, was deeply offended by you. You abandoned and rejected something which he held very dear. The most important thing in his life. He despised you for it."

"What? How dare you!"

I stopped suddenly and turned to face him, horrified and angered by what he was saying. Before I could respond he held up his hand to quieten me

"Oh yes, Mark, he hid it well. He was always cordial, always civil to you. But he no longer saw you as his brother in God. Your blood relationship was not enough to counterbalance your lack of Faith."

. "So much so that he preferred to leave all our family's property and belongings to a stranger? I asked, my voice strangled and strident.

"Indeed so. He made his choice. Philip Sullivan was an orphan, a devout Catholic and an excellent student. Jack wanted to do something for him beyond his work as a teacher. I know he discussed it many times with Father Kelly, the Headmaster."

"And what was his relationship with Phil all this time? Do you believe it was really innocent?"

"Don't be ridiculous with your implications, Mark. Jack was celibate. There is nothing unnatural about that. He was dedicated to God. Remember, this is a man who at one time nearly joined the priesthood. However, you had forfeited his respect and to Jack's mind, did not deserve anything from him. Besides, you were working, already established with a house and a family. He saw no need to leave you anything."

"But the house and the cottage held so many memories of our childhood together. How could he brush that aside for the sake of a stranger? And to only mention me fleetingly in his will as 'my brother!'"

"I'm surprised he even did that. To him, you were certainly no longer his brother in God. I hardly think he considered you to be his brother at all any more."

"I can't believe it. I can't believe he thought that."

"Oh he did, Mark, he did. And you're going to have to accept it. Nothing you can do will ever change things now. I know you've been wondering about Jack's motives, probably coming up with all sorts of answers, all sorts of possible reasons for his behaviour. But in the end it was very simple. It all came down to the fact that you are no longer a Catholic. He could not tolerate it. It's really as simple as that."

He stood gazing at me in the half-light, his eyes boring into me from under the brim of his trilby. I felt like screaming, shouting, lashing out, but I was frozen, motionless. My fists clenched and unclenched by my sides.

So it all came down to that. My hurtful dismissal of the Church all those years ago; was that at the root of Jack's spurning of me? I felt that God had had the last laugh; but how petty of an all-powerful God! Bitterness welled up in me, and contempt for this little man, this very little man in front of me. Then I was aware that Father Byrne was speaking to me.

"Do you want to walk further with me, Mark? Or have I answered all your questions?"

I felt he was enjoying this now, and I desperately wanted to get away from him before I said something unworthy of me, something I would later regret.

"No, Father Byrne. You've told me enough, and you've been very honest. I don't like it, but I must live with it. Now I want to walk a while on my own."

"So be it, my son. Would you like my blessing?"

"Blessing?" I laughed hollowly. "You must be joking. No, I would not!"

He shrugged and turned away, and we parted.

I walked a long way that night. My steps led me down dark roads; empty suburban streets in reality and comfortless cul-de-sacs in my mind. Eventually I found myself wandering blankly round Sefton Park, blundering among the trees and bushes, and when, some time later, I emerged onto the road again, my feet were soaked by the damp grass and my shoes covered in mud.

Although I disliked Father Byrne and detested the religion he represented, his words had the ring of truth. They had shut the door firmly to any other avenue which I might have been tempted to explore. And despite my years of rejection of Catholicism, it never occurred to me then, brought up as I was, that my family's priest might resort to falsehoods.

Tears blinded me as I thought of Jack and the lie I must have lived all those years, thinking that he still cared about me as a brother, never seeing, never realising the depth of his dislike for someone like myself who had let him down so completely. I rubbed the back of my hand roughly across my eyes. Memories of childhood days and laughter, happy times shared in North Wales, jokes and stories – all dust, all worthless in retrospect. I felt sick, and empty.

I walked on and on, and finally I found myself by Otterspool Promenade, where the thirty-foot tides of the murky Mersey scour the sandstone embankment. The tide was in, and the moonlight shone on wavelets on the water. I leaned on the rail and peered down into the cold, swirling currents. Depression folded me in its pallid grip. Where did all this leave me? Nowhere, seemed to be the answer. I'd gone looking for an explanation of Jack's will, hoping to rationalise it, yet it turned out that the answer was staring me in the face. Perhaps the most obvious explanation, and the one I was least disposed to admit. Jack, in the end had rejected me as a non-Catholic. My loathing of that stifling religion came flooding back,

And the other trails I had followed? Bob Downs, at the funeral, had as good as accused Jack of homosexuality, but there was no evidence of that from those who knew him well. Ruth Morris had been a dead end, and Edie Barton, although her revelations had shocked me, had shed no fresh light on Jack's actions. My trip to Belgium had been abortive and irrelevant, and had proved nothing. Two things, however, remained to puzzle me. What had happened to change Jack's life back in the late sixties? What could be so important that he had mentioned it to Ruth Morris, but without telling her what it was? And who was it, Jack or my father Harry, who was paying out money over the years, apparently to support Phil Sullivan, and why?

Those puzzles remained. However, perhaps Ruth had over-dramatised Jack's comments to her. And Father Byrne had convinced me that Jack had chosen Phil to leave everything to because he was a devout Catholic and a favoured pupil, so perhaps he had, in fact, been supporting him as an act of charity for longer than that. In the end, none of it seemed to matter. Jack had rejected me, and I had to live with that. The cottage had gone, as well as the house in Liverpool, and I could well imagine Phil laughing behind my back. And Edie too – she had done all right from my father and Jack, getting a nice place to live in, while I was excluded.

But when I thought of Edie, the thought of our night together came flooding back to me. I remembered the sparkle in her eyes and the warmth of her body, her laughter and her teasing. I realised that however much I fought the feeling, I wanted to see her again. I knew I should just go home and forget her, but that was easier said than done. I decided to give her a ring. I walked along the prom and headed back up towards Aigburth, until I came to a phone box, but when I dialled her number there was no answer. I sighed and put the receiver down resignedly. It was probably for the best, after all.

Depression and something akin to despair enveloped me again. I caught a bus into town and wandered aimlessly for a while by the Pier Head, where the great ships used to come and go, and the busy ferries once plied across the Mersey. Then, seeking forgetfulness, I made my increasingly unsteady way by gloomy streets and various insalubrious bars to Upper Parliament Street. Here some of the basements of the elegant old Georgian houses had long been taken over by a variety of clubs for people of different nationalities, and I visited more than one of them.

I drank beer in the Somali club, where I rubbed shoulders with dark-skinned seamen from far away, then crossed the road to the Al Ahram club, where nominal Muslims drank hard liquor and a belly dancer shook her beaded veils to the sound of North African music. The heat and fug of the small room, combined with the blurring effect of the alcohol combined to relax me and take me away from my dark thoughts. Some time well after midnight, I staggered out into the cold damp air, and someone kindly helped me to find a taxi.

Emily had been asleep in bed for hours when I got back. She must have wondered where I'd got to. I tiptoed clumsily up the stairs and fell into the bed in the back room which I had known for so many years, and sleep came like a great rushing blackness to suck me into unconsciousness.

I slept the heavy sleep of the drunk, but woke surprisingly early. I showered to clear my head a little, and went downstairs to get some breakfast before heading for home. I took Emily a cup of tea in bed and went to my room to collect my things. In the morning light, all Father Byrne's rantings about Jack and my betrayal of my religion seemed like a sick joke. It was hurtful, of course, to even think that Jack and my father might have thought less of me than I believed, but I would have to live with it.

I was looking forward now to getting home, getting back to normal. It was Friday morning, which meant that I'd had whole week off work, but I would be back in school on Monday, ready to start afresh. The length of time since I'd seen Jenny meant that it would be easier, perhaps, to gloss over my visit to Maes-y-Bryn and my night with Edie. I hoped she'd be more interested in my trip to Belgium. I was sure now that she'd come back, once she'd had a chance to let off steam. Pretty sure, anyway. I thought I'd give her a ring that evening and talk to her.

But I didn't need to. When I got home Jenny's little Peugeot was parked outside and I sensed that something was wrong. I let myself in and found her in the living room, too distraught to be surprised by my reappearance.

"Look at this! Look at this, will you!"

I cast a glance around at the overturned furniture, the emptied drawers, the broken ornaments, the smashed glass in the photos, the books cast on the floor – all the general mess and chaos of a burgled house.

"What's going on, Mark? What's all this about?"

Jenny's voice was trembling and she looked wan and disorientated despite her smart suit. Some wisps of carefully tied back hair were escaping and straggling around her face. The tone of her voice sounded as if she blamed me for what had happened.

"I don't know, Jenny. What's happened?"

"We've been burgled, that's what's happened. Surely even you can see that. While you were away!" Her voice was strained and accusing.

"What have they taken?"

"I don't know yet. Nothing obvious. They've left the TV and the video. Oh God, what a mess!"

She sank down on a chair, while I had a quick look round, checking upstairs, where drawers had been tipped out and wardrobes ransacked. But I couldn't see anything missing either. I ran back downstairs.

"When did this happen?"

"Tuesday night I think. But nobody noticed until yesterday evening, when Mrs Banks looked through the window. Then they couldn't contact us. You'd disappeared, of course, and they didn't know where I was staying, so they had to wait until this morning and ring me at work. I came straight here."

"Has anyone called the police?"

"Yes, Mrs Banks called them. She let them in with her key. They took a statement from her and said they'd have to wait until we got back to find out what was missing. There was nothing much they could do at the time; the burglars were long gone by then, and the house was secure because they'd closed the door behind them. I gave the police a ring earlier; they should be here soon."

The police, when they came, didn't stay long. They didn't seem too hopeful from the start, and when we said we couldn't see anything missing, they gave a metaphorical shrug and left, merely saying they would be in touch if there were any developments. I didn't say anything about any suspicions I might have. I was afraid it might lead to awkward questions from Jenny about my trip to Maes-y-Bryn.

It hadn't taken me long to arrive at the conclusion that we'd been burgled by the men I'd seen in Wales and then again the next morning in the village street, waiting in their car. It was too much of a coincidence otherwise. After all, I'd never been trailed before, and equally, I'd never been burgled before. At first I'd thought they were something to do with Edie; now I wasn't so sure. I tried to think what I could have that they might have wanted.

We started to tidy up the house, but as we did so, all sorts of things were going through my mind. If there was nothing obvious missing, it suggested that the burglars were looking for something in particular. But what? And who were they?

Whatever it was, maybe it was something I hadn't had very long; otherwise, why hadn't they come looking for it earlier? It was then that I thought of the papers I'd acquired from my dad, the ones that had pointed me towards Belgium, towards the possibility of German gold. But who else could know what was in that box of stuff from forty-five years before?

When we'd put the place as much to rights as we could, we

swept up and I put the kettle on while Jenny went to have a shower. She hadn't done much more than grunt at me so far, and my hopes of starting again on a friendlier footing began to seem overly optimistic.

Warm from the exertion of sweeping up, I began to take off my fleece, and as I did so I felt a piece of paper in the pocket. I pulled it out and stared at it. For a moment I didn't recognise it, then I saw that it was the note from Edie with the unknown phone number on it. I sat down by the table and smoothed it out and as I did so, curiosity crept back into my mind as to her whereabouts. At the same time I realised that if I really wanted to find out, this could be the best clue I had.

I took the note across to where the phone hung on the wall of the kitchen and dialled *01425 58996*. All I got was the number unobtainable tone. Disappointed, I put the phone down. Then a thought struck me. It was an outside chance, but worth a try. I went and got my father's tattered old address book out of my bag. If the number on the note belonged to someone Edie knew, maybe my father knew them too. When I flicked through the book, though, I realised that all the numbers were old. The pages were yellowed and worn at the edges, rubbed thin by frequent thumbing, and some of the names were almost illegible. There appeared to be no numbers added as recently as the last five years, the time since my father had known Edie.

I turned the pages anyway, and as I riffled through them, something caught my attention. I turned back to the page in question, and opened it out. A number stared at me from the page: *01425 58896* – only one digit different from the number on Edie's note. It looked as if my forensic skills with the pencil shading had let me down slightly. But surely this could not be a coincidence – the number was too similar, an easily mistaken *8* instead of a *9*. And the name gave me a sudden thrill of excitement – *Peter Ashby*. The address was somewhere in Leicestershire, which meant nothing to me, but the name *Peter*, or as he was probably known, *Pete*…that could mean a lot. A thought began to germinate.

My mind racing, I took out my father's diary and turned once more to the date *5th September 1944*. Hands trembling with the emotion of discovery, I read again the blurred and faded words: *Pte and I separated from section*. But now, when I looked at the smudged forty-five year old ink in which it was written, instead of *Pte,* I saw *Pete.* It seemed so obvious; the clue had been there all along.

Misled by the difficult script, I had jumped to a conclusion, but now my mistake was clear. *Pete* was the name of my father's companion on that wartime occasion in Belgium and my guess was that this was the Peter Ashby in his old address book. If so, there was a lot more to find out from him than just Edie's whereabouts. But why would Edie have his number anyway? Why would she, apparently, have rung him yesterday morning? Could that be where she had gone? I wanted to know, and the next step was pretty obvious.

Chapter Nine

"You don't know me, but I think you may have known my father."

Silence. For a moment I thought I'd been cut off. When he spoke again, the tone was guarded, very different from the rather jolly voice that had first responded when he picked up the receiver to answer my call. I was in luck, I thought, to find Peter Ashby still living at the same address.

"Who's this speaking, please?"

"My name's Gilgarran. Mark Gilgarran. I think you may have been in the Army with my dad, Harry."

"Why do you think that?"

"I believe he mentioned you" – I didn't tell him where – "and I found your phone number in his address book."

There was a long pause before he finally answered.

"Well, yes. Yes. It's true, I was."

"I wondered whether I could come and talk to you about your experiences."

"Oh dear."

Another silence. It sounded as if he had placed his hand over the mouthpiece. In the background I faintly heard a woman's voice asking *"Who is it?"*, then a brief muttering that I couldn't make out. Finally he spoke again.

"I knew you'd get in touch sooner or later. You'd better come here. Then we can talk. When do you want to come?"

"How about today?"

"Today? That's very sudden."

"Well, no time like the present."

"No, I suppose not." His voice was doubtful.

"I've been making some enquiries recently. Into the War"

"Oh. Where have you been doing that?"

"In Belgium."

"Belgium?" A stifled gasp.

"Yes. I've been doing some research. I hoped you might be able to help me to fill in some of the gaps."

Although I'd never met him, I fancied I could visualise him, an elderly man with grey hair, motionless in his tidy living room, telephone receiver pressed to his ear, thoughts tumbling through his brain while half-forgotten events came racing out of a misty, violent past to trouble him once again. Eventually he spoke.

"All right then, Mr Gilgarran. I'll see you later on today. I'll be at home. Maybe you could ring me again when you have a better idea of when you'll be arriving."

I thanked him and agreed to call later on. Then I rang off. As I replaced the receiver, I realised my hand was shaking.

I comforted myself with the thought that I should be able to find out anything I wanted to know about my father's involvement in wartime events from Peter Ashby, without any threats from touchy Belgian locals. He might even know something about my father's or my brother's relationship with Phil. After all, it seemed that he must know Edie.

I went back upstairs and sat on the bed to pack my few things back in my bag. From the bedside table I picked up the book which I had got out the previous day to read in bed, but which I had never looked at.

Stuffed between the pages was something I had put there to use as a bookmark. I opened the book and looked at it .It was a leaflet from the hotel in St Hubert, which they had given me when I paid my bill, with the receipt for my night's stay stapled inside it. I glanced at it casually, calculating how much it had cost me, translating Belgian francs back into pounds.

Then, at the top of the leaflet, I saw it: *Hotel de la Paix; Prop. Sophie Hermans.*

I froze. For an instant I caught my breath. So there was a Sophie in St Hubert after all, running a well-appointed hotel at the heart of the village's life. Was this was the girl my father had met in 1944? If so, it was inconceivable that the men I had met in the bar didn't know who I was talking about, which meant that they were consciously trying to mislead me. Which in turn meant that they had something to hide. And the way they treated Alain when he tried to reveal what they were hiding, now suggested that he was telling the truth. And the truth was a secret to be kept by them.

I reckoned my conversation with Peter Ashby was going to be very interesting after all.

There'd been an overnight frost, and the roads were white with salt, although when I reached Leicestershire a watery sun was trying ineffectually to brighten the sky. Jenny had gone from the house again before I left, storming out in a fit of white-faced fury when I told her what I intended doing.

Once I left the motorway I had to stop once or twice to check the way. The village of Kingsthorpe lies well off any main route, on a junction of four straight roads. The Ashbys lived in a pre-war semi on a small estate on what would once have been the edge of the village, but which had subsequently been surrounded by new developments

I drove cautiously down the narrow road, looking for their address. I spotted it, an unremarkable house with a car on the driveway, and pulled in to the side, parking with two wheels on the pavement to let other vehicles pass. I got out and locked my car, strode up the paved path, and taking a deep breath, rang the bell.

The man who opened the door was smaller than I imagined him, his shoulders a little stooped, and in his fawn cardigan and light blue slacks it was hard to visualise him on the D-Day beaches or battling through Normandy. Yet the pale eyes in his round face had seen more violence than most men of my age could dream of. This is the mistake we make too often about our elders: we forget they were not always old.

He anxiously smoothed his wispy grey hair away from his lined forehead, and despite his smile there was a hunted look about him as he ushered me into the living-room. It was as tidy as I had expected, although the suite was a little worn, and the armchair near the fire, padded with an extra cushion and doubtless an old favourite of his, did not match the others. There were one or two tired-looking watercolours on the walls, and a few photographs in frames on the old-fashioned sideboard.

"Sit down, Mr Gilgarran. Would you like a drink? Tea, coffee…"

"Tea would be lovely please. And call me Mark."

I sat down on the sofa and Peter Ashby went through to the kitchen. I heard him talking to someone, presumably his wife. Then he came back and sat in the chair by the fire, which, on this chilly morning, was burning with the steady glow of smokeless fuel. He turned his gaze on me for a long moment, as if he was summing me up, perhaps comparing me to my father, the comrade with whom he had shared so much danger and privation. I found it unsettling, and shifted uneasily in my seat.

"So how can I help, Mark? What exactly do you want to know?"

I paused. Where to start? I decided to start by telling him what I knew, or had guessed from what I had pieced together. So I told him about the diary and my trip to Belgium, my explorations in the wood and the finding of the SS badge. And I mentioned my theory that he and my father had found something – I didn't say what I thought it might be – and buried it there, in the wood. His face was grave as I spoke of these things. He rested his elbows on the arms of his chair and steepled his fingers before him, tapping them nervously against his lips, deep in thought as if about to reach a decision.

He seemed to be preparing to speak in reply when the door opened and his wife came in with a tray of tea and a plate of biscuits. She put them down on the coffee table and straightened up, a woman in her sixties with fair hair turning grey and the remains of striking good looks about her. She smiled at me with eyes whose twinkle seemed overlaid with sadness, and I had an immediate feeling that I'd seen her face somewhere before, although I couldn't place it.

"Hilda, this is Mark. Harry's lad." Peter's voice sounded wistful.

"I know that, Peter." She shook my hand, studying me carefully as she did so. "He's got a look of his dad about him, hasn't he?"

"Mark wants to know more about the War, Hilda."

"I know that too, Peter." She sighed and looked away, then turned and went out of the room, closing the door behind her.

Peter poured tea for the two of us and offered me a biscuit. Then he settled back in his chair, and began to talk, and at once I sensed a certain bitterness underlying his quiet tones. I listened quietly with increasing fascination.

"Being friends in wartime, being comrades in arms, is not the same as peacetime friendships. Normally we see our friends when we want to, enjoy each other's company, have a laugh. The best friends you have you can rely on – you think – but how often do you put it to the test? Friendship's fun, but it's casual as well. You go through periods where you don't see each other, sometimes you drift apart.

"Wartime in the Forces is not like that. You're thrust together with people you don't choose, you've got to trust them even if you don't like them. You can't just walk off, or ignore them. But when you have a friend, a true comrade, there's a special bond. Not only do you see each other every day, but you trust each other with your lives. You suffer hardship together, you're hungry together, you risk death and wounds together. That's special.

"Harry – your dad – and I met in 1942 in England. We were in the same platoon and the same section. We were both privates to begin with, but Harry was a year or two older and a bit more serious than me. He got promoted to Corporal, but we still stayed together. Being in the Army then was quite fun and we felt we were getting ready for a useful role. We missed home, of course, especially Harry, who had a wife in Liverpool, but I was quite happy to enjoy myself. The girls liked a man in uniform!

"Then when it all started properly it was bit more serious. We were lucky on D-Day; we landed on a quiet part of the beach and there wasn't too much fighting. But after that there were some terrible times. During one attack I was wounded, not seriously, but I was knocked out. Some of our men had been killed and I was lying there almost in the open – it was in an orchard, actually – in range of a Jerry machine-gun. Harry grabbed the Bren – he was a killer with that gun – charged from tree to tree and wiped them out. Then he dragged me to safety. He got a medal for that, and he deserved it.

"We watched each other's backs on many occasions, and we made it through the Battle of Normandy and up to the Somme. Then we pushed north to Brusssels and Jerry folded before the tanks and the armoured division. It was like 1940 in reverse, only this time the Germans were the ones doing the running. When our unit got close to Brussels, there was a bit of a lull. Monty and the Yanks were debating about the next move, so for a fortnight or so we were in that area, patrolling, picking up groups of Jerries who were trying to catch up with their own troops. That's when we were billeted for a while near St Hubert."

He stopped talking, and sat forward on the edge of his

armchair, picking up the poker to stir the fuel on the fire. He seemed use the pause to weigh up how he was going to describe what happened next. I waited in silence for him to continue. At last he put down the poker, sat back again and went on.

"One day our platoon went out on patrol. I think there'd been a message about some Germans trying to get through, and we went out looking for them. We were taken out from St Hubert by truck and dropped off. We went several miles then on foot. At one farm we came to, we were told that German soldiers had been there earlier looking for something to eat. The farmer's daughter was milking their cow, and they demanded milk. She refused, said they didn't have any to spare, so one of the Germans shot the cow. Then they beat the farmer and his daughter, took all the food they could carry, and left. For some reason, I don't know why, this seemed to make Harry really angry, more so than I'd seen him before. Sometimes it takes just one thing like that, after all the violence you've seen over several months, to tip you over the edge.

"Anyway, he was really furious, muttering to himself and cursing the war, and the Germans. It was an hour or so later that we made contact with some Jerries – I don't know if it was the same ones – and there was a bit of a pitched battle. They can't have been very good quality troops, because in the middle of it, Harry noticed a couple of them creeping off behind a hedge, trying to escape. He grabbed the Bren and went after them, and I went with him. There were bullets flying everywhere. Our lads were keeping their heads down, waiting for a chance to attack, but we just got up and ran after these two.

"We followed them the length of the hedge and across a couple of fields of crops. We had to wade an irrigation ditch and we lost them for a few moments. When we saw them again they were making for cover in a small spinney. They had to cross open ground to get there, and they took a chance and ran for it. Harry dropped to the ground and let them have it with the Bren. They were cut down before they got half-way.

"We walked over to check they were dead, and we could hear gunfire from where the other lads were. Then it went quiet. We headed back, but when we got there the unit had gone without us. It turned out they'd taken some bullets, so they had to make a decision to get the wounded back rather than looking for us. So we set off on our own.

"We made a beeline back to our billet, which was in a group of farm buildings outside St Hubert. It was starting to get dark when we came to a small road near a wood. As we were about to cross, we heard a vehicle, and we took cover in the shadows. It might have been one of our trucks, but you could never tell. When it came into view, we saw it was German, bold as brass, driving along as if they were still in charge of the place. To tell you the truth, I think they were lost, and didn't realise how close they were to some of our positions.

"We saw the swastikas on the wings; then the SS badges on their collars. Harry didn't stop to think about anything – the back of the truck could have been full of stormtroopers, for all he knew – but he just let fly with the Bren. The truck swerved and crashed, I got one of the soldiers with my rifle, and it was all over in a few seconds. It was a good feeling afterwards to be still alive.

"But it was when we had a look in the back that things took a different turn. We found one dead soldier – the bullets from the Bren had gone right through the truck and killed him outright – but we found something else, much more interesting. There were several boxes in the truck – wooden ammo boxes. But when we opened them they didn't all have ammunition in them

He paused. So it was true. I realised that I'd been hoping it would all turn out to be imagination, and that his story would confirm it as such. Now excitement wrestled with anxiety inside me.

"What was in the boxes, then?" I asked, although I was pretty sure what the answer was going to be.

"It was gold. Gold bars, some of it, melted down probably from stolen jewellery. There was other precious stuff – rings, crucifixes, silver monstrances and chalices taken from churches – a real treasure chest. And then there were some boxes of files – no use to us, but obviously important to the SS. Harry took some of the documents with him – they were lying on top in a big envelope. I don't know why, because neither of us could read them. Maybe he thought they'd turn out to be important. I don't know. He stuffed them down the front of his battledress blouse, and I never saw them again.

"Well, what were we going to do next? Jerry had stolen all

that gold and other stuff – no-one except us knew now where it was, and no-one was really expecting to get it back. It didn't take us long to reach a decision. We decided to bury it in the wood. We had to bury the bodies as well, so that no-one would be drawn to the spot. It was hard work, carrying, digging, covering everything with dead branches. It was late by the time we'd finished. And then we burnt the truck. We tried to leave as little trace as possible of what had gone on.

"If we could hide that treasure, and come back for it later, after the war...we'd be rich, make no mistake about that. We didn't worry at the time about how we'd convert it all into ready cash. We'd cross that bridge when we came to it. The SS thought it was going to be their pension fund...now it would be ours."

Peter Ashby ceased talking and gazed into the fire, lost in recollection. The silence went on so long that I began to doubt that he was still aware of my presence. I wondered whether he would ever start talking again. Gently, I prompted him.

"And did you ever return? Did you find your treasure?"

He turned his eyes on me, slowly, as if coming back from a long way away, and his look gradually hardened into one of contempt mingled with scorn. When he next spoke, it was with surprising vehemence, his voice heavy with bitterness.

"Return? Oh yes, I returned all right. It was the autumn of '45, soon after I'd been de-mobbed. I got in touch with Harry, but he'd just started a new job at the time, and couldn't risk taking time off, so he said he'd leave it to me. I thought it was a bit strange, but he said he didn't want his wife to find out about it.

So I went back on my own. I borrowed a friend's van, and drove down from Leicestershire. It was a bit of an adventure, and I was full of excitement and anticipation. I thought when I got back my life would be changed forever. I found the wood, and went in with a spade to dig up my fortune. I hoped that if I found the gold and found a way to change it into cash, I would contact Harry and share it with him. I went into the wood at dusk, so as not to be seen. I drove up there with no lights on, but it was bright moonlight, just like the night when it all started, so I could see quite clearly what I was doing.

"Well, I found the place, and at once I realised something

had changed. The branches had been moved and the ground had been turned over. I got my spade and dug and dug – I began to think I was in the wrong place – but in the end I had to give up. There was nothing there except soft soil and earthworms.

"The bastard had got there before me. Harry – your father, my mate – who'd pretended he couldn't get away, had been and gone without telling me, and taken the gold with him."

"How did you know it was Harry?"

"Come on, Mark, it's common sense. Who else could it have been? Nobody else knew about it. And who else would know exactly where to dig for the boxes? You see, we'd buried the bodies several yards away from the boxes, and they hadn't been disturbed. No, it was someone who knew just where to look. That could only be one person, couldn't it? We didn't tell anyone else about it."

"Did you get in touch with my father? Did you ask him about it?"

Peter Ashby laughed caustically.

"I certainly did. I made sure I got in touch with him. He denied all knowledge. Said he was as surprised as I was. As if he expected me to believe him!"

Peter Ashby stopped talking, and sat staring blankly ahead, his fists clenched on the arms of his chair, his face closed and white with remembered anger and indignation. My mind was rapidly turning over the information he had just given me. It didn't sound like my father, whom I knew as a straightforward and honest man, and loyal to his friends.

"If it's any consolation," I said gently, "our family didn't seem to profit from all this. We never had much money to spare, even though my dad worked all his life. We had no luxuries to speak of, just an ordinary working-class sort of upbringing."

"I'm glad to hear it, Mark. Don't expect me to feel sorry for you."

"There's nothing to be sorry about. We were perfectly happy. I never knew anything about any ramifications of this gold business before, so why would it affect me now? What does puzzle me a bit, though, is where did the money go? If my dad did take it, as you maintain, why didn't we see any profit from it? What could he have done with it?"

"I really don't know. Why should I?"

His voice was testy now, and he stared past me as if unwilling to meet my eyes.

"What your father did with *our* money is nothing to do with me. He made sure of that!"

He rose suddenly, as if to indicate that our conversation was over. As he did so, I remembered the other thing that I wanted to ask him; important, but pushed temporarily to the back of my mind by his wartime reminiscences.

"Do you know someone called Edie? Edie Barton. A friend of my father's. She's living in his cottage now."

His eyes flickered up suspiciously at my question, and he hesitated; then he shook his head with an exaggerated air of finality.

"I don't know her. But yes, I remember she did ring when Harry died. And again a month or so back when your brother passed away. She thought I ought to know."

"So where did she get your phone number from?"

"I don't know! Maybe Harry had talked to her about me. Maybe she looked in his address book. Really, Mark, it's not that difficult. She probably rang lots of people at the time."

Something in his manner failed to convince me, but at the same time made me think that it would be pointless to pursue it. I stood up, and stretched out my hand. He took it rather unwillingly.

"Thanks for seeing me, Peter. I'm sorry your friendship with my dad ended the way it did. But I'm glad you've told me what you know, even if it doesn't really explain where all the money from your treasure ended up. Maybe we'll never know. Maybe it's best that way."

He let go of my hand and shrugged.

"Oh, one last thing, Peter. Did my father ever know a Belgian girl called Sophie?"

Did he pause momentarily? It was hard to tell.

"Not that I know of. He was a married man. He generally left that sort of thing to the young single men."

"So he didn't even know such a girl casually?"

He shook his head with an air of finality.

"Never mentioned her to me."

He stared at me candidly. I was about to press him on the matter, than decided it would be pointless to pursue it further.

112

Even if he did know something, which seemed likely, he obviously wasn't going to share it with me, and I didn't want to antagonise him.

"I'd better be going," I said. "Do you mind if I use the toilet?"

"Of course not. Upstairs on the right."

I ran up the carpeted stairs and into the bathroom. When I'd finished, I flushed the toilet, and came out, turning as I did so to close the door. The next room was obviously Peter and Hilda's bedroom, and the door was ajar. Looking in, I couldn't help noticing that on the bedside table was a photograph in a frame, and I realised straight away that I recognised the people in it. Glancing down the stairs, I pushed open the door, tiptoed into the room, and picked up the photo with trembling hands.

They were both much younger then, and Hilda had changed markedly in the intervening years. She was beaming brightly from the picture in what may have been a rare moment of happiness, and her arm was around the shoulders of a younger woman who glowed with the beauty of youth, although her face was troubled behind the smile.

And the younger woman was clearly Edie Barton; a different, straighter hairstyle and different clothes, but there was no mistaking her.

There was a certain similarity between the two women, and I wondered for a moment whether this was why Hilda had seemed so familiar to me. But her resemblance to Edie wasn't all that strong. Another reason that I still couldn't pinpoint nagged at the back of my mind, a further connection that I couldn't make. I was about to replace the photo when I heard Hilda's low voice behind me.

"You've been a long time, Mark."

Then she saw the picture in my hand.

"Ah. I was afraid of that."

"This is you and Edie Barton, isn't it Hilda? Why have you got a photo of the two of you together?"

She opened her mouth to speak, but was interrupted by Peter shouting from downstairs.

"Hilda! What's going on up there? I thought Mark was leaving!"

She stiffened at the sound of his voice, and a shadow of fear passed over her face. Then she clutched my arm and whispered quickly to me, almost hissing.

"Meet me in the *Copper Kettle*, the café in the village, in half an hour. There's something you *must* know."

The *Copper Kettle* turned out to be a typical old-fashioned tea-shop with gingham tablecloths and wheel-back, dark wood chairs. The waitresses wore black, with white aprons. Most of the clientele were middle-aged females with shopping bags, chatting animatedly over pots of tea and sandwiches.

I ordered a coffee and a cake, and sat watching the door and idly scanning the *Times* I'd bought in the newsagents which also served as the village Post Office. Time passed, and I was beginning to give up on Hilda, when at last I heard the tinkle of the bell on the café's door, and she came in up the two steps, flushed and anxious, and looking nervously over her shoulder. She calmed down a little once she was seated and had given her order.

"Sorry. Sorry I've been so long," she murmured. "It was Peter. He kept me talking after you'd left, then he wanted to know why it was so important for me to go to the shops. I don't think he realised I was meeting you, though. I hope not, anyway."

"Don't worry about it," I replied. "I'm glad you came. I want to know what it was that you had to tell me. Can I get you something to drink?"

I called the waitress over and ordered the pot of tea that Hilda requested. We chatted idly until it arrived, then, when Hilda had poured herself a cup, she pulled her chair up close to the table and began to speak in a low voice so as not to be overheard. I listened with growing amazement to her story. She began with a question.

"You saw the photo of me and Edie, didn't you?"

I nodded.

"And Peter no doubt told you that he didn't know her. That's right, isn't it?"

Again, I acquiesced.

"Well, you can probably guess that that's not really true. But the whole thing is rather complicated. So it's probably easiest if

114

I start at the beginning.

"Back in 1945 I was in the ATS. I was serving in Germany, and I met Pete and Harry when I was stationed in Hamburg. I liked them both, but Harry was already married, and Pete was a lively, cheeky young fellow in those days. I fell for his charm, and we started going out together. Sometimes Harry would come with us, other times he'd stay in the billet and write home to Sarah, his wife. Sometimes we'd all three go to the pictures or for a meal together."

It was then, when she spoke about having meals together, that it came to me – the other reason why Hilda looked familiar. I recognised her now as the mysterious, unknown woman in the photo I had found amongst my father's things.

"Anyway," she went on, "Pete and I got pretty serious, and the upshot of it was that we decided to get engaged to be married. This was in June 1945. The War was over, and Pete and Harry were due to be de-mobbed soon. I hoped that if we were going to be married, it might help me to get home sooner as well. When Harry got his de-mob date, it was a few weeks earlier than Pete, and I began to realise just how much I was going to miss him. What I did then was wrong, very wrong, and I've paid for it all my life.

"I slept with Harry. Pete was on duty, and there was a party on in the Mess. Harry and I went together, we had a bit too much to drink, and we got a bit too close to each other. We started kissing, pretending we were just friends saying goodbye, then we got a bit maudlin and weepy. Perhaps we were consoling each other, I don't know. Anyway, we ended up at my billet and from then on it all seemed inevitable. It was soon after the war, and I suppose we'd all got into those sorts of habits. During wartime we'd all relaxed our morals a bit."

She smiled wryly.

"Yes, Mark, I know you think your generation invented the permissive society, the swinging sixties and all that; but you should have been around in 1940 and the next few years after that! Anyway, Pete found out. How could he not? We were all so close. He was furious, but not as terribly angry as he was a few months later on when he found out I was pregnant. By then, however, we were married; I made sure of that."

A cold feeling had taken hold of the pit of my stomach. I

guessed what she was going to say next, and the implications were shocking.

"Edie was born in April 1946, and I'd got home sooner than I expected. I'd been de-mobbed as soon as the Army found out about my condition, and Pete had been home for several months. He had no job, and no prospects of getting one. All the jobs had been snapped up either by men who never fought, or by the first soldiers coming home. Pete was too late for that. He was also seething over the other business – you know what I mean?"

I nodded.

"Yes," I said. "Peter told me all about the Nazi gold."

"Well, to cut a long story short, Pete got in touch with Harry, told him that he had a daughter, and that we couldn't afford to keep her, because he didn't have a job and Harry had cheated him out of his share of the treasure they'd found."

"Do you really believe that?" I cut in sharply. "My father was a decent man. I can't imagine him cheating anybody."

Hilda gave me a long, hard stare.

"Well, we certainly didn't get anything from him. And we were struggling to make ends meet. Pete was on the dole for quite a while. So we told Harry the baby was his and asked what he was going to do about it. Pete wouldn't keep her. He wouldn't countenance it. And Harry didn't want to wreck his marriage. He had a little boy of his own – Jack, your brother. So he took Edie away to Liverpool and quietly had her adopted. After that he never actually set eyes on her again, not for years. Until comparatively recently, in fact. Sarah knew nothing about it at all, thank God. It would have destroyed her, I'm sure, and none of this was her fault."

Hilda paused, and I signalled numbly to the waitress for another coffee. This latest piece of news was the most devastating revelation of the last few days. It seemed now that Edie Barton and I were related; and I had just slept with my half-sister. Not only that, what was worse was that she had had an affair with Harry, my father. *Her* father. It was unthinkable. Did he not recognise her? Had she met him and trapped him into it without admitting who she was? No wonder I had been so drawn to her, and found it so difficult to shake off thoughts of her, if we were so closely bound by blood. Where did I go from here? I found myself staring aimlessly, motionless in my seat, the chatter of the café seeming quietened by remoteness. I was dimly aware that Hilda was speaking again.

"I lost touch with Edie; well, in fact it was deliberate. There was no point in keeping in touch, or so I thought. Pete forbade it, anyway. Then, when she would have been twenty-one, I couldn't keep my yearning to myself any more. I'm a mother, when all's said and done. I wanted to know how she was getting on. I contacted Harry, and after I threatened to tell Sarah all about it – I wouldn't have done, really – he very reluctantly put me in touch with Edie. He'd been dutifully paying money for her upkeep to her adoptive parents, the Bartons – she'd taken their name, of course. Harry still knew where she was, although he never saw her either. She knew nothing about Harry; or about me, until she got my letter. But by then she'd got a job and set up on her own. When I say got a job, she'd had a succession of low-paid menial jobs. She'd been a problem at school, left at fifteen, and worked as a cleaner, factory hand, barmaid – don't ask me what else …"

Her voice trailed off. She took a little lace handkerchief out of the handbag which she was clutching on her knees and blew her nose. I saw that her eyes were bright with tears. I waited for her to continue.

"I was so pleased when she replied to my letter. I'd found it very hard to put everything into words after so much time. But eventually a reply came, inviting me up to Liverpool.

Edie was living in a little bed-sit in West Derby. It was cramped and depressing, but she kept it clean and tried to make it homely with bunches of flowers and pictures, and teddy bears. She loved cuddly toys. She even learned to make them herself. Maybe they helped to make up for the family we should have been She was still in touch with the couple who'd adopted her, but she'd led them a merry dance over the years, and I don't think there was much love lost between them.

"At first she was surly and kept me at arm's length. She couldn't believe who I was and what I was telling her. I probably told her too much, too quickly. But I didn't tell her about Harry. At last, when she made up her mind to trust me, she clung to me and sobbed her heart out, and called me "Mummy" over and over again as if she was making up for all those years without me. Her moods changed very suddenly, you see. If you've met her, you'll know that's often still the case."

I smiled bleakly and shrugged in agreement.

"After that we kept in touch. When Pete found out, he wasn't best pleased, but eventually he came round to it."

"And was she here earlier this week?" I interrupted

She stopped, considering her answer to what was, after all, a simple question. I was about to prompt her to continue, when she froze, eyes drawn towards the window, her mouth open in fear. I turned and followed her gaze, in time to see Peter Ashby's face pressed against the steamed-up pane. Then he came rapidly up the steps, flung open the door, whose usually melodious bell clanged wildly with the impact, and strode towards us. He stopped and shoved his face towards Hilda. He was livid and spitting with anger

"A bit of shopping, was it? No wonder you were acting oddly. I know what you've been telling him, you stupid bitch. Well, your conversation's over! And as for you," – he turned to me – "you're not welcome here, you son of a thief. Get out before you get hurt!"

"And if I don't?" I tried to sound calm and composed, but my heart was thumping in the face of such fury from the older man, and my hands had begun to sweat.

"If you don't," – here he placed both hands on the table, lowering his face close to mine, as his voice sank to a hiss – "or if you come back, I will kill you!"

I looked at Hilda, who gave an almost imperceptible nod.

I got up, put a five pound note on the table, and mustering what dignity I could, made my exit. As I left, I saw Peter grab Hilda's wrist and drag her to her feet. The other people in the café, whose tea-drinking had been disturbed and their conversations stilled by the incident, watched aghast as the two of them stumbled outside, a hitherto respectable local couple who would now be the cause of some curious gossip.

The violence in Peter Ashby's manner, and his threat to my life had been all too real. How we forget! This elderly gentleman had killed before, on more than one occasion. He had lived through times when his own life was in continual danger, and had come through it. Beneath it all, the grey hair, the slacks and cardigan, the respectable lifestyle, was the ruthless training of a hardened infantryman, and the deadly skills that went with it. I did not doubt that his threat was real.

There was obviously no future in my staying in Kingsthorpe. I was unlikely now to learn more, and besides, I was seriously worried for my own safety. Then suddenly, like a bombshell, a thought struck me. Those two men, who had tried to waylay me at Maes-y-Bryn after my night with Edie – were they involved with this? Were they hitmen working for Peter Ashby, and not, as I had naively thought, boyfriends of Edie Barton? And what then, was her involvement in this? Was she part of some plan of Ashby's to get back at my family? My God, it was bad enough that I had slept with her, if she was my half-sister! But what other revelations might be forthcoming? Whatever resolutions I might try to make about not seeing her again, I knew now that I would have to.

With legs like jelly, I got into the car, started the engine and headed north. It was Friday afternoon, I was tired and apprehensive, and all I desperately wanted to do now was get home and do some thinking. But instead of going straight to Yorkshire, it was imperative that I went back via Liverpool and checked on Emily again, and after that, tried one way or another, to contact Edie.

Emily! She was alone in the house, apart, possibly, from Phil. And what use would he be? I couldn't rely on him to keep her safe. I didn't even know now whose side he would be on. I would not be able to forgive myself if Peter Ashby's hired men had sought Emily out and caused her harm in the search for money that he thought my father had cheated him of.

I was already breaking the speed limit by the time I left the village, and when I reached the open road I floored the accelerator and drove as fast as I dared towards the M1.

Chapter Ten

The house was in unaccustomed darkness, which made me immediately suspicious, and I fumbled clumsily with the keys, nearly dropping them in my haste to open the door. I was desperate with fear at what I would find inside, but cautious at the same time. The hallway was unlit and silence reigned. I paused for a moment, listening. Then, in the deathly stillness I fancied I heard the sound of tortured breathing, almost whimpering, coming from the kitchen. But there was no sign or sound of any heavy-handed thugs in the house.

I pushed open the kitchen door, and in the faint light I could see Emily sitting in her usual armchair by the fireplace. I took a chance and turned on the light. There was no-one else there, no-one waiting to surprise me, and I breathed a little easier. But the sight of Emily shocked me. She was staring straight ahead, her eyes unfocused, rocking slightly and moaning quietly

"Are you all right? What's happened?"

I dropped to my knees by her side and took her hand in mine. She grasped it tightly and turned her head to stare at me, and some life came back into her expression.

"Emily! You've got to tell me what's happened! Has someone been here? You've got to tell me!"

She seemed unable to speak. I went into the kitchen and fetched a glass of water. She bent her head to the glass and drank a little, moistening her lips with her tongue and swallowing with difficulty. When she spoke her voice was weak and hoarse, and seemed to come from a long way away.

"Two men...two men. Frightened me. Kept asking questions, questions..."

"What about, Emily?"

"About you...Jack...Harry..."

"What sort of questions?"

"About the War. About the gold. Harry's gold."

"And what did you tell them?"

"Nothing, nothing!" Her voice was a little stronger now. She clutched my arm and pulled herself up in her chair to face me. "But I knew it would come to this in the end. I should never have let them in."

"What did you know, Emily? What are you talking about? You must tell me!"

My voice was urgent, but she ignored me. A look of horror had come ever her face.

"Look upstairs, Mark. What have they done to Phil?"

"Phil was here?"

"He came back while they were searching the place. He surprised them upstairs. Then there were noises... I don't know what happened. He hasn't come down again. Oh, quickly, Mark, go and see!"

I straightened up and almost ran from the room, taking the stairs two at a time. Phil was in the main bedroom, but there was no rush. I knew that straight away from his vacant eyes and open mouth, and the grey pallor of his skin. He lay crumpled on his side on the floor, and the sticky red puddle on the bedroom carpet had come from the fractured hollow in the side of his skull where he had been brutally struck. At his side lay the poker from the downstairs fire, dark with congealing blood.

The room was in disarray, with evidence of a struggle, and of a rapid but thorough search having been carried out by violent men who, I guessed, knew what type of thing they were searching for. No doubt they had hoped to get information from Emily or Phil, but to give him credit, it looked as if Phil had fought rather than tell them anything, and they must have despaired of Emily, whose state of shock must have rendered her incoherent and apparently senile.

But I was stunned and horrified. Not even my intuition about Peter Ashby's hitmen and my presentiments about what they might do had prepared me for the reality of this violence. I had no reason at all to like Phil, but this ... this was totally different. Sympathy flooded through me as I thought that it could equally well have been me lying there, beaten to death by these ruthless men. And where would they strike next? They had not found what they were looking for, and even my protestations that this stolen fortune did not exist would carry very little weight with my father's former comrade, obsessed as he seemed to be with getting his own back on my family.

But even as I ran back down the stairs to tell Emily, the thought went through my mind that it was bizarre that Peter

Ashby would tell me so openly about his feelings towards my father and our family, and then send his thugs to carry out such a crime The link was far too clear. Perhaps he was prepared to dispose of any other witnesses, myself included, as he had apparently got rid of Phil.

As I reached the bottom of the stairs the phone shrilled piercingly in the quietness of the hall, making me start physically. Recovering, I snatched up the old black bakelite receiver.

"Mark?"

I knew the voice instantly, and a wave of mixed emotions swept through me.

"Edie! Where are you?"

"I'm at Maes-y-Bryn. I need to see you. I've phoned your house but there was no answer. I didn't know where you were."

She sounded upset, and I refrained from saying that she was a fine one to talk. Where, after all, had *she* been? I felt too concerned about her to be angry. Despite the circumstances, hearing her voice again stirred the sexual attraction I had felt before; but at the same time, knowing now about our blood relationship, I felt deeply protective towards her.

"Can you come out here? Please! Come straight away!" She sounded anxious and stressed.

"Of course, of course, I'll come as soon as I can. I've got a few things to sort out, then I'll be over. Give me a couple of hours or so."

I didn't say what it was that I had to sort out. It wasn't the type of thing you could just say over the phone. I'd save that until I was face to face with her.

"OK. But try not to be any longer."

I put the phone down thoughtfully. I was worried about Edie. She sounded very disturbed on the phone, but whose side was she on? Was she in danger as a relative of ours, or was she, perhaps understandably, in league with Peter Ashby and her mother? Were they all in this together? If that was the case, I would have to tread very carefully when I went to see her.

But the first thing now was to call the police. I went back into the kitchen and told Emily what I had found upstairs, and she wept for a little while, although more from the shock than from any love for Phil. I made her a cup of the strong tea she enjoyed, after which she seemed a little more composed. So much so, in fact, that it was she who stopped me from ringing the police straight away.

"Think about it, Mark. The men who did this have got away. Phil's dead, the poker that killed him must have your fingerprints on it. Lord knows, you've used it often enough. You've got a really good motive, and you've had the opportunity."

I stared at her open-mouthed. She pulled herself upright in her chair, and when she went on it was very much the Emily I knew talking.

"You look like a goldfish. Don't look so surprised. I haven't spent a lifetime reading Agatha Christie and P.D. James without learning anything. You must get away, get an alibi and I'll ring the police a bit later."

She was right, of course. She so often was. She went on.

"You go out the back way, and come up the street to the car as if you'd just left it parked there. I'll wait a while until you're well away, then I'll dial 999 and ask for the police, and when they come I'll do my senile bit and tell them Phil must have disturbed a burglar. Now go! Go on!"

I kissed her gently and turned to go, but paused in the doorway.

"Can you remember anything else about these two men, Emily?"

"Well, I can't see very well now, Mark, as you know. My eyes are going. But I could hear them all right. And there was one odd thing. When they spoke to each other it was in a foreign language."

"What language was it? Did you recognise it?" I thought of the two men I had encountered at Maes-y-Bryn.

"Was it Welsh, do you think?"

"I'm not sure, Mark." She knitted her brows with the effort of remembering. "It might have been, but I can't really tell you. You know I know nothing about languages."

If it was Welsh, I thought wryly, at least it meant Peter Ashby was using local labour to do his work for him at Maes-y-Bryn. If Edie was involved, I'd need to be really careful going out to the cottage. It could be some sort of trap. If, on the other hand, she wasn't involved...

It could still be a trap, but with Edie as the bait. These men might already be in the house with her, using her to make a phone call to lure me out there. From the tone of her voice on the phone, she was thoroughly frightened. The adrenalin surged in me again. I realised at once that Edie might be in deadly peril. I would be taking a risk going to Maes-y-Bryn, but I had to get to her.

I called goodbye to Emily and rushed out through the back door into the yard, and from there into the gloom of the passage which would lead me, unremarked, I hoped, back to my car.

I knew the men I was up against weren't stupid, I was pretty sure of that, and I had no intention of walking into a trap. Instead of motoring straight up to the cottage, I parked in the car park at the *Cross Keys* inn, where I hoped I looked like just another customer, then faded into the shadow of the trees and climbed over the pig-netting fence onto the moor. I slipped and slithered over the boggy stream beds, then climbed steeply through waist high heather under the waning moon. Moving cautiously, it took me the best part of an hour to reach the fields above Maes-y-Bryn. I'm no Royal Marine Commando but as youngsters we had spent hours and days playing tracking and hiding games across these fields and moors. This was no different, except that now it was for real.

After my strenuous short-cut on foot across country it seemed like an age before I eventually drew closer to the narrow road above Maes-y-Bryn. In the shadows I made out the outline of a car parked on the grass at the top of the hill, pulled close in under the shelter of a small stand of birch trees. Moving closer, but still hidden by the old stone wall, I thought I could see a figure slumped behind the steering wheel, but I couldn't be sure. Then a match flared, and I dimly saw his face. *I thought: Not as professional as all that then.*

I was pretty sure he was alone. So where was his companion? I crouched by the wall, my trainers squelched in the damp grass and the scent of moss and lichen in my nose. What would I do in their position? I thought rapidly.

They'd obviously been following my movements since the time of Jack's funeral, probably seeing where I would lead them in their search. They'd been at the cottage when I was there with

Edie, and must have decided to try to capture me then and get information from me. I had no doubt their methods, in that lonely spot, would have been ruthless. The next day at my own house, I thought I'd given them the slip, but at that point I'd had no idea who they were or what they wanted. Now I realised that they'd been looking for a chance to burgle the house; and still they'd clearly been unsuccessful in finding what they wanted.

Now they'd raised the stakes by murdering Phil. They'd be feeling under pressure to complete whatever mission they were on, and their patience would be wearing thin.

They'd be waiting for me; waiting for me to arrive by car, and they'd want to make sure I was out of the vehicle and cut off from any escape route before they moved in. I guessed that both of them would still be outside the cottage, waiting to trap me when I went in to meet Edie. I no longer felt like a detective; instead I felt the animal fear of the hunted. But anger, too, was growing in me; anger at what they were doing and determination not to let them have their way.

Carefully, I worked my way back from the road and across the hillside at the back of the cottage. I skirted above the garden and crept down towards the lane on the other side, crouching motionless by the hedge and scanning the semi-darkness of the road for a figure or a movement. There was nothing. I was about to change my position again when I saw a faint ripple of moonlight, then a pinpoint, a gleam. I realised that what I was seeing was the dull reflection of light on a leather jacket, and on the face of a watch as the man checked the time.

I retreated slowly to the slope behind the cottage. Built so close to the steep hillside, there was a narrow passage cut out around the rear. I reckoned that I could get into that passage and reach the back door, out of sight of the road, without being seen by either of the watchers.

With infinite care I climbed through the hedge into my father's old potato patch, and wormed my way down to the retaining wall. I slithered down into the gap between the hill and the cottage wall, and an instant later I was at the door, tapping quietly and insistently.

A moment later, the door swung open, and Edie was framed in the light. Before she could even speak, I pushed her inside and into the living room, where the curtains were closed. To my relief, there was no-one else there.

It was then that I got a good look at her, and gasped in shock. Her cheek was swollen and puffy, and her left eye was bruised and bloodshot. She was trembling. I put my arms around her and held her close.

When she had calmed a little, she told me, whispering, how the two men had come earlier that evening and forced their way in when she opened the door. They had questioned her about me, and hit her when she refused at first to co-operate. Then they'd made her phone me; first at home, and when I wasn't there they'd tried the house in Liverpool, where, by chance, they'd found me.

"I'm sorry, I'm sorry," she muttered several times. "I was so frightened."

"Don't worry, it's not your fault," I whispered, trying to console her. "I'm pretty sure I know who these men are. It's a good job you didn't refuse to help them. Who knows what they would have done."

"Who are they? Tell me!"

"It's a long story, Edie, and I don't know all the ins and outs of it. What I do know is that they are searching for something, and even if they don't find it, they may not want to leave any witnesses alive. They've already killed Phil!"

A look of utter horror came over her face, and her skin turned pallid. Her eyes were wide open and staring, and her breath through her gaping mouth came with difficulty. Then her legs seemed to give way and she sank down on the sofa and hid her face in her hands, sobbing.

"Oh the poor boy! The poor boy!"

I glanced around anxiously. We had no time to lose, but one thing I wanted to do was to give Emily a call to see how things stood at her end. I looked for the phone, but it was gone. They'd obviously thought of that.

"There's a phone in my bedroom." Edie was following my train of thought.

"Thanks Edie."

I ran upstairs to Edie's bedroom and looked around, but couldn't see the extension anywhere. Obviously they'd thought of that too. Frustrated, I went part way back down the stairs.

"I can't find it. They must have taken it."

"Let me look."

Edie came upstairs and crouched down by the bed. She groped under the valance for a moment and came up triumphantly clutching a phone.

"There you are. There's never room on the table, so it usually ends up on the floor. Or under the bed."

Our luck was in. These men were certainly vicious and determined, but their attention to detail was suspect. I took the extension from Edie, and when I picked up the receiver I heard the dialling tone. In the light from the stairs I punched in Emily's number. I seemed to wait an age before she answered.

"Can you talk?" I asked.

"Oh Mark! It's you! Yes, but I've got bad news."

"What, Emily, what?"

"I called the police, but when they came with their flashing lights and everything, Mrs. Kelly from next door but one came out and stuck her nose in. She told them she'd seen you arrive and then drive off later. When they asked me if it was true, I had to tell them. I tried to tell them that it was a burglar, but they said there was no sign of a break-in. Then they asked me where you'd gone. When it came to it, I couldn't tell a lie. I just couldn't. They're on their way now."

"Don't worry, Emily," I answered as calmly as I could. "It's not your fault. Sorry, I've got to go."

I put the phone down grimly.

Oh Emily, I thought. Thanks a lot, Emily. But with your good Catholic upbringing, what else could I expect? Telling lies is a sin, after all, no matter what the circumstances, I suppose.

I rushed back downstairs. Edie was still apparently overcome with grief at the news and I had some trouble getting her to listen to me. I finally got her to understand that we had to go, and go quickly and quietly I didn't want to get caught by the men outside; nor did I want to take my chances with the police finding me at the cottage with a woman who'd so clearly been assaulted. I didn't have enough faith that they would look beyond the obvious. And I couldn't be sure whose side Edie would choose.

I got her to change into jeans and trainers and a dark jacket, and explained my plan.

"We can't go back to my car. The police are on their way;

they'll probably come past the pub where it's parked, and they'll be on the lookout for it anyway.

"First, we need to get out of here and get away. I need a chance to think about what to do."

"How are we going to get away?"

Edie's voice was faint and there was a note of pleading in it.

"Out the back. We'll have to go across country. I think I know where we can get a vehicle. Then we'll get as far away as possible. Come on now, Edie!"

I turned the light out in the hall and we went quickly through the back door and swung round behind the cottage. I helped Edie up the wall into the potato patch and we eased ourselves through the hedge and onto the hillside. The moon was fading in and out of the cloud, and darkness was our friend. I couldn't see either of the watchers, and I hoped they couldn't see us.

I took Edie's hand to help her along, and using the shadow of the old wall for cover, we stumbled, bent double, up the hill and out onto the moor. I breathed a little easier after we had crested the brow of the hill, although we had a couple of miles to go on foot, and I didn't want to risk any of the paths or lanes.

We worked our way around behind the hill by the lake, and as we did so I was aware of lights behind us. Turning, I saw headlights spearing the sky, and the revolving blue lights of police cars travelling at great speed up the narrow road towards Maes-y-Bryn. We hurried on.

Edie seemed to be in a state of shock, and hardly spoke. We came to a fence at the edge of the moor, and I helped her over it. On the other side we were in a swampy wood of lichened birch and scrub, where we had to wade ankle deep in icy water. Branches whipped at our faces in the darkness and the peat bog clutched at our legs and made the going hard. Eventually we reached another fence and scrambled over it into what I remembered was a huge open field of many acres, which fell away in a great sweep from where we stood.

We had not gone far when we heard the sound of movement and heavy breathing. We stopped dead, crouching close together and fearing the worst, my heart beating madly and my ears and eyes straining for a sight of whoever was there, hidden in the night. A cloud was over the face of the moon and we could see little.

Then we sensed creatures around us, and smelt the sweet scent of ruminating beasts. In the dim light we saw that we had stumbled into the middle of a herd of black cattle. I heaved a sigh of relief. It was short-lived, for, a moment later, the moonlight strengthened as the clouds thinned. What I saw made me clutch Edie's hand and push her behind me. Together we started to move backwards. Twenty feet away was a huge Welsh Black bull with menacing down-curved horns. The ring in its nose caught the light as it moved its massive head, and it rumbled deep in its throat as it peered at us. It pawed the ground angrily, and began to move towards us.

"Stay calm!" I whispered. "It's probably only curious."

Very gently we retreated, keeping our eyes on the bull. I remembered that not far behind us was a small broken line of crags, and below them a very steep slope of rough grass and bracken. *Cattle don't like steep slopes, I thought.* We had just reached the edge of the rocks when the bull made up its mind and began to run, slowly at first, then with gathering speed, in our direction, the ground shaking under the impact of its heavy hoofs.

Abandoning any pretence of calmness, we turned quickly and slithered downwards over the shallow cliff, half sliding, half falling. The bull stopped right on the edge above us and I fancied I felt the hot exhalation of its angry breath. We, however, couldn't stop ourselves so easily, and we both rolled and tumbled down the slope, being scratched by brambles and bumping elbows and knees on the hard ground. Part way down the slope we came to a halt. Edie was whimpering slightly.

"Can you walk?" I asked her, and after a moment she pulled herself together and gingerly got to her feet as if to check.

"Yes," she whispered. "I'm OK. Let's go on."

Lower down, the slope flattened out and the grass was shorter. We had some way to go to reach the next fence, and out in the open, even in the feeble light of the moon, I felt conspicuous. The bull was invisible in the darkness at the top of the slope, and had doubtless lost interest in us by now, but out on the grassland we seemed acutely visible. However, we reached the fence without incident, and clambering over it, continued for some distance through rough fields with scattered clumps of stunted trees and bushes. Edie was clinging to me and sagging with tiredness. We were both frightened, wet, and battered and bruised but I knew we hadn't far to go, and with an effort we kept going.

After what began to seem an age, we reached the wall which gave onto the access track to Bryn Pritchard's farm.

I'd known Bryn since we were teenagers. He was a little older than Jack, and I remembered how I had watched in admiration as he bounced and roared up the grassy lane on his scramble bike, his hair slicked with Brylcreem as he headed for a night out in Wrexham. In those days the lane was unsurfaced, muddy in winter and rutted in summer. Now it was smooth tarmac until it reached the gate to the farm, where there was a turning area, for the lane itself was a dead end. Beyond this point, the track was stone and old cobbles for the last hundred yards or so down to the farmyard.

I had kept in touch with Bryn over the years, and I considered him a friend. I was confident that he would help us to get away, although my plan was hazy. Bryn was a hard and resourceful man, and not one to bow easily to authority. He had grown up on the farm, but had spent some time in the army, rising through the ranks and seeing service in the Middle East and Northern Ireland. Eventually his father's deteriorating health had left him too frail to cope with the rigours of running a Welsh hill farm, and Bryn had come home then and taken over the farm. Since his father's death he had run the place with his wife Megan.

We stumbled down the track into the farmyard, which, apart from the soft glow of the moonlight, was in darkness. My heart sank. The dogs began to bark as we approached, first the border collie chained to his kennel in the yard, then another dog from inside the house, the sound echoing hollowly in the quiet.

Down the right hand side of the yard had once run an old whitewashed shippen and haybarn. On a previous visit I had been shocked to see it had been demolished.

"You got to move with the times, Mark, haven't you?" Bryn had said brightly, but I had merely mumbled in reply, horrified at what I considered to be vandalism.

The building had been replaced by an open Dutch barn, in one end of which Bryn now usually kept his car parked. It wasn't there. I knocked on the door of the farm-house anyway.

There was no reply, no stirring within. Only the dog's barking became more frenzied. My heart sank.

"What now?" Edie's voice was weary.

"I don't know. Let me think." I took her hand and pulled her with me into the dark shade inside the big barn. There were some hay bales there, and we sank down gratefully on them, resting our backs against the stack behind. After a while, as we remained quiet and motionless, the barking of the dogs became less persistent, then slowly died away.

In truth, I had no idea what we were going to do. I hadn't thought beyond reaching Bryn's farm and asking him for help, asking to borrow his car, or for him to give us a lift somewhere. Now we were there, and he wasn't, I was going to have to think again. On foot, and with me wanted for murder, I couldn't see us getting very far. Maybe we should just give ourselves up to the police. Edie would be safe enough from the police, but what about Phil's murderers? They would still be at large. And I certainly didn't fancy being arrested, with no way then of proving my innocence. And in any case, I was reluctant to let Edie go. We sat on in silence as I waited for some solution to my predicament to strike me. Tired as I was, with the illusion of temporary safety in the dark, I found myself gradually relaxing with the sweet scent of the hay in my nostrils, recalling childhood romps in other barns. After a while, my eyes began to close.

Suddenly, Edie clutched my arm.

"Look!"

Headlights were coming towards us. Coming swiftly down the road. Then we saw them start to swing up and down as the vehicle bumped over the unmade track, and as it got closer we heard the sound of its engine. It was too late to run. Like frightened rabbits we cowered back out of sight, clinging wordlessly together.

I expected the vehicle to drive right up to the farmhouse, giving us a chance to sneak out round the side of the barn and make for the thin wood that edged the field on that side, but at the last moment it swung its nose towards the barn, and the headlights swept towards us, blinding us. In a desperate attempt to avoid being seen, I pulled Edie with me and we rolled sideways over the bales and dropped out of sight as the vehicle entered the barn and stopped only feet away from us. We lay on the dusty floor, hardly daring to breathe. The engine was switched off, and the door opened. We heard feet hitting the ground, the door slammed, and steps came towards us.

A torch shone over the bales, and then a figure, grotesque and distorted by the shadows, was bending towards us. Another dark shape seemed to be hovering in the background.

"There's no point trying to hide. I saw you as I drove up. Get up now and let's have a look at you!"

Shamefaced we rose to our feet, brushing the dirt and the hay from our clothing and our hair. I cursed inwardly at being caught out so easily; it made me feel like the amateur I was. It was a salutary lesson for any similar situations in the future, but fear had quickly given way to relief. For the voice was not that of a thug or a policeman.

It was Bryn's.

Chapter Eleven

Our hands clasped round hot mugs of tea, and with dry socks supplied by Bryn, we sat by the stove in the farmhouse kitchen and discussed our plan of action. The old oak grandfather clock in the hallway ticked on with its slow, immemorial beat, but we all knew we didn't have much time. We'd given Bryn and Megan a quick run down of the situation, describing as well as we could the two men we'd escaped from at Maes-y-Bryn. They were shocked by what had happened to Phil and Edie, both of whom they knew to some extent.

"The police stopped us on the way up the lane," Bryn was saying. "But it was only the local bobby, Barry Rogers. There was a squad car outside, and there were some other officers in the house, but no sign of anyone else."

"They hadn't found anyone there then?"

"Not as far as I could see. But," – he held up a hand to stop my next question – "we were passed by a car going down the lane in the opposite direction. He was travelling really fast, and had to swerve to avoid me. You know how narrow that lane is, and he didn't slow down, just swung two wheels onto the grass verge, skidded and slithered and shot past really close. It gave us a real turn, I can tell you."

"Did you see what sort of a car it was, Bryn?"

"Hard to tell. It was so quick. I was too busy trying not to hit him."

"Could it have been a BMW?"

"Could've been, I suppose. Yes, I think it was that sort of size and shape."

"I thought as much," I answered slowly. "It will have been the guys who've been tracking me. The ones who killed Phil and beat up Edie. I saw the car hidden under the trees above Maes-y-Bryn.

"So now they've taken off to avoid the police. They must have taken a chance and got away down the lane after the police cars passed their car without seeing it. They could be anywhere now. The police are on a murder inquiry. They know I'm in this area, so they'll come looking, probably checking all the properties round here. I can't let them find me. Not yet. Not till I know what's really going on. But we've no car – they'll find mine in the car park of the Cross Keys. – and we've nowhere to go ..."

I was thinking aloud, but Bryn interrupted me.

"You've got to get away. You need to get as far away as possible while we sort things out."

"Easier said than done, Bryn. First of all, I can't see how I can get away now without being stopped by the police on the road, and on foot how far will we get? Where will we go? Secondly, if we do get away, how will we be in a position to sort anything out?"

"I've got an idea. I've been thinking. You can't get out down the lane past your fathers' – I mean Edie's – place. You'll drive straight into the arms of the police. And even if you reached the junction before there and turned left, they'll probably have that blocked as well. But there is an alternative. It might work."

"What's that, Bryn?" My voice was eager.

"You know the old drove road that runs along above here?"

"The old lane that was always overgrown with brambles and bushes? It was fenced off in places, wasn't it? What use would that be?"

"Well, over the last couple of years it's been tidied up. It's a proper bridleway now, with gates and everything. It gets used a lot by pony trekkers from the centre near the village. They've got rid of most of the obstacles and all the blockages have gone."

"You're not suggesting we make our escape on horseback? Very romantic, but a little impractical!" I hoped I didn't sound too sarcastic.

"No, Mark." Bryn laughed. "Not horseback. Better than that. Why not take the old Land Rover? It's round the back of the barn. It'll be a rough ride, but you should be able to make it along there as far as the road below the village. Then if you're careful you can get away, wherever you decide. But don't tell me where you're going. Just phone me some time tomorrow to make contact."

I thought quietly for a moment. I glanced across at Edie, who looked weary, dishevelled and disorientated. Her left eye was bloodshot and that side of her face was turning yellow. I still wasn't really sure what she was thinking.

When she spoke, her voice was very quiet at first, her eyes downcast, not looking at anyone in particular.

"Bryn's right, Mark."

She paused, and when she went on her tone had strengthened. She raised her eyes and looked into mine, and there was more determination in her expression.

"Bryn's right. We've got to get away. It's got to be worth a try. We might have thrown those thugs off the scent for now, but if the police catch up with you, you'll be in real trouble. They'll think you killed Phil, even though we know you didn't. We owe it to him to make sure the real murderers get caught. And we need to find out who's behind all this."

I bit my lip, not wanting to come out there and then with my suspicions about Peter Ashby. Instead I asked:

"And how do you think we can do that if we're on the run?"

"I may be able to help there, Mark." Bryn's voice was calm and confident.

"You remember when I was in the army? Did you know that I was in the Military Police?

I did know that, but I had to admit I'd forgotten.

"I made a lot of contacts in various services. I won't go into all that now. But I think they could be useful. If you and Edie get yourselves away and lie low for a while, I'll make some enquiries and see if I can't find something out. If you can give me any ideas of your own, any clues, I'll follow them up and if you phone in from time to time I'll let you know how things are progressing.

"Now, let's get going. We've got to make sure you're well clear before the police come asking questions. And before anyone else does."

The old Land Rover coughed into life. It smelled of diesel fuel and leather, mixed in with scents of old hay and sheepdogs, and a glance in the back showed a pile of empty sacks. The canvas top was torn in places and the seats sagged, but it started, and that was the main thing. Bryn still used it occasionally, so he said, but unlike a lot of farmers, he still enjoyed walking the fields with his dogs, so it didn't get used all that much.

I eased it into gear and we bumped carefully across the farmyard. Bryn opened the wooden gate at the corner of the house, and we passed through the gap in the wall and ground up the old track that joined the drove road a few yards higher up, the heavily treaded tyres digging deep into the soft grass, the engine whining in low gear.

Once on the drove road, I could see that the gradient was easier, and I stopped for a minute to shake Bryn's hand through the window, and to thank him again.

"Take care now, Mark. Drive carefully, think about where you two are going, and give me a ring tomorrow. Either myself or Megan will be sure to be here."

As he spoke, his wife appeared at his elbow, clutching an old haversack which she thrust into my hand.

"Just some sandwiches and a flask of coffee. I think you may need them."

I took them gratefully. Then they turned, and I saw their shadowy figures making their way back down to the farm. I'd been right to trust in their friendship. They'd accepted my story without question, and had offered help beyond what I had expected. Knowing that Bryn was doing all he could to find out what was going on meant that for the moment I could concentrate on one thing. And that was putting as much distance as possible between us and the two lots of people whom I did not wish to find us.

Conscious that at any moment police cars might be approaching Bryn's farm in search of us, I lifted the clutch and we set off again. The headlamps were not as bright as a modern vehicle, but I could make out the green road between the trees, churned up in places by the passage of horses' hoofs. The branches had been trimmed back to allow riders to pass, and although in the narrow places they scraped along the sides, the Land Rover was able at first to make progress without too much difficulty.

The track climbed steadily, and I stayed in four-wheel drive, wary of getting stuck. In places, stones and boulders had spilled across the way, and we bounced gingerly over them; in others trees grew close to the edge, and we had to squeeze between them and the stone wall on the other side. Anxiously, I scanned the track ahead, hoping that we would not encounter any insuperable obstacles.

We climbed slowly over a brow, and the trees became more

sparse. I could see the line of the old drove road ahead, its edges marked with grassed over stones, the remains, perhaps, of ancient walls. Shadows of tree and rock, thrown by the moon, lay across the sheep-nibbled pasture, and frost lay on the grass. From this high point, we could see the dark outline of the hills across the valley, pinpricked with the lights of a few houses. It was late now, and I wondered if folk not yet abed were watching our lights as they swept across the hillside and asking themselves what was afoot. Would they be ringing anyone to report this unaccustomed night-time movement? I hoped not, but I turned off the lights anyway, and drove some distance by the light of the moon.

We began to descend, gradually at first, then more steeply, and the bushes began to draw more closely together once more. Then the trees began again, the darkness closed in, and I was forced to switch the headlights back on. The track became steeper and narrower, just cart width now, and the surface changed from grass to loose stones, slippery and gouged by the passage of hooves and running water. I remembered then where we were.

We were dropping down to the ford, where the drove road crossed the Afon Cyfynwy, a tributary of the Alyn. I knew it was a sharp drop into the stream, which here was about two feet deep, and I began to worry, because the climb out was even more abrupt. I hoped that if the route had been improved for horses, it would be all right for us. But I was wrong.

As we reached the bottom of the small valley in which the stream ran, I saw that the bridleway had been diverted to make the stream crossing easier, but the gap between the trees where the new route went was too narrow and too sharp a turn for us. We had to carry straight on, and I realised too late that we were dropping off an undercut bank into the bed of the stream. I braked, but even in four-wheel drive it was too late to stop us slithering and bouncing down into the bed of the stream.

Trying to make the most of our momentum, I floored the accelerator, hurtled across the stream in a great shower of spray, and managed to get the front wheels up out of the water on the other side. For an agonising moment I thought we were going to make it, then all four wheels began to spin, and we stopped, the bonnet tilted up at a crazy angle, but going nowhere.

I tried again, but if we couldn't make it with a run at it, we weren't going to do it from a standing start. The tyres spun, gravel spurted, we rocked forward, then sank back again. I tried a couple of times, with the same result. I put the clutch in, pulled on the handbrake and cursed roundly.

"What now?" Edie's voice was weary and despondent. The thought of setting off on foot again was unattractive to both of us. I thought for a moment.

"Shift over here, Edie"

I slipped out of the Land Rover, and the cold water swirled around my legs, soaking my feet for the second time that night. Edie moved across into the driver's seat and clunked the engine into gear. She revved up and let out the clutch. I threw my shoulder against the back of the vehicle, and pushed with all my strength, feet sliding on the wet pebbles.

The Land Rover moved forward promisingly, then stopped again, hanging on the lip of the bank. For a moment I thought it was going to climb free, then the front wheels lost traction, and I had to move quickly to avoid being crushed as it lurched back again. When I'd got my breath back, we tried a couple more times; but the second time I had less strength left, and we got no further, if as far. By the third attempt I was totally spent and gasping like an old man. It was no use.

Defeated, I waded round the stranded Land Rover, opened the door and got into the passenger seat. We sat in silence for a while.

"Any ideas, Edie?"

"Not really."

"We may have to walk."

She snorted. There was another silence as we reluctantly contemplated setting off. Then she spoke again.

"How about digging? Have we got a spade? We could maybe dig out a bit of the bank. It shouldn't take much to make a difference. We were nearly out of it the first time."

It was a possibility.

"We can try. Look under those sacks. There should be something we can dig with …"

"And the sacks! We could put them down to get more grip."

Galvanised into action, I jumped out again while Edie climbed over and hunted in the back for something to dig with,

138

but when she joined me at the front of the Land Rover, her enthusiasm had drained away.

"There's nothing, Mark. Nothing we can dig with. I think we're well and truly stuck after all."

I brushed aside her disappointment, for I had spotted something which suddenly filled me with renewed optimism.

"Oh no we're not! Look at this!"

I pointed excitedly to the front of the vehicle. I was surprised I hadn't thought of it before. There, fixed to the front, was a winch.

It took me a while to work out how to control it, but once I had, it didn't take long to unwind enough cable to hook on to a reasonably sized oak tree, and with the combination of engine power and winch hauling, we bounced out of that gully like a cork out of a bottle.

We hugged each other crazily, rewound the cable and jumped in again. After the stream crossing, I guessed that the worst was over. We climbed out of the little valley, skirted a headland, and came onto quite a good track through a wood, which lost height steadily until we came to the farm of Mynydd Isa. Here Edie jumped down to open the gate, and we sidled through the darkened farmyard, the engine barely doing more than tick over. I didn't want to risk waking anyone.

Unfortunately, our luck was out. As we passed through the yard, the security light came on, the dogs started to bark, and the cattle grid clattered loudly as we crossed it. A light came on in a bedroom, a window was flung open, and we heard a voice screaming at us in Welsh.

All hope of passing unnoticed having gone, I gunned the engine and we roared up the rough track to join the minor road to the village. I turned away from the direction of Maes-y-Bryn, and headed for Llandegla and Ruthin, aiming to come round in a big sweep to reach the motorway which would take us north.

I'd often wondered where I would run to if I needed to get away. Sometimes I used to toy with the idea of running away when I was fed up with school and Jenny was getting on my nerves. I used to think about just setting out for work one morning, but not arriving and not coming home in the evening either, and leaving everyone else to sort it out. I used to wonder where I'd go.

When it came to it, the decision seemed simple. I was heading for the Highlands. I know all the sayings about "if you want to hide a leaf, hide it in the forest," and the conventional wisdom about losing yourself in the big city; but cities are full of people, neighbours, policemen and other sets of eyes and ears. I reasoned that the Highlands cover a vast area, and that if no-one knew where we were headed for in the first place, they would have no reason to look for us there, and no idea where to start looking if they did. And besides that, it was a gut instinct. I've done a lot of mountaineering in Scotland, and it seemed almost like my home ground.

We had a long drive ahead of us, in a vehicle that wouldn't do much more than sixty miles an hour and it was already into the early hours of the morning. But by the time we reached the Charnock Richard services we needed fuel and I was finding it all but impossible to keep awake. Edie had been asleep for some time, curled up uncomfortably on the passenger seat, her head padded against the window with my fleece.

I signalled and pulled off the almost deserted motorway into the services. Edie woke briefly as we stopped in the car park outside the cafeteria, but I merely switched off the engine and fell asleep myself where I sat. We slept for half an hour or so, for my part troubled by vivid dreams of death and pursuit, then I woke with a start, conscious that we couldn't afford to waste time on this part of the journey where we might be easily spotted. We needed to press on. First, though, I had to use the toilet, and so did Edie.

We went inside, feeling strangely conspicuous, even though there was nobody much around at that time except a few lorry drivers. The service station had that unreal quality of night. Bright lights in the darkness; a place apart from the rest of the world where people pass without acknowledgement; the roar of traffic on the motorway; and the pall of weariness that goes with night-time driving.

We came back to the Land Rover together and climbed inside. I reached for the haversack Megan had given us and pulled out the flask and the food. The steaming coffee helped to revive us, and we sat in silence with our thoughts.

"Where are we going, Mark? You haven't said."

I hesitated. Should I tell her? Perhaps the less she knew the better. On the other hand, I wanted to trust her. After all, she was my half-sister, and there was a strong if confused bond, which might even be some sort of love, between us. Besides, what harm could it do? She'd be with me in any case.

An image swam into my mind of towering heather-clad peaks, tumbling burns and scattering deer, and of eagles circling and water lapping on untrodden sands.

"Knoydart," I answered dreamily. "The last wilderness. One of the most beautiful places on earth. Think of it as a seaside holiday. You'll love it."

"I hope it's not too cold!"

"Don't worry. I'll make sure we can stay warm. More coffee?"

I poured the hot drink, and we sat cupping it in our hands, staring out through the windscreen. Suddenly I stiffened. A police car had swept purposefully into the car park in front of us and stopped by the service station doors, its red and yellow stripes garish against the white paintwork. Only the fact that its blue lights weren't flashing stopped me from panicking completely.

The doors opened and two policemen got out of the car. They turned to face us, adjusted their caps on their heads, and strode grimly towards us. I reached for the ignition key, then immediately realised the futility of trying to outrun a motorway patrol car in a Series I Land Rover, and let my hand drop.

The nearest policeman gestured to me and I slid open the window. I was aware of his bulk and the baton on his hip, and the light gleaming on the handcuffs at his belt. His radio crackled with ignored messages. Were any of them about us, I wondered.

"Excuse me sir, is this your vehicle?"

I cursed the farmer at Mynydd Isa. Who else, I thought, could have reported the passage of Bryn's Land Rover? How else would the police know what vehicle they might be looking for? My own car, I guessed, was either still in the car park at the Cross Keys, or in the police pound being searched minutely and dusted for fingerprints. *Damn all stroppy Welsh farmers!*

"Is this your car, sir?"

The voice was less patient now. My answer was confused.

"Yes, officer. I mean, no, it belongs to a friend."

He paused, as if about to query my reply, then smiled faintly.

"You must have some good friends, to lend you a vehicle like this."

Was he being sarcastic? Out of the corner of my eye I could see his partner strolling round the back of the Land Rover. It seemed an age as I waited tensely for his questioning to continue. How much did they know, these motorway policemen? Did they know that they were involved in a murder inquiry; indeed, that they were speaking to the chief suspect? Or had they simply been told to stop Land Rovers like Bryn's?

"We used to have one of these," the policeman went on evenly. "It's a classic, isn't it? We used to take it to the Land Rover trials. A bit underpowered, though, compared to the new ones. Still, it's so nostalgic to see one. And good that it's still being used on the road."

Sweat was trickling down my armpits. What was all this about? Was he playing for time while his partner checked the details? I could hear the other copper's radio booming with incomprehensible messages. Then he came looming back to join his companion by the driver's door. He leaned menacingly over his partner's shoulder.

"Would you mind stepping out of the vehicle, sir?"

I got out slowly, debating whether to run or not. The two policemen led me to the back of the Land Rover. Was I in for a kicking? I clenched my fists. Then, slowly, realisation dawned. One of them was pointing at something.

"Look at this, sir. You've obviously been in a bit of mud recently. Which is, of course, a good place for a Landie! But your number plate and the rear lights are almost obscured. The lights are pretty small anyway on these old models. I'd advise you to clean them up before you continue. Otherwise, sir" – here he chuckled, and the sound rang incongruously in my ears – "I may have to arrest you!"

I let out a long breath. *Thank God, so they knew nothing, after all!* They had received no message about us. They were simply genuine Land Rover enthusiasts, happy to chat in the middle of a long boring shift. I could have kissed them!

"Of course, officer, of course! Thanks for pointing that out. I'll give it a good clean before we set off again."

The two of them strolled back to their Volvo, turning to

wave to us as they got in. I couldn't help wondering how they would feel later on if they realised that they had had a murder suspect in their hands and done nothing about it. Still, that was their problem. And I took back the imprecations I had heaped on the head of that little Welsh farmer. Perhaps, after all his shouting, he'd just gone back to bed.

Fort William was just waking as we got there. It was about nine o'clock and the shops were opening. We'd timed it about right, as we had some important purchases to make. You can't set off into the hills without being prepared, and we'd brought nothing with us.

I'd shaken Edie from her slumber as we came over the summit of Rannoch Moor. She had fallen asleep to the steady rumble of the Land Rover's engine as we drove up the A74, through Glasgow and up the winding shore of Loch Lomond. As we crested the top of the moor the sun was rising in a clear sky, although mist lay like pale rags over the cold bogs and lochans that sprinkle that great expanse of wilderness. The summit of Buachaille Etive Mor, sheathed in snow, shone pink in the growing light, and the Three Sisters of Glencoe brooded over us as we descended to the narrows at Ballachulish, where the sea loch lapped into the heart of the hills.

"It's beautiful," Edie murmured. She'd never seen the Western Highlands before. "But I'm cold!"

Now, parked between the main street of Fort William and the little by-pass which edges Loch Linnhe. I made a shopping list while Edie snuggled against me, more in an attempt to keep warm than out of affection We needed sleeping bags, a stove, cooking pots, warm clothes, rucksacks, food ... The list was long. I decided against a tent, hoping to use an old mountain bothy I knew of.

When I'd finished the list, we walked up to the end of the main street, where I knew there was an outdoor shop which also had a café. Gratefully, we settled down with a cooked breakfast and a cafetière of coffee. Edie had bags under her eyes and her hair was a mess. The side of her face was an interesting colour by now. There was vulnerability about her, which in spite of, or because of the situation between us, and the uncertainty of our position, inspired a surprising feeling of tenderness in me. We still spoke little, and she seemed prepared to let me take the decisions about what to do next.

Revived by the food, we made our purchases. I looked for good value equipment, not worrying too much about its weight, as I envisaged simply carrying it once to the place I had chosen for our hideaway. We bought some cheap boots, looking for comfort rather than high specifications, since we weren't intending to go mountaineering. The pile of stuff looked daunting, and the bill was quite large. I hadn't much cash left, and my cheque book was at home. I handed over my credit card, and signed the slip ruefully, thinking of all the equipment I already had back at my house. I shrugged mentally. What else could I do? At least the shop didn't have an electronic till with a card-reader linked to a computer.

"Was it a good idea to pay by credit card?" Edie's voice was quizzical.

"Probably not. But have you got enough cash to pay for all this?" I gestured at the pile of equipment.

"No, of course not!"

"So what choice have we got?"

"Can't the police trace a credit card purchase like this?"

"I should think so, eventually. But I would guess that when they're using those signed slips it takes at least a week, maybe longer, before they send them off. So we should be all right for a while. But I don't really know."

We carried our purchases back to the Land Rover, then went to the supermarket to buy food to last us as long as possible. Dried food, sauces, pasta and rice and porridge went into the basket, along with easily cooked vegetables such as peppers, tomatoes and mushrooms to cheer up our meals. Dried milk, tea, coffee were amongst the essentials, and, as an afterthought, candles and a bottle of single malt whisky. It would be hard work carrying all the food into the hills, but at least I was confident that we wouldn't starve for a while. I left Edie to load the food into the Land Rover, and went to find a phone

Bryn answered after the first couple of rings. He didn't have much new to tell me. The police had come to the farm and questioned him, but he had deflected their enquiries and convinced them that we hadn't passed that way. He had gathered that I was the prime suspect in Phil's death, and that they knew nothing of the two men that I was sure were the true criminals.

"I'm doing what I can," he went on. "I've rung a couple of contacts already, and I've a few more I can try. It would help, though, if you can give me any more leads, Mark. I got the impression last night that you knew more than you wanted to say, at least in front of Edie."

"You're right, Bryn. I've got a theory of my own."

Then I quickly told him about my visit to Peter Ashby, my feeling that it was he who had set these men on me and my family, either to gain recompense or simply as an act of revenge. I said a little about what had happened between myself and Edie, and how I was unsure of her role in this. At that stage I didn't want to tell him that she was my half-sister, though. That needed some thinking through and a heart-to-heart with Edie herself. I hoped we'd have time for that over the next few days.

"I think I need to pay Peter Ashby a little visit," Bryn went on grimly. "It's certainly the best lead we've got. I'll find out what I can. Ring me the day after tomorrow, if you can get to a phone."

I hung up and walked slowly back to the car park. The sun was rising in the sky and the air was warming up, but weariness was catching up with me. Edie was sitting in the passenger seat waiting for me. She gave me a tentative smile as I got in and reached down for the ignition key to start the engine. I was just about to put it in gear when she called out.

"Stop! Stop, Mark, I've just remembered what we forgot to buy. *Matches!* No point having all that food if we can't light the stove. I'll go and get some. I've got enough cash for that in my handbag."

I switched off the engine, and she turned as if to pick up her bag, then stopped suddenly and put her hand to her head in a gesture of frustration and anger.

"Shit! Shit! I haven't got it! I must have left it in the cottage when we rushed out. It's got everything in it. My cards, my address book... everything. Shit!"

I certainly couldn't remember seeing her with it since we left Maes-y-Bryn, but it didn't seem like the end of the world to me. Where we were going there wasn't much call for credit cards.

"Don't worry, Edie, I've got a bit of cash."

I fumbled some coins out of my trouser pocket and handed them to her. She took them, slid out of the door and disappeared back up towards the main street. I rested my head against the door pillar and closed my eyes. Jumbled images danced unbidden across the inside of my eyelids as my subconscious fought for the dreams it had been denied for most of the last twenty four hours. I'd almost drifted off to sleep when Edie opened the door and climbed in again, brandishing a couple of large boxes of matches.

I yawned, shook myself and started the engine again. We turned out of the car park and headed out of Fort William on the road to Gairlochy. The great hump of Ben Nevis towered into the sky behind us, but we were going into the wilder lands further west, where we could lie up for a long time if necessary and never be found. Or so I thought.

Chapter Twelve

The trees of the Dark Mile near Achnacarry enfolded us in almost subaqueous green shadows as we drove slowly along the narrow road to Loch Arkaig, and the peaty brown waters of the burn thundered endlessly in the waterfall as we crossed the old stone bridge. It was a beautiful morning of what would normally have been heart-lifting clarity, ideal to be heading for the hills; but instead we were brooding, distracted and exhausted.

The long, bumpy road along the lochside is a dead end, and so has managed to preserve its feeling of remoteness. Only a few little caravans, permanently installed in small clearings in the woods, and inhabited mainly by fishermen in the summer months, give a hint that it is not entirely undiscovered. We drove most of the length of the loch, dazzled intermittently by the sunlight shimmering on the slight breeze-driven waves, until we reached the last of the trees.

I pulled off then to the side of the road, and drove as far as I could out of sight into the birch scrub. The silence when I turned off the engine was like a heavy presence. We sat quietly for a while without moving, reluctant at first to tackle the job of sorting all our gear, loading it into the rucksacks and setting off on the long walk into the wilderness.

Finally, we stirred ourselves and moved. We got everything we had bought out of the Land Rover and started to sort it out. Edie was moving as if in a dream, and I wasn't much better. With the sun on our backs we made up our loads, discarding surplus cardboard and plastic wrappings from the food supplies, and started to pack our rucksacks. I was anxious now to get going. Haste made us clumsy, and weariness was in our bones.

"Can we make a cup of tea?" Edie's voice, when she spoke, was strained, almost tearful, and pleading.

I hesitated, then thought, *Why not? After all, what difference would a few minutes make?* I got out the stove and took my water bottle to fill it at a clear little burn that trickled through the woodland on its way to the loch. We settled ourselves on our camping mats and sleeping bags while the water boiled in the billy-can.

The hot tea was wonderful, and I broached a packet of biscuits for us to share. Warmed by the sun that filtered through the leafless branches, I lay back comfortably, drained my mug and put it down. Edie's eyes were closed, and I felt sleep tugging remorselessly at my own eyelids. What harm could it do to close them for a moment?

I woke with a start, shivering. I looked up through the trees. The sun was obscured now by cloud, but I could tell that it was well past its zenith, and sliding down the sky. Edie was wrapped in her sleeping bag, still soundly dreaming by the look of it. It was an effort to move, but I did so, dismantling the stove and loading it with the mugs and billies into my rucksack. I let Edie sleep as long as possible, then gently shook her awake.

"Time to be going," I whispered.

She got up stiffly and reluctantly, and we packed the sleeping bags and mats away. Then it was time to set off, leaving the Land Rover hidden in the wood, shouldering our packs and heading on foot, like other fugitives before us, for the hidden folds of the hills. Prince Charlie came this way after Culloden, stumbling through the bogs in buckled shoes, heading for Glen Pean, and many months more of hunted wandering until he finally made his escape back to France.

The surfaced road ends before the head of the loch, and a track continues on past the abandoned houses at Strathan and forks right into Glen Dessarry. Some distance further along the glen, the track ends at Upper Glendessarry House and a footpath continues indistinctly up the wide glen beyond.

Our breathing noisy in our ears, we climbed steadily into the hills, the path rising ever higher above the burn in the valley bottom. We crossed several tributaries, scrambling down into the gullies and, with an effort, up the other side. In some places the going was soft underfoot and the muddy turf slippery; in others the bare rock slabs showed through the grass and heather. Edie, unbalanced by the unaccustomed weight of her pack, found it hard and frustrating work, and cursed several times under her breath. But at least that was better than sobbing. It showed she had the toughness to get angry rather than just give up.

The afternoon was well advanced by the time we reached the summit of the climb at the pass of the Bealach na Cloich Airde. We slipped off our packs, and sat gratefully on the boulders by the side of the path. We ate a couple of bananas and swigged water from our bottles. Despite the cloud, there was little wind, and we were both warm from exertion. Sweat from the rucksack straps had left damp marks on Edie's shirt, and she grimaced as she wriggled her shoulders and rubbed them to try to ease the stiffness. We spoke little.

Silence pressed in upon that remote spot. No birds sang, nothing moved, and the chuckle of the burn was muted. The only sound was the whisper of the slight breeze in the rough grass. The steep hillsides sloped up inscrutably before and behind us, littered with the rocky debris of countless millennia. Evil, death, and the dangerous preoccupations of men, already seemed a distant memory.

Suddenly I started. An unexpected movement had caught the corner of my eye. We were being watched! The adrenalin surged as I swung round, my heart racing, in time to see a red deer stag, as large as a small pony, bounding effortlessly across the mountainside. I slowly relaxed again, and then, joyously, I saw others; twenty or thirty deer moving away, pausing to gaze inquiringly at us, then loping gracefully and noiselessly away, and vanishing into a fold in the hill. We were left with the rustle of the grass and the peaty scent of a Highland glen. I couldn't, however, help a slightly uneasy feeling. What other unseen eyes might be watching our progress?

"Come on, Edie," I muttered, swinging my pack onto my back again.

"Let's go before we get cold. In any case, I'd like to be down at Loch Nevis before nightfall."

She gave me a bleak look, screwed the top back on her water bottle and got ready to follow.

We carried on, gently downhill now, passing close to the two shining lochans cradled in the narrow valley. A little further on we crossed to the other side of the burn, part wading, part boulder hopping, and picked up a better path trending easily down the mountainside through the heather. We crossed a final rise, and then, by unspoken mutual consent, stopped, awestruck, in our tracks to take in the scene below.

It was getting close to sunset now, and the afternoon's sullen clouds were finally lifting again, like a pale grey theatre curtain with a darker bottom edge. The sun itself was still hidden, but below this edge, the visible rays of the sun shone out in a gold fan, spreading their touch over mountainside, sand shore and sea loch.

Where the light touched the scattered boulders, they gleamed pale grey, almost white, propped by dark shadows against the green and russet hills; and seams of quartz glittered with unnatural brightness across the rock faces. Half a mile away, down the slope below us, the beaten silver of Loch Nevis crawled with motionless waves, like drying oil paint tugged into ripples by the painter's invisible finger, and the water lapped in distant silence on a shining crescent of perfect white sand. Further away still, the loch curved out of sight through the narrows at Kylesknoydart, hemmed by the slopes which rose on either side to long ridges marching down towards the Atlantic.

"You were right," Edie murmured. "It is so beautiful. I've never seen anything like it."

She closed her eyes briefly, breathed deeply and opened them again. She seemed to have regained some of her normal cheerfulness, and turned to smile warmly, if a trifle wryly, at me. She hefted the weight on her back, and then it was her turn to exhort me.

"All right, Mark, let's go. Let's get to our new home before dark."

The old wooden door of the bothy creaked on its iron hinges as it swung open. It had been closed but not locked, and inside there were signs that it might have been recently occupied by mountaineers. A couple of used gas cylinders and some empty packets of camping food left behind by thoughtless people were evidence of a previous visit. I was angry at the rubbish, but pleased at the same time that they had, by chance or design, left some wood for the fire. There didn't appear to be any sign of habitation at the moment. I breathed a sigh of relief.

The bothy was a squat stone building of one room, with a roof of rusted corrugated iron held down by cables lashed to heavy stones outside. There was a stone-flagged floor, a fireplace at one end and a raised sleeping platform with room for two people in comfort or four at a pinch. In front of the fireplace, someone had set a short plank across a couple of logs to form a makeshift seat. Apart from the doorway, the only light came from a small window with four cracked and grimy panes.

As the sun went down, dragging with it the remaining warmth of that early spring day, I knew that the cold would come creeping up. We donned fleeces and warm hats, and while Edie set up the stove on a stone slab, I set about lighting the fire.

By the time the fire was lit and crackling up the chimney, a cup of tea was ready, and we sat together on the wobbly bench, staring into the flames, enjoying the hot drink and taking turns to swig from the whisky bottle. Just at that moment, things didn't seem so bad. I was in the Highlands, in the hills, away from danger, and sitting comfortably shoulder to shoulder with a women who meant a lot to me, one way or another. I knew we had a lot of talking still to do, and that our problems were still unresolved, but for the time being I was prepared to relax and let events take their course.

By the time we had finished our drinks, it was almost fully dark and I set about lighting some candles. An excited exclamation from Edie made me turn round, and in the beam of my head torch I saw her holding up an old candle lantern which she had found in the corner.

With that, a couple of other candles stuck in old tins which we had found, and the light from the fire, the place seemed almost cosy. We unpacked the food, and got on with preparing something to eat. Hunger and exercise are always the best ingredients of a camping meal, and we tucked in eagerly to what we would probably have turned our noses up at back home.

Afterwards, I took the pots outside to the stream to wash them, and on the way back, collected some driftwood to try to keep the fire going overnight. When I got back to the bothy, Edie was standing by the doorway, her arms folded across herself to hug in the heat, gazing pensively out over the starlit water.

"How long will we be here, Mark?"

"I don't know. It depends what Bryn's managed to find out. In one way, I hope to God it's all resolved as quickly as possible. I hope Bryn can find out definitely who hired those men, and what they're after, and clear my name with the police. I trust him to do it, and do it quickly. I'll walk to the Post Office at Inverie tomorrow and give him a ring to find out how things stand. But at the same time I feel I could easily stay here for a long time.

Just you and me and the hills."

Edie leaned against me and rested her head against my shoulder. She shivered and then gasped almost theatrically with the cold. I put my arm around her; her arm crept round my waist, and we stood in silence for a while, looking down the peaceful length of Loch Nevis, listening to the breathing of the sea on the shingle. A myriad bright stars cartwheeled imperceptibly across the night sky, fading gradually as the rising moon silvered the quiet waters.

After a while we went inside and I built up the fire as far as I could. Edie spread our camping mats on the sleeping platform, and we crept into our separate sleeping bags, still wearing most of our clothes. It was early as bedtimes go, but we were both exhausted. Our tiredness postponed any problematic exploration of our relationship, a fact for which I was quite grateful. I kissed Edie goodnight, but it was no more than a friendly peck. In minutes, or less, I was fast asleep.

When I woke the fire had almost burned away, and the first pale light was creeping through the window. Edie was still sleeping. I rolled over and crawled carefully out of my sleeping bag so as not to disturb her. I slipped my feet into my boots, picked up the empty water bottles and went to the door, easing it open to stop it creaking. Outside, the air was chill, but the sun was rising and the sky was clear. If anything, it was more still and silent than the previous evening.

I walked a little way from the bothy and peed in the heather, gazing down the loch. Too early in the year for midges, I noted with satisfaction, despite the good weather. Far out on the glassy water, I spotted a small fishing boat looking as if it had been painted into the scene to add interest. As I watched, it started up its engine, and the quiet *put-put* of the diesel carried clearly to me across the distance as it turned and headed away, its wake bright white against the grey of the loch.

I went to the stream and rinsed my hands, splashing the cold water on my face and neck. A proper wash and tooth cleaning could wait until after breakfast. I filled the water bottles and went back to the bothy, which stood squat and solid against the backdrop of rock and heather. From the stone chimney a wisp of woodsmoke from the dying fire rose vertically into the windless air.

I went inside, lit the camping stove and put water on to boil.

"What time is it?" Edie's voice was reluctant and thick with drowsiness.

"Early. But the sun's nearly up. It's a beautiful morning and I'm making tea."

Soon she was clutching a warming brew, sitting up but still huddled in her sleeping bag. She made no attempt to converse. Her face, still showing the marks of bruising, but less obviously now, was grim, and her mind was far away behind apparently unseeing eyes. For the last thirty-six hours we'd been too busy with action, and too tired and confused to talk much. Today, I sensed that all that would change. We both needed answers to try to make sense of what was going on. Together we might be able to piece together the jigsaw. We had a lot of talking to do. But first we needed breakfast.

While Edie went outside to pee, in the growing warmth of the morning, I got the porridge on and soon afterwards we were sitting on a stone bench in the sunlight in front of the bothy eating the comforting hot oats and drinking coffee.

After breakfast we did the housework together. We washed up, aired the sleeping bags and tidied the food and cooking things. Then we spent some time gathering driftwood for the fire that we would light again later that evening. An old wooden fish crate cast up on the shore was a bonus. We set the firewood we had found against the wall to dry out thoroughly, then walked up to a small stand of birch and pine trees which nestled under the steepening hillside a hundred yards or so behind the bothy. Here we added to our supply with lying dead branches which we dragged back behind us.

When we had finished, we set off for a stroll along the beach towards the mouth of the Camusrory river. We took off our boots and walked barefooted through the sand. And at last, we began to talk.

"So," I asked, taking the plunge, "where did you get to?"

"When?"

She turned puzzled blue eyes on me. The question had been on my mind for so long that it was almost a shock when Edie appeared genuinely not to understand what I meant. Although, to be fair, the question I wanted answering was not so much "where?" as "why?" And I didn't want to let her know how much I knew about her relationship with Peter Ashby, my father and myself. I wanted to hear it from her, if possible.

"After we spent the night together. At Maes-y-Bryn."

"Oh yes. That." She pursed her lips thoughtfully and paused again. After a little while she went on.

"I went to see my mother."

"Why? Why did you leave without a word?"

"I was confused."

"Not half as confused as I was when I woke up in the morning. I don't make a habit of sleeping with women I hardly know. In fact I don't make a habit of sleeping with anyone these days. But that night was special. In more ways than one. I wanted to talk to you. I wanted to know what it all meant. Why did you get me to stay in the first place?"

"I don't know. That's why I was confused. I was lonely, I suppose."

"I see," I replied rather curtly, "so in that case anyone would have done really?"

"No, no, not at all!" She stopped and turned to face me, looking up into my eyes. "I didn't mean it like that. I'd fancied you since we first met. You probably don't remember. You'd called round to see your dad on your way to Snowdonia. I think you were going climbing. You seemed quite excited about it. You said hello, but you were much more interested in talking to your dad. Then we met again once or twice after that."

"But you gave she impression you didn't remember me to begin with when I called to see you at the cottage."

She lowered her eyelids modestly, then opened them again and looked steadily at me.

"Sorry, Mark. Typical woman, aren't I? I just didn't want to give you the idea I'd been thinking about you at all. I had no inkling either that that evening would turn out as it did. I know it shouldn't have done. But as the hours went by I realised how much I was attracted to you. And of course you were Harry's son. I suppose that's one of the reasons why I so wanted to be comforted by you. And it was also, ironically, the reason why…"

She stopped in mid sentence. She raised her hands in a gesture of helplessness, and let them fall again to her sides

"…the reason why it shouldn't have happened," I added gently.

We walked on a little way, our feet scuffing the white sand until we reached an outcropping of rock which ran down to the beach. We stopped and settled down on the tide-smoothed stone, whose contours were warmed now by the sun's rays.

"It's all right, Edie," I went on. "I know about you and Harry. I know the background. I can accept all that. What I can't understand is how you could have had an affair with him. He was your own father, for God's sake!"

She stared at me, her eyes wide and panicky. I think she was just beginning to guess at how much else I might know that she had tried to hide from me.

"So you know that? How could you …?"

"I'll tell you later," I interrupted roughly. "When you've answered me. How could you do it? How could you? It's unnatural. It's illegal. It's…it's bloody shocking. "

This time when she answered she sounded almost relieved.

"Well, the simple answer is: I didn't."

There was silence for a moment, broken only by the lapping of the waves. Then it was my turn to feel relief flooding through me. Those two words of Edie's were music to me. But I waited for her to continue. There were too many half told tales in all that had happened recently for me to accept a simple denial.

"All that stuff I told you, Mark, about moving to Tyddyn-y-bont and meeting Harry, that was all true. Except that it wasn't by accident. It was quite deliberate. I'd found out that he was my father and I wanted to be near him. I also hoped he'd help me out, to be honest. I was in a bad way generally, and short of money. He was pleased that I'd come looking for him.

"But he still didn't want to acknowledge me openly as his daughter. It would have been too complicated, too many questions to answer, too many people to be shocked. We were spending so much time together, though, that in the end word got around locally that we were having an affair. So we let them talk. It was the easiest explanation of our closeness. I think Jack was the only other person who knew the truth. And after a while, I almost began to believe it myself. You see, I'd never known Harry as my father. When I met him, I was an adult and he was a stranger, and he was very attractive to me. And, of course, because of our relationship he was always kind and loving. If I hadn't known he was my father I think I *would* have wanted to have an affair with him. I can be very impulsive."

Edie looked thoughtfully down at her hands, the fingers linked across her thighs, and stretched out straight legs, wriggling her brown toes into the warm white sand.

"So is that why you slept with me? On an impulse? Don't forget, I'm your half-brother"

She turned to look earnestly at me.

"No, Mark, no. I didn't even think about you being related to me. I'd hardly ever seen you before. To me you were just a rather gorgeous man, who I'd thought about a lot since I first met you. When you turned up on my doorstep, I couldn't believe it was happening…"

"But you made sure it did!"

"I know, I know. And it was wonderful. I don't regret it at all. But when I woke up, early in the morning, I was really worried about it. You were still asleep. I lay there watching you as the light grew and the birds began to sing in the garden. Then I got up very quietly, made myself some coffee and crept out of the house."

"And went to see your mother?"

"That's right. Who else would I go to?"

"And what did your mother say?"

"She was very understanding. She said I should follow my heart. Go back and find you and see if we could work it out."

"Work it out?" I exploded. "When you're my half-sister?"

She shrugged.

"My mother said that if you didn't know about our relationship and neither did anyone else, why should it really matter? It's not as if we'd be likely to start a family at our age, is it?"

"And where do I stand in all this? What about my feelings?"

"That would be up to you, Mark."

I was shocked, but at the same time excited. I gazed for what seemed an age at her upturned face, her eyes like a clear sky, bright blue and limitless in their possibilities, laughter lines fanning from their corners. Her hair shone pale gold in the sunlight, and her nose was wrinkled expectantly.

Then I kissed her. Her mouth was soft and her tongue eager as I pulled her against me, and it was some time before we let go of each other again. When we finally did, we remained holding hands. No words were spoken, nor needed.

After a while we strolled on along the beach, and I told Edie about my conversation with her mother, although without mentioning what I had discussed with Peter Ashby, and his reaction.

"How did you get in touch with them?" she asked, puzzled.

"You'd written the number on the pad by the phone. It went through to the next sheet. All it needed was a little detective work."

"That's typical of me," she muttered glumly. "I'm always scribbling numbers on the pad. I can never remember them, even the ones I should know well."

She went on to confirm the story of her background, growing up in Liverpool, a fragile, confused and unruly girl who gave her adoptive parents a harder time than they deserved.

"But there's more, Mark. Things you still don't know. My mother and Peter had just about adjusted to my situation – although Peter was never happy about it. I think he would have preferred to forget all about me.

"What they weren't prepared for – no parent ever is – was that I then went and got myself pregnant. There was never anything in the relationship, it was just some young man I met on a night out – I was like that then – but I was saddled with an illegitimate baby. Like mother, like daughter, some would say."

She grimaced.

"Harry had stopped paying money for me when I was twenty-one – seems old nowadays, doesn't it, to become an adult? But I was in no position to support a child. In fact, I'd had a bit of a breakdown. I suppose I was a bit fragile, mentally. So history repeated itself, as it so often does, and my mother had to persuade Harry to go on paying to support my baby."

Edie's voice began to quaver and her grip on my hand tightened and she pulled me to a halt. She turned to me and I saw that tears were running down her cheeks.

"The poor little thing was adopted, just as I had been. Then when he was about eight years old the couple who'd adopted him split up and he ended up with foster parents. But he was quite happy with them, I think, in Liverpool."

"And what was the name of your son?" I asked, although by now I was certain I already knew the answer. Her answer, when it came, was almost inaudible. I had to strain to catch it.

"Philip. It was Pete's father's name."

"Aah. Now I understand."

So much was clear now; the secret Jack had kept from Ruth Morris back in the late sixties; the money paid by my father to support Phil; the legacy of the house in Liverpool and the cottage in Wales, and the money left to Phil to atone for his growing up alone, outside the warmth and security of the family. But – and there was one very big but – what about Edie's relationship with her own son, I wondered?

"You told me you weren't related to Phil. Why did you lie to me? Why did you cover that up?"

Edie wiped away the tears and steadied her voice.

"Because there is – was – no relationship. I didn't see my son after he was taken away for adoption. I met him again for the first time after I had got to know Harry. Jack brought him out to the cottage one day. At first he had no idea who I was. Phil didn't know anything then about his relationship to Harry. He just thought he was a favourite pupil of Jack's. And he was quite smug about that. I have to say, although I knew he was my son, I didn't really like him. I found it hard to believe he was mine. And when he eventually found out about the situation – it was a slip of the tongue that gave it away in the end – he didn't much like the idea of me being his mother either. In fact, he gave every impression of hating me. It was very upsetting."

"I can imagine it must have been. I had no idea all this was going on. It's all rather hard to come to terms with."

"I know. And then the worst thing was Harry dying. I thought he might leave me the cottage at least, but it was on a joint mortgage with Jack, so it reverted to him on Harry's death. Poor Harry, he never really had a house of his own. And Jack was living in the house in Liverpool, so he kept that too.

"Then when Jack died, I know you were horrified, Mark, that he didn't leave the house and cottage to you. But I, for my part, thought he might leave the cottage to me. After all, I was living there. But no. It was all left to Phil. I'm not sure how much Jack really thought of me after all; and Phil was his protégé. So I had to start paying rent to my son, who disliked me so much and could legally have evicted me from my own house. But to be fair, he did respect the conditions of Jack's will about my tenancy."

"And now he's dead," I put in gently.

"Now he's dead, yes, and I feel sorrow, but not enough. A mother should feel more, but I can't. I don't know what to feel, I really don't."

We turned around and started to head slowly back to the bothy, seagulls wheeling overhead and oystercatchers piping at the water's edge in their neat black and white plumage. As we walked, Edie turned the conversation to our immediate plight. Who, she wanted to know, were the men who had killed her son and threatened both of us, casting us in the role of fugitives.

And so I told her the whole story, both of what I had found out for myself and my trip to Belgium, and Peter Ashby's description of the burying and the disappearance of the Nazi treasure. And I ended with a portrayal of the anger and hatred felt for Harry and his family by his old comrade-in-arms.

"So what did happen to all that treasure, Mark?"

I shrugged impotently.

"Search me, Edie. It certainly didn't come to our family. And it doesn't look as if Phil inherited it either. I think maybe Peter Ashby thinks we've got it in some secret cache. But we haven't. So even if he's sent his hit men to get us, we can't tell them anything. And after Phil's death, who knows what they're capable of!"

Reminded by our conversation of the predicament we were in, I glanced at my watch, and then at the sun, now high in the sky. I really wanted to get to a phone sometime today, and that meant a long walk. We covered the remaining distance back to the bothy a little more quickly, and had a hasty lunch of biscuits and cheese. Then I grabbed a water bottle and some cereal bars to snack on, and set off again on my own, moving swiftly round the shore, this time crossing the River Carnach at the shallows and tackling the steep climb to the pass of Mam Meadail which rises to nearly two thousand feet.

Even moving down the glen to Inverie at a pace which was not much less than a jog, it took me the best part of four hours to get there. Scotland is famous for its beautifully sited red phone boxes, and the one outside the little post office in Inverie is amongst the best. I gazed down the tranquil loch towards Mallaig as I listened anxiously to the sound of the phone ringing far away in Bryn's farmhouse. But the voice that eventually answered was Megan's.

"He's not here, Mark. He spent most of yesterday ringing contacts and waiting for answers. Then he set off very early this morning to visit Peter somebody."

"Peter Ashby?"

"Yes, that's it. Peter Ashby. Down in Leicestershire. Then he rang not too long before you did. Said he'd missed Peter Ashby, but he'd got a trail to follow. It was a bad line and he was in a hurry because he was running out of money. All I caught before he was cut off was that he was heading back North. I'm sorry, Mark, that's all I know at the moment."

It wasn't much to go on. After I had left the Post Office, I stood irresolute in the road for a moment or two. North? That could mean anything. Back to Wales, Liverpool…or Scotland? And where could Peter Ashby have got to?

As I emerged from the phone box and turned to my left to set off, a thick set man in workman's overalls came out of the Post Office and got into an Inverie estate Land Rover which was parked outside. He started the engine, then stuck his head out of the window as he passed me.

"D'ye want a lift?"

I hesitated, then glanced at my watch. It was after three o'clock already, and a long way back.

"Yes, please. That would be very kind. Are you going towards Gleann Meadail?"

"Ye're in luck. I'm going as far as the wee wood, but I can drop ye a little further on at the Inverie River crossing. Jock Hamilton's my name."

He thrust a large freckled hand out at me and shook mine with gusto. I climbed gratefully into the vehicle. This would save me a couple of tedious miles of the return journey. As we jolted up the hill, he engaged me in conversation.

"Are ye staying at the bothy, then? At the head of the loch? Calum McKay said he thought someone was up there when he called with the ferry just now. Rab Grant from Mallaig told him. He was away up there to fish last night. Said he saw smoke from the chimney and someone on the beach this morning."

It seemed pointless to deny it, so I agreed that that was where we were staying. Jock dropped me at the river bridge, and turned back down the track. I thanked him, and watched him go, a big hand waving to me from the Land Rover.

So our hiding place was common knowledge already. I'd overlooked the fact that to the few inhabitants of this wilderness landscape, the slightest thing out of place is noteworthy. I felt an urgent need to get back to Edie as soon as possible.

It was almost dark when I finally reached the bothy, stumbling with weariness. Edie had lit the fire and water for tea was boiling on the stove. Heated as I was by then with exertion, it seemed snug and warm when I came in out of the cool evening air, and almost like coming home.

I told her the inconclusive result of my phone call and she replied non-committally.

"I don't suppose it matters for the moment. Will you try again tomorrow?"

"I might do." I was conscious by now of what a long walk it was to the phone, but didn't really want to admit how tired I thought I might be in the morning.

"I might leave it until the day after. Bryn could have more news by then if he's back at the farm."

After we had eaten and washed up in the burn under the stars, we stoked the fire and sat in our sleeping bags drinking coffee. The burning wood flickered in ever changing colours and patterns at the heart of the blaze and the dancing flames cast weird shadows on the grimy bothy walls. After a while I broke out the whisky, and we sat and sipped the warming spirits as we chatted softly in a new found intimacy, although I guessed must have appeared occasionally distracted. After a while she commented sympathetically:

"You seem really anxious tonight, Mark."

"I suppose I'd really like to know what's going on out there, Edie. I hadn't really thought through how cut off we might be here."

She laughed.

"I thought that was the reason we came here. To be cut off. It doesn't matter though, does it Mark? Not for the time being. Let's just enjoy being together for the moment."

"You're right," I replied more cheerfully. No-one but a few of the locals knows we're here. And they have no idea *who* we are. So we're quite safe for the moment. Nobody, not even Bryn, knows where we are."

I was aware then of a long pause before Edie answered, in a very different tone from which all buoyancy had suddenly disappeared.

"I'm afraid...I'm afraid that's not quite true, Mark. My mother knows. And...and I think Peter may too."

"What? What are you saying?" I sat upright, startled, spilling some of my drink. "How could they know? Unless...No, tell me I'm wrong!"

"Yes, Mark." Her voice had gone very small. "I'm sorry. It was me. When I went to get the matches in Fort William I gave my Mum a quick ring. I had to tell her about Phil"

"Yes, of course you did" I said rather bitterly, "I thought you were a long time. Although I thought then it was just because I'd dozed off that it seemed so long. But for God's sake, what did you tell them?"

"I told them what you'd told me. That we were heading for Knoydart. By the sea. I heard my Mum repeat it, and I think Peter was listening. I heard him in the background. He sounded very angry."

"Oh my God!" My voice was anguished.

"I'm sorry, I'm sorry!" She was sobbing now. "I had no idea that Peter might be involved in any of this. As far as I was concerned I was just telling my Mum. In a way, it made me feel safer. At least, it did then. It doesn't now!"

There was absolutely no point in being angry. What was done was done. And there was no point in moving now. It would be too dangerous, and I was already tired from my trip to Inverie. We'd move at first light. Where to, I hadn't decided. But we could easily find somewhere else in the Highlands, I was sure of that.

I poured more whisky.

Later, when the bottle was empty, I went outside again to pee. The air was cold, the stars gleamed on the ripples on the loch and the ridges were black against the sky, but everything was still. The very slightest of breezes ruffled the grass and I could hear the call of wading birds near the shoreline and an owl hooting from the wood. No doubt other creatures were abroad, but I couldn't hear them. I turned and went back through the old wooden doorway into the comparative warmth of the bothy.

We lay in our separate sleeping bags, cuddled against each other. I could feel the shape of Edie's body against me, and I put my arm over her, holding her tight. I think we were both feeling very cautious about our relationship, although I, for one, felt better for having discussed it. But neither of us wanted to take it any further that night than a friendly cuddle. What the future would hold on that score, we could wait and see. Despite my forebodings, the effects of exercise and alcohol meant that sleep came easily that night.

Chapter Thirteen

I woke with a start and was instantly aware that it was later than I had intended. I had slept heavily and dreamlessly, lulled by exercise and the whisky I had drunk. I could see the dust motes dancing in the rays of sunlight flooding through the window and the open door of the bothy, and the air was already warm. Edie's sleeping bag lay empty beside me, and the fire was out. I sat up and rubbed my eyes, which felt sticky and blurred, peering out at the hazy view of loch, mountain and sky. There was neither sight nor sound of Edie. Hastily I shrugged myself out of my sleeping bag and swung my legs down from the platform on which we slept. I clumsily pulled on my trousers and padded barefoot out into another glorious morning.

I went to the burn where it rippled over the pebbles, and splashed some of the water over my face and neck. Somewhat revived by its clean, cold touch, I straightened up and looked around. The sun was already above the high hills, which should have made me anxious to get moving, given the danger of discovery which we faced after Edie's revelation the night before, but the almost tangible serenity of the scene calmed me and made me pause.

The sun's strengthening rays were bathing the bothy and the shore which had briefly become our home, with warmth and light. The faint, intoxicating scent of gorse floated to me from the edge of the nearby wood and the softly moving air stroked the skin of my face and arms with gentle fingers. I looked up and down the beach for Edie, and at first could see her nowhere. I shaded my eyes with my hand and squinted into the sun, down across the bright sand to the loch, where the tops of the marching wavelets sparkled with stars of golden light and shimmered in a dreamy haze. Then I saw her.

At first, against that bright background, it was difficult to make her out clearly. She was emerging from the sea's edge, rising slowly from the clear water with each stride, spray around her legs, and droplets glistening on her skin, as she raised both hands to push back her blonde hair from her face. No doubt it was icy in the water, but the air was clearly warm on her naked brown body and she made no rush for her clothes. Instead, she paused at the very edge of the loch and turned to face the sun. She spread out her arms as if to welcome its comforting warmth, then sank down in the sand and lay supine and motionless.

I watched her for a moment, and then, my breathing quickening with excitement, I began to walk slowly down the beach towards her, conscious of the grains of sand and tiny shells crunching almost imperceptibly under my bare feet. To my heightened senses the calls of waders and gulls sounded loud in my ears, and somewhere, an early bee hummed, perhaps sickening itself on the brilliant yellow flowers of the gorse.

She lay with her feet right at the edge of the lapping tide, her legs together but her arms thrown wide. In that defenceless position the flesh was taut over her belly and the swell of her ribcage, little pearls of water glittering against the skin, her nipples standing tightly up from her breasts. *Was that due to the cold of her immersion in the loch, or to something else?* To me in that slowly creeping moment of time she looked like an angel fallen from heaven. Her eyes were closed, but I could tell at once that she sensed I was there.

She half opened her eyes and gazed languidly at me as if from a secret, infinite distance, the half hidden pupils seeming almost cornflower blue between the narrowed lids. There was, perhaps, some unspoken challenge there...or was it an invitation? For she made no attempt to cover herself up, although her abandoned clothes lay in a straggled heap within reach. After a moment, still without speaking, she shifted her position slightly, letting her legs separate and moving her feet apart. I stared down at her, swallowing hard, and felt the stirring in my loins. I was aware of the blood beating in my head, but all external sounds seemed to fade, except for the persistent buzzing of that one loud bee.

Conflicting thoughts struggled in my mind. *This is your sister, your half sister, you shouldn't, you shouldn't...don't worry, we've decided that that doesn't matter...well she has...but you can't do it, not now you know...maybe not, but she's so lovely, so golden in the sunlight, so open to me...what difference will it make now...no-one need know...*

I knew at the back of my mind that time was pressing, and

that there was an urgent need for us to be on our way, but that logical reasoning was swiftly losing out to a different sort of physical urgency. Her legs appeared to move just a little further apart, and without any conscious decision I stepped between them, my bare feet pressing warmly against the inside of her ankles. In that brief moment she was perfect to me, within the overall perfection of that morning.

Desire tugged remorselessly, overpoweringly, at me. I was mesmerised by her body, my eyes moving from her now smiling face and outstretched arms, to the shadowed V at the top of her legs. Trembling with anticipation, I began to sink on one knee in the warm sand to get closer to her, stretching out my hand...

The droning of the bee suddenly seemed even louder and clearer...

"Jesus!"

I straightened up and spun on my heel, clenching my fists by my side in fury at my stupidity. Panic seized me. Behind me, Edie, startled from her languid mood, rose awkwardly and reluctantly to her knees.

"Look!" I pointed with a stabbing finger down the loch.

The droning had become a metallic roar, and now we could clearly see the motor boat speeding towards us, its bow slapping the water, the wave curving back in a white crescent on either side. *Damn, damn, damn...*

They had found us. I was immediately sure of that. Our hideaway had become a trap.

Cursing, I turned and grabbed Edie's hand, pulling her roughly to her feet. She snatched up her abandoned clothes with her other hand.

"Run!" I shouted, and we stumbled together up the sandy beach, feet sliding and toes struggling for a grip as if we were running in slow motion. I pushed her ahead of me, conscious even in this desperate situation of the way the muscles moved under the skin of her flanks and how the damp sand clung to her bare back as she ran as if for her life.

We had reached the slope of short grass below the bothy when I heard the screech of metal as the motorboat was driven straight onto the shore, its propeller grating on the small pebbles below the tideline.

We hurled ourselves in through the door and grabbed our

boots. I had left a rucksack packed with a few emergency things, and now swung that onto my shoulder.

"Come on, Edie, *come on!*"

An agonising moment passed as she hopped on one leg, tugging on trousers and throwing on her shirt, before we were ready to leap out of the door again and try to make our escape. If the window had been at the back instead of the front, I might have been tempted to try to smash it and get out that way. But we were too late anyway.

As soon as I poked my head out of the door, I heard the sharp report of a handgun, and a bullet struck the stone wall of the bothy not too far from me. They obviously meant business this time. Inwardly I cursed Peter Ashby, and Edie, who had as good as given him a map of where to find us. And as I ducked back into the bothy, the thought went rapidly through my mind, *had that performance on the beach been simply to make sure we didn't get away in time?* Perhaps I was about to find out.

I flattened myself against the wall next to the window, peering out through the cobwebbed panes. Two men were running up the beach, close now to the bothy. Even from a quick glance, I knew instantly that I had seen them before, in the Welsh hills far away. Both were fair haired, and one was wearing a black leather jacket. And both were wielding automatic pistols. As they ran, half crouching like men who might expect to be fired on in return, they called to each other in a foreign tongue. At first I couldn't make it out, then it dawned on me with awful clarity as the second man called to his faster companion.

"*Josef! Vorsicht! Er könnte ein Arm haben!*"

I froze. These men weren't English, nor were they Welsh. My mind racing to make sense of what I had just heard, I put my hand to my brow. I felt cold. What a fool I was! Suddenly it all came clear; it all made sense. These men had absolutely nothing to do with Peter Ashby, and Edie had as much reason to fear them as I had.

But who else would be interested in Nazi gold from the Second World War, and long forgotten, murdered SS men? I knew as soon as I asked myself the question. These were bitter men, ruthless, evil men, the descendants of Hitler's Nazi servants. They were certainly Germans, probably part of one of the clandestine organisations dedicated to looking after the interests of former SS members. *Odessa*, something like that. I'd read a book about it once. Men who would stop at nothing to protect their own and to get back what they believed to be theirs. But how had they found us?

Speculation was cut short as they reached the wall of the bothy, one either side of the open door. After only a second's hesitation they burst into the room, one behind the other, swivelling in opposite directions to cover all angles, pistols clasped high in both hands and knees flexed in copybook fashion. Edie jumped across to where I stood and pressed herself against me. I put my arm round her protectively

"It's them!" she screamed, shaking in fear and anger. "The men who hit me! At Maes-y-Bryn!"

"*Hände hoch!* Hands up!" Josef was shouting at us, gesturing with the barrel of his gun. "Stand not together! Hans!"

We were too slow to follow his instructions, and his partner grabbed Edie by the arm and dragged her, staggering, away from me. I raised my hands slowly, and Edie reluctantly followed suit. I noticed that in our haste, she hadn't had time to fasten her shirt.

"Search them, Hans!" Josef was saying, and Hans shifted his pistol to his left hand and ran his right over Edie's body, although with her shirt hanging open as it was, I don't know what he thought she might be hiding. He slowly checked around her back and under her armpits, then ran his hand down the outside of her legs. She grimaced as he then ran his hand firmly up between them.

When he'd finished checking Edie for hidden weapons, he did the same to me, finding nothing. Even my Swiss Army knife was in a pocket of my rucksack. They seemed to relax a bit more when they had finished searching us, but I was the first to speak.

"What do you want? Why are you following us? Why did you kill Phil?"

At this, the one whom I'd heard called Josef laughed

"You think it was us who have killed him? Not the English police, they don't think that. Your police! They think you have done it! They search for you. But we find you first!"

"How did you find us?" I couldn't resist the question.

"Thank Edie. We have taken her handbag from that cottage when we came to speak to her. She has not noticed. But in it she had an address book. We have found "Mum" there and been to visit. Nice people, they tell us Knoydart. So now come to look. In Mallaig, ferryman mention people stay here. So we come, say hello." He grinned humourlessly.

"What have you done to them? What have you done to my Mum?" Edie's voice was frantic.

"Nothing. Don't worry. They tell us, so we do nothing. Otherwise, Mum maybe very ill. Maybe even dead. Your father, old man, very frightened. He do exactly what we say. Very helpful!"

Edie's face was tense and tight with emotion. She half lowered her arms and took a couple of paces forward.

"You bastards!" She spat the words in Josef's face. He stared at her calmly, but Hans placed a hand against her chest and pushed her roughly back across the room.

I tried to imagine the scene in the Ashby's quiet semi-detached house, the threats at gun point and the terror reaching across the years, haunting Peter Ashby long after he thought it was all forgotten. Except that he had never forgotten it either, for different reasons. But Josef's description of him as very frightened did not fit well with my memory of him. Quiet and elderly he might be; worried for his wife's safety, naturally; but not, it seemed to me, a man who scared easily. If he had given them the information he had, perhaps there was a reason for it.

"You still haven't told me what you're looking for, what you want from me." I tried to make my voice as normal and conversational as I could.

"You don't know?" Josef laughed grimly again. "Perhaps you forget the things your father stole. Our things. Took from my grandfather and his comrades when he kill them."

"Your things? That's a funny way to describe all those treasures the Nazis stole from the people of France! Stole or bought with the blood of innocent men and women." I thought of the ransacked churches and bank vaults, the betrayals, the silent bodies swinging from lamp posts in small French towns, and the anger surged inside me.

"Those things? Legitimate spoils of war" – the phrase was obviously well rehearsed, and his tone dismissive – "These things they were entitled to take. But then your father kill and steal everything."

I was astounded by the fiction he had convinced himself of.

"Well," I replied, "wherever it came from in the first place, I've no idea where it ended up!"

"Liar!" He stepped closer to me and brandished the pistol uncomfortably near to my face. "You know where it went!"

"I'm sorry, I really can't help you." I tried to stay calm and reasonable. He remained standing inches away, his face thrust at mine. His mouth was clamped tight shut as if to suppress his fury, but his eyes were bulging and staring. Out of the corner of my eye I could see Edie looking at me with puzzlement. *How much did she really know about all this?*

"You must know! Your brother leave everything to Phil. But he has not got it."

"Phil's dead, remember. You killed him. And I'm damn sure he never had all your precious gold either."

"Maybe not, maybe not…" He sounded less sure now. "So you must have it."

"And if I've got it, what makes you think I haven't changed it all into cash and spent it, or given it away? What do you know that makes it worth while coming here to Britain, killing, risking arrest and imprisonment for something that may no longer exist?"

But an idea had already crossed my mind after the burglary at our house. The men were not just looking for gold or treasure. They were looking for something specific that they guessed was in my possession. The thought began to crystallise gradually in my mind as I spoke. A memory came to me of musty German documents amongst my father's things, official, boring lists … unimportant, apparently, at the time, but perhaps teeming with hidden significance …

"Or is there something in particular you are looking for? If so, perhaps you should tell me what it is. Then maybe I can find it and we can come to some sort of deal over it." I tried to sound conciliatory.

"*Vielleicht.* Perhaps." He looked across at Hans and ran his tongue nervously over his lips. He shifted his grip on the butt of his pistol. Then he must have come to a decision.

"There is one thing that we want, Mr Gilgarran A file. Stolen from my grandfather's SS unit along with everything else. A list of names. Important to my organisation. It means nothing to you or anyone else. But we've been looking for it for a while. A long while." He was attempting to sound casual now. *If it was all so casual, why were they killing for it?*

"And if I give it to you?"

"We can, as you say, have an arrangement. Maybe, after all, no violence necessary. But I tell you" – his voice was harsh and stern again – "any problem from you, your friend die."

He swung the gun slowly until it was pointing at Edie's stomach.

"Now, where is it? You tell me!"

I took a deep breath and thought hard. Where was that file? I searched my memory. I remembered finding it and putting it on one side while I went through the letters and so on.

Yes…then I'd put it back in the box. And the box…I'd put in the boot of the car. I'd driven to Belgium and back, I'd been to Liverpool, home to Yorkshire, then to Leicestershire and back to Liverpool. And all the time that box of documents had been in the boot of my car. It had been there when our house was burgled – that made sense now, as well. And it had still been there when I rushed off to Maes-y-Bryn to find Edie, finally leaving the car in the car park of the Cross Keys, most likely to be found later by members of the constabulary.

Suddenly and inappropriately, I laughed out loud. Josef and Hans started nervously, tightening their grip on their pistols, and Edie gave me a sour look of incomprehension. It wasn't funny at all, really, but if my reasoning was sound, those almost certainly incriminating documents that our German friends wanted back so badly, were already in the hands of the British Police.

The catch now was that, without revealing the identity and the doings of Josef and Hans, I would have difficulty convincing the police of my innocence of Phil's murder, especially after my flight from the scene of the crime. And if Josef and Hans remained hidden, the chance of Bryn persuading the police was equally small.

But the immediate danger was that if I revealed the probable current whereabouts of the file, the Germans might see no further use for either of us. An image of two bodies being dumped at night in the loch swam before my eyes. I hesitated.

"Where is the file, Mr Gilgarran? *I'm waiting!*" Josef's voice was perceptibly more impatient now, the gun waggling ominously in front of me. The silence was broken only by the sound of our breathing, and somewhere outside, far off, beyond our little world of fear and menace, the gentle put-put of a fishing boat's motor as it crossed and re-crossed the loch.

"It's in my car." I was stalling, trying to think what to say next. "It's hidden in a disused quarry in North Wales."

If I could get them to take us back down there, and I could find a way to contact Bryn, maybe the police could catch them red-handed with us as prisoners. I hoped that would convince them that I wasn't the guilty party. But it might not be too easy to engineer. They would watch us like hawks. After a moment's reflection, Josef replied.

"Can you take us there?"

He was falling for it.

"Of course. But what's in it for us?"

"Your lives! What else?" Josef grinned cruelly. I thought I saw Edie wince.

Inevitable really. My bargaining position isn't too great at the moment, I thought.

The moments crawled by. No doubt we were all thinking furiously in the silence, working out the different implications of any course of action. I knew that if I led them to the file, they would have no further use for us, and would most likely dispose of us to cover their tracks. At the same time, they needed us, and particularly me, alive until the file was in their possession. That was the only strength in my position, but I would have to appear to co-operate, otherwise they would doubtless get rid of both myself and Edie.

Turning all this over frantically in my mind, I glanced out of the window, looked away, and then, astonished at what I thought I had just seen, carefully turned my eyes and looked again. The fishing boat I had heard was now drawn up at the edge of the water, close to the two Germans' motor boat. A man in fisherman's clothes was calmly tidying mooring ropes and making everything ship shape on his boat. But that, surprising though it was, was not the most remarkable thing I could see.

For closer to me, already crossing the stretch of grass that separated the beach from the bothy, was the slight figure of an elderly man, crouching as he walked and carrying something shrouded in an old sack. As I watched, fascinated, he paused and in one movement drew out the contents, letting the sack fall where he stood. The sunlight gleamed on dull metal and as he grasped it at hip level with practised ease I recognised the outline of a World War Two Sten gun. So Peter Ashby had found us as well. Relief was my first emotion, followed by fear of the violence that might be about to take place.

I didn't have long to contemplate all that. Peter Ashby reached the wall of the bothy in a few more strides, and from where I stood, still with my hands raised, I could see him through the open doorway, hidden from the sight of Josef and Hans, who were facing in the opposite direction. Ashby saw me at once, and raised his index finger to his lips, warning me to give no hint of his presence.

Josef was speaking again.

"So, Mr Gilgarran. You have make your mind up? You help us to find the file, and you may live. You will have good times still with your woman. If not, perhaps it is we who have good times with your woman before you die."

He laughed coarsely and eyed Edie lewdly as he spoke, but I was not about to have the chance either to answer him or to feel anger at his threats.

In one swift movement, Ashby swung into the bothy, the sunlight streaming blindingly through the door around him, crouching and screaming at the top of his voice. He fired one round into the roof, and the detonation was deafening in that confined space. Josef and Hans, startled and disorientated by this sudden apparition, turned to find themselves staring down the barrel of an old, but seemingly still lethal submachine-gun.

"Drop the guns! Drop the guns!" Ashby shouted in the voice of someone very near the edge of real violence.

The two Germans didn't hesitate to obey, letting fall their pistols with a clatter on the stone floor, and raising their hands in turn.

I bent to retrieve the guns

"Not so fast, Gilgarran!" Ashby jerked the Sten in my direction, and stepping forward, kicked the two hand guns into the corner of the room.

"Stay back. My quarrel's with you as well!"

Having a machine-gun, even a very old one, pointed at your chest makes for a very powerful argument and, shocked and scared by Ashby's words, I stepped immediately back again and raised my hands, fear flooding through me in a way I had not felt when threatened by Josef's pistol. Then, I felt I had some chance of bargaining my way out of it. Now, on the other hand, I was facing an unpredictable threat.

Did Ashby wish to bargain, or had he come to kill me? I remembered his threatening words to me in that tea shop so far away in Leicestershire. For the first time in my life, I felt in real danger of opening my bowels instinctively through pure terror. I realised that I didn't want to die. Josef and Hans, pressed back against the wall, didn't look too confident now either.

I glanced out of the window. The fisherman was standing in the shallow water, one hand on the gunwale of his boat, staring up the beach in consternation. He had obviously heard the shot and the shouting, but, irresolute, unsure what to do, he was a motionless picture of consternation. I guessed Ashby had hired him without telling him what he was getting involved in. At that moment I desperately hoped he would do something, anything, to get me out of this situation.

I tried to steady my voice.

"Where did you get the gun, Ashby? I thought that was more a commando weapon. You were regular infantry, weren't you?"

"It's surprising how many weapons came back from the War, Gilgarran, one way or another. You never knew when one might come in handy. Like now."

"What do you want, Ashby?"

"You know what I want, Gilgarran!" His voice was scornful. "You know what your father stole from me!"

"I've told you, I know nothing about that!"

"And as if that wasn't enough," he went on, not listening to me, "you shag my daughter and murder my grandson!"

I stared at him uncomprehendingly.

"Your daughter?"

"Yes, my daughter. Edie." He laughed harshly, bitterness spilling out of the sound. I turned to look at Edie, whose mouth had fallen open in an almost comical O of amazement. So she didn't know either.

"But I thought…"

"I know what you thought, Gilgarran. And what we made your father think too. Does that make it better or worse? But yes,

Edie's my daughter. After the War I couldn't afford to look after her. I was bitter. I blamed your father for my lack of funds. So I made sure he paid for his betrayal in the long term. It wasn't hard to convince him. I think he almost wanted to believe it."

Relief that Edie was not my half-sister after all flooded through me and made me almost want to smile; but that emotion wrestled within me with fury at what Ashby had done to my father

"So my dad thought all that time that Edie was his daughter. And he had to pay out money for her when he had a family of his own to support?"

"It served him right, the thief."

He spat viciously on the stone floor. I couldn't believe that any man could have given up his daughter in cold blood like that, and harboured such a grudge for so many years. Yet, at the same time a rational part of me was genuinely relieved at this sudden revelation that Edie was not my sister or my half sister; in fact, was not related to me at all. It meant that there was nothing to stand in the way of our relationship. Except a Sten gun pointed at me, and as I remembered a moment later, feeling ashamed and aghast that I could forget, even momentarily – my marriage to Jenny.

Peter Ashby was speaking again, hatred spitting from the corners of his mouth.

"You're a bastard, Gilgarran, a bastard like your father. First he steals my money, then you take my daughter…"

"Hang on, Ashby, you know it wasn't like that…"

"Oh wasn't it? So why was she so upset that she came running back home to tell her mother? I couldn't believe it!" His voice was rising as he worked himself up to a new pitch of fury.

"And then, and then…you find out that Phil has inherited your family's money. So you murder him! My little grandson!"

There were tears in his eyes. He beckoned to Edie to come and stand by him. She stayed motionless, and he gestured again, impatiently now. White faced and shaking, this time she obeyed.

"I'm going to kill you, Gilgarran. It's what you deserve."

"Don't be ridiculous, Ashby." My voice was trembling. "You'll never get away with this."

"Won't I? Don't be too sure of that. With all the confusion about what's gone on here, who knows what these two German gentlemen may be accused of. And I'll decide what happens to those two bastards when I've dealt with you. And in any case," he added chillingly, "what makes you think I care whether I get away with it or not? Killing you will be satisfaction enough for me."

He moved the Sten forward in his grip, the barrel aimed at my chest. I stared helplessly at the dark circle of the muzzle. It seemed to grow as I watched. I could see Ashby's finger stroking the trigger, preparing to squeeze it, and waited for the agonising moment when he would finally fire. My mouth was dry and my pulse was racing, the blood beating in my temples.

How had it come to this? To die at the hands of my father's wartime comrade. How could that happen? A man who had shared so much with my father, a man who owed his life to my dad…how could all that comradeship turn to wasted lives and so much hatred! I thought back over recent events…just over a week ago – a long week ago – I had been nothing but a teacher with slightly rocky marriage and a predictable job in a pleasant Yorkshire school…and now, on the one hand there was Edie and all the excitement that went with that…and on the other…unfathomable secrets…intrigue…death…

The tension was almost unbearable. I perceived an age, outside the constraints of normal time, in which nothing was happening. Then many things happened all at once.

Edie, as if making an almost impossible choice between two impulses, threw herself, with a rending cry, in front of Peter Ashby, knocking the submachine-gun sideways. Simultaneously, I heard the rattle of the Sten as it loosed several rounds, one of which smashed a pane in the window; then a deafening bang as the ancient gun exploded in Ashby's hands.

Edie fell into my arms with a moan and I lowered her inert body to the ground. Through the smoke of the detonation I could see Peter Ashby slumped against the opposite wall, bleeding and obviously seriously injured by the blast from the ruptured gun, if not already dead. And the two Germans, Josef and Hans, reacting quickly, were already scrabbling on the floor in the shadows of the corner to find their pistols.

I knelt by Edie. She was unconscious but breathing, and through her ripped shirt I could feel blood on her back. She was obviously badly hurt, but I guessed that her injuries weren't life threatening. As I crouched there, the boatman burst into the bothy, panting and clumsy in his long boots. Thrust into a situation for which nothing had prepared him, he looked around the room, his expression startled and fearful, trying to make sense of it. It must have taken some guts even to come and see what had happened, but fishermen, by the nature of their calling, are courageous and pretty resourceful.

For a moment he was between me and the two Nazis, and I took my decision quickly. I knew that Josef and Hans were interested only in me and my information, Peter Ashby looked to be already beyond anybody's help, and I hoped the fisherman would have a radio on his boat to call for help for Edie. I had to leave her. It was hard, but I had to do what was best for all of us. I had to run while I still had the chance. I straightened up, grabbed my rucksack and launched myself headlong through the door.

Behind me, Josef and Hans were struggling to get past the fisherman's burly form, and by the time they got through the door and turned the corner of the bothy, I was into my stride and running hard towards the wood.

Chapter Fourteen

Seen from a boat crossing the mouth of Loch Nevis, the sharp cone of Sgurr na Ciche comes slowly into view, stabbing the sky like an Alpine peak, perfectly framed by the wild hills on either side. The small village of Inverie and its fields and woods stretching towards the Long Beach look to have been crowded down to the sea's edge by the encroaching wilderness of the Rough Bounds of Knoydart. Towering into a sky hazed by heat and distance, Sgurr na Ciche looks like an illustration from a fairy story, ethereal and misty blue, home to elves and unicorns, beckoning yet unreal, locked distantly and inaccessibly behind a mazy barrier of hills.

Zoom in though, and from the head of the loch it swiftly becomes a solid, challenging mountain, a magnet for Munro collectors, rough slopes of grass and heather narrowing to a stony summit, the path finally zigzagging through steep rock bands to reach the very top, more than three thousand lung-searing feet above its sea-lapped base.

Get closer still and the hill narrows down to the next few yards of tussocky grass and a constant scanning for the best line of ascent, using deer tracks where they appear, abandoning them again when they veer off the chosen route, picking a way around bogs and low bluffs, climbing all the time.

This was my home ground and I felt comfortable here. Although I had no clear plan, I felt confident that on the heights I could outmatch the two Germans in their town clothes and unsuitable footwear, drawing them away from the bothy and onto terrain where I hoped, one way or another, that I could get the better of them.

I crashed, panting, through the undergrowth and fallen branches of the little wood, feet sliding on hidden roots and clutched at by brambles. The trees were mature, a mixture of Scots pines and deciduous trees and I was able to pick a swerving course through the cover. I must have been out of sight, for no shots were fired. Beyond the wood, the hillside rose steeply at first, grass interspersed with small crags and patches of bare, glacier-polished slabs. If I could climb over the brow to the easing of the ridge beyond the first rise before Josef and Hans cleared the wood, I knew I stood a good chance.

I went at it hard, gaining height quickly with vigorous but careful strides, zigzagging slightly up the slope to make the best use of my foot placements. The sun was high in the sky, there was little wind, and I was soon sweating. Although I had had a long walk the day before, I had woken refreshed by my long sleep. I knew that I had good basic mountain fitness from many mountaineering trips over the years, and the adrenalin gave an added effortless surge of energy. I climbed that hillside very fast, hands occasionally pressing on my knees to give extra leverage, sometimes grasping at rock edges as I picked my way between the outcrops.

I crested the brow with relief, and risked a glance back. The two Nazis were just emerging from the wood. Behind them I could see the bothy by the shore, and as I watched the fisherman appeared, carrying what I guessed was Edie in his arms, walking with short hasty steps under his load and heading for the beach and his boat. I prayed that she would be all right. Then I turned quickly and carried on, moving faster now on the gentler slope.

The ridge was flatter here for a while, and a lochan lay cradled under the next steepening a couple of hundred yards away. I crossed that area with long strides, sinking slightly into the soft ground and relishing, even in those circumstances, the fresh scent of crushed bog myrtle under my boots. I uttered a secret prayer of thanks for the recent good weather, which had rendered the boggy ground merely spongy, but wet enough, I hoped, to be a problem for Josef and Hans in their town shoes.

Part way up the next craggy section of the ridge, I looked back. Far out on the loch, I could see the fishing boat heading out from the shore towards the narrows. My pursuers were clearly in sight now, small figures lost on that great sweep of grass, but too far back to take a worthwhile shot at me. In any case, I argued, why would they try to kill me now? They still needed the information I had. There would be time for killing later. I pressed on, more relaxed now. I knew they wouldn't catch me now on that mountain until a time of my choosing.

I reached a subsidiary peak on the long ridge, and standing on that high point I quickly swung off my pack. I had dried dates and apricots in the top pocket, and I ate a few mouthfuls of those, then drank deeply from my water bottle. I scanned the hillside below, and saw the two Germans, still dogged in their pursuit. In the still air I faintly heard them as they called to each other, like hounds on a scent. I had been climbing hard for nearly an hour. I put the bottle away, dropped down the little saddle beyond and contoured steeply to the east into the gully between Sgurr na Ciche and Garbh Chioch Mhor.

Reaching the saddle of Fidean na Ciche I could look northwards down the rough rocky bowl of Coire nan Gall towards Loch Quoich. The chill breeze blowing through the shadowy gap on even this still day rendered its English name, often translated as *the Whistle,* appropriate. Slowly now, keeping my breathing steady, I climbed the last rough section of path up to the summit cone.

When there was nowhere higher to go I stopped on that neat rocky peak, turning to survey the hawk's eye view of the surrounding land. To the north, east and south, majestic mountains marched away to the edge of sight. To the west, the gleaming waters of Loch Nevis led the eye towards the sea and the isles of the Hebrides. I was warm with exertion, but the air was cold in my nostrils. As I turned, taking in the breathtaking panorama, I felt as if the world was spinning dizzyingly below me. But the awe-inspiring nature of the vista could not distract me from what I had to do.

My plan, such as it was, had evolved as I was climbing. I would lead the two Germans onto the summit by what was clearly the only feasible route, then bypass them, using my rock climbing skills to traverse the crags on the north side of the peak, regain the saddle and head down again while they were still searching for me up here. Even if they spotted me, by then I would be so far ahead that they would never get near to catching me on the descent.

I had another bite of food, and slipped on my windproof jacket. I didn't have long to wait. Soon I heard the sound of voices calling and then stones being clumsily dislodged underfoot, and knew that they were climbing the last section of scree path. They would soon be in sight. I didn't hesitate any longer. I ducked down the slope to the north side of the peak, and carefully began to descend the steep grass ledges. As I did so, I gave a last backward glance and caught a quick glimpse of Josef cautiously approaching the highest point of the mountain, outlined against a blue sky feathered now with wisps of high cirrus cloud. I imagined that he expected to find me trapped there, unable to find another way down. Well, I intended to surprise him.

The slope I was on was exceedingly steep, composed of slippery grass, unstable turf ledges and shattered rock. Normally I wouldn't have dreamed of venturing onto such dangerous ground, but in this case there was no alternative. I worked my way carefully downwards, placing my feet across the slope and angling my upper body outwards, digging in the edges of my boot soles as far as I could, like a skier on a traverse.

Gradually the rock outcrops became firmer and more consistent and I was able to scramble across them, working my way back eastwards all the time. However, it was steep work, and several times I had to pause and steady my nerves, calling on all my reserves of rock climbing experience. There was moss and lichen on these untrodden rocks, and damp leached from plant filled cracks. And all the time, beneath my feet, the drop beckoned me, sweeps of broken cliff falling to jumbled scree slopes and far, far below, an apron of rough brown grass and dead bracken.

I wondered what Josef and Hans were doing, out of sight. Were they by now pacing nervously, waiting, glancing at their watches, wondering where I had gone to and where I would re-appear; or were they searching the slopes for me? Were they still together, or had they split up, hoping to ambush me in this remote spot, so far from help?

All the while I kept on moving, breathing slowly and steadily to mask my fear, looking for handholds and trying to follow natural lines across that shattered face. It was going well, I thought, and I was making progress, until I rounded a corner and found myself faced by a vertical gully, undercut at the bottom and filled with rotten rock and vegetation. I managed to get both feet onto some reasonable footholds while I contemplated the problem.

The only solution seemed to be to climb up the edge of the gully to where it faded into the mountainside and a crumbling ledge ran across above a steep slab of better rock. But quite apart from the apparent difficulty of making the necessary moves, another problem was that as I climbed upwards, the summit ridge was also declining towards the saddle. This meant that when I reached the top of the gully, I would not be very far below the area which I imagined Josef and Hans to be patrolling. But there was nothing else I could do.

I eased myself upwards, reluctantly trusting my weight to grass tussocks which seemed to barely adhere to the stone backbone of the hill beneath, fingers seeking support from minute and friable wrinkles in the rock. Soil trickled from below my feet as I climbed gingerly on, falling almost soundlessly into the abyss, and several times my boots skidded breath-stoppingly on slimy patches. But at last I was level with the slab.

I surveyed it carefully. It was a fairly compact stretch of rock about five yards across, with one or two crack lines that might afford reasonable handholds, and about eight feet below the top it was split horizontally by a crack, the bottom side of which formed a narrow flake edge running almost its full width, which looked as if it would provide secure toeholds while I moved across.

Below this point, the rock became mossier, wetter and less trustworthy, and fell dizzyingly to an overhang, below which I could see only the sunlit scree, many hundreds – or was it thousands – of feet further down. Above the slab was the grass ledge, three feet wide and sloping, tufts of vegetation and small white flowers growing in safety in their own little alpine garden. They were in their natural environment here; I was not. The ledge of turf where they grew looked insecurely attached to the rock, small pebbles and soil filtering continually from it. I didn't feel like trusting myself to it. I would take my chances on the slab. At least that looked solid.

My position at the side of the gully was quite precarious, and because of that, it was an easy enough decision, in principle, to make the first move. It needed a long stride, though, until I was safely established on the slab. I felt around with my right hand for a good hold on the rock to balance my leftwards lean. I found nothing to trust. In the end, praying silently to no-one in particular, I clutched a substantial tuft of coarse grass, and swayed across, the toe of my left boot just reaching the top of the flake, and the fingers of my left hand curling gratefully over a small, but positive handhold.

But just as I lurched into the move, the tuft of grass in my hand gave way under my weight, pulling out of the soil, loosening stones and earth, and with it one bigger rock, which just missed my leg as it fell with a thud. Then it bounced into the gully, clattering from side to side and echoing in that silent place as it fell, until it flew down over the overhang and spun like a discus into the light and the space, falling rapidly out of sight. I heard one or two more crashes as it completed its descent; the same route, more or less, that my body would take if I slipped now.

I'd always thought that falling would be a very violent death. Knowing, as you parted company with the rock, that pain was imminent. The helpless silence, just the air hissing around you as you fell through emptiness. Would you scream, curse, cry out? Then the first impact: sudden shock, limbs breaking, skin tearing, blood bursting from wounds. Would you feel the pain straightaway, or would shock numb it? Falling further, bouncing, tumbling, hitting rocks, teeth breaking. When will it stop? Will you be dead, or just seriously hurt? Will you die there, merciful blackness closing over you, or lie in agony, waiting for rescue that may never come?

I shoved such thoughts aside. More immediately, I wondered, had I drawn attention to myself by dislodging that stonefall? It had rung out as the only sound on the mountain apart from the wind in the grass and the sound of a raven croaking as it scanned its territory for dying deer and fallen sheep. I shrugged to myself. I could do nothing but carry on. I stepped a little further left along the flake, looking down and placing my toes carefully on the rock edge, seeking the next fingerhold to ensure my balance. My left hand felt a deep crack and I grasped it with relief ...

"Give me your hand!"

I looked up, shocked. I had been concentrating so hard I had blotted out everything except the next move. Now I found myself looking into Josef's face. I realised, of course, that he must, as I feared, have been drawn to me by the sound of the falling stones. He was half squatting on the ledge a few feet above me, holding on with his right hand to the loose rocks, stretching out his left for me to grasp. His smooth soled shoes, their polished leather wet and muddied now, were insecurely placed on the sloping grass that I had rejected as unsafe. He was either very foolish or a braver man than me.

"I can help! Give me your hand!" He gestured and nodded encouragingly. Then it dawned on me. He thought I was stuck; that I had somehow slipped and got myself into what looked to him a very dangerous position. And I knew how much he wanted me alive. He was genuinely trying to save my life, even at risk to his own. I admired him for that. But I knew as well that once he had no further use for me and what I knew, he would be quite prepared to kill me. I couldn't put myself in his power again. I gazed into his pale eyes for what seemed an age. I knew what I had to do.

"Come on, Gilgarran!"

His voice was urgent now. I reached up slowly with my right hand, and he leaned a little further forward and stretched out to grasp it. I knew it wouldn't take much to overbalance him. I grabbed his fingers in my fist, not allowing him the chance to take my hand firmly in his, and yanked violently, not the gradual weight transfer he was expecting.

He toppled forward, headfirst, losing his hold on the rock with his right hand. His feet skidded off the ledge, and he fell straight past me. I leaned desperately away as he fell, and narrowly managed to avoid his clutching hand. I was worried that he would grab me and pull me with him, but I succeeded in fending him off. In the instant in which he passed me, however, sliding inexorably down the slab, he grasped at my leg, tugging momentarily but heavily at me. I lost my footing on the flake, and slipped. For a moment I felt his weight on me, and the strain on my left arm and hand, wedged in the crack, was immense. I thought I was going. Then he lost his grip, and shot away down the gully, like a ghastly swimmer in a grisly, vertical flume. He bounced out over the lip, and I heard him screaming, imagining him flailing at the air for what seemed a long time. Then I thought I heard a distant thud.

It is no small thing to kill a man, even one such as Josef; even when there seems no alternative, but I had no further time to reflect on it. My own position was far from good. I was hanging by my left arm, which had been wrenched in that final moment before Josef let go and fell, and blood was oozing from my hand. My feet were dangling, and I had swung round like a slowly opening door, so that I was facing outwards from the rock. I had no strength in my injured left arm to pull myself back up. I found myself gazing for a moment down the corrie towards Loch Quoich, thinking inconsequentially that it would make a good photograph, the distant view framed by the gully walls. Then, coming quickly back to reality, with a desperate effort I wriggled around so that I was facing the rock again.

The flake was now somewhere on the level of my knees. I could get my foot back onto it, but couldn't make the step up without some help from my hands. My left arm wasn't much use, but I felt around with my right hand, and finally found a small protuberance of rock which I could pinch between my fingers. Using this with all the strength I could muster, I was able to lever myself back up, terrified all the while that if my numb left hand slipped from the crack while I was doing so, I was gone.

Eventually I was upright and back in balance, and crossed the rest of the slab relatively easily, although the blood was pounding rapidly in my head, my mouth was dry and my breathing was hoarse and laboured. There were a few more yards of difficult ground to cross beyond the gully, and then, to my relief, the angle began to relent.

My relief was short-lived, however, as a moment later I saw Hans weaving between the boulders in my general direction. I guessed that he had heard Josef's cry as he fell, and was coming to investigate. I ducked down, hoping he hadn't seen me, and pondered. My damaged left arm and shoulder were painful now and would be almost useless in any physical struggle.

I couldn't risk his catching me. Besides, at close quarters I was under threat from his pistol. Once he realised Josef was dead, he might shoot me out of hand, in revenge for the killing of his partner. And, despite all my plans to avoid the two of them, if he spotted me now, I was back to square one. I still had to try to use the mountain to help me.

"Josef! *Wo bist du?*"

He was calling now, his voice tinged with anxiety and mounting apprehension. Forgetting my own fears for the moment, I tried to imagine how Hans might be feeling. He was, after all, alone on unfamiliar terrain on a high mountain in unsuitable clothing, and separated from his partner. Uncertainty and disorientation would, I hoped, be creeping up on him. I glanced at the sky. Bad weather clouds were beginning to move in now, tearing and reforming as they scudded across the above the peaks on the freshening wind. The atmosphere was changing rapidly from brightness to cold, threatening grey, and wisps of mist were staring to cling to the higher summits. I guessed that Hans would be on his nerve ends by now. It wouldn't take much to confuse him. Psychologically, I estimated that I was in the stronger position.

I risked another look, raising my head stealthily between the boulders. Hans was about thirty yards away, but coming closer. I had to distract him, quickly. I looked around for a rock, the biggest I could throw with one hand. I found one about the right size, one that I hoped would roll and bounce. I picked it up and hefted it in my good hand.

"Josef!"

Hans called again, his voice hoarse now, the stress showing in it. I peered out from my hiding place, and saw him paused, his hands cupping his mouth like a megaphone as he shouted. Then he lowered his hands and stood gazing around, irresolute and perplexed. For a moment his back was to me. I rose to a crouch and hurled the rock as far as I could back towards the gully. I was in luck. I heard it land on the steep slope, then bounce again. Then there was a rattle as it fell through the crags and over the drop of the cliff. Not as loud as I had hoped, but enough to draw Hans' attention.

He made towards the sound, calling again, searching now on the very edge of the precipice, and dropping out of my line of sight as he scanned the mountainside for some sign of life. Quickly, I shrugged off my sack, grabbed my map and compass from the top pocket and some food and water. Then I undid one of the shoulder straps and opened the top flap, hoping to make it look as if it had been dropped. I hurled it as far as I could, watching it disgorge the rest of its contents as it flew through the air. I hoped Hans would find it and decide that I had lost it as I, too, had fallen. When he found it I hoped that he would think that he was alone on the mountain and give up the pursuit. That was my hope.

Then I ran, bent double at first, skulking through the outcrops of the declining ridge, gradually straightening up and stretching out more confidently as I descended the slithering gravel and loose stones of the rough path to the saddle. When I reached it, I glanced back towards the summit, but there was no one in sight. I gave myself a moment to drink some water and let my breathing settle.

Then I heard the voices. Two of them, high above me, their faint echoes torn and distorted by the wind that was now ripping through the gap. *Two* of them? How could that be? I had seen Josef fall. I had heard his scream. Had he, by some incredible chance, landed on a ledge not so far below me? Was that the thud I thought I had heard? Was he badly hurt, unable to move? Or had he been rescued by Hans, and even now the two of them were resuming their pursuit? Fear coursed through me. It was like hearing someone coming back from the grave.

If Josef could survive that fall and return intact to the chase, how could I ever get rid of him? For a moment, a feeling of helplessness swept over me. The voices came again on the wind, closer now, clearly two men shouting to each other, but I could make nothing out. I shivered involuntarily. After all my terrifying antics on the summit crags of Sgurr na Ciche, the hunt was still on. I took a deep breath.

Stay calm, stay calm. You know you can outrun them on the descent.

I turned and launched myself down the gully, stumbling and nearly falling in my haste, unbalanced by my stiffening left arm, until I managed to settle after a few yards into a lopsided downhill jog. I was sure I had enough of a start to gain the lochside long, long before they would have any chance of catching me.

To that extent at least, my plan had worked.

Chapter Fifteen

The sea was steepling into wind-whipped crests, building into a confused jumble under the gathering storm. Where the currents of Loch Nevis met the open waters of the Sound of Sleat the boat began to struggle to make headway. Piling into the growing swell, I could sense the engine straining and hear the propeller shaft knocking angrily. As we crested each wave, rocking momentarily before racing down its other face, the motor screamed shrilly as the blades cleared the water surface, and the knocking grew steadily worse. I began to wonder whether I would make the safety of Mallaig harbour, so close now and yet still tantalisingly out of reach.

From the moment I had re-launched the motorboat and started the engine, leaving the Germans stranded in the hills, I had realised that all was not well. In carelessly running the boat up the shingle under full power, Josef and Hans had obviously damaged the prop shaft. In the comparatively sheltered waters of the inner loch, the uneven vibrations had been little more than an irritation. Now, battling against tide and waves, with the wind building to near gale force, and the visibility decreasing each minute as the rain showers swept up the sound, I was becoming more and more worried for my safety.

Suddenly there was a series of loud metallic bangs from the back of the boat and, to my horror, the engine cut out. Whether it was a result of the damage to the prop shaft and the strain placed on the motor, or something else entirely, I didn't know. I'm no mechanic. But whatever was the cause, it resisted all my frantic attempts to restart the engine. Without any forward propulsion to enable us to steer a course, we lost way immediately and began to drift helplessly, tossed this way and that on the swell. Waves were already breaking over the gunwales and swamping the cockpit. The weight of water in the boat made it still more unwieldy, and it began to list one way and then the other as the liquid swilled about in the bottom. Clinging with desperation but little effect to the tiller with my bad arm, and attempting to bale with the other hand, I began to fear we would capsize at any moment.

Then it started to rain. Not just the intermittent showery rain that had been in the air for a while, but a drenching squall that lashed at me with heavy drops borne on cold gusts of hurtling air. The cheap waterproof jacket I had purchased a few days earlier in Fort William was not equal to this onslaught of Highland rain, and I was soon trembling with the chilling effect of the weather as well as my fears of foundering. If I ended up in the water, I would surely drown.

The squall passed over as swiftly as it had come, and the air cleared a little. The sea, however, was no less mountainous. I tried to keep the bows to the oncoming waves, although at the same time I knew I was drifting further out into the sound and away from Mallaig. I tried to stay calm and concentrate on the immediate task of keeping the boat upright, while salt spray splattered over me, stinging my eyes and affecting my vision.

I was drifting rapidly with the outgoing tide, my body temperature was dropping rapidly and I could see no way out of my predicament. I might have felt in control on the mountain, but that was certainly not the case here. There seemed to be nothing I could do except cling on, buffeted by the waves, and pray. *Pray? Who to*? I wondered miserably. I'd given that up long ago. It would have been some comfort to me now, I admitted to myself. But still I couldn't bring myself to do it, except in a roundabout sort of way, no direct appeal to Jesus, or perhaps, as I thought, with some bitter irony, it should be to St Jude, to whom Emily had so often prayed for me. I muttered generalised invocations and imprecations, and hoped for the best. While I was still alive, something might turn up. The wind might slacken, I might be spotted by a fishing boat making for shelter in Mallaig…

My luck was in. An age went by, or so it seemed to me in my helpless state. Then, at last, I thought I heard something other than the roar of the wind and the slap of the waves. A steady sound, reassuring and powerful: the hum of a marine diesel engine, growing from wishful thinking into blissful reality. I screwed up my eyes and peered ahead of me. I was worried that even now I might be missed in that confusion of sea and sky and greyness. Then out of the dank mist a shape loomed, detaching itself from the gloom and forming itself into the welcome outline of the Mallaig pilot boat, figures in yellow oilskins visible by the bow rails.

For a moment I thought they were going to run me down, and I waved frantically, trying to cross my arms in front of my face and wincing as I did so. But I needn't have worried. They had seen me before I saw them, and with practised skill they drew alongside. Seconds later, I was aboard and hustled into the steamy warmth of the cabin, my wet jacket removed and blankets wrapped around me. Somebody thrust a mug of steaming soup into my chilled hands, poured from a large tartan thermos flask.

Then I noticed the policemen, and my heart sank.

A local sergeant and a constable, uniformed under their waterproofs. How much did they know? I guessed that even here in the Highlands they would have had some communication about me. I cursed inwardly. I'd come all this way to hide myself from them, and had ended up by delivering myself straight into their hands. And did I yet have any new evidence to support my story and my claims of innocence? I thought not. A dead man in a mountain bothy and an injured woman. A boat that wasn't mine. And no sign of the men who were supposed to have murdered Phil and tried to kill me. How could all that help me clear my name? It didn't look good. I bowed my head and huddled miserably into the rough blankets, cupping the soup in my hands.

I heard the engines roar again and felt the boat lean as we turned under power to head back towards Mallaig harbour, towing the half swamped motor boat behind us.

Then, seconds later, I became aware of someone making space for himself in the midst of the animated group of crew and policemen in front of me, and once again, with relief, I recognised that comforting voice.

"Bryn!" I looked up, and there he was, smiling and reassuring me with quiet confidence. He seemed at home amongst the local constabulary, and that instantly gave me hope.

"How're you doing, Mark? You had me really worried. It's good to see you alive. We didn't know what had happened to you ..."

"Edie!" I interrupted, half rising from my seat. "Where is she? Have you seen her? Is she all right? Is she alive? Has she gone to hospital? Can I see…"

"Steady on, Mark. Calm down! Yes, she's alive. She was pretty poorly when Rab brought her back in his boat, that's for sure. She'd lost some blood and she was stunned and in quite a lot of pain. The doctor had a look at her and decided to call for a helicopter. They took her straight to Inverness. They'll look after her there, I'm sure. I think it was mainly flesh wounds. No bones broken, nothing internal. At least, I hope not. Ashby's dead, though."

"I guessed as much. I didn't think he'd survive that explosion. But how do you know what happened to him? And when did you get here, Bryn? How did you know where to come?"

"I followed Peter Ashby. At some distance, because he'd left before I got there. And I only had a rough idea where he was headed. It was fortunate that his wife remembered the name *Knoydart*. But I had no idea whereabouts exactly.

"However, something else Mrs Ashby said gave me an idea about why these two men were so interested in you and Edie. I rang a friend in Military Intelligence, and he made some enquiries with the police in Belgium. My fears were confirmed when they told me what they knew about two particular men with known Nazi connections who seemed to match the descriptions you'd given me. They'd already had them under surveillance for some time, but they had information suggesting that they'd slipped away and taken a ferry to England.

"I began to wish then that you had told me where you were going. Then I could have come straight to you and warned you. As it was I didn't get to Mallaig until after ten at night. And that was only on chance. I checked it out on the map, and that seemed to be the best starting-off point. You could have been anywhere.

"There was nobody around at that time of night, when I arrived, and of course I didn't want to rouse the police until I knew what was going on. It wasn't until this morning that I got a clearer picture. Your two German friends had arrived last night. They found out from a local fisherman –"

"Rab Grant?" I interjected.

"Yes." Bryn looked surprised. "How did you know?"

"News travels fast round here." I gave a wry grin.

"Anyway, they found out that there were people up at the bothy. They knew it must be you and Edie. They hired a motor boat and set off this morning to pay you a visit."

"And Peter Ashby?"

"I missed him too. He spoke to Rab as well, and Rab offered to sail him up to the head of the loch. He said he was going to meet his daughter and surprise her."

"He was certainly right about the surprise!"

"Of course he had no idea that either Peter Ashby or the Germans had any evil intent. It's not something you really expect, is it?"

"So when did you find out what was really going on?"

"When Rab got back here with Edie. He confirmed Ashby's death. He was understandably shocked at what he'd seen and got involved in. He'd radioed in as he was sailing down Loch Nevis, but his message was a bit garbled, and it seemed quicker by then to let him come straight back here, rather than go out looking for him. The pilot boat was out anyway at the time, looking after some Russian fishing boat that was in trouble out towards Rum.

"As soon as Rab landed, he met the sergeant here and told him what had happened." He gestured to the policeman, who smiled as he took up the story.

"Sergeant Watt. Pleased to meet you, sir. Although, of course, the circumstances could be more pleasant. We were pretty surprised to find you'd all landed up on our patch. We'd had the general alert from CID of course, about the murder in Liverpool and the fact that you were on the run, but we never gave it a second thought. It was assumed you'd still be in Liverpool or North Wales."

Despite the sergeant's pleasant demeanour, I was still suspicious.

"Are you going to arrest me?" I asked bluntly.

"I don't think so, sir. Of course, CID will want to question you. But apparently they'd already questioned your aunt and she'd told them about the two foreign men who, she said, had murdered Mr Sullivan. The problem was that there was no proof of their existence. What's happened today, though, and Rab's evidence, backs up your story.

"What you do need to tell us is what has happened to the two men now. How did you get away from them? Rab said the last time he saw you, you were running off up the hill, with them in pursuit. That was quite a few hours ago. They obviously didn't catch you. So where are they now?"

I sipped quietly at my soup for a moment, relieved to no longer be the chief suspect. As I did so I gathered my thoughts. Then, haltingly, I told them what had happened high on Sgurr na Ciche. I described Josef's fall, and went on to say how I heard two voices calling when I was on the saddle. I couldn't decide which was more frightening: to have killed a man, or to have watched him fall so far, as if to his death, and then find he was still alive, a walking ghost.

"We're waiting for back-up from Fort William and Inverness," Sergeant Watt explained after listening thoughtfully to my story. "Then we'll start a search for these two. From what we've heard though, they aren't men to be approached lightly."

It was late afternoon in Mallaig when we climbed ashore. The rain had stopped and to the west, sunlight was showing again under a dirty skirt of cloud. Here, though, in the grey harbour town, the air was chill, the light was flat and the streets were empty. Bryn took me straight to his hotel for a hot shower and something to eat. I realised then just how exhausted I was, both physically and mentally.

A long shower made me feel better, and seemed to ease my aching arm, but I was still chilled after my time on the loch, and Bryn had to lend me some dry clothes. The hotel rustled up some food, and we ate by the open fire in the dining room. Then I went wearily back up to the room, lay down on the bed and promptly fell asleep.

Late that evening, Bryn woke me. Emerging reluctantly into consciousness again, I learned that several CID officers from Liverpool had arrived in Mallaig and were waiting downstairs to interview me. They had driven up at high speed after receiving a call from Sergeant Watt, and were understandably eager to continue their investigations. The new developments in their inquiries into Phil Sullivan's death had shed fresh light on the matter. I pulled on some clothes and went downstairs to the hotel lounge.

Inspector Keenan was a dour man, and thorough. His approach was like that of someone assembling a difficult jigsaw from which certain pieces were missing. Fortunately for me, it transpired that he seemed now to have found enough of the pieces to start to see the picture, and was beginning to imagine what the blanks might be.

Nevertheless he was keen to find out what I had to say about the events of the last few days. He took out his notebook and glanced at it, refreshing his memory as to the details. Then he began to question me closely, making fresh notes from time to time. I recounted the whole story again, and eventually, he seemed satisfied with my answers.

"You'll be relieved to know, sir," he went on, "that information which has come to light seems to show that your story may be true."

Then he began carefully to explain, in his turn, how he had interviewed Emily in Liverpool, and how, despite what she had told him about the two men with foreign accents whom she had inadvertently allowed into the house, the evidence had at first clearly pointed to me. No witnesses had been found to back up Emily's story, and forensic were still sifting through the evidence.

Then they had visited Maes-y-Bryn, and found that I had vanished from there with Edie. Our abrupt disappearance had only served to strengthen the police suspicions – in these types of circumstances, as was to be expected, running away is generally taken as proof of guilt.

In the course of their inquiries they had spoken to Bryn. He had been careful to give nothing away, but had promised any help he could give. In view of his background in the Military Police, and the discovery that he and Inspector Keenan had some contacts in common, his offer was taken seriously.

Soon afterwards, they had found my car in the car park of the *Cross Keys,* with the file and the box with the letters still in the boot. This had proved most interesting to them, and an officer with some imagination had made a connection of sorts between the letters that I had left on top and the two foreign men. They had come across the maps and the diary and had puzzled over them for some time without evolving any convincing theory.

"Then Bryn contacted us," Inspector Keenan went on. "He had made some inquiries of his own, and had been down to see

Peter Ashby. Ashby wasn't there, but his wife told him that two men with German accents had called at the house earlier. There had been arguing and raised voices, and threats. Then eventually Ashby had told them where to find you. Or at least, he gave them as much, or as little, detail as he knew himself. They'd left immediately then, and a little later he'd set off after them, after giving Hilda a brief outline of the situation

"Bryn called a friend in intelligence, and the pieces fell into place. They'd heard from the Belgians that they'd been tracking the movements of these two Germans for some time. Apparently, they belonged to an organisation – the *Heldschutz* – dedicated to helping former Nazis."

"Is that something like *Odessa*? I read a book about that once."

"That's right, Mark. There's more than one organisation like that. And a lot of people still prepared to pay good money for new identities, passports, papers and so on.

" In fact, both Josef and Hans were the grandsons of SS troopers. The Belgians knew they'd come to England some time ago, but had no authority to follow them.

"So it all gradually became clear. But at the same time you were in a lot of danger, it seemed. So it came down to a mad rush north to Scotland to try and get there before all hell broke loose. But it seems Bryn was a bit too late after all."

"So where does all this leave me now?"

"In the clear, sir, as you'll doubtless be pleased to hear. We will still want to take a statement from you, but I think we can be sure that our two German friends are the real culprits in all this. You are free to go."

He closed his notebook with a snap and smiled faintly. Was it really that easy? Or was he playing some long game of his own? Relief at not being arrested as a suspect was, in any case, mitigated by the awareness that Hans and possibly Josef were still at large, more dangerous than ever, and likely to come looking for me again. The file they wanted was now definitely in the possession of the police, and I was not sure that when they realised it was out of their reach, they would not be tempted to eliminate me as a witness against them, if not out of pure revenge for my part in it all.

It was after midnight by now. Bryn and I went back upstairs.

He had a bottle of *Bunnahabhain* in the room, and we poured ourselves a couple of glasses.

"Cheers!" I said mechanically, although I felt far from cheerful. I took a good swallow of the malt whisky, and felt it burn its way down, the warmth spreading from it as it did so. By the time we'd had a couple of drams, I felt more relaxed and ready for sleep again.

"So what happens next, Bryn?"

"A good night's sleep, Mark. Time enough tomorrow for tomorrow's worries."

Chapter Sixteen

The ward in which Edie was recovering seemed almost unnaturally tranquil after the violent circumstances in which we had parted. Through the windows I could see the sunlight gleaming on the wet rooftops of Inverness, a small town by southern, English standards, but nevertheless the heartbeat of the northern Highlands. Beyond, the waters of the Beauly Firth streaming under the leaping span of the road bridge were whipped into white-topped cones by the steady breeze. I realised I'd only ever been to Raigmore Hospital once before when visiting a friend who had had a skiing accident at Aviemore. Bryn had kindly driven me up from Mallaig, that morning then gone straight back to tie up loose ends with Inspector Keenan, and to glean any more information about the fate of Peter Ashby and the two Germans.

Now, as I quietly crossed the ward, Edie suddenly spotted me.

"Mark! Thank God!"

She struggled to sit up, obviously in considerable discomfort, and reached out to grasp my hand tightly.

"Thank God you're alive," she murmured. "They've told me nothing about what's been happening. Of course, I didn't know much about anything yesterday in any case. They were operating to take bits of shrapnel out of my back. It's still bloody sore."

She winced as she lay back again.

"I can only lie on my side at the moment."

"You saved my life, you know," I murmured. You could have been killed."

She shrugged. "Maybe. You're worth it."

"Your father's dead, Edie. I'm sorry."

I could see no point in beating about the bush.

"Father?" Her tone was at once quizzical and scornful, and as she spoke she grimaced. "He disowned me, he never acknowledged me, and I didn't know he was my father until minutes before he died. I'll lose no sleep on his account. If anyone was my father, Harry was. *Your* dad, not mine. But how I wish *he'd* been my real father." Her voice was tinged with regret and bitterness.

"Try not to think about it, Edie. The past is gone. I'm sure my father loved you, really."

I hesitated. Should I go on and say what I really wanted to? I decided to go for it.

"And I ... I ... don't forget ... if it helps ... I love you too."

She squeezed my hand when I said that, and I bent forward and kissed her on the lips, but chastely because we were in a hospital ward and the prune-faced woman in the next bed was watching us closely in a disapproving sort of way and looked as if she was about to ring for the nurse.

"Now that we know the truth," I went on, "there's no reason why we shouldn't be together. If you want us to be, that is."

"I do. I do. Of course I do. But Jenny? What about her? You are still married to her, aren't you?"

"I suppose so. But I doubt whether she'll be waiting anxiously for my return. She's been pretty horrible to me recently."

"Is that perhaps because she's been worried about you, do you think? Worried about the direction things might take if you carried on trying to find out the truth about Jack and Harry? Perhaps it's because she really cares about you."

"Well if it is, she's gone a funny way about it. Jenny being unpleasant to me doesn't exactly encourage me to be nice to her. But maybe she can't see that. Maybe she just expects me to be charming to her whether she treats me well or not."

"She *is* a woman, Mark," Edie chided me. "You must try to understand the way her mind works."

Don't resort to that irritating "We're-all-part-of-the-sisterhood-you-men-wouldn't-understand" routine ...

As if she could read my thoughts, Edie opened her eyes wide and innocently, and smiled teasingly at me, and in that moment I wanted her so much I would have forgiven her anything.

"I'll have to get back home, Edie. There's things to sort out. I'm catching the train" – I glanced at my watch – "in just over an hour. I'll come back and collect you in the car when you're discharged."

"The sooner the better."

She leaned forward again. I felt her breath on my cheek and caught the scent of her as whispered in my ear.

"I'm fed up being in bed on my own. Come for me soon!"

"Of course I will."

I kissed her on the cheek and stood up. I wished I could snatch her up there and then in my arms and carry her back to my home, *our* home, as I hoped it soon would be. Instead I smiled inanely and walked away, pausing at the door to blow her a kiss. She waved in that sort of childlike way adults do when they're in love, and I felt myself melting with affection. Then I saw Prune-face looking at me blackly, so I straightened my features, turned and headed off down the corridor.

I had plenty of time to think on the train journey south. In between reading the *Times* which I had bought at a platform stall and scanned for any mention of my escapades (there was a small paragraph on an inside page: *Search for teacher in murder case moves to Highlands,* but very few accurate facts); swaying down the train to the buffet car for a sandwich and a coffee (whatever happened to dining-cars?) and dozing uncomfortably with my head wedged against the window, I mused on the situation I found myself in.

I realised that I had as good as asked Edie to move in with me, and yet in reality I still knew very little about her. And Jenny might still be waiting for me with an olive branch, although I somehow doubted it. In any case, I had some big decisions to make.

My job? What would the Head make of it all? Perhaps he would be prepared to excuse my unplanned absence when he knew what had really happened. Or not. I didn't get on with him any better than I did with Jenny at the moment. In fact, it wouldn't break my heart not to have to go back there, although it might make getting another teaching job slightly problematical.

And what about Jack's will? My search for the truth had led me into all sorts of unexpected avenues. I had found out a lot about my family's secrets, but did it come any closer to explaining my brother's motivation in cutting me out? Was it the Catholic thing, my lack of faith, after all? If so, that was disturbing.

But, most worrying of all, in the immediate future, what about my two German friends? Would the police catch them before they caught up with me again? I felt fear stir in my guts. I must try to make a clear plan, or at least collect my ideas as to what I would do on all these counts, before I got home...

I woke up just outside Lancaster, my face against the window and dribble on my chin, filled with lethargy and feeling no desire to do anything except find my bed and go back to sleep. If only it were that easy. I trailed my way down to the bus station and found I had an hour's wait for a bus. Bored and fractious, I filled the time by browsing in Waterstone's bookshop and having a coffee, then went back and caught the bus.

The journey seemed interminable. Although there were few passengers, we seemed to stop at every hamlet and crossroads on the way, and it was early evening by the time I alighted in our village street. It was already going dark, and when I got to the house there were no lights showing. I breathed a sigh of relief. I could do without a confrontation with my wife for the time being. That could wait.

I turned, inconspicuously I hoped, into the drive at the side of the house, feeling instinctively in my pocket for the door key as I did so. It wasn't there. I cursed inwardly. Where was it? As I asked myself the question, the answering image came immediately into my mind. It was with the car keys, of course. I seemed to remember that I had left them lying on the seat of the car when I'd abandoned it in the *Cross Keys* car park. But I couldn't be sure. All I knew was that some time during the adventures of the last few days, they had disappeared. Now I couldn't get into my own house. I would have to knock on Mrs Banks' door and borrow her key. And she'd want to know what was going on, naturally, even though I really didn't feel like talking about it.

I hesitated on the doorstep, dithering. As I did so, I became gradually aware of the sound of music playing gently somewhere. In consternation, I pressed my ear to the door. It was coming from inside the house ... *There'll be Bluebirds over the White Cliffs of Dover* ... it sounded like the nostalgic 1940s album I'd bought on the ferry coming back from Belgium. But it was very unlike Jenny to sit in the dark listening to music like that. Besides, her car wasn't there, so neither, I assumed, was she. Other explanations presented themselves. Had I, or someone else, left the CD player on permanent replay for the last week?

That seemed extremely unlikely, too. So, I was left with the most frightening possibility. Was there someone else in the house?

Perplexed, I listened for a while, motionless and fearful, my heart beginning to thump heavily in my chest, weighing up the options. Then slowly, carefully, more out of curiosity than bravery, I tried the handle of the door. It was an old wooden barn door with vertical planks and a brass handle as well as the Yale lock. The Yale was obviously snicked back, because as I turned the handle, the door swung almost noiselessly open. Someone had clearly been in the house. The question was, were they still there?

I eased myself into the darkness of the hall. The music was louder now I was inside. Vera Lynn had given way to a rousing rendition of *It's a long way to Tipperary,* enough to cover the sound of my movements. I tiptoed across the hall, past the kitchen and up to the door of the sitting-room. I peered cautiously round the jamb of the door, straining to make out shapes in the semi-darkness. The curtains were open, and in the vague light from the street, I was sure I could see someone sitting on the sofa, which was at an angle to me, so that the figure I saw was partly obscured by its arm and back. Then, as I watched in trepidation, he leaned forward, as if resting his forearms on his thighs and clasping his hands between his knees, and as he did so, the light gleamed dully on his leather jacket.

No! It couldn't be! How could he have got there, from the Scottish Highlands, so quickly? I pressed myself against the wall beside the doorway, the adrenalin of fear coursing through me, and my mind racing.

Here, in my own house! Was it Josef, whom I thought I had killed once already, or was it Hans? Or were they both there? If so, I was in a lot of trouble. Perhaps one of them was somewhere upstairs, about to descend at any moment and trap me. I glanced nervously sideways at the staircase which rose from the hall into the blackness above.

But even as I did so, anger wrestled with the fear inside me. How dare they pursue me into my own home? They'd done enough damage already, and it was time now to confront them, to show them that they couldn't just come here, not just to England, but to my house, and do as they liked. I was about to move, to reveal myself, when common sense took over at the last minute.

They're armed. You've no weapon. Don't be so stupid. If you're going to do anything, call the police ...

I made my decision and turned to go. As I did so, the music stopped as the track ended and my footstep rang loud on the wooden floor. I froze, but it was too late. I heard a click as the CD player was turned off, and a louder, metallic sound as of a weapon being cocked.

"Who's there?"

The voice had a foreign tinge to it. My heart sank, but I didn't reply.

"Don't move. Turn to face me. Raise your hands!"

I turned back through the doorway and saw the light reflected on the barrel of the automatic pistol. The man's figure loomed large behind it.

Slowly, I raised my hands, as instructed. I had no choice. I didn't feel so brave now. In fact, I was terrified. Back to square one, it seemed. All my performance on Sgurr na Ciche, my risky escape down the loch, my rescue by Bryn and the pilot boat, had all been a waste of time. I was caught again, and this time, what was worse, in my own house. In the darkness I still couldn't make out the face of the man who was now moving slowly towards me, but I could feel the threat.

He had almost reached the doorway, the gun still pointed menacingly at me. He stopped and carefully stretched out his left arm, feeling for the light switch. An instant later the room was flooded with brightness. In the sudden glare, dazzling to eyes accustomed to darkness, I started with amazement. I recognised him immediately. But it was not who I was expecting.

"So we meet again, Monsieur!"

His gaze searched over my shoulder for a moment, as if expecting some sort of trap. Then he lowered the gun, transferred it to his left hand and offered his right hand for me to shake. His expression was guarded, but less openly hostile than when we had last spoken, so long ago it seemed, in that café in St. Hubert.

"What the hell are you doing here?" I asked, as I grasped his hand without any great enthusiasm. "You scared the life out of me."

Do I need to be scared?

"There are people you need to be frightened of, Mark. I think you know who I mean. But fortunately, I am not one of them. Sit down and let me explain. There are things you need to know. You may find some of them surprising. And it may take a little while."

He put the gun away, stepped back and gestured towards the sofa and armchairs in the sitting-room. I closed the curtains, turned the lamps on and switched off the main ceiling light.

"Whisky?"

He nodded in assent and I poured two stiff glasses. Not until I had handed one to him and was settled myself with the malt cradled in my hand, was I ready to listen to his story.

"Go on, then," I muttered somewhat truculently. "Amaze me."

"Oh yes," he murmured softly, and for the first time a faint smile made its appearance. "I think I will be able to do that."

For a moment he closed his eyes, as if gathering his thoughts, maybe deciding where to begin. Then he began to speak, gently but at the same time with the air of one who does not expect to be interrupted.

"When we last met, I told you my name was Jean-Luc. I didn't, however, mention that I am a member of Belgian Intelligence, attached to the Anti-Nazi Brigade. My job is to track down former Nazis and their descendants and to either bring them to justice, or to ensure that they do not profit from their crimes of fifty years ago.

"I have been aware for some time of the movements of two men in particular, Josef Stiegmuller and his partner Johann Gruben – Hans to his friends, such as they are. They are both members of the *Heldschutz*, an organisation dedicated to protecting the interests of Hitler's former Nazi colleagues, particularly the SS. Are you aware of its existence?"

"I wasn't, until yesterday. But I certainly am now!"

"I had learned," Jean-Luc continued, "that they were searching for a file that contained much information about stolen French treasures, and also incriminating evidence that could be used against former SS men, some of whom were still alive. A file that disappeared during the German retreat through Belgium in 1944. No word had been heard of it since.

"I knew that they had recently travelled to England, and I assumed they had found a fresh lead, which was unusual after all these years. I had trouble, however, getting permission to follow them, both from my own organisation and from the British authorities. They seemed to think I was too personally involved.

"I was particularly interested, you see, because it appeared that this file in question had vanished near my own village in 1944, and the story, in various guises, was, how shall we say ... well known locally."

Which of course you denied when I asked you about it ...

"Naturally, I couldn't mention it to you until I had checked you out further ..."

"Further than going through my belongings in my hotel room?" I ventured to interrupt. He had the good grace to look slightly sheepish as he replied.

"I apologise for that. Your return that night cut short my investigations. I expected you, like most Englishmen, to spend more time in the bar drinking our Belgian beer. I didn't even have time to put your things back. It was amateurish of me. I felt ashamed. You should never have known I had been in the room. But it gave me a good guide to what was going on. The one thing I couldn't be certain of, was whether you were really who you seemed to be. I had to find a way to be sure of that."

"But why were you so interested in me and my doings? Did you think I would lead you to these two men? Did you set me up? You realise I could have been killed by them?"

The indignation must have been apparent in my voice, for he shook his head vigorously.

"No, Mark, I was intrigued for a different reason."

"And that was ...?"

"If I were to tell you that my name is Jean-Luc Hermans, would that give you a clue? And that my mother owns the café in St. Hubert?"

I set down my whisky glass with a slight rattle on the coffee table. I began to sense what was coming. So, it turned out that *Sophie* Hermans was Jean-Luc's mother ... In the silent pause Jean-Luc was fumbling in his jacket pocket for something. He pulled it out and placed it on the table between us, and it glinted in the light. I knew what it would be before I saw it.

An army cap badge, lovingly cleaned and polished. A cap

badge of the King's Regiment. Not just any cap badge, but the cap badge given by my father to a young woman called Sophie in wartime Belgium. I was immediately certain of it. I sat motionless, staring at it, overwhelmed by the implications. As I did so, Jean-Luc placed a faded envelope on the table next to the badge.

SOPHIE PIRON, SAINT HUBERT, BELGIUM was the simple address printed in bold block capitals on the front.

"Read it!"

I took up the envelope as if it were a sacred relic, and gingerly drew out the single sheet inside. It was stained and brittle, and worn, as if it had been frequently handled over the intervening years. I found my hands were trembling as I opened it out. It was dated October 1944, the address *"Somewhere in Holland."*

"Ma chère Sophie," I read, in what was unmistakeably my father's hand. A little firmer, perhaps, the writing more upright and carefully formed than in later years, but definitely the same. It was in French, with one or two minor grammatical errors, but competent enough for a self-taught working man of his time.

"Thank you," it went on, *"for two wonderful days. You are the loveliest person and helped me to forget this awful war for a few hours. I will always remember your loving kindness, and I hope you, too, will keep the memory of our short time together.*

Who knows? Perhaps we will meet again one day after the War. Until then,

Affectueusement,

Harry."

I sat in silence, still holding the letter, still staring at it as if to suck more information from it. But I knew it said quite enough as it was.

"A nice letter, is it not, Mark, though brief? My mother did indeed keep the memory of those few hours with her brave English soldier. How could she do otherwise? For only a few short weeks after she met your father, she found out she was pregnant.

"Yes, Mark, it was *I* who was the memory she kept of your father after he had left to chase the Boches back to Germany, gone with his comrades, his band of brothers, into a different world, and eventually back to the wife my mother didn't know he had.

205

"Harry – your father – *my* father – never came back. He never wrote again, he made no effort to get back in touch. But my mother treasured the memory of their short *liaison.* To her he was always a hero, a liberator. I grew up believing that, for a long time. Only later did I grow bitter when there was no word from him, while my mother struggled alone to bring me up. However ..."

"Don't forget," I interrupted rather angrily, mindful of the dreadful secret that had cast a shadow over my father's life, albeit from a totally different source. "Don't forget that my father knew nothing of your existence. He didn't shun you deliberately. Don't blame him for that."

"Would it have made any difference if he had known? I think not. My mother was just a wartime conquest, soon forgotten."

"My father wasn't like that. You didn't know him."

The silence was long and heavy. Jean-Luc looked down at his clasped hands, then sighed, sat up and roughly brushed the back of his right hand across his eyes.

"Exactly. My point exactly. I never knew him. Never. However – as I was going to say – after I got over the bitterness, I found that I did, after all, want to know something about him. I wanted to know my family – if I had one. But I had no trails to follow, none at all. A name – Harry. An infantryman. My mother couldn't even remember his regiment, or wouldn't tell me. Eventually she showed me the cap badge, and I made some enquiries. I found out it was the badge of the King's Regiment, but I still couldn't track him down. A lot had changed since the war. The regiment had amalgamated with another and they had no records that could guide me to him. My mother didn't really encourage me in the search Perhaps she was resigned to it all by then, and didn't want to damage his life by suddenly catching up with him with a grown son. Anyway, I never found him."

"It wouldn't have helped your search," I put in, more kindly now, "that his real name was John."

"I know that now, of course. I know a lot more now. More than when we met in St Hubert. Then I was suspicious. Why had you come asking about SS men, stolen gold? Nobody knew, or so we thought."

"We?"

"The village. It was our secret. Carefully guarded for forty-five years. Then someone arrives who appears to know about it. Could it really be you, I wondered? Could you be one of my unknown relatives? That's why I went through your things. I was very excited, Mark, as you can imagine. My dream, my lifetime's search was coming to an end. But I was still cautious. The letters in your room showed me who my father was. Can you imagine, seeing your father's handwriting for the first time, proving that he was a real person? But how had you come by them? Were you who you claimed to be, or had you acquired them in some way? I wanted absolute proof before I spoke to you about it."

"So, I presume, that's why you broke in here?"

"Yes."

"After you'd already broken into my hotel room?

"Yes."

"And did you find what you were looking for?"

"Yes."

Jean-Luc reached again into his jacket pocket and slid his final proof onto the table.

A faded photograph of a young man in battle dress, smiling with the slight cockiness of someone who has faced danger and violence and survived. Not quite the twin, but near enough, of one of the framed pictures hanging on the living-room wall, along with several other black and white photos of deceased relatives.

"It came with the letter he sent to my mother. I have looked around your house, Mark, and seen the photos of your father. Now I am sure."

He stood up, and something unspoken immediately made me do the same. He stepped towards me and reached out to grasp my hand, smiling almost shyly, and I realised why the gesture was uncannily familiar; why it had seemed so familiar that first time when he shook my hand in the bar of the Hotel de la Paix, what seemed now like a lifetime ago. It was Harry, my father, that he reminded me of, in the way he moved, in his courtly civility.

Can you inherit such things? Is it in the genes? It would indeed seem so, and if I needed any other proof of his identity, it was there as large as life before me.

Jean-Luc let go of my hand and spread his arms.

"Now, at last, I know. You are indeed my brother."

He put his arms around me and hugged me, and I felt tears in my eyes as he did so, tears of emotion and confusion.

"Life is strange, Jean-Luc, very strange" I said a little later, after we had eaten a simple supper together and sat sipping the last of a bottle of champagne that I had found in the fridge, while we began to get to know each other a little better.

"I've lost the brother I thought I always knew so well, who turned out in the end to be a mystery to me, and now instead I've found the brother I never knew existed.

"And tomorrow you must meet my aunt Emily. Sorry, *our* aunt!"

Chapter Seventeen

"Things happened in wartime, Mark. Things which would not be acceptable normally. But when young men are put in such positions, who are we to judge their actions? Harry, your father, would never have done such a thing normally. Men didn't talk about it when they got home from the War, naturally, and their wives didn't ask."

We had told Emily briefly about everything that had happened since my flight from the house only a few days previously. So much had happened: rescuing Edie from Maes-y-Bryn, the flight to Scotland, the death of Peter Ashby. Such a lot in such a short time. And finally, the revelation of my father's wartime liaison with Sophie and the outcome of that relationship.

I hadn't really expected Emily to be all that shocked – she was far too worldly-wise for that – but I thought she might have shown a little more surprise than she did. Instead she allowed Jean-Luc to kiss her on both cheeks, and greeted him calmly, as if it were a normal occurrence for unknown nephews from foreign countries to suddenly turn up on her doorstep.

"I knew Harry had secrets, but I never enquired too closely about them. It was none of my business, and anyway, a man has the right to keep certain things to himself. Some things are too painful to talk about. Oh, listen, there's the kettle whistling."

Emily eased herself out of her chair and pottered through into the back kitchen, emerging a few moments later with three mugs of steaming milky instant coffee on a tray.

"Get the biscuits down, Mark. I'm sure Jean-Luc would like one with his drink."

I got the tin down from the cupboard and opened it, revealing a selection of shortbread and digestives. As I did so, I glanced at Jean-Luc and saw him frown slightly as he tasted the coffee, but of course he was far too much of a gentleman to comment. In fact, I think he was fascinated by the whole thing. Meeting his English aunt, seeing the house where his father had lived, visiting the terraced streets of Liverpool for the first time, not as a tourist, but as someone whose family roots were there…

compared to all that, the slightly unusual food and drink were easily taken in his stride.

Jean-Luc seemed genuinely delighted to have discovered us as relatives after such a long wait; and if he was pleased to meet me, I in my turn was elated at what he had had to tell me. In fact, the story he had outlined to me late the previous evening was quite fantastic. However, coming after all the other recent revelations and discoveries concerning my family, I accepted it with no other emotion than deep satisfaction, for he had much to tell me about the aftermath of my father's skirmish by that Belgian wood in 1944.

We had sat up until well after midnight, Jean-Luc talking quietly and assuredly as he filled in the gaps in the story which my efforts had failed to complete.

In September 1944 his mother, Sophie, had been a girl of twenty. As I already knew, she had met my father at the hotel in St. Hubert, and intoxicated with the excitement of the Liberation, she had been whirled off her feet by the presence of smiling Tommies in uniform. Their youthful air of power and confidence seemed such a contrast to the downtrodden, if defiant air of the men she was used to. How could she resist? So much I had worked out already, but there was more.

Sophie had a younger brother, then a lad of twelve, desperate to join one of the local Resistance groups. He had gravitated towards the Communist-inspired Belgian Army of Partisans, who liked to take a more active role in their fight against the occupying forces than the other Resistance networks in the area. He had run errands for them, braving German patrols and checkpoints with the invincible cheekiness and confidence of youth. He knew the woods and field paths as well as he knew the village streets, and would roam far and wide through the countryside, scavenging for extra food for the family, turning his hand to a little poaching when he could.

As the German retreat began, he took also to looking for souvenirs on his forays, bullets and shell-cases, once, to his great excitement, an abandoned sub-machinegun which was welcomed with enthusiasm by the young men of the Resistance.

Then, on an unforgettable evening in September 1944, he was heading home from one of his expeditions in the fading light when he saw a German truck, an SS vehicle, trundling past the wood where he had discreetly hidden himself on hearing its approach. He crouched uncomfortably in the brambly undergrowth, peering out through the branches, consumed with hatred, wishing he could do something to puncture their persistent arrogance, longing to be able to halt their passage with a sudden burst of overwhelming firepower and terrible harm. But he was only twelve years old, he could do nothing, and he had the sense to know that.

Then, as he watched with his face twisted in impotent fury, willing something dreadful to happen to these men who had done so many terrible things to his people, the longed-for, the impossible miracle occurred.

A burst of machinegun fire, the truck swerving, crashing. Answering fire, an SS trooper trying to run, cut down almost immediately, then silence. The boy crept forward, anxious to know the source of this miraculous intervention. When he saw the two British soldiers, his first instinct was to break cover and greet his heroes, the Tommies who were liberating Belgium yet again, but something in their grim demeanour made him hold back.

Instead, he observed them with growing excitement as they carried the bodies into the wood, then came back and began unloading boxes and sacks from the truck.

To begin with, the boy couldn't understand what the soldiers were doing, or why. Until, that is, one of them let slip one of the sacks and from it rolled a golden chalice, the rising moon gleaming eerily on it as the man bent to retrieve it.

Realisation dawned quickly then. The boy had heard of the Nazi habit of stripping all sorts of treasures from the countries they occupied, and he quickly guessed that these Britishers had decided, rightly or wrongly, to appropriate this windfall for themselves. He crept closer and closer until finally he lay hidden in the darkness on the damp grass only yards from where they were digging, his elbows spread and his chin resting on the backs of his hands, thinking furiously.

The soldiers were edgy, looking round frequently, and more than once the boy thought they were staring straight at him. Each time he waited anxiously for the gruff shout of discovery, the scuffle, the strong hands pinioning him. Yet each time it was a false alarm, and he breathed again, but not daring to move away for fear of making a noise.

"So he lay there until it was over." Jean-Luc spoke in a low voice, as if to himself. He paused and took another sip of whisky.

"He saw them bury the bodies of the SS men, the boxes and the sacks. He noticed also that one of the soldiers was carrying something as they left the place – that was probably the file that Josef and Hans traced eventually to you.

"He followed them to the edge of the wood, trembling with fear and excitement. Then, as they were about to leave the cover of the wood, he saw one of them – the corporal – stoop and pick something up off the ground. It was ..."

"... a swastika armband," I chimed in before Jean-Luc could finish the sentence.

"You knew?" He looked surprised.

"I've got it. My father – our father – sent it home to England, to his wife."

"And a few days later he seduced my mother."

A long pause. Jean-Luc sat in stern-faced silence, as if struggling inwardly with a nagging resentment.

"It wasn't like that," I murmured, fearing his reaction. Eventually his expression softened.

"I know that. Now."

"And Sophie's – your mother's – brother. What was he called?"

"Maurice."

"Aah. Of course."

"You've met him. In St Hubert."

"I know."

Jean-Luc paused for a while, deep in thought. Then, after a few moments, he resumed his narrative.

"The boy – Maurice, my uncle – waited until the soldiers had set fire to the truck and moved on. Then, damp and cold, he crept home, hugging his secret to him. He said nothing to his sister, even when he saw her later on, getting very friendly with the English corporal. Then, when the soldiers had gone from St Hubert, he informed his friends in the Resistance. They went by night to the place and dug up the boxes, the gold, the stolen treasures. They left the bodies where they were. It wasn't until the end of 1945 that the villagers decided to move the bodies, and bury them again at the edge of the cemetery in an unmarked grave.

They were good men, in their way, a lot of those young men of the Partisans. Rough, uneducated, some of them – not like the former officers who made up the backbone of the Belgian Legion. And they were all hardened by war. But they used all the money they made, or most of it, to help their own village. It was their secret, *our* secret – the village's secret. Nobody ever spoke of it to outsiders. No-one ever knew. But then, some months later, one of the Englishmen came looking for it…"

"Peter Ashby?"

"I guess so. But it was all gone by then. He dug and dug in that wood and they all laughed behind his back. Nobody told him anything and he left empty-handed. Since then nobody has ever inquired about that wartime incident in St Hubert. Those Germans were nameless casualties of a heartless war. Their families never knew what happened to them, or where. Why should anyone come looking? We had grown to think that no-one ever would. Until a week or two ago."

"When I arrived."

"Exactly. But I'm glad you did, Mark. Otherwise we would still never have met, and I would still be dreaming fruitlessly about the family I never knew."

I mused for a moment on what Jean-Luc had told me. Then a thought struck me.

"You said the Resistance used *most* of the money to help the village."

"That's exactly what I said."

"So what happened to the rest of it?"

He smiled briefly, as if suppressing an inner excitement.

"I wondered when you'd want to know about that! Some of the proceeds of the discovery were given to Maurice and my mother. The Resistance felt they'd earned it, especially when they knew about my mother's condition. She had enough money to buy the hotel and set herself up there. Of course it wasn't like it is now. It was a little run down and all the facilities were old. It needed a lot of money spending on it. But she could afford it. She's run it ever since, and it's been a good business for her.

"But she didn't spend all the money she got. She put some aside for her English soldier. She went on loving him, you see, or the memory of him. She wanted, if she ever saw him again, to be able to give him back some of the treasure he had captured from the Germans. So there is still money in a bank account, for her beloved Harry, or his descendants."

"But you said she stopped looking for him. Why would she keep money for him?"

Jean-Luc shrugged and spread his hands in a gesture of incomprehension.

"She was a woman. She didn't need this money. Who knows what she was really thinking?"

"Have you asked her about it?"

"We haven't spoken about it for many years. Now, though, I think she will want to speak about it. She will want to meet you, and make sure, after all this time, that you get the money that was destined for her English lover."

"And how much money might that be?" I asked tentatively.

Jean-Luc looked casually down at the nails of his right hand, then glanced up at me and held my gaze.

"Gold is a very precious metal. The Nazis knew that. There was a lot of it in those boxes. Now, with interest, there is in that bank account the equivalent of around two hundred thousand pounds."

I gasped. It was a huge amount of money to me and could mean that I would never need to work again. At the same time I was uneasy about it.

"But who did all this wealth belong to, Jean-Luc? I mean, before the Germans stole it? Shouldn't we be trying to give it back to them?"

"Too late for that, I fear, Mark. Even if we could have traced where it all came from back in 1944 – which I doubt – by the time I was old enough to know anything about it, the gold had been traded and the other treasures sold off. I think now that the villagers, including my mother, were perhaps wrong to do that, but we cannot change what is past."

"Then what about you, Jean-Luc, and your family? Shouldn't you have this money?"

"I can assure you, Mark, we don't need it. My mother has the hotel, which provides a good living on top of the money she kept and invested. Maurice, my uncle, has a haulage business which has always been very successful. They don't need it. You're a teacher." He paused, and smiled wanly. "If you've still got a job, that is. How well paid are you, for what you do? I think this money will be very handy for you."

"And yourself? You work, don't you? Why would you do what you do if you are so well off?"

"Because I hate the Nazis. I hate what they did and what they stood for. And I am determined that such a thing will never happen again, not in my lifetime; not ever. So I have dedicated my life to hunting them down, to winkling out the neo-Nazis, and anyone else who poses a similar threat to the security of our democracy or that of Europe."

I was quite surprised by his vehemence, but I believed him.

And so as we sat in the warmth of Emily's kitchen, sipping the comforting milky coffee she had always made for me, I felt that most of the mysteries which had plagued me over the last few weeks had been resolved. On the plus side, I had found my half-brother and was apparently about to inherit a lot of money. I was looking forward to seeing Edie again, and it seemed I was in the clear with the police.

Against that I had to set the deaths of Phil and Peter Ashby, and the fact that the two Nazis, Hans and possibly Josef, were still looking for me. However, with Jean-Luc by my side I felt a lot safer on that score, and I knew that the police were on their trail, so that worry had diminished to some extent. One other thing still nagged, however – Jack's rejection of me. I couldn't resist mentioning it to Emily.

"You know I spoke to Father Byrne."

"Of course I remember that, Mark. I don't know what he said to you, but he must have upset you. You came back very late that night."

Tactfully, she made no further comment on the state in which I had returned, although she'd obviously guessed. So much for her being asleep when I got in

"What he said upset me very much. I wonder whether you'd agree that it's true."

"You'll have to tell me what he said first."

"Of course. To cut a long story short, he told me that Jack

despised me because I didn't go to church any more. That's why he cut me out of his will. That's why he didn't even mention me by name. Is that true? You knew more of what Jack was thinking than I did."

There was silence. Emily sat motionless, as if frozen. I began to wonder if she had even heard the question.

"Tell me, Emily." My voice was urgent, almost pleading. "Tell me. You must know." *She must, she must.*

"That was a terrible thing for Father Byrne to say." When it came, her voice was clear, and disapproving. "Sometimes men – even priests – can be so harsh, so ... so ... un-christian."

"But was it true what he said about me and Jack?"

"No, Mark. I don't believe it was true at all. The reasons were different from that. Quite different."

I suppressed a desire to urge her to go on. I knew the words would come when she was good and ready.

"Jack knew about that file, the one the Germans wanted. And the other stuff, the gold or whatever it was. I think your dad told him. He seemed to know it was dangerous – neither of them told me why – but he didn't really know what to do about it.

"He was worried that whoever came looking for the file and the gold would find you and hurt you in some way. I think that was why he seemed to make sure as many people as possible knew that he'd left everything to Phil. I didn't realise at first that he'd included the house and the cottage. That seemed hard on you. But at least that way he thought you'd be safe.

"You may have hurt him, Mark, by your lack of faith, but he never wanted anything bad to happen to you. You were still his brother."

"It seems odd, all the same. Why didn't he talk to me about it? Maybe we could have worked something out together."

"I don't know, Mark. I think he was rather confused towards the end. Not as clear in his mind as he used to be."

Another thought struck me.

"If Jack thought there was danger attached to this file, the money, the inheritance, why did he leave it all to Phil? He must have realised he was putting him in danger. And God knows, Phil paid the price!"

Emily shook her head wearily and blew her nose. She seemed close to tears.

"I don't know, I don't know. He wasn't thinking straight. I'm sure all he really thought about was protecting you. You were his brother."

"So why didn't you tell me about this before?"

"I wanted to keep out of it. I didn't want to interfere. I suppose I hoped it would all blow over. I'm sorry. Maybe I should have said something. I knew you'd be angry at first, but then you'd make the best of it, and just get on with your life. And if Phil hadn't given you that box of Harry's stuff from the war, that's what might have happened."

Oh no, Emily, I couldn't have let it rest anyway. But if he hadn't given me that box, I would not have found Jean-Luc, or gained a fortune. We cannot see all things ...

"What I don't really understand, Emily, is how these Germans tracked down the file. After all these years – forty-five years since the end of the war – they suddenly turn up and seem to know all the details of who's involved, who might have it. How did they know where to come?"

Jean-Luc, who had been listening quietly to our conversation, sat forward in his chair. Emily, with the two of us waiting for her to speak, suddenly looked very small and very old.

"I don't know, Mark. I've been thinking about it a lot."

"Did Jack tell anyone else?"

"No, I'm sure he didn't. He was always very careful of what he said. And quite suspicious of other people. You know that."

"But you did say he was rather confused when he was ill, before he died"

"I agree with Emily on this." Jean-Luc's voice was calm. "Your brother realised the significance of the file, probably more than you do, Mark. He'd lived with the secret for many years and knew how dangerous it was. I don't think he'd have mentioned it to anyone else, not even at that late stage"

We sat in silence for a while, listening to the hum of traffic on the main road, the clatter of a bin lid in a back yard, the sound of voices calling.

"Did Dad tell anyone about all this?" I felt I had to ask the question. Emily looked slightly shocked.

"Harry? No. It was his burden. He carried it for years. It destroyed his happiness."

"But you knew about it?"

217

"Very little. But I know that it preyed on his mind. He'd spoken to me earlier about killing those SS men in that truck, and he seemed worried about it. I couldn't understand why. There was something, you know, odd about it. It was war, after all, and Harry was already a hero, although he wouldn't have thought so. And he'd killed before. That's what soldiers do. That's what they're trained to do. There's nothing very remarkable about it. So I'd already guessed there was more to it than he'd told me."

"So you're pretty sure he didn't tell anyone else?"

"I'm certain, Mark."

"How can you be sure?"

"I know, believe me. He bottled it up for many years, as you now know. But near the end, when he was getting ill, but before the cancer took over his life, and he began to find he couldn't cope with it any longer, he desperately wanted to share it with someone."

"And did he?"

"No, I've told you that already." Emily's gentle voice sounded momentarily testy.

"There was nobody he could share his secret with anyway. He asked me what to do. So I suggested that to finally get it off his chest, he should go to confession."

"Confession?" I must have sounded startled. Jean-Luc looked up sharply.

"Yes. Don't sound so surprised. You may have forgotten, Mark, but that's what Catholics do. And Harry had known Father Byrne for many, many years. Ever since he came here from Ireland just after the war, in fact."

"Ireland?" The word was a chorus from myself and Jean-Luc. Our eyes met and realisation dawned suddenly.

"You don't have to repeat everything I say, Mark," Emily chided me.

"Maybe not," I replied, as Jean-Luc and I rose swiftly to our feet. "But what you've just said could turn out to be very important. I'm sorry to dash off, Emily, but we'll have to leave you now. Thanks for the coffee. We'll be back later, but right now we've got to go and see someone, and the sooner we get there the better."

Chapter Eighteen

The door was of heavy wood, large and black, the brass letter-box and doorbell shiny with much polishing. Gloom overhung the privet-hedged pathway, and jackdaws squabbled in the dark boughs of the garden's spreading trees. A sense of foreboding hung in the air – or was it just in my mind? – and I shivered slightly as we paused on the doorstep.

The presbytery, of dark brick, squatted in its own grounds behind an encircling wall, a little way away from the church itself. In contrast to the mock-Gothic building where Mass and Benediction were celebrated by a faithful congregation joined together beneath the light-flooding stained glass, this was a place of shadowy introspection. How many faithful parishioners, I wondered, bothered to tread this pathway to speak of their concerns to their parish priest? It was not a welcoming approach.

Jean-Luc nodded, and I placed my finger lengthily on the bell push. The sound echoed shrilly and emptily through the otherwise silent building.

I paused, then rang a second time.

Nothing. He's gone. We're too late…

I rang yet again, and we waited once more for long moments. Finally Jean-Luc shrugged and we began to turn away. As we did so, the door swung noiselessly open, and turning back, I saw Father Byrne's housekeeper standing in the hallway, giving us both a blatantly unfriendly stare. With one hand on the doorknob, she seemed to be blocking the entrance with her bulky but round-shouldered body, standing as if the weight of the years had sunk her in upon herself.

I took in at a glance her greying hair pulled back in a tight bun, her thick glasses and her expression of nervous truculence. I imagined the years of faithful service to a man above reproach, and how all that loyalty, I guessed, would soon seem shattered and wasted. From the look of her, something had already happened to disturb her normal routine; something to make her both suspicious and defensive.

"Father Byrne's not here."

The tone was flat, and the lie did not come easily to her.

Even as she spoke, I heard the sound of movements and whispering from a room at the back of the house. Overcoming my natural politeness, I pushed past her with a muttered "'Scuse me" and hurried down the dim hall, which smelled of furniture polish and overcooked vegetables, with Jean-Luc close behind. I wanted to be the first to confront Father Byrne.

I found him in his large study, dressed in a black cassock and sitting calmly at his leather-topped desk. He was writing carefully with a fountain pen on a pad of notepaper by the light of a green-shaded lamp. As I entered the room, he signed the letter with a flourish, folded it and placed it in an envelope. He swivelled the chair to face me as he ran his tongue along the flap, then closed and sealed it, watching me coldly as he did so over his steel-rimmed reading glasses.

"Your letter of resignation, *Father*?" I emphasised the word sarcastically.

"You might call it that."

"And what would *you* call it?"

"Explanation, perhaps? An explanation of how an Irish patriot who gave his life to the service of an English parish is now being hounded for his loyalty to his wartime allies."

"Hounded?"

"I know why you are here, although I don't recall inviting you into my house. But I have never underestimated you, Mark. You're not stupid, and neither, unfortunately, is your illegitimate sibling. Once he arrived on the scene, I guessed it was simply a case of how long it would take you to make the connection. Where is he, by the way?"

I looked casually over my shoulder, but to my consternation there was no sign of Jean-Luc. I managed to hide my surprise and merely shrugged.

"Not here, as you can see."

I'm not sure he believed me entirely, but he seemed to relax slightly.

"Tell me," I went on, "why a priest would want to cause such trouble to parishioners who had always trusted him?"

He threw back his head and laughed harshly, then smoothed back his thinning hair with his hand.

"Priest, you say? Yes, maybe. But an Irishman first, priest second. You must remember how we hated the Brits, all of us,

220

my family, my friends. We'd all lost loved ones, good men, loyal men, shot down by British soldiers during the Risings. And for what? For wanting our country back! Sure is it any wonder then, that when Germany declared war on Britain, we saw it as an opportunity to fight back. Many's the German agent we fed through our ports during those years. Galway, and a lot of smaller harbours we used to get them safely in, and to get information out to disrupt the British war effort."

"And yet after the war you came over here to live in our country?"

"And why not? I was posted here. The people of Liverpool have always welcomed Irish priests. They love them. So many of the people have Irish roots themselves. The connection goes back a long way. And how could I refuse, since they asked me?"

"And how many trusting people have you betrayed to the Nazis since the war?"

He looked away then, as if slightly uncomfortable, but soon collected himself. Calmly, he studied his fingernails, but avoided my eye.

"Sure, that would be telling, now. That would be my secret, Mark."

"But have you no shame, no honour? How could you live this life for so long?"

"Now wouldn't that be an easier question. The priesthood is a good life for a man like me. The work's not too onerous, and there are a lot of *admiring* women in the parish who take, shall we say, a real interest in the needs of their priest."

He smiled thinly, showing a line of yellowing teeth, and a wave of revulsion swept over me. I glanced around the book-lined study, with its leather armchairs and well-stocked drinks cabinet.

Yes, I thought, a very nice life for a traitor in our midst. And who would believe that so long after the great conflict, Englishmen were still at possible risk from believers in Hitler's evil ideology?

"And now, Mark, how can I be of help? Although I've enjoyed our little chat, I'm a busy man, you know." He laughed mirthlessly.

"You know perfectly well why I'm here. To bring you to justice. You and your henchmen."

"Henchmen? You've been reading too many thrillers, my son. I have no henchmen, as you call them."

"Then who were you talking to when we came in?"

He put on a puzzled look for a moment and hesitated before answering.

"Ah. That would be young Father O'Connor. He was just leaving on some home visits. He wanted my advice. These young priests often need my guidance on delicate matters."

"I'm sure they do. But you won't be giving them any more advice in future, I'm afraid. Instead, you'll be explaining yourself in a British court of law."

"And why would that be?"

"Don't play the innocent. You're implicated in the death of Phil Sullivan and the assault on Edie Barton, and the attack on us in Scotland. In fact, everything those two German thugs have been up to since they started following us."

"Implicated? In what way? I doubt you'll find any connection between myself and their activities."

I knew myself that was probably true. However, I went on.

"But we know that my father confessed to you. He told you everything. That's the only way those Nazis could have found out about the file and the gold. You're the link!"

"Supposition! Pure supposition! Who knows what goes on within the confessional? No priest is allowed to repeat what he is told. Your theory would never stand up in court."

Sickeningly, I knew at once he was right. I stood without speaking for a moment, thinking hard, my eyes sweeping nervously round the room. In the silence, a police siren sounded above the hum of the traffic on Wavertree Road. I became aware that almost opposite the doorway, in which I was still standing, there was another door leading into a further room. The door stood slightly ajar, and in the darkness beyond I thought I caught a movement. Focusing on the door, I saw it open another inch, and then I was almost certain I saw the gleam of eyes in the shadows. I looked away again, trying not to betray the fact that I had noticed anything.

Instinctively, I knew. It was Hans. Hans, or Josef, returned like a recurring nightmare from Scotland, seeking sanctuary and shelter with the only ally they had. It had to be. Who else would stand, half-hidden, listening to the conversation we were having?

If I was right, this changed everything. It made the chance of bringing Father Byrne to justice much greater, but at the same time placed me in immediate danger. I took a deep breath.

"So. You're prepared to abandon the other two, are you? Deny their existence, after they've done all the dangerous work. Josef's already had a very nasty fall, and Hans has had a rough time of it in the mountains. Who knows where he is now?"

"Frankly, I don't know who you're talking about."

"Oh come on, you've as good as admitted it already."

"Maybe, in your mind. But I wont be admitting it to anyone else. No-one will be able to prove a connection. I've made sure of that."

"You know the police are looking for Josef and Hans? What if one of them comes to you for help or protection?"

"I've told you. I know nothing about them. I accept no responsibility for them. As far as I'm concerned they don't exist."

"So the fact that myself, Jean-Luc and the British police are on their track means nothing to you?"

"Nothing at all."

"And the reality of the situation being that those German bastards will eventually be caught and punished for murder is none of your business?"

Father Byrne swivelled his chair back to his desk, turning his back on me. He stared fixedly out of the window.

"This conversation is over. Goodbye, Mark."

"NO! It is not!"

The voice of Hans rang loud in the quiet room as he flung the door wide open. His eyes were wild, his hair uncombed and his cheeks unshaven. He looked as if he had been sleeping in his clothes for several days. He would have cut a pathetic figure, were it not for the automatic pistol pointed straight at my chest. I felt my bowels contract. With difficulty, I kept control of myself and managed to steady my voice.

"Hello again Hans. Nice to see you. Shame we couldn't meet in friendlier circumstances."

Father Byrne swung around again and sighed theatrically, although his voice when he spoke was calm and resigned.

"Hans, Hans! Always so impetuous! Now what have you done?"

The pistol moved jerkily to cover the old priest. Hans' voice, when he spoke, was high and strained.

"You betray me. You look after yourself. You must help me!"

"And what would you suggest we do? Now that you've proved beyond doubt to our friend here that there is a connection between us?"

"Kill him!"

The gun swung back to point at me. For the first time I noticed the silencer. What could I do? Was this the end? And where the hell was Jean-Luc? And what could they possibly achieve by killing me now? Something seemed to have made Father Byrne think along the same lines. His voice, when he spoke, was harsh and contemptuous.

"Don't be ridiculous, Hans! Put the gun away! There's been enough killing. And no doubt as we speak this gentleman's bloodhound dog of a Belgian half-brother will be creeping around somewhere. No, I suggest it's time we beat a dignified retreat, you and I, together. We'll take my car."

Hans grunted uncertainly and seemed to acquiesce, but still kept the gun trained on me. Father Byrne picked up a leather travelling bag which had been out of sight next to his desk and rose to his feet.

"Goodbye, Mark," he said calmly. Would you give my regards to your aunt, and apologise to her now, that I wasn't able to say farewell in person."

I had to admire his cheek.

He walked over to Hans, gently placed his hand on the barrel of the pistol, pushing it down so that it pointed at the floor. He gave me a wintry smile, then he took hold of the German's arm and the two of them turned together and vanished through the door that Hans had come in by. Afterwards there was silence for a moment. *Should I follow them? No, stupid idea. I'd just had a let-off. Don't risk your life again. But where* was *Jean-Luc?* Not for the first time, I dithered.

I heard their footsteps in the passageway, and the sound of whispering, followed by raised voices as if they were having some sort of altercation. *Let them,* I thought. *Soon they'll be gone for good. Well, let them go. Much good may it do them.*

I walked slowly across to the window behind Father Byrne's

desk and gazed out at the scene he must have surveyed a thousand times. Then I stiffened, immediately tense again. Through the large panes of the sash window I saw what he must have seen himself a few minutes previously. At the side of the building was an untidy, semi-circular lawn and beyond that a small tarmac parking area with a couple of vehicles standing on it, an Escort and an old Rover which I guessed was the parish priest's intended getaway car. From here a driveway led around the back of the church to join the small public parking area which gave access to Sycamore Street and eventually to the main road.

None of that was unusual of course; but what had caught my eye was the two police squad cars parked under the trees opposite the building, their white and red bright against the greys and greens of the church grounds. Officers were moving purposefully and silently under the shadows of the old trees, and over the roof of one car I could see what I took to be the helmet of a police marksman and the small black circle made by the barrel of a rifle trained on the building.

A moment later I started at the sound of quiet footsteps behind me, and turned to see Jean-Luc standing at my shoulder.

"It's nearly over now," he murmured.

"Where the hell have you been, Jean-Luc?" I was taut and angry, and it showed in my voice.

"I went to call the police."

"And left me to get shot?"

"But you didn't. I was only gone for a few minutes, and I was just there in the passageway behind you when Hans was threatening you. He would have died before he pulled the trigger."

"I wish I could share your confidence. Why didn't you just shoot him?"

"Because it's important that the police are involved in this. We don't want to be accused of murder again, do we?"

There was silence for a moment, an expectant silence. Then I heard the rattle of a bolt being drawn on what must be the back door of the presbytery.

A pause. Then it all happened, so quickly that it was difficult to follow the sequence of events.

Father Byrne, his cassock flapping like a crow's wing,

running, stumbling, turning, pointing at his accomplice, shouting …*"Get him, get him!"* Hans, the gun still in his hand, startled to see the police, confused by the priest's betrayal, hesitating. Father Byrne reaching the police line, an officer pulling him into cover behind a tree. Voices calling *"Armed police, armed police, put the gun on the ground, put the gun on the ground…"* A muffled shot – was it Hans? … followed by the thump of a heavy rifle round. Hans throwing up his hands as if in surrender, knees buckling as he slumped to the ground and lay motionless. Then a movement in the trees, a dark figure fleeing – Father Byrne, taking advantage of the policemen's concentration on the violent scene before them, and the fact that no-one ever really suspects a priest of being involved in evil. Swiftly, he was gone, round the corner of the church and out of sight, heading towards the main road and the bustle of people and traffic.

"Jean-Luc! He's getting away!"

I glanced sideways at him and his face was grim.

"Come on, Mark!"

We rushed out of the back door, our hands raised, Jean-Luc holding up his Belgian police badge. It took only seconds to explain the situation to the police inspector in charge, but it seemed like hours. Quickly, we were into one of the cars, the blue lights flashing and the siren wailing. We raced down the narrow driveway and out into narrow Sycamore Street, funnelling through the parked cars to the junction with Wavertree Road.

Which way? I tried to think what his plan might be. He'd had to leave his car, so he was on foot. Would he catch a bus, or a taxi? To the station, or the docks? We paused for a split second, the officer at the wheel maybe having the same thoughts that I did. Then we must have seen it at the same time, a little way down to the right.

A commotion, people in the road, cars backing up, a stationary bus not quite at the stop. Our driver managed to squeeze part of the way through the traffic; then we had to walk. The bus driver was standing in the road, white and shocked, and gabbling excuses

"I didn't see him. He just ran out. Ran across the road. From nowhere. I couldn't do anything. Oh my God." He covered his face with his hands.

The figure lying at the front of the bus seemed strangely shrunken, twisted by the impact and obviously beyond help. Blood covered the side of his head and face.

Two middle-aged women were kneeling by the body, and one of them was praying, the same words, repeated over and over again: *"Hail Mary, full of grace, the Lord is with Thee ... Holy Mary, Mother of God, pray for us now and at the hour of our death, Amen."*

The other woman stood up with some difficulty and I overheard her speaking to the police officer.

"... Father Byrne ... parish priest ... lovely man ... don't know what he was doing ... came from nowhere ... in a hurry ... ran across ... driver couldn't stop ... what a way to lose him ... under a bus ... lovely man ... such a lovely man ..."

His battered leather travelling bag lay in the gutter. It had burst open with the impact, and apparently unnoticed by the gathering crowd, a golden crucifix and a silver chalice had spilled partly out of it. I glanced at Jean-Luc.

"Nothing changes there, then!" He nodded thoughtfully.

I crouched quickly and picked up the bag, closing it to hide the contents. I saw one of the policemen watching me.

"I'll take that, thank you, sir," he said courteously as he stepped forward to receive the bag.

"I don't know what he was doing with that stuff, officer. It looks valuable."

His reply was delivered in a neutral tone, apparently devoid of irony.

"I expect he was trying to rescue it from the gunman, sir. I'll make sure it's returned to its rightful place."

I handed it over meekly.

Nobody, I thought, would ever know the truth about Father Byrne. He would be buried with all the honour due to a man of his calling and there would be fulsome praise for him at his funeral. Parishioners would weep and exchange happy memories of weddings and baptisms, and his passing would be recorded with sadness in the pages of the *Universe* and the *Catholic Herald.*

But nobody would know the evil he had wrought, and how he had worked to betray his adopted country. Maybe it was fitting that for an Irishman who had chosen to work unsuspected in the treacherous shadows, the end should come in a faceless suburban street in Liverpool, with no ultimate acclaim from the powers that he served so faithfully.

Coming out of my reverie, I heard the sounds of the street, the hubbub of voices, the crackle of the radio in the police car and the sound of an approaching ambulance. I shook myself. Maybe it *was* all over now. All the mysteries, all the danger. Maybe I could put it all behind me and get back to some sort of normality, sort things out with Edie and Jenny and find out what had happened about my job …

Jean-Luc put his arm around my shoulders.

"Come on, Mark. Time to go."

Yes, I thought, time to go and sort out the loose ends …

Chapter Nineteen

The Land Rover was still where I'd left it the only the previous week – it seemed years ago – hidden and abandoned-looking in the undergrowth. A fine early morning rain was falling, and cloud hung around the flanks of the hills. An air of desolation reigned and there was no-one about, not even a fisherman, as we started the vehicle. I'd got my car back from the police and driven Bryn up from Wales to collect the Land Rover, and we'd stayed the previous night in a B&B in Fort William. We reversed the vehicle carefully out of the bushes and proceeded back down the loch in convoy, with the wipers splashing intermittently across the screen. At Spean Bridge Bryn headed south in the Land Rover, and I carried on to Inverness to collect Edie.

I went by Laggan and Newtonmore and picked up the A9 at Kingussie, passing the distant snow-capped Cairngorms at Aviemore. It's an easy run from there to Inverness nowadays, and I was soon at the hospital.

"I thought you weren't coming. I've been waiting ages."

Edie's greeting was less than enthusiastic. She'd been watching television with some of the other patients in the dayroom when I arrived, and was patently bored, desperate to get away and not in a particularly good mood.

"I'm sorry, Edie. It's a long way from North Wales to here. I brought Bryn up to collect the Land Rover …"

"It doesn't matter," she said in a voice which suggested that it most certainly did.

"Just take me home."

"You're quiet," I said, after I'd helped her into the car and we were heading south. Rain was still falling persistently and the clouds were dark and heavy on the hills.

"What did you expect?" Her voice was surly and sarcastic. "Singing and dancing? I've been thinking."

I sighed inwardly. Women have an apparently infinite capacity, I thought, for spoiling what should be good moments by concentrating on the wrong things. Still, to be fair, she'd had a lot of things to think about.

"I thought you'd be pleased to see me," I murmured hopefully. My mind went back to the warmth and promise of our last meeting in the hospital ward. Selfishly, I wanted her approbation.

"How do you expect me to be pleased about anything at the moment?"

"Well, I *had* rather been looking forward to seeing you again, you know. I thought perhaps you might feel the same."

"Great. You obviously haven't given much thought to the reality of how I might be feeling right now."

"A bit more welcoming perhaps?" I knew it wasn't the right thing to say, but I could feel myself bristling. "I've come a long way to fetch you, you know."

"And so you should. This is all your fault, Mark. If it wasn't for you none of this would have happened!"

I was taken aback. For a moment I had to concentrate on pulling out to pass a slow-moving caravan. Once we were safely back on our side of the road, I replied, biting back my anger.

"I think that's a bit unfair, Edie ..."

"Do you? Do you really?

I managed to stifle an impulse to snap back at her, and tried instead to hold out a rather feeble olive branch.

"I'm sorry. I'm sorry about what's happened, and about the way you feel. But I'm sure we can work through it together."

"Together? *Together?* That's a bit presumptuous, isn't it? And what do you mean by 'work through it'? You make it sound like a piece of homework. I've lost my son, my father – two fathers, if you like. My mother will probably never speak to me again, I've been shot at, my back's still killing me, and God knows whether I've still got anywhere to live! How is it possible to work through that?"

She had a point, I suppose. When she put it like that it sounded shocking, unbearable. I know I should have tried to calm her down and talk her round, but I was furious at her attitude, and typically, I just clammed up. We drove in silence for a while until she turned away, reclined the seat back and closed her eyes. She dozed then for much of the way.

Past Perth and Glasgow and over Beattock summit I drove

for several hours without stopping, too fast probably, venting my anger on the accelerator. I was quietly simmering, wondering who this woman really was, so loving, and so loyal a few days ago in the face of danger, yet now pushing me coldly away when we had a chance of happiness, as I thought, together.

Eventually, and not before time, I pulled into Killington Services on the M6. We weren't all that far from my house by then, but we needed fuel and I wanted a break from driving and a coffee. Edie roused herself, rubbed her eyes and got sleepily out of the car. The sun had finally emerged and the air was warm. I was expecting a frosty silence, but, to my surprise, as we walked towards the café, she linked her arm companionably through mine.

"Sorry I was a bit bad-tempered earlier," she murmured. "I'd let things get on top of me."

I let it go and said nothing until we'd both been to the toilet, ordered drinks and sat down at a table looking out towards the lake.

"Things may not be as bad as you think, Edie."

"How do you make that out?" The tone was still ironic, but the smile was back in her eyes.

"Well, your mother for a start. I think you'll find her surprisingly supportive. She missed you, you know, all the time she didn't see you. But she lived in fear of Peter – your father. In fact, I think she was terrified of what he might do to her – or to you."

I recalled the vicious look, the hatred on his face in the *Copper Kettle* as he warned me off, and the moment of certainty that he was going to kill me in cold blood in the bothy in Scotland.

I glanced at Edie. She was sipping her cappuccino, holding the wide cup with both hands, not looking at me. She put the cup gently back in the saucer.

"Go on."

"You were worried about having nowhere to live."

"True. Cheer me up on that score. If you can."

"Well, Phil inherited the cottage, Maes-y-Bryn, from Jack, didn't he?"

"Yes."

"And Phil was your son, wasn't he? The son you never really

knew, but your son notwithstanding. And Phil wasn't married, was he?"

"Of course not. Get to the point, Mark."

"I'm getting there, don't worry. The point is, you're Phil's next of kin, aren't you?"

"I suppose so."

"So you should inherit Maes-y-Bryn from Phil, shouldn't you? I can't think of anyone else who could have a claim on it."

She looked up at me then, and smiled, an uncomplicated smile of relief and understanding. Then she leaned over and kissed me on the cheek.

"Perhaps we could live there together, after all!"

Already I could see her making plans, as women do.

I gazed out of the window for long moments. Coots and tufted duck were swimming on the lake, and the hills beyond were emerging green and clear as the afternoon sun finally burned off the cloud. A mallard struggled to take off, webbed feet pattering over the water as it tried to gain height. I felt poised, on the cusp. I knew it was a turning point. Now that it came to it, how should I act?

I thought of Jenny, of how severe she could be, and how little, after all these years, was left in our relationship. I thought of my career, in tatters at the moment, and going nowhere. It was time to be bold. *Could we live there together?* I took my decision, as I knew I would.

"Of course we can. Of course we can."

She took my hand and squeezed it.

"But there's more to the story, Edie. I've got more to tell you. Things I've found out recently."

I ordered more coffee, and she sat quietly while I told her about Jean-Luc, and my father's relationship with his mother, and the finding of the gold. I recounted Jean-Luc's tale in some detail, ending with the revelation that I'd found out not only that I had a half-brother, but that I had inherited a large sum of money. Edie's eyes grew wide.

"So we're rich!"

We're rich? I hesitated. I was wary of Edie's immediate assumption that she had a share in the money. *My* money. After a moment I went on.

"Not rich, exactly, but comfortable for the time being. It's enough money to give us a breathing space, to decide where we go from here."

"Oh Mark. So we do have a future, after all."

She snuggled against me and put her arm round me. I've never been too keen on public displays of affection, but her body was warm and her scent reached me so I relented and stroked her hair.

It was dark when we reached my house. There were no lights and no sign of Jenny. There was nothing to indicate that she'd been there since my last visit. I found some beer in the fridge, and a bottle of red wine, and rustled up something to eat. Then we sat together on the settee and put the television on, although I don't think either of us took much notice of what was on the screen. My mind kept revolving, going over recent events and thinking about the future.

"Do you mind if I have a shower?"

Edie's voice interrupted my thoughts. She stood up and stretched.

"Of course not. The towels are in the airing cupboard in the bathroom."

As she was going upstairs I called after her.

"It's getting late. I'll be up myself in a minute." I turned off the television and the lights, double-checked that the doors were locked – I'd got nervous about that since finding Jean-Luc in the house. Also, I still wasn't absolutely sure whether Josef was alive even now and seeking revenge, although I pushed that thought easily to the back of my mind.

I went lightly up the stairs and into the bathroom to wash and clean my teeth. The shower door was still steamed up, and the smell of shampoo lingered, but Edie wasn't there.

When I'd finished, I went onto the landing and saw that the light was on in the main bedroom. I hadn't really thought about our sleeping arrangements – or at least, I'd thought about them quite a lot, but typically, had decided to let events take their course.

Edie was sitting on the side of the bed – the one I'd shared with Jenny until the last couple of weeks. She was wrapped in a white bath-towel and was drying her hair with a smaller one. She turned and smiled as I came into the room, then put down the hair-towel and got to her feet. She came to meet me at the foot of the king-size double bed.

The bath-towel was knotted above her breasts, contrasting strongly with the brown skin of her shoulders and arms. She looked at me levelly, unsmiling now, but with the hint of a twinkle at the corners of her eyes. Then, without shifting her gaze, she undid the knot and let the towel slide to the floor.

The last time I had seen her naked, she was spread-eagled on a Scottish shore. She was no less beautiful to me now. I stepped forward and kissed her on the lips then pushed her gently back onto the bed. Because her back was still sore, and painful to lie on, we had to find other ways of making love, but that proved not to be a problem. The bed seemed suddenly like a different bed entirely. Latterly, its size had provided an excuse for Jenny and me to sleep without touching. Now, in the course of our activities, we appeared to explore every corner of it together.

Later, we lay tired and satisfied in the darkness, our arms around each other and our legs entwined, until gradually we drifted into sleep.

"I hope you know what you're doing." Emily sounded resigned. She'd been fond of Jenny. "You know all I really want is for you to be happy."

"Thanks, Emily. I know. And it's Jenny who left *me*, remember. Although I may have given her cause to," I added hastily. "But it was her decision in the end to walk out."

Emily gave me a sharp and disapproving look, as if she knew I was being economical with the truth, but said nothing.

"Don't worry, Emily," Edie chipped in brightly. "I'll look after him. And in Harry's house, too! It'll be great for us to be living there together. I know I'll be able to make him happy!"

And who could fail to believe it, I thought, with Edie looking, to my eyes, more attractive than ever, her face filled with a glow that I hoped I had more than a little to do with.

I left her chatting to Emily and making a shopping list of things she could go and get for her before we left. That, combined with her natural charm, would help to bring Emily round, or so I hoped.

I found Ruth Morris at home, and told her the whole story as quickly and concisely as I could.

"So are you satisfied now, Mark?"

"Satisfied maybe isn't quite the right word, Ruth. Phil's death was terrible. And I'm not happy that Peter Ashby got my father to pay for his daughter's upkeep for all those years. That was sly, evil even. But on the other hand, Edie's the best thing that's come out of all this for me. And I'm glad that I've managed to untangle it all in the end. Not only that, but I've acquired a half-brother – Jean-Luc – and quite a lot of money."

"And you're happier now that you know why Jack didn't leave anything to you?" She sounded anxious.

"Oh yes, I am. And it's nice to be sure that Bob Downs was way off beam with his allegations at the funeral. I think Jack may have been misguided, but it's touching, reassuring, you know, to think that he was wanting to shelter me from any problems. He was naïve, I think, but it showed he hadn't lost his brother's love for me. That's good to know."

Ruth nodded vigorously.

"Yes, yes. You needed to know that, Mark."

"And the secret that Jack wouldn't confide in you. The one he said would change his life. We know what it was now."

"Do we?"

"Yes, of course! It's obvious, really. It was about the time that Phil was born. My father must have told him about Edie and everything. It must have been a great burden to him. But naturally, he didn't want to tell anyone else. Not me, not you, nobody."

"Yes, Mark, I'm sure you're right," she agreed. But she looked very pensive as she said it and for some reason I wasn't altogether sure she was convinced.

The visit to Bryn was much more straightforward. We went directly to his house from Liverpool, without stopping at Maes-y-Bryn. He'd got back from Scotland the previous day without mishap, and now had some news for me. News I was glad to hear.

"Have the police picked up Josef yet?" was one of the first questions I was eager to have answered.

Bryn laughed, but there was no humour in it.

"Yes, they found him all right. Smashed to pieces on the

north side of Sgurr na Ciche, below the crags. You did a good job, Mark. He'd fallen a long way. Nobody could survive that"

I was relieved, but still a little puzzled.

"But the voices I heard … I thought I heard Hans calling, and Josef replying … I've been worrying about that on and off ever since."

"You heard voices all right, Mark. But it wasn't your German friends. Josef was already dead. No, it was two walkers, Munroists, coming down from the next summit. They saw Josef fall, and then they saw you running away. They were shouting to you to stop, to come back and help!"

"I'm glad I didn't!"

"I bet you are!"

"And are the police considering charges against me?"

"No, no. You don't need to worry on that score. They know what was going on all right; and they've talked to me and Jean-Luc. It'll all be hushed up, don't worry. MI5 wouldn't want anything getting out about neo-Nazis roaming unhindered through Britain."

"And what about the file that caused all this trouble?"

"The police have passed it on to MI5. They'll make sure through their own clandestine channels that the message gets back to anyone who might still be looking for it. I think you're safe enough now from any more unwelcome visitors."

We settled in quickly at Maes-y-Bryn; after all, it was already Edie's home, and I felt immediately comfortable in what had not long before been my father's house. I already knew the surrounding area very well, and soon felt like a local. Jenny showed no real inclination to patch up our marriage – she was too preoccupied with her job – and divorce proceedings were soon under way. The house in Yorkshire that we had bought together nearly twenty years before was put up for sale and we made quite a profit on it. Jenny had already moved on, to a flat in Lancaster. Sad, though, I couldn't help thinking, when your home, where you were once happy together, becomes simply in the end, a profitable investment.

I left my teaching job by mutual agreement. Headmasters don't take kindly to staff having a few weeks off for unspecified personal reasons, and for my part, I was happy to leave. Edie went back to her job at the engineering firm and I spent a few months pottering round the house and walking on the hills, revisiting old haunts. Sometimes I'd stroll across the fields to spend some time with Bryn and Megan, or help them with some of the farm chores: the daily rhythm of feeding stock and milking, the annual rhythm of haymaking and harvesting.

Other times I'd get up early and go rabbiting with my .22 rifle. As the sun rose I'd be sidling down the hedgerows, netted with dew-silvered spiders' webs, leaving dark footprints in the damp grass. I'd creep through into the stubbled fields and line up my sights on a fat doe feeding on the aftermath, and that evening we'd give thanks for the garlicky rabbit stew bubbling in the pot.

Sometimes at a weekend we'd drive down to Snowdonia together, to the harder, rockier hills to be found in the Glyders and Carneddau. Edie enjoyed the walking and scrambling we did on the wild ridges, and when I suggested going rock-climbing, she quickly agreed. She took easily to the vertical world of the Welsh cliffs. Together we did quite a few of the classic routes on the Idwal Slabs, the Milestone Buttress and the towering East Face of Tryfan. She climbed without apparent fear and her fluid movements and effortless balance made up for any lack of strength. I felt sure that with practice she would be able to cope with much harder ascents.

I believed at the time that sharing the intimacy of danger and difficulty on the crags, joined by the lifeline of a climbing rope, could only strengthen the bond between us.

We had enough money in the bank – I'd opened a joint account after all, at Edie's suggestion – for me to do all that without worrying too much for a while. I also went to Belgium once or twice to see Jean-Luc and to get to know Sophie, his mother. It was strange, but rather delightful, to stay in the *Hotel de la Paix* in very different circumstances and with different status from my first visit. We talked about my dad, and I found it deeply moving to hear Sophie expressing the love she had kept for her English soldier down all those lonely years. It also made me very proud.

I was very much in love with Edie, and she reciprocated at times with passion that brooked no refusal, as if she was fulfilling a desperate need to make up for the years of insecurity when she lacked the affection first of her parents, and later of a husband. But her mood could change rapidly, and she could sometimes be distant and critical, which would worry me and start me questioning our relationship. Then the period of coldness would end, as usual, with tears, then laughter and a breathless rush to bed, where the supple accommodation of her body would smooth away all my worries.

Edie still regularly attended the Catholic church where she had met my father, never missing Sunday Mass, and getting involved with various committees which meant that she was out several evenings in the week. It was refreshing to note, however, that her faith had never interfered with her lack of sexual inhibition. At first I let her go to church on her own, or, sometimes, drove her down to Mold and passed the time reading the Sunday paper in a café while she was at Mass.

A little while later, during that autumn term, all that changed. I got a part-time teaching job in a Catholic school near Wrexham, and was immediately impressed with the behaviour of the pupils. It was as if the sense of community and shared beliefs had a powerful influence beyond the normal discipline of the school.

Perhaps there's something in this after all, after all these year, after all the doubts and scorn...

After a few weeks I started going to church again. This time it was voluntary, not the overwhelming straitjacket of growing up in a Catholic household, and the requirement to believe everything literally that had been beaten into me at school.

I thought Edie would be pleased, but she did nothing to encourage me. In fact, at first I felt she was a little disapproving after some of the things I'd said to her about Catholicism. But I really quite enjoyed it, and got pleasure from getting to know other members of the congregation, even though I became gradually aware that they included more than a couple of fellows that Edie had previously gone out with, including her building contractor friend. In fact, she still attracted a lot of admiring glances, but, I was proud to be seen with her, and confident of the trust between us.

So, all in all, after the upheavals and revelations of the previous months, I was able to bask in the knowledge that life, for me, had never been better.

Epilogue

I've been looking through some boxes of stuff that belonged to Jack. We acquired them along with the rest of Phil's things – not that there were many things apart from some surprisingly expensive clothes and a lot of books. What did startle us, though, was a Halifax Building Society pass book with around twelve thousand pounds in the account. Where, we wondered, had someone in Phil's situation got that amount of money from?

It's mid-October and Edie's gone to a Christmas Fête meeting at the church. One of her friends picked her up, and she said she'd get a lift back, so I've settled down with a beer in the spare bedroom to idly leaf through the papers in this box of Jack's belongings. A lot of it is of no interest to me, nor, I imagine, to anyone else. Old birthday cards, theatre programmes, invitations, newspaper cuttings including a couple of articles that he had published in the *Daily Telegraph* ...

But what's this? A handful of letters addressed to Jack in an unknown hand. I open one and scan down the single sheet to the signature – *Steve*. Who can this be? Steve Tomlinson? He's the only Steve I know. Why would he be writing to Jack? He saw him every day in school until Jack's retirement on grounds of ill health. The letter, however, is more recent than that, just a couple of years old.

I begin to read from the beginning.

Dear Jack,

What are we going to do? I know Phil Sullivan is your nephew, or at least half-nephew, but what he's doing is evil, especially after the way you've looked after him at school and helped to coach him through his A-levels.

But if you don't pay up, he'll destroy us both, I'm sure of it. I'm not ashamed of our relationship, but I know Beth couldn't cope with it if she found out. I don't imagine your family would be best pleased, either. It would destroy everything you've stood for over the years. And I'd lose my job, of course

I don't think we have any alternative at the moment. It's the only way to keep him quiet. But I can't stand the smug look on his face. If only he hadn't found us together like that – but it's too late now.

Remember, I still love you,

Steve.

I take a swig of my beer, but my hands are trembling and I feel chilled inside. I read the letter again, in case I've misunderstood it, but it only seems plainer this time. I put it down and pick up another one, dated a week later.

Dear Jack,

Thank you so much for what you are doing. I hadn't, however, realised that Phil was demanding so much. It means Mark will get nothing. Am I being selfish? Perhaps so, but I'm desperate. And in any case, the choice is that Mark doesn't get what he's never had, and probably won't miss, or on the other hand we are both ruined and our reputations destroyed.

In any case, it's morbid to think of you dying. You will probably shake off this illness and go on for another fifty years. That would serve Phil Sullivan right. Thank you again.

All my love,

Steve.

I sit back, staring sightlessly at the wall. It's unbelievable. Or rather, no, it isn't. It makes perfect sense. This is it. This is the real explanation at last, not Father Byrne's, not Emily's, not the one Steve Tomlinson gave me. This is what I had been searching for – the truth. And now that I've found it, I really rather wish I hadn't.

But it's suddenly so obvious now. The secret that Jack would not share with Ruth Morris, was not, after all, the secret of my father's illegitimate child; it was the life-changing discovery of my brother's own sexual proclivities. It's clear as well that Bob Downs' allegations at the funeral were not unfounded at all, only wrongly aimed. I can understand now the friction between him and Jack, and I recognise with dreadful clarity Steve Tomlinson's attempt to put me off the trail with his version of the truth, cleverly twisted to suit his own ends. Clever – but not quite clever enough.

So it turns out that Phil Sullivan was a blackmailer – that

doesn't altogether surprise me, but my sorrow at his death is somewhat mitigated now. And my own brother, it seems, was not deliberately rejecting me, but was helplessly caught in a trap woven of his own desires. That, at least, gives me some forlorn satisfaction.

I need to share this with Edie. She'll be shocked by the revelation about Phil, who was still her son, after all. We'll talk it through, though, and in the end I'm sure she'll be as glad as me that we know the reasons behind Jack's eccentric will at last.

I glance at my watch. It's getting late. Strange, I thought I heard a car coming down the lane a little while ago, but it can't have been Edie, or she would have come in by now. Maybe I'll just go out and check.

I put the letters back in their envelopes and replace them in the box. I tread softly down the stairs into the living room where the stove is burning with a homely glow and the silence is broken only by the measured ticking of the old clock and the creak of the floorboards under the patterned rugs.

Leaving the house, I realise that I have forgotten to turn on the outside light, but it doesn't matter too much as the moon is full and the night is still. A little way away, in the wood across the meadow, an owl hoots, a quavering, ethereal sound that speaks of a world we do not know. Yet I am aware that all around me the darkness is full of quiet, unsuspected activity.

There is no sign of a car, but it's a beautiful night and I decide to stroll up the lane a little way. At the top of the hill I stop suddenly as I realise that under the birch trees a saloon car is parked. I'm not sure I recognise it, but then that's not surprising as I'm not very good on modern cars. I start to walk towards it, but something, some instinct, makes me stop a yard or two away. At first I can see nothing, just huddled shapes, but next I hear a sound and turn my head to catch it more clearly – Edie's voice, but not a voice as such, not speaking, not words, just a sound, muffled from within the car, rising to the climactic moan I know so well. Then her face, pale in the faint cold light, turning carelessly to the window, eyes closed, her expression the ecstatic mimicry of pain that goes with release, abandon.

There is no mistaking it.

Shock sweeps paralysingly through me, and a wave of

misery follows.

So soon? Have I, after all, lost her so soon?

I step closer. The man is wearing a dark suit. In the shadows it's difficult to make everything out, but he looks as if he is panting and I can see clearly that his hand is pushing up beneath my Edie's skirt, moving urgently between her bare legs ...

Suddenly, he is aware of me. Surprised in the act, he swivels round, and the moonlight gleams on the starched dog collar of our parish priest ...

Postscript

This little cottage in the middle of the village suits me quite well now. It's a manageable size, and no garden to speak of. I like being able to hear the sound of the church bells, and I like to walk down to the river and sit on the old clapper bridge that I remember from my childhood visits.

It's only a few yards from here to the village shop, and, perhaps more importantly, it's not far to go to the comfort and welcome of the *Drover's Inn,* where I often get my dinner. I have an arrangement with Trefor, the landlord, to keep something for me – sausage and chips or something simple like that, and if I want to take it home he'll wrap it in tinfoil for me. That saves me from getting into a session and drinking too much with some of the locals, which I must admit, I have been doing a bit too often recently. Perhaps now, though, I'm starting to get a bit of a grip on things again. It's not been easy, though.

Edie's still at Maes-y-Bryn, my dad's place, and that hurts. That hurts like hell. Especially as we didn't really part on the best of terms, as you'd expect. She's let Emily stay on in Liverpool, so that's something I suppose. But when we came to split the joint account, there was very little in it and I've no idea where my money's gone. I've never been too good with financial matters, investments and so on. My solicitors are still working on that one. I've been too embarrassed to tell Jean-Luc, but Bryn, as usual, has been very supportive.

As I mentioned, I had been drinking too much, and was getting into a routine where I was in an alcoholic fog most of the time. Then something totally unexpected happened to snap me out of it. It was about a week ago now…

When I opened the door at the second knock, she was standing there looking rather worried and mournful, a pleasant-featured woman of about my own age, her curly pale brown hair dampened by the light rain.

"You don't know me, I think," she began hesitantly, "but my name's Edie Barton."

For a moment I was speechless. Frankly, I gaped at her. The

243

words appeared to make no sense at first.

"Aren't you going to ask me to come inside?" She smiled weakly. "We've got a lot to talk about."

My mind raced, searching for the significance of what she had said. Slowly, a vague but seemingly impossible idea began to crystallise in my mind. At last, with an effort, I pulled myself together and opened the door wide.

"Yes, yes, of course," I mumbled. "I think you'd better come in."

At first she didn't know where to begin, but once I'd poured the tea she told me at some length about her childhood growing up in Liverpool, and about her adoptive parents. She told me about leaving home and moving to the bed-sit in West Derby, and about the friendly blonde girl called Nancy who'd lived alone in the room opposite her, across the landing. Even before she described her, I knew who she meant. When she'd left, Nancy had promised to forward any mail, but she'd never heard anything from her after that…

I didn't remember everything she told me about the intervening years and her efforts to find her true parents, until she came to the moment when she had read the newspaper reports – *"Search for teacher in murder case"* – about me vanishing to Scotland. Seeing the name Edie Barton – her own name – made her take a close interest, for obvious reasons, and eventually she'd put two and two together and with a little help from Directory Enquiries, had tracked down Hilda Ashby.

"Hilda told me everything, you know."

"So you're telling me that you are the real Edie Barton! Peter Ashby's child? And no doubt you realise my father was tricked into paying for your upkeep until you reached the age of twenty-one?" Bitterness seeped into my voice, and the words came out like gall.

"Not tricked, exactly." She paused and swallowed nervously. I could see her hands were shaking, and she twisted them together to steady them. After a moment she went on.

"Not tricked, Mark. You see … Harry – your dad - he really was my father."

"That's not what Peter Ashby told me."

"Of course not, of course not! *He* believed I was *his* daughter. Or at least," she added bitterly, "he believed that one of us was. Not me, though, in the end. My identity had been well and truly stolen by then. At the last he thought it was that Nancy woman who was his daughter. Hilda had to convince him of that, naturally. You saw the sort of temper he had. She didn't know what he might have done if he'd known that the child he thought was his own really was Harry's. She told me all this when I went to see her. And the tragedy is that because of the way things worked out, Hilda also ended up believing for the last twenty-odd years that Nancy was her daughter, instead of me."

I sat forward in my armchair in silence, head bowed and hands clasped together, trying to come to terms with her astonishing news.

"So you really are my sister," I admitted slowly at last, as much to myself as to her. "My half-sister."

"I truly am."

She smiled, and I saw her warmth then, and her resemblance to our dad. My suspicions had melted away as she was speaking and I knew instinctively she was telling the truth.

"I hope you're prepared to have me in the family," she murmured.

"Of course. Of course I am. And I tell you what. I'll put the kettle on again. Then we'll have a whisky. And after that we can start trying to work out how to get our own back – our houses and our money to begin with. And the first thing we must do is to find out exactly who *she* is."

"Do you mean who I think you mean?"

"Yes. I mean that woman I thought I knew so well. The woman I loved once, but who turns out to be a complete mystery to me, a stranger, a different person altogether. The woman with no name of her own, except a forgotten name from a long time ago – *Nancy*. The other Edie Barton. We need to find out who on earth she really is ..."